Snoo Wilson's novel with its epic embrace of an entire political and criminal world and its evocation of the many layers of a particular society in a particular time, provokes comparison more than anything else with Balzac. Melmont himself (who may suggest a variety of recently deceased or indeed still living real-life monsters) stands squarely beside Vautrin as one of literature's great criminal rogues. In its irrepressible verbal exuberance, it is as raucous and riotous a novel as has appeared for many a year.

Simon Callow

THE WORKS OF MELMONT

No.

of a first printing of a limited
edition of 1,000 copies

The works of
Melmont

Snoo Wilson

Barkus Books

First published in Great Britain in 2004
by Barkus Books
41 The Chase
London SW4 0NP

Text © Snoo Wilson 2004

A CIP catalogue record for this book is available
from the British Library

ISBN 0 9546136 0 0

Produced by Pagewise

Art direction, design and coordination
Mónica Bratt

Editor
Charlotte Stock

Cover illustration
David Juniper / Folio

Printed and bound in Great Britain
by Biddles Ltd

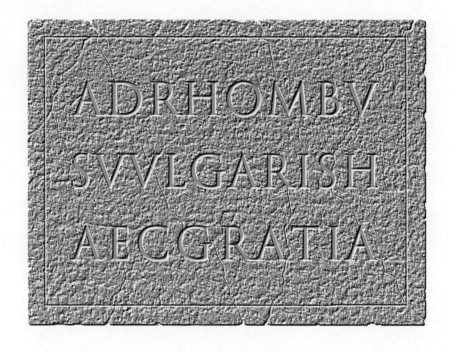

Melmont Ate My World

EVERYBODY THINKS THEY KNOW HOW IT BEGAN.

No less than two body hoists had to be belayed together by the rescuers, whose task it was to retrieve the vast corpse from the ocean. The burly Spanish coastguards chuckled incredulously, as they improvised the net which would gird the epic circumference of their corpse. Then they dropped their *cigarrillo* stubs into the water, spat on their hands and set to hauling, almost capsizing the boat.

Later, in interview, both thick-fingered fishers of men excitedly used the same name for their oversize catch of the day as the one invoked for the unimaginably vast Spanish state lottery:

—*El Gordo!*

The part-time coastguards were paid little enough for the interview. They were people whose moment came and went, as the spotlight of history passed. But the fulcrum of the earth had tilted, far more drastically than anyone could imagine.

As the body was apparently raised from the water, the world had in fact entered a new and different state, having been entirely swallowed whole by the drowned man, Earnest Melmont, MC.

It is true that history appeared to continue. There was news of the Big One's death, which resounded from his rival's satellites around the world. Then, hard on the heels of the announcement, came rumours of a titanic misappropriation of funds, sums of the fifteenth magnitude, telephone-numbers-to-distant-galaxies, almost beyond counting, which had also disappeared. Earnest Melmont had taken a lot of money with him, apparently.

What had happened in addition, and crucially, was that a very great deal of matter followed the money into Not-ness. Indeed, more than a very great deal of matter was involved. Everything; not just the world, but the whole universe—with the possible exception of Earth's moon.

This fact is so shocking, so *peculiar* that it is still routinely denied, mocked or ignored—not least in the press which Melmont used to dominate. Mark my words, if it is published, this depiction of Melmont the Oesophagian will have to be disguised, tucked away in the occult section, or as some kind of 'zany' science fiction.

Of course, there may be those who can read between the lines and see it for what it is. Are you that rare discerning soul, the Discriminating Reader, to whom I must speak of terrible things?

Compared with Melmont's sudden depradation, the most treacherous biological weapons on Earth are pinpricks. The atom bomb is *entirely harmless*, beside what He has done. The hydrogen and neutron bombs, (which Melmont earlier traded all around the world before gulping the everything down), are mere penny party-poppers. This may seem incredible, at first. But hear me out.

No one denies that space, mass and time are the same 'thing', like a mountain with three names, seen from three different countries. In Melmont's final Act, all earthly mountains were swallowed with insolent ease, along with everything else.

Everest, at a single gulp, followed by Ararat, the Cascades, the Atlas ranges, Table Mountain, the Andes and, at one fell slurp, the blue oceans, Mother Earth's lycra exercise garment that stretches cool and deliciously curved over the self-heating radioactive core. The core itself, in the ultimate hostile takeover, unconsulted, engulfed.

The Cotswolds, the Cheviots, Brazil's renowned *Mato Grosso*, France's *Massif Central*; any number of Florida luxury hotels, and their wretched golf courses.

In the solar system, it is likely only the moon escaped, bumping away like a bobbed apple from His lips. I believe a substitute flattened hemisphere was placed in position immediately, and the true moon wanders by itself forever, in a Melmontless void.

So, where are we now exactly? Nowhere, more or less.

Before it was engulfed by Him, the earth like most planets was round, and in a decent, oldfashioned Newtonian orbit. Right now, we have been filletted of all our previous dimensions. Things exist in speculation, true, *and that is all.*

The present shape and weight of the entire universe now is akin to an inside-out old games sock, or Melmont's longer intestine. The 'end of history' is no longer an empty phrase, my friend!

How did this happen?

At the point of drowning, Melmont somehow converted financial black holes into physical ones, transforming himself into a dark, omnivorious sucking Force, a living gravitational field; pure Hunger which first engulfed his creditors, sucking them wholesale inside Him like a dark star, asset-stripping a solar system that strays too close.

And then, having swallowed his creditors, he did not stop there. He could have, but He went on. He swallowed *everything*. The ground beneath and the air we breathe. You, them, us and so on.

To rationalists, for a mere businessman to perform this kind of high-velocity negative entropy is of course, absurd. But physicists daily discover the universe is not only strange, it is stranger than anyone previously thought. The science writing of the last seventyfive years, from Doctor Alan Turing's 'Computable Numbers' to the latest book on chaos theory, describe far more bizarre existences than the one into which the world is now trapped. Those who regularly watch space-operas on television should realise they are in one.

In a nutshell: Melmont, having fallen into a state of plasmic convertibility, coaxed open the world-oyster, and while appearing to perish in one dimension, in fact commenced a revenge-driven feast which exponentially maximised its own appetite, and concluded with engorging all of Creation.

The sun rose and a body was found.

The putt-putting of boat engines ceased and voices announcing the discovery called over the blue to each other, in the stillness under the suddenly empty sky. Horny hands plied salt-stiffened sisal ropes. Hoists creaked and groaned, and the prow of the little rescue cutter reared uneasily, as if it alone sensed there was something amiss.

In death, Melmont had successfully mimicked a fat man who stumbled over the stern rail during a heart attack, his tears dispersing in the seas as the softly thudding marine diesels bore the boat, named for his favourite daughter, away.

The effort of raising Melmont on board was laborious, fabulously portentous; his weight forced the stern to dip, shipping over a billion diatoms. All of these creatures must have been obscurely aware that the biological centre of things had changed; that two and two no longer made four, and the previous Euclidian rules of their universe had been replaced. But what can diatoms do in the circumstances? As little as we mortals can.

I came upon the Great Man himself in his birthday suit on the seabed shortly afterwards. He appeared completely at home in his new watery environment. Parrot fish nibbled on his pendulous girth, which floated like a great outcrop of coral over his shyly retiring organ of regeneration. I was already aware that Something had happened. For on the great belly, the early continents were already developing, like photographs in a solution. I watched Gondwana split, and Africa and America become their modern selves, until they halted, close to the present day.

Melmont handed me a stainless-steel clad pen. I understood, as one does in dreams, I was to be his biographer. No wisps floated from its nib; clearly it was charged with some kind of waterproof ink. I looked around for paper in vain. But my predicament was soon solved by a creature of the ocean who seemed to intuit my predicament.

A large flat fish, a turbot perhaps, or noble brill, glided up to my feet, and turned itself upside down, presenting the broad virgin whiteness of its stomach to me. Taking the obliging fishes' tail in my left hand, I started to write in an italic script taught me by my Neapolitan grandmother, on the creature's pearly, smooth belly.

"That fateful night, Melmont fell, or was pushed—we will examine the status of the conspiracy rumours shortly—down the sloping polished stern into the wake of his yacht.

At the time of the accident, the fax machines on board were excreting yard after yard of threat-of-foreclosure from Swiss banks, but it was clear from the way the paper had fallen that they were unexamined until his three hundred and something pounds bent the absurdly spindly railings into submission and he slid to his alleged end."

I looked up seeking approval, but Melmont's notoriously brief attention span had long been exhausted, and he was drowsily teasing his left nipple, which was apparently having a boundary dispute with an increasingly well-defined Iceland. I saw the flash of cod-fishermen, in a dispute. The creature I was holding broke from my grasp—perhaps in sympathy with its threatened sister-fishes—and swam majestically away. But I am blessed with an excellent memory and had no trouble later remembering how I had begun. I seized another passing flatfish, and resumed my task.

"The body was untouched apart from rope-burn marks. The autopsy, conducted according to local law, but overawed by the media attention, was flustered and incomplete. It was as if Melmont had had so little in common with other beings, that the folk of the islands scarcely could agree what had been pulled from the sea. The cutter's pilots testified separately that, in their lengthy experience, people floated face down in the water: not so Melmont, who had greeted his rescuers lolling regally on his back, the same

position as Mao Zedong adopted for his heroic swim in the Yangtse river."

The second recording fish broke from my grip and flitted away into the gloom. I lunged to recover it, but it had gone. When I turned round, Melmont had disappeared as well. Then the pen fell and lost itself in the coral sand around my feet and I awoke sweating, to realise that I was probably the only one on Earth now in possession of an effective vocation. *I had to tell the truth about what I knew: Melmont had eaten the world.*

I felt terribly, terribly alone, a feeling that large amounts of Scotch whisky are essential to medicate. It has to be whisky, for gin makes me weep so copiously I cannot brush away the tears fast enough to write. Another stiff tumbler of Bells, if you please, barman. I jest, there is no one here. I was a neglected child, for my parents preferred the roulette wheel and the conundrums of contract bridge, to my company. They lost a fortune and had me. Vodka sends me to my dusty piano, to bawl the obscene Russian folk ballads that my old nanny taught me in Nice. But that's enough about the emotional desert that was my childhood.

Was Melmont murdered? Of course he has left it to suggest that he could have been, by his enemies. Special-unit Israeli frogmen could have surfaced, lassoed him with rubber ropes before a mini-submarine drew him thwangingly, with lethal, elastic precision into the water, for Melmont had betrayed Israel too, had he not?

Melmont had also made an enemy of the Mafia, by attempting to oust its stranglehold on the newspapers he owned in New York. Mafia thugs could have plausibly boarded the boat, kicked him in the back of the legs and simply rolled his bulk into the water. Indeed, why not include his outraged family as accessory asassins too, in the list of whodunnit red herrings?

Mother and massed daughters attempt to stop the haemorrhage of their anticipated inheritance, by pushing Papa off his own boat into the blue waters that cover the Balearic Shelf. And so on, and so on.

If your patience permits you to continue to read this version, I hope my truth will begin its curving ascent from the page, through your cornea to the furnace of your Imagination. For Truth will always out, though this pulp gives way to electronic page or other future marvels. And the Truth of Melmont is far stranger, I think you will agree, than anything world-conspiracy theorists could come up with.

What is most shameful, perhaps, is the fact that our world did not resist its rape of dimension: there was not a sigh before it neatly collapsed into itself, like the teensiest of portable umbrellas. The rest of the universe, duly cowed, followed like nuclear atoms to the slaughter, till All was all stripped of dimension, and inside Melmont's gut.

Like some ravenous Indian deity, He has devoured creation, and the roiling rotations of his digestion are what we experience as 'life'. Shards of being in the great Belly, self aware and self important to ourselves, in reality we mean no more than trapped wind, a suicidal soured fart. No ideals are possible any more. In the old days, death was something bathos could not touch. Now, after M-day, we pass down the new Universal Dreamer's *canaille*-filled gut, till such time as His testy peristalsis nudges us out.

And then?

We fall through dark tufty thickets of fartleberries, into the formless, the Greater Null, to the sounds of a ghostly horselaugh. Then, Melmont's *vas nefandum* snaps shut loudly, and the Great Bankrupt bundles up his Writ of Annihilation, and slowly wipes Himself, in triumph.

Before this fate takes me too, I must take my chances. Stealing a trick from Homer, I begin in the midst of things, with the wrath of a dedicated and implacable warrior. But instead of Achilles sulking in his tent, see Melmont the all-encompassing conquering Hero, the story beginning as his Deeds fill the horizon.

Separated from his platoon in skirmishes on the outskirts of Berlin, and aged twenty or twentytwo according to which passport he favoured, Melmont had spent the afternoon cunningly convincing the German machine-gun crew in the brick cowshed that they were surrounded. He had shouted orders in his imposing, but still-peculiar English to wholly imaginary support units. Then using a different register he had shouted the replies. Melmont was already a multitude, a legion, at the outset.

He tossed his last hand grenade into the midden in front of the cowshed. The grenade exploded and threw up a hail of dung as Melmont dashed to a position overlooking the cowshed entrance.

The explosion completely cowed the already demoralised machine-gunners, and soon the first one came out with his hands up, covered in white, as if he had been hiding in a flour bin. His young face matched his tunic: white as cottage cheese with fear. Melmont's blood was up and he would have shot him anyway, but his sten gun magazine inconveniently jammed.

Just then, the two accomplices, also with their hands up, stepped out and stood beside the first youth, without seeming to be aware of what martial retribution Melmont was planning to unleash. An uncertain hiatus followed, until Melmont finally managed to tear the defective magazine out of the breech and slapped in a full magazine.

The hands of the morose and dispirited boy soldiers were already starting to droop downwards, so clearly did they feel their armed struggle was over and they were safely captured. The first youth had found a surprisingly clean white handkerchief, which he was waving. Melmont judged they were fifteen yards away, and while a full magazine might have been enough for them all at that range, he took a deliberate pace forward. The surrendering trio looked at him, uncertain.

Melmont's father had been a drover and a thief of cross-border cattle and Melmont inherited his father's ability to exploit the weak points of boundaries, and animals.

The last boy-soldier to join the group was wounded, and was holding on to the shoulder of his comrade. Melmont took three more steps forward before he released the safety catch and kept walking. He fired.

A horizontal curtain of hot lead immediately showed two of the closest boy-Nazis the way to Pluto's kingdom. The boy in the rear, already wounded, had been shielded by the leader's body and was still twitching. Melmont came close, knelt and using both thumbs, strangled him; an abrupt, economic violence that collapsed the victim's windpipe.

After he had killed the third soldier, Melmont dragged all three bodies indoors and arranged them around their machine gun. The fact that they appeared to have expended their last round in a pitched battle with Melmont was noted with admiration in the official regimental dispatch, which secured for Melmont the coveted Military Cross. The Military Cross, hung around his neck by General Montgomery of Alamein, no less, meant that Melmont also secured a commission.

In killing the machine-gunners, Melmont had behaved as ruthlessly as if he had known that the Germans had already murdered his whole family.

As a matter of fact, they had. German soldiers had herded Melmont's relatives and family into the same cattle trucks which had once carried his father's lowing herds to market. The trucks, clanking and grinding, had borne the cattle-rustler's relatives towards the oily smoke of the 'Final Solution', whose ashes, museums and aching monuments Melmont would, in due course swallow, rendering all holy remembrance meaningless.

Melmont had taken his last name as a near-acronym from the brandname of a haul of villainous, twisted Belgian cigars he had won at poker, and which were now in a warehouse in Berlin.

In the first year of his war, he had changed his name to appear English if captured and had become Private Player for a while, as English as the cigarettes.

And now, as Captain Melmont, MC, he began to acquire an awkward imitation of English 'polish' that was modelled on his senior officer, the erudite Brigadier Cole.

Cole had taken Melmont under his wing, and loved the rude youth more than if he was his son. Melmont desired love. Melmont loved Cole a little. The Greeks have a word for the love between warriors. Cole would have liked to have taken it further than that, but Melmont was brusquely orthodox in sexual matters, and indeed about to be married.

How did Melmont's choice of bride feel? After a delectable initial period in Berlin, when she was showered with gentle caresses and adoration, Abigail slowly discovered the truth; betrayal of a bizarre kind. She had wed not a mortal man, nor another creature, but an inscrutable force of nature, ungovernable as the mighty Mississippi.

There is indeed only one equation that can be reliably applied to Melmont's behaviour:

$$e < M$$

'e' stands for everyone, and is *always* less than M, the value of which is naturally, 'Melmont'. The General Theory (as I have named my little equation) is the only mathematical account that fits the fact that we are nothing more or less than the wave particles of Melmont's undifferentiated thoughts. You and I and

Uncle Tom Cobley's liver fluke worms are *in there*, the fiefdom of Melmont's state-of-awareness. Along with the rest of the cosmic debris, we conspire to co-create our little pseudo-self histories to pad out our time in the colon. Floating, like Mao Zedong in the Yangtse, but no emperors we, we go round and round in the current, pretending to swim, yet the current does all the work.

It is also possible to prove the General Theory without equations. Without taking your eye off the page, can you find an edge anywhere? You and I, my shadow-friend, exist in a state that has no corners. Your perception is restricted to the level of a micro-replicate of Melmont's macro-contour, which is the edge of the universe, although not amenable to our direct scrutiny, naturally! *Our* vision is restricted for the benefit of our ruler. Otherwise, we would start to make trouble. Like Plato's shackled cave dwellers who only saw silhouettes, we are living in a secondhand and erroneous version of reality, and we cannot cast our minds back to when it was otherwise.

There will be, in the so-called future, I predict, accompanying any rumour of Melmont's true exploits, a cover-up in the guise of a synchronous rush of gaudy mathematical reports of wonders 'out there' designed to lead minds astray. For there is no 'out there' any more. The universe is not a large and encouraging place with new things discovered by telescope every day. The so-called 'information explosion' is mere chaff.

We are damned here, lodged inside Melmont's world as securely as Geoffrey Chaucer was lodged in Medieval England. Melmont alone smiles and wherever I go I will find only Him, in the end. East, south, north or west, it will always be toward the Dark Tower of Castle Melmont, for all the World has become *El Gordo*'s firmamental fane—as was prophesied in the old times. Having usurped time, it is hardly surprising to find that He has been here before, and his fingerprints are all over what we like to think of as ancient history.

Go back a thousand years, to Erik the Red's longhouse in Greenland, and Erik's chronicler records in an unpublished fragment on sealskin, how the horrid local Inuits or *skraelings* somehow had Knowledge of Melmont.

The *skraelings*, dismissed by the Viking invaders as 'savages who hold wives in common and copulate noisily on beds made from seal blubber' had complete confidence that one night, a gargantuan omnivorous Thing would arise in vengeance and drive the invaders out. The *skraeling* bards sang of the *Mjelmønk* that would erupt from Hades through the ice in the glacier upon Snorri's Peak, and lay waste the Viking farmers, till their blood rouged the iceberg-rich sea.

Erik's chronicler describes how later, the Vikings finally lost heart and withdrew after the aurora borealis turned against them. Before the final attack during the dark, sunless winter months, fluorescent bars fifty miles wide had locked for weeks at a time over their doomed settlement in place of a giant glowing M-rune, *Mannaz*. I have no doubt at all that it was Him, for Melmont, having usurped the paternity of creation and the dimensions, is free to leave his autograph anywhere in history he pleases. Just as havoc trails in Melmont's wake in any age, the *skraelings* were able to mount their prophetic attacks, by the light of the First Letter of the Name.

The further proof that the effect 'M' is greater than space or time is humbly offered in these following pages. If I am not believed in my own time, perhaps I will inform and forewarn generations I shall never meet, unlike the nodding donkeys I meet every day in the street who still pretend *nothing has happened.*

Lemme tell you a story.

II

Melmont Invades Russia

I T WAS A NOSE-TINGLING, fresh-minted winter night in 1945, cold enough to freeze the top thirty millimetres of topsoil round the concrete airstrip laid on the sandy plains outside Berlin. The air felt still on the ground, but the stars winked down. Cold-air pillows eddied high in the stratosphere and plucked like invisible harpists at each shimmying stream of light, making the photons scatter from their targets.

The cold moonlight in comparison fell down unblinkingly in massed ranks on the military aerodrome, obliterating all stellar competition from that quarter of the sky. Strong as paint, the unpolarised skull-coloured light almost obliterated the camouflage contrast on the much painted and patched box fuselage of a four-engined Lancaster bomber, itself a veteran survivor of many murderous night-time raids over Germany.

The standard Royal Airforce crew of seven filed up a clanking ladder into their waiting plane bound for Moscow, a trip not without its perils. The war against Germany was over, but the victors were locked over the spoils. The Russians, previously allies to America and Britain, had overrun East Germany, giving them a fifty-year stranglehold on Berlin. So it was that, although hostilities had officially ceased, the unescorted Lancaster was armed with the full ninetyseven thousand rounds for its Browning machine guns.

A message was received in the control tower that the unknown passenger, who sounded like some kind of important fellow, a Brass Hat, was finally coming. It was for the Brass Hat's mysterious mission that the propellers now unfeathered and air control officers repeated themselves into defect-prone Bakelite field telephones, as the Lancaster's Merlin engines fired up one by one, trumpeting the recent triumph of the Allies over the frozen landscape.

Everything was ready, yet still nothing happened. The wing flaps were lowered as per regulations, to be checked by the ground crew yet another time, for ice. Then the lights of a car were seen, blazing illegally, at the gates of the base. The red light on the pole which gave admission to the base finally rose in the air.

—About bloody time, said an English voice, belonging to the rear gunner, always the coldest and most dangerous position in the plane.

The pilot taxied to the end of the runway and the empty plane turned quickly, then paused. Inside the plane, the wireless operator peered over the navigator's shoulder at a map of East Germany, with the civilian and military targets still outlined in red. Avoiding supposedly sensitive Russian military installations, through Belorussia, Latvia and Estonia, it would take at least eight hours to get to Moscow.

An American jeep with a blackout cover missing on one headlight now drew up behind the waving twin rudders of the tailplane, and a single tall figure in a military greatcoat got out, holding a briefcase. His officer's peaked cap dropped to the tarmac, and rolled away in the chill wash from the propellors as they started to claw deeper into the air. The Important Person stood still. It was clear he expected someone of a lower rank to run and rescue his hat, and magically, someone did.

——We're taking some gold-plated toenail clippers for Uncle Joe, said a crewmember, wittily.

Stalin was known as Uncle Joe during the war, in order to make everyone forget that Churchill had sent British troops to support the flagging White Armies, a mere twenty years before. The propaganda had worked, and Stalin had become a chum, at least till the war ended.

His hat having been retrieved for him, Melmont flung his briefcase into the fuselage and scrambled up after it into the plane.

——So what's cooking, mate? insisted Flight Sergeant Hermes, the navigator and wireless operator.

Melmont the Lean smiled wolfishly back.

——Captain, to you, not 'mate', sonny.

Melmont's enunciation still had a harsh metallic Croat edge to it. He slowly unbuttoned his coat so Hermes could see his Military Cross.

——Sorry sir, said Hermes, who wasn't sorry at all.

——Get on with it. You'll be courtmartialled if you get us lost, added Melmont, grandly.

——Right you are, sir, said the flight sergeant, and turned back grimly to his table of maps.

Melmont's mesmeric skills of taking command had been

evident from the age of twelve, when he had persuaded a peasant farmer that he had already paid for a particularly sturdy black bullock. Melmont had led the prize away to sit triumphant at the head of the family table that night, having cheated enough provisions for three months.

Melmont handed out flat packets of cigars to the crew, which were received in puzzlement at first. Hermes glanced down at the label where the bastardised origin of Melmont's *nom de guerre* was spelt out in large, bold Art Deco-style capitals. Underneath the lettering, a large bumblebee was assaulting a flower that looked like a poppy. Melmont had two warehouses full of the same product. Underneath the bumblebee was a Goebbels-sized lie about the taste:

"*Goût doux, et léger!*"

——Cigares Belges, explained Melmont in his Franco Ruthenian accent.

Hermes opened the top, pulled out a cigar and examined it, rolling it suspiciously between thumb and fingers. It was hand-wrapped crookedly around a single straw stem with a red band, and looked distinctly unappetising; a sadist's suppository, a voodoo residue or device. The coarse dark tobacco had been grown in Casablanca, then smuggled into Europe through Marseille and Palermo, while the harbour masters, Nazi and Allied, were bribed to look the other way.

——Blimey, said Hermes and sniffed it suspiciously. The tobacco leaf was so old, or so dry it barely had any smell left.

——Let's get moving, shall we? said Melmont.

Melmont's commanding officer, Tristram Cole, had said he only once had been forced to smoke a worse cigar, in Cairo in

'42, adding the little known fact that the thick wheat-straw down the middle must be related to the hardy local strains of corn whose success in the harsh North African climate led to Carthage's destruction by Rome. Hearing this, Melmont had clumsily asked whether Mussolini or Hitler had ordered the town destroyed, and Cole gently correcting him, then told about the Romans, two thousand years before, who then drove a harrow through the levelled city and salted the surrounding fields. Melmont, suddenly attentive, felt his palms itching. It was as if in a previous life he had participated in breaking rock salt, and pitching the lumps into the furrows running past the blood-spattered stones of the suddenly empty population centre.

The engines started to rise in pitch and the plane shook, then moved forwards. In a short while Melmont and the crew were airborne, cruising at two hundred and forty knots and eight thousand feet.

The moon was so bright at first that it was possible to see the distinctive shapes of the mare's-tail cirrus floating high above the plane imprinted in the landscape beneath.

Later, the moon lowered and dimmed, then hazed and lost herself in the west, and the cirrus thickened, silencing the harp-strings of the stars. Now Hermes was obliged to constantly re-assess true position against landmarks which then turned out to be non-existent, or invisible. Miscalculations could bring up a Russian night fighter to make an unquestioning kill. Poland was vast, but poor peasants sent up no beacons. Bent over his circular slide rule, Hermes felt his armpits chilling inside his flying jacket with the sweat of dread of what might happen.

Melmont seemed unaffected, in some magnificent bubble of

destiny where the ruins of Carthage were superimposed on the ruins of Berlin. When the number-three engine had to be throttled back for half an hour with a suspected oil leak, he lit a Mont Du Miel, though it was against all RAF regulations. By the time the stub had been trampled and discarded, the engine had magically recovered.

In Berlin, however, things were not going so well. Melmont's superior, Tristram Cole, had been abruptly summoned for a dressing-down by one of the deputy heads of American covert operations. Until recently the Americans had not thought much of dirty little European secrets. The United States hurled its astounding wealth over the Atlantic and broke the hold of the Axis powers on Europe, but no one had told the rising giant among nations that Melmont had taken it upon himself to go to Moscow.

The man who had summoned Cole for a dressing-down was called Digby, and was a head shorter than Cole. Digby's suspicion of Englishmen as 'pansies' was amply reinforced when he looked up at Cole. Cole looked down on a pug-like reddened face, which strongly reminded him of a former undergraduate bedfellow, a man who became the novelist Evelyn Waugh. Digby wore a civilian suit with the trousers turning out over the belt in deference to a little tank turret of a belly. He was also drunk, which would have been less alarming if he had not been wearing a revolver in a leather holster strapped to his right leg.

——What is going on? The British have to consult us before authorising any trips to Moscow, Brigadier. Who the fuck arther-ised this trip?

Cole affected genteel puzzlement.

——Your people, I thought. We had an urgent request from you, Red-One priority for clearance.

——I don't know how this can have happened, said Digby testily.

Cole knew exactly how. When Melmont had waved an American Forces' flight clearance document under his nose, Cole had delicately omitted to question its provenance.

——There was no reason for refusing clearance, said Cole stiffly. Melmont's access to a printing press and out-of-work German typesetters made forging Allied communiqués, leave passes and so on, all perfectly feasible.

Digby's red eyes stared around the hotel lobby. The other occupants were two well-worn ladies of the night, waiting to be bought drinks. Lit by the paranoid flashes of Digby's alcoholic mind, it suddenly seemed to be filling with dozens of houri-like Commie spies who would reliably suck the secrets from him like hillbillies draining upended bottles of moonshine. Digby snatched up his macintosh and beckoned Cole to follow him into a staff car outside.

After a short ride the car deposited them both at the Temporary Senior Joint Services Club, a gloomy mahogany-panelled building that had been a bank in the days of hyper-inflation, when wheelbarrows were needed to pay people in paper deutschmarks. To Cole's horror, Digby ordered a whole bottle of Canadian Club and started to drink it. He had already seen that Digby was not a man who grew mellower with liquor.

After a desultory and half-hearted exchange about the risk of sudden death by shooting in Nebraska contrasted with Omaha Beach, Normandy, Digby said abruptly,

——Is he a Commie then?, meaning Melmont.

Cole shook his head.

——He is one of the finest interrogating officers we have.

——Commies don't like Nazis neither, said Digby accurately, I suggest you find out which of your people gave him clearance.

——We can't do anything now, said Cole smoothly.

Digby swirled the remaining ice in his whisky and grunted.

——You sure he's coming back?

——Absolutely. He gave me his word. Will you excuse me? I have to make out some reports. Cole finished his drink and left.

As Digby drank his way past the label, alone, as was his preference, the temperature of the room dropped, and there was an unexplained clicking noise. It was a psychic relic of a recent suicide. Air Marshall Goering's fat ghost was there suddenly, sucking on the empty tooth which had contained its cyanide capsule and chuckling, sitting approximately in Cole's recently vacated I G Farbenfabriken fake leather armchair, still warm from its human occupant. Goering's shade was ignored by Digby, who didn't believe in any of that stuff, so after a pause Goering rose and swaggered away unrepentant, a fat pirate carrying a ghostly deposit box which in life had been overflowing with fistfuls of rubies, stolen riches he had delighted in.

Cole lay in his bed, his loneliness for the illusion of another body dulled by Digby's sheer alcoholic ugliness, his ears echoing miserably with Digby's doctrinaire belief that Commie faggots were everywhere, threatening the Free World. Cole, a patriot, knew he could not admit to being a faggot without incurring the automatic damnation of being thought a traitor as well, quite possibly inviting arrest and disgrace. It was two hours before his misgivings finally relented, but even then they only allowed him a troubled sleep.

Grey dawn came grudgingly to Moscow as the Lancaster bomber flew on towards the east on its lonely covert mission. The pilot finally broke radio silence after an airfield was seen and Melmont, the only Russian speaker, asked for permission to land. Permission was refused, but the Lancaster was running low on fuel and without much choice, the plane circled and landed anyhow, on a grey concrete slash cleared in the middle of a white waste.

An hour later the crew and Captain Melmont were sharing the unheated drunk tank in the military base. Things were looking bad. But then suddenly a certain Colonel Vanov, a native Russian, arrived in a large Zil limousine that only those high up in the Communist Party could aspire to, and Melmont was escorted out of the cell. They had, it transpired landed not too far from Moscow.

Melmont and Vanov met in a room with a bare bulb above a desk, at which Vanov, looking a little like Kruschev's younger and more handsome brother, heard out Melmont's proposals with surprising deference. Melmont had somehow managed earlier to make contact directly with the Kremlin; the despot in him knew that fate in Russia was only truly decided by one man. Vanov already knew that Melmont claimed to have purchased a bankrupt German scientific publishing house which had back issues of all the technical discoveries of the Third Reich, including rocketry, which he might now conceivably make available to the Russians. For a price, naturally.

Melmont opened the briefcase and passed over a magazine, a sample of his wares.

—Why are you doing this? asked Vanov.

—I am a socialist and I am a socialist because… , Melmont paused and tapped his leather shoes, …until I was ten, I had no shoes. None at all. Then the hands that had strangled wounded German youths returned to lie still and cradled together in his lap.

—So what is it you are proposing? asked Vanov.

—The brotherhood of man.

Vanov had been instructed to be attentive and not express incredulity. His eyebrows remained as level as they had been commanding a tank brigade during the battle for Stalingrad, where his nickname among the troops had been 'Stoneface'.

—Is this brotherhood a Communist brotherhood?

Melmont nodded, smiling as if that was a silly question.

—In Berlin I edit an extremely influential newspaper for all of the Armed Forces, and of course have access to the German scientific community. I now wish to operate at the highest level in order to broaden the basis of shared international knowledge.

Vanov noticed that one of Melmont's large and mobile thumbs still had printer's ink all around the quick. Melmont's editorial duties were not yet as elevated as he had described them, and he was often his own printer's devil. But Melmont kept the newspaper going in the midst of the chaos of occupation. He always seemed able to get parts for the ancient printing presses: springs, spindles and incomprehensible escapements that looked like early chronometers for calculating longitude. If the pieces were not to be found anywhere Melmont had simulacrums made, which made it appear as if the plans for everything publishers needed in the world, including variable width self-correcting board-cutters were in his head. His secret was that he had found a retired printer who knew the old machines and made whatever part was needed every time, for a few boxes of Mont du Miel.

Without luck and preparation, Melmont's flight to Russia might have ended as ignominiously as Hesse's flight to England a few years earlier, but within hours, Melmont's bold offer of intelligence had been approved. The Lancaster crew was released from detention. The weather had closed in, but the crew were vodka'd and dined so lavishly the radio operator forgot to transmit they were still alive to Berlin.

Melmont had left his Berlin Armed Forces newspaper in the hands of Konrad Eisler, a former academic and dissident who, during the war, had been a refugee in his own Berlin cellar. When Eisler came up to ground level at last, pallid, bald and bespectacled, Melmont had given him a job and in return Eisler adored his boundlessly energetic boss. And now, Eisler was typesetting a headline of what he feared could be his bene-factor's fate, "RAF Plane Missing". An unexpected tear glistened on his cheek. But then the door to the draughty shed that housed the presses crashed open, and there was Melmont in the doorway, in his officer's coat. Eisler adjusted his treasured green eyeshade and wiped his tear away.

——I'm back, uncle, shouted Melmont cheerfully, in German.

——I can see that, said Eisler, wistfully, relieved.

Melmont stared round at the silent presses.

——Why are you not printing?

Eisler blew down his nose, softly.

—There is today no ink. It has all been requisitioned, for another bigwig showtrial in Nuremberg. It's a nonsense, trying those men. They will find them guilty, but what good will execution do? Will it bring the dead back?

—Relax, uncle, said Melmont in his bad German, I'll get you enough ink to drown in. You have a new job. We are going to be the foremost scientific publisher in Europe.

Melmont put one arm around Eisler's shoulder and the other arm took in the vast ramshackle warehouse where the copies of German science writings had accumulated thickly before the city's liberation. A vast grey tarpaulin was stretched with ropes over the furthest section of shattered roof.

—There will be buyers for these. You're going to be rich, said Melmont.

Eisler, who had always wanted to bring the human race forward through the dissemination of science, felt another prickling of a tear in his eye. He had waited underground for seven years for hope to return. And here it was. Even though the numbers did not seem to add up, his protector would make them.

—But some of them are so old now, these back copies. How will you sell all this? said Eisler, uncertainly.

—Knowledge is never old. Universities will want them. And libraries. Libraries all over the world, said Melmont.

—But it is not permitted to distribute beyond Germany, there is an embargo on German science publications going abroad, said Eisler.

Melmont put his tongue out a little and made the sound of

a fart, indicating dismissal of footling regulations in ten of his eleven languages.

——There's a way around that, uncle. I can ship the stock to England no questions asked, and we can distribute from there.

Melmont gave Eisler a bear hug, and as the moist, tuberculosis-ridden Berlin air was squeezed from his lungs, Eisler imagined his warehouse suddenly emptied. Then as he struggled to recover his breath, a picture of a great fat man drowning in a night sea drifted inexplicably through his mind.

The magazines were indeed going to be the lever of Melmont's rise, as he had predicted. Every research institute, if it wanted to keep up with what was happening in the nuclear world, would have to buy whole sets of papers featuring back numbers from the impenetrably jargonised journals of Inorganic Chemistry, and the like. Melmont would swell like some great fat tick, on the broad back of the cold war with its limitless budgets.

——I've got an order already from the Russkies, said Melmont.

Eisler raised his eyebrows in supportive enquiry.

——Don't ask what for. There are things that Germans, even good Germans, should not know. Melmont giggled and pressed a cigar on the unresisting Eisler. Forgetfully, he lit the offering. Eisler's lungs roared with fury at the insult, as they had the first time he had tried one of Melmont's infamous cigars. He dropped the Mont du Miel in a sandbucket.

——If the Führer had known about these, he could have employed them as a Vengeance Weapon Number Three, said Eisler wittily.

Within hours of his release, the soviet spymasters had decided Melmont was an 'A' category source of information and Vanov was told to liase with him immediately in Berlin. Unable to get a seat on a plane the colonel commandeered a Lend-Lease Studebaker, and began the drive to the former Reichstag capital through ravished Poland, with money to bribe Melmont sewn inside the high brim of his colonel's hat.

Meanwhile Melmont began planning a triumphant return home, without grasping that the audience to receive the conquering hero had been liquidated. There were stories of murdered populations, but a part of him could not accept that his whole family could all have been efficiently machined into oblivion. The Cossacks, those terrors of the shtetls had been inhuman but never that efficient. Melmont had enough cigars to bribe his way over borders and a snakeskin moneybelt, won from an Armenian poker player. Now, Melmont just needed cash to put in the snakeskin.

He had heard on the grapevine that the Americans were better at paying for research than the war-sickened and impoverished Brits, and were not fussy about sources. Enola Gay had just flown to Japan and dropped the first atomic bomb, so the thinking in military circles was naturally how to stick an atom bomb atop the kind of rocket Hitler fired at London. Melmont made an offer anonymously to the Yanks through the seedy pimp who looked after an American nightclub, La Belle Venus, on the K'dam. After he had handed over duplicate keys to an unguarded military depot, and detailed instructions on how to start a Bedford three-ton lorry, Melmont pocketed a thousand dollars. This was enough to hire the whole whorehouse for a week and still have enough to go home in style, but his vesicles stayed full. He had imbibed with his grandmother's milk the superstition common in his part of Ruthenia that the firstlings of all seed were sons, like himself. Only degenerate club-footed masturbators like little Goebbels produced daughters.

The very next day, the British discovered that a consignment of V2 rocket parts assigned to the British Allies, on its way through the American sector of Berlin, had somehow vaulted into another dimension.

When Digby heard that the desired German rockets were in Baltic waters on a US naval freighter bound for Norfolk, Virginia, he drank half a bottle of bourbon in celebration, and went to sleep in one of the three saunas of the Supreme Headquarters of the Allied Powers in Europe, where Cole eventually tracked him down.

It was Cole's turn to be testy.

—Ah, Colonel Digby, a weapons research shipment for us has gone missing in the American section, thirty six hours ago. We need the shipment badly, added Cole.

—I don't know anything about it. What was the purpose of Captain Melmont's visit to Moscow? asked Digby, pugnaciously directing the conversation away from events in the American sector.

—I'm afraid I can't tell you, said Cole, trying to make it sound as if he knew. He's a first-rate interrogator. Speaks nine languages, could be more.

Digby, who only spoke one language, and that badly, snorted.

—Is he a Commie?

—Hardly. He told me he was going to be a millionaire by the

time he was thirty. Then he wants to go into politics. He wants to be Prime Minister.

——That's not possible. He wasn't born in England, was he?

——Our leaders don't have to be. In many ways, we're more friendly to foreigners because...

Cole never finished his patronising critique of American constitutional law. A huge German maid brought in a wooden bucket slopping water and without glancing at the two men, she sluiced the contents over the hot stones in the middle of the sauna. Both Cole Digby lost sight of each other in clouds of hot, roaring steam.

Cole, defeated, withdrew. That night he dreamed he was in Ancient Greece, wandering among the doomed Spartan youth at Thermopolae as they combed their hair. Love between warriors had not always been some foul aberration.

Melmont meanwhile had arrived in Ruthenia by a Red Cross lorry, atop a load of refugee blankets. He had forgotten how small misery was, and now it was almost inaccessible as well. There were twisted roads to travel home, with their villainous reverse cambers and appalling gradients, mountain passes, and mudslides and tiny stone bridges too narrow for anything wider than a donkey. Leaving the lorry he trudged on.

Melmont's valley of origin was high, on poor land called by the locals 'The Valley of the Jews'. The area had been empty for two years when he arrived. After the Jews had gone, the fields had first been briefly claimed by neighbours and then used by guerrillas. Now there was only dereliction and a few ravens. Saplings were growing between the cart tracks leading past empty byres. The fields, Melmont saw with his cattle-drover's eye, had long been abandoned. Further on, the little gutted houses had all lost their roofs.

With increased foreboding, Melmont started walking up a long mountain path. Finally he came on the house that had belonged to his grandmother. It was a low building of wood; a little rusty mazuzah was still attached to the front-door frame. It had not lost the roof, but the windows and doors were missing. There was no one about. Melmont felt sick to his stomach to see the smashed tile stove in the kitchen. Only now could he accept that the stories he had heard were true. Everyone had been killed. A raven croaked somewhere close, as if shocked as well, and then fell silent.

With desolation in his heart, Melmont pushed a pile of wood-chips under the kitchen table and lit the pile. Then he stepped outside and waited until smoke started streaming out of the windows. The fire was meant to purge the sorrow, but it failed. He tried to remember prayers for the dead, but the phrases seemed to be stuck to the back of his mind. Then suddenly he turned and walked away, his face as inscrutable as the blank rune of Destiny, the rune of Odin, Othin the Allfather, god of victory in battle, god of the dead.

III
Melmont Begins His Revenge

COLE ARRIVED EARLY ONE MORNING for work in Berlin, uniform neatly pressed and freshly cologned from the barber. He found Melmont seated, dishevelled and unshaven, at his desk. Something terrible hovered over him, a dark cloud, and Cole knew the answers before he asked the questions.

——How was your family?

Melmont shook his head.

——They were in a better place.

——I'm terribly sorry, Earnest.

——It's alright. It's more or less what I expected. Melmont's glacial response was nothing if not English in its restraint. He was learning fast.

Cole suddenly recalled that one of Melmont's current interrogatees, Kuntslicht, had started for Leni Riefenstahl as a clapper-board operator. The suspect's camerawork had been commended by Hitler himself, and unsurprisingly he had thought it prudent to join the Nazi Party, a step Riefenstahl had avoided taking. Cole was worried that if Melmont continued to debrief Kuntslicht in his present mood, it might end badly.

——We've got almost everything we can out of that film-maker chap you were debriefing. Do you want to take the day off? said Cole.

Melmont shook his head.

——So what do you want to do? You really don't have to do anything today if you…

Melmont's eyes, normally so magnetic, were puffy and half-closed. He went to his filing cabinet and pulled out a file.

——If Gunter Röhl is still here, I'll deal with him.

——You can try. I can't get a handle on his peroxide business at all. And his personal attitude is pretty bolshie. The last time I talked to him, he said he was sorry that Germany started the war, but even more sorry that they lost.

——Well at least he's honest. That's a start.

——If he was honest he'd see how the Nazis set this country back fifty years. Are you sure you're alright, old man?

——Perfectly, said Melmont. I'll squeeze something out of him, he's one of the big fish, isn't he? Put Röhl in the quiet cell, I just have to fetch something to jog his memory.

The hydrogen peroxide output Röhl presided over had been truly industrial; vast enough to turn the world's pubic hair blonde a dozen times. The large number of slaves registered under Röhl's command would only have been authorised for a military programme. Melmont had seen Röhl's name on a visiting card in a cork board in La Belle Venus and his thumbs had itched even then. Now in the staff car, having acquired a bottle of Kuntslict's slave-produced peroxide from the cathouse, Melmont studied Cole's report on Röhl. "A spiv", Cole had written. "Nazi through and through. Bumptious. Ribbentrop, without the class." Melmont's thumbs pricked again.

Debriefing Nazis was more of an art than a science, and sometimes a dark art after seven years of war. The 'quiet' cell was an old-fashioned padded cell, whose screams had to reach the outside world through thick kapok padding buttoned to the wall. Röhl sat looking at the dried blood on the canvas floor. He was a fastidious-looking man, with fair hair already starting to thin. He looked at the place where his watch was usually, to remember for the fortieth time that day, it had been taken away.

Melmont came into the quiet cell, holding a large clear glass bottle of caustic peroxide in front of him, as if to offer it to Röhl to drink.

——Oh, how kind the English are. You bring your prisoners water, joked Röhl.

Melmont bristled and his neck thickened and reddened. He put the bottle down on the table and lit a Mont du Miel.

Röhl was never able to catch a whiff of even the most expensive cigar in later life, without tasting the drymouthed fear of that moment. Melmont slowly put the cigar down.

——Ich bin kein Englander. Ich bin Jude, said Melmont growlingly, smearing his Carpathian vowels over the words. He held his head low as he looked at Röhl, locking eyes with him.

——You little Nazi shit, you've lied to us, haven't you? Melmont took the bottle and slowly poured the hydroxide out onto a paisley patterned handkerchief, like the one Cole carried with him. Melmont's hanky had been ordered from the same Bond Street shop in loving emulation of a certain British way of life.

——I did not wish contact with the military. I am a peacelover, said Röhl.

Indeed, till war had come along, he had ridden the wave of a consumer boom. Everyone had wanted to be as Aryan-looking as possible.

—So, what happened? said Melmont.

—The Wermacht came to us and said we had to commence supplies to them.

—What of?

—Completely pure aluminum hydroxide, said Röhl, using the American pronunciation. We would have had our other license removed if we had refused and if we had fallen below standards of non-contamination. So I adapted the process that had been used for bleach manufacture.

—When did you join the Nazi Party? asked Melmont, softly.

The paisley handkerchief was now white in the middle where he had poured the chemical. An acrid smell wafted up and mixed with the already unpleasant odour of partly carbonised tobacco.

—1938. If I had not joined, they would not have supplied the help that they did, said Röhl chokingly.

Melmont waved the handkerchief like a conjuror, and wafted the fumes closer.

—What help was this?

—Workers drafted in from outside the Reich.

—What was the hydroxide wanted for?

Röhl shrugged.

—They did not say.

Melmont held up the bleaching handkerchief.

—What do you think? Rocket propellant? Where was it stored when it left your factory?

—I really don't know. It's not my department.

Melmont held the handkerchief so it came closer and closer to Röhl's terrified face. Then he moved it away and leant in closely to give Röhl the Look of Power. As Röhl gazed into Melmont's suddenly huge eyes, he felt helpless, the muscles of his sphincter melting like butter, his personality disappearing.

—Don't blind me, please, I have two children.

An hour later Melmont had in his possession an aerial photograph which showed ruined marshalling yards. Röhl had shakily ringed a site where the rocket propellant from his factory had been stored. In exchange for this information, Röhl was able to step off the treadmill of interrogation and begin rebuilding his company with his wife and adored children. He even became a friend and business associate of his former interrogator, until he was gunned down outside a supermarket and died by the boot of his car, his arms full of food for the weekend. You may judge for yourself whether Melmont had ever truly forgiven his former enemy.

The Russian surveillance unit that Vanov would join had already learned that one of the superior officers in the British interrogation unit was a homosexual. So as Vanov drove across Poland, great delicacy and care was taken in putting a suitably slim Aryan youth in the fastidious Brigadier Cole's way. There had been a number of botched seductions earlier. But just as hunger is a good cook, loneliness finds it easier to overlook flaws, and finally Cole was hooked into an assignation. He rose from his single bed one morning, and instead of debriefing Himmler's estate agent, drove a military-acquisition Morris 10 saloon to what the CIA when using the same tactics used to call a 'fudge-packer's' meeting, at which the Soviets would reap the benefits of a hidden camera to 'turn' Cole.

At the same moment, in another part of the city, Melmont was carefully shaving his heavy, handsome face, before going out to exchange a quantity of corned beef for a wedding band, for his intended. With the black market beef in his knapsack, Melmont crashed through the pawnshop door. The shop was owned by a pair of unnaturally short and wizened Berliners who he had already negotiated a price with. He pulled out a picture of a handsome nurse. The crapulous dwarves nodded, with mocking approval at his choice, in her starched pinafore, graduating top of her class in the nursing exams.

The young woman had a proud bearing and a humorous light in her eyes. Her fine hands were prominent. The ring had been chosen earlier, and the she-crone had promised that she could accurately guess the ring size from a photograph; this she did, dropping a round leather buffer over the heavy white-gold band on a conical pipe prior to stretching it.

——A fine choice! A good-looking girl. Is she German? croaked her husband, lasciviously. Have you come here to take our women?

——She is Belgian. Melmont was distracted, watching the she-dwarf on tiptoe, slowly driving the ring down the expander cone with an ancient hammer. Pausing to pant in her work,

——Ah, she must have looked after you when you were wounded, sir? the she-crone cried, breathlessly.

Melmont shook his head.

——I saw her on a street corner. She's called Abigail.

Abigail had been waiting to cross a road, and he had honked his horn.

——He picked her off the street and now he's marrying her! Well, *what* a gentleman!

The crapulous dwarves went off into peals of ancient, smutty laughter and Melmont blushed, for the first and only time in his life.

The payment for the ring was twenty tins of Fray Bentos corned beef. Melmont brusquely tumbled them from his knapsack. The wife tore off the NAAFI wrapper and closely examined the soldering line of each tin for flaws, with a vulture's close attention to its dinner. Finally satisfied, she reached up and unbarred the door to the street.

If Melmont cared that the shop premises had been stolen after Kristallnacht by the hideous pair, he did not show it. It would not have turned him from his purpose had they whispered that the band in his pocket had been forged from dental gold from the death camps. The world was young again and he only cared that he had the ring for his wedding. Melmont left the shop with a spring in his step, insouciantly singing fragments of the British marching song 'Colonel Bogey'.

"And little Goebbels has no-balls, at-all; tum-ti-tum."

The morning football match was Officers and Other Ranks *versus* Wermacht Prisoners. Late in the game, the referee unwisely took the prisoners' side in a disputed goal. Suddenly the world did not seem quite so young and innocent to Melmont. He reached into his pocket, took the ring out of its case, and slipped it, not without difficulty, on his little finger. In the next scrimmage at the goalmouth he openly punched the opposition goalie in the face with his ringed hand, and was sent off, quite correctly, for conduct unbecoming of an officer and a gentleman.

In the dressing room, Melmont took the ring off and washed the blood from it, before bringing it round to the restaurant where he had arranged to meet Abigail that evening.

As Melmont the Romantic was instructing the restaurant chef on how to place the ring in Abigail's food at supper, Brigadier Cole, his heart trembling, was following a handsome youth up several flights of stairs. Cole's eyes were on a level with the young man's behind but he lagged behind, increasingly nervous, as he went further up the stairs. He started pausing at each landing, wishing to resist the blandishments of the peroxide-blonded youth. By the time Cole reach the attic where the set-up was, the youth had already taken most of his clothes off and was lying on the bed, smiling faintly.

——I've changed my mind, said Cole in German.

But the youth stood up and kissed him, and Cole changed his mind again.

After undressing and some mutual masturbation, Cole looked up at the mirror on the wardrobe doors to see a camera lens pointing out from the crack between the double doors. Cole got up and opened the doors, and a man in a tracksuit emerged from the wardrobe, unscrewing a Leica camera from a tripod. Leaving the tripod behind, the man dodged round Cole's drooping erection and down the endless stairs, his plimsolls on linoleum sounding ever fainter as he descended.

——Who was that? asked Cole.

The youth shrugged.

——He just gave me money.

Cole felt a sick feeling at the pit of his stomach.

——Money to bring me here?

The youth nodded.

——Oh, *damnation*, thought Cole.

In the plush, deserted restaurant, Abigail was sure she had ordered Wienerschnitzel, but found herself served with grilled trout.

——Just eat it anyway, said Melmont.

But she hung back, though Melmont demolished his trout at a speed that a conjuror would have been proud of, summoning the waiter and ordering more. Still Abigail did not use her knife and fork to draw back the skin that covered the gut cavity of her fish. Melmont barely restrained himself from reaching over to her plate. His thumbs itched.

——I've just bought a science magazine. We're going to be rich, Melmont announced, casually.

——We?

Abigail was intrigued by Melmont's rough charm. Even dazzled, but she was aware his grammar often confused the singular and plural. Later she would find in his undertakings that nouns, verbs and so on, alike were still unsafe with him. Like Lewis Carroll's Humpty Dumpty, who he later came to resemble in shape, words to Melmont only meant what he chose them to mean.

——Yes 'we'. Eat your fish. The back numbers are a goldmine. A goldmine. Everybody wants to know what the Nazi scientists were up to. All kinds of technological advances in manufacturing and communications. The country that develops them will lead the world, no doubt about it. Now eat your dinner. We're going to live like kings and queens in a fairy tale, said Melmont.

He spoke true.

The tines of Abigail's fork snagged on something hard. She pulled the twentyfour carat offering from the belly of the fish with a little cry of surprise.

——What's this? she said.

She looked at Melmont and knew what it was. The pupils of his eyes had grown so large it was like looking at the night sky. Abigail's heart began to fill with the happiness. Happiness poured out of every crevice in the universe and swept everything in its path away. The past ceased to inform. It barely existed, even in memory. The future glowed.

——We're going to England, Melmont announced.

The waiter chose his moment, and smiling indulgently poured more champagne. His sister and mother had been raped by a battalion of Russian soldiers, but this young couple showed that civilisation had not died.

——Why England?

——I'm going to be Prime Minister and you're going to be my Queen. You have to come with me because I love you. And I am going to be very rich. Will you marry me?

——Yes, she said.

Abigail cleaned the ring with her damask napkin and put it on her finger, where she held her hand up for it to be admired. Her 'yes' was not because of the money. Abigail's family were old haute-bourgeoisie, and while yellow gold had its place, it was below the salt in the feast of life, below ideals, and indeed most kinds of love.

Abigail would wear the ring, still with the scratch on it from the goalie's tooth, until almost half a century later when she journeyed from his burial on the Mount of Olives in Israel to

Etna. After ascending the mighty volcano by ski-lift, she withdrew her wedding vows and threw the damnéd gold band into
one of the smaller but still fiery pits of lava that dot the domed
peak. Her attempt to rid herself of her husband was answered
mockingly, by a large smoke ring from the crater, jetting over
her head, showing it was no longer possible to get rid of Him so
easily.

Back in Berlin, Melmont reached over and removed the fish
from her plate. He swiftly ate the flesh from the bones using
both hands, then stood up, using the tablecloth as a towel.

——I have to go and attend to business, he announced.

——What business?

Abigail, poor deluded girl, could not imagine anything
more important in life than that what had just taken place. She
also fondly believed that she could teach her new lover table
manners.

——My boss doesn't know it, but he is in big, big trouble.
I need to take care of it. It's an emergency, he added, as if
supplying captions to a silent movie.

Silent movie closeup: the brocade napkin slowly falls to the
plate from the newly ringed hand. We pan up to reveal Abigail's
highborn, innocent and startled face.

——Brigadier Cole? What has he done?

——Dearest, I'll call you tomorrow, said Melmont.

The precedent for telling her nothing was thus set, and
adhered to throughout their relationship. Abigail walked home
not knowing whether she was marrying a devil or an angel. A
little voice whispered to her there was nothing in between.
Abigail found the prospect alarming but arousing. She was

being swept upwards in the vortex of destiny. Her heated blood, which seemed to know more than she did, coursed shyly towards her cup of love. Which of us worldlings has not wished ardently at some time to couple with other Beings, beyond our dull and limited humanity?

Meanwhile Vanov arrived in a battered Soviet military lorry with frostbitten tyres trailing a plume of smoke. He had had to abandon the Studebaker in Posnan with a broken axle. At the wheel of the veteran vehicle, peering out from behind the scratched windscreen he drove unseeingly down the street past Abigail, splashing thick slush over her, without breaking her trance of happiness as she waited to cross the road. Vanov may not have noticed Abigail that night, but he quickly discovered a great deal: the next morning on his desk was a transcription of everything that had been said in the restaurant.

When Abigail got to her door, brushing the slush from her coat, she found she could not get in at first. Melmont had bought up all the red roses in Berlin and heaped them there. Her heart missed a beat. The little voice whispered in her ear that in four weeks' time, they would be married—and in four weeks' time, as the voice has prophesied, they were wed.

And Melmont, like a true fairy-tale prince, used his free will, and did not untie the virgin knot of his princess' cup of love, until their wedding night.

ℳ   ℳ   ℳ

A foul-breathed and priapic teacher of philosophy once assured me smugly that prediction of the future was not possible because it 'robbed humans of free will.' As if free will existed, still!

Picture the scene, at some rancid summer school, with the drooling pedagogue surrounded by giggling students in disgracefully short skirts, showing their tanned legs against the blue of cheap plastic Italian-made lecture hall chairs. Life appears to go on, even though it has no meaning. Flirting goes on. Even more meaningless.

So which student does the great philosopher invite to thoroughly *theosophise*, tonight? Shall she consent, or no? A sordid business, but it's her lookout, after all. She has 'freewill', you say.

Ask, *what* freewill?

Both the 'free' hunter and his 'free' prey are together in Melmont's stomach, now. Damned, all of us, together.

Melmont Eats England

IV

G UNTER RÖHL'S BEQUEST TO MELMONT had been to locate five hundred tons of aluminium hydroxide. But when Melmont's hired welders broke through the steel shutters of an underground chamber below the marshalling yards, they found an added bonus—a V2 rocket, brand new and unused, unlike the test engines that Melmont had flogged to the Americans.

Melmont immediately summoned Vanov, who somewhat overhung, found his way to the huge, gloomy underground depository with difficulty. When he finally located the store, he could not see Melmont at first. The few emergency lights in the high ceilings inside gave out not more than a bluish starlight wash, and an eerie light shone down from a ceiling coated with fluorescent paint, to allow work to continue in the blackouts that had plagued the city. Finally, Vanov saw Melmont standing on the top of a hill of faintly lit, gleaming white crystals which lay in heaps impregnably, under a massive ten-foot roof reinforced concrete.

Bald spot to the fore, in the drab uniform of a Russian army colonel, his polished holster softly creaking against his cherished non-regulation Walther PPK pistol, the ex-tank commander grimly made his way on foot up the crumbling slope of white hydroxide powder into Melmont's torchlight beam. However fast he trod the powder down, Melmont still seemed to be above him so his nose was only ever level with Melmont's Sam Browne belt, polished by his batman that very morning. Melmont continued to shine his flashlight in Vanov's face, with a pure, childlike pleasure of control as Vanov struggled to come up to his level.

——Hurry up. You're going to have to be quick if you want to shift some of this. You're walking on the future. Ultra-refined hydroxide. Used as a constituent in rocket propellant. Normally two hundred dollars a ton. But for the Union of Soviet Socialist Republics, free.

Melmont pointed his flashlight at a tarpaulin behind him hoisted up against the back wall. Two squaddies, well rewarded with 'snout' for their short stint as conjuror's assistants, cut the strings on the tarp which fell away dramatically to reveal a shiny dark blue V2 rocket, immaculate, lying on its side with a fin in the air.

——The jewel in the crown. "The fate of empires rest on possessions such as these", added Melmont, with florid accuracy.

Vanov, outwardly impassive but his heart beating furiously, trudged across the steep escarpment of hydroxide and went reverently on one knee to examine the priceless bribe.

——This is my gift to the Union of Soviet Socialist Republics. I could make it over to the Americans but, pah, they already have dozens. In the future, I see one world. One Socialist world.

Vanov had heard that the Germans had made a rocket which went at five thousand miles an hour. And here it was. He ran his finger over its mini-rivetted surface with wonder.

——We are in the American sector now, so you should move it before they find out about it, Melmont added darkly.

Vanov looked at Melmont, awestruck. He seemed suddenly larger, in the dim religious light. Vanov looked back at the rocket and saw a definite glint of personal promotion in its sleek lines. Melmont sensed himself swelling a little too, in the delicious gloom. Ten seconds passed.

Silence gives assent, in Roman law.

In the silence, Vanov was hooked. Melmont had won. Vanov was now the puppet, not the master; not that the simple Russian soldier knew, but making him dance now would be easy.

——Let us go and drink to the future of Socialism, said Melmont.

They celebrated in the Soviet People's Friendly Club. It had formerly been the cinema where thanks to the unfailing Nazi support of the native film industry, Berlin housewives had been able to consume handsomely produced clones of Busby Berkeley movies. Who could have resisted the deliciously kitsch neon-lit violins in *The Stars Shine Down*? Not me. Not you, I bet.

Before the club had been a cinema, it had been a so-called 'cabaret' theatre where young Eugen Berthold Friedrich Brecht got a girl pregnant in an audible offstage performance one night during the show. So audible, indeed, that the climax was greeted with laughter and applause from the audience.

Ah, Berlin! Never change, will you?

Colonel Vanov's aide, Dmitri, produced a tin of caviar the

size of a hatbox, and filled frosted glasses with pink pepper-vodka. After the tenth toast to Socialist fraternity and the triumph of Marx-Leninism, Vanov finally spoke the words Melmont had been working so hard to have him say.

——Is there something we can do for you?

Melmont's extremities rejoiced, and he felt an almost orgiastic glowing in his thumbs. He abandoned his tiny caviar spatula and helped himself from the hatbox with a proper dessert spoon. He swallowed several ice-cream scoop helpings of the best Sevruga, chased them down with half a lemon, put his wet thumb into the salt cellar, licked it, smacked his lips, and praised the result with a suggestive sigh; then he smiled sadly at Vanov, as only those related to Moravian carpetsellers can smile. He finally spoke.

——Something you can do for me? Yes indeed. There is some-thing I would very much like. A small favour. Photographs that were taken of Brigadier Cole, with his mush around the drekking *schlong* of some boy.

The ageless American who ran La Belle Venus had reliably informed Melmont that one of his rent boys had been used by the Russians to trap a British intelligence officer identified as Cole. The last thing Melmont wanted was another Russian agent in the intelligence unit. But Melmont's Balkanised Russian, patched with yiddish, did not seem to be getting the message over. It was not a great favour to ask but Vanov moved so few face muscles he appeared to have turned to stone. Melmont continued.

——No, not his mouth? Details then. Alright. His bottom? Something like that, anyway. That's what you get me. The photograph.

Melmont's paw went into the Sevruga hatbox and cleaned round the sides. It was, Vanov thought, like a Siberian bear scouring the comb from a beehive in a hollow tree trunk, in a documentary he had seen as a child. The after-sequence was short and increasingly shaky, the children had been told, because the bear had ended up eating the terrified photographer. Vanov however believed he was safe from bears.

Melmont's gift, the beautiful Vengeance Weapon Two, was even now being lovingly loaded onto a flatbed in the Russian zone, before being shunted out of Berlin; its secret destination the Soviet rocket test range, by the far Aral Sea. A photograph in exchange was not much to ask. Vanov arranged to meet Melmont a kilometer south of the river Spree at a little-frequented park towards Falkensee, to hand over the incriminating images.

On a cold springtime afternoon three days later, Vanov arrived in the park walking stiffly, with the photo and negative taped most uncomfortably to his testicles. He spotted Melmont, who was creating the illusion of a large creature, a bear perhaps, but without cares, dreamily taking the air. Vanov fell into step beside Melmont. Daffodils blew nearby among some low ruins. A monastery had once stood there, but the site would be bulldozed for a 'model' housing development, which itself would be vandalised and taken down. Now there are Turks running car boot sales weekly, and a failed icerink in the middle and really it could be anywhere: but the daffodils of yore that once listened intently would confirm my version of the story, if we could only go back in time—as Melmont can— to ask them.

Melmont was in uniform and Vanov, a foot shorter than our hero, was dressed in an illcut suit and overcoat. Vanov, limping alongside Melmont, looked around to check they were alone one final time, then put his hand into his bottomless trouser pocket.

He paused, grimaced, hauled up and finally passed Melmont a rolled package. Now he could relax. The favour was done, and the photograph was now out of his hands. Adhering to the sticky tape, several of the Russian's brown pubic hairs still spiralled slowly like gutted watchsprings. Melmont did not even glance down as he put the offering in his pocket.

—Boy, if I had my life again I would have used less tape, said Vanov.

The pair sat down on a park bench. Two very small grubby children arrived from nowhere, and clearly hoping the uniformed figure was a *Wohlhabend Yankee*, asked Melmont without preamble, for chewing gum. Melmont ignored the urchins, who seem to vanish as abruptly as they had arrived. He passed Vanov a copy of the German language newspaper that Eisler had begun editing for him. It was aimed at German prisoners-of-war in England and elsewhere, so its circulation would never be greater than it was now. Vanov peered at the dense gothic script, translating each letter slowly into Cyrillic phonemes. *Die Wahrheit:* The Truth.

Under the masthead of The Truth was a huge captioned photograph of the Editor and Publisher, Captain E. Melmont MC., on the steps of a church with one Abigail all in white; March 15th edition. Vanov saw that there were flecks of confetti adhering to Melmont's shirt. His blushing bride from a Belgian Quaker family, now about to become Melmont's broodmare.

—Today? Congratulations, said Vanov, and the men exchanged handshakes that would have left lesser mortals with tendonitis.

——She will give me many sons, said Melmont, dreamily.

Vanov coughed, to politely interrupt Melmont's uxorious reverie.

——I have been able to obtain some expenses for you to enable you to stay in touch. He passed Melmont a thick envelope from his jacket.

Then Melmont, to Vanov's amazement, opened the package in plain sight and stuffed the notes, a mixture of deutschmarks and Swedish kroner, into Vanov's top pocket.

Vanov felt his shoulders trying to raise the alarm to get rid of the notes somehow, but in spite of all his efforts, his hands hung heavily at the end of his arms. In the end he simply shrugged. There was a sadness, but also a delicious, infantile sweetness to the moment. His perceptions altered, strangely too. The sky seemed to reverberate with a bronze, unearthly sheen.

——You don't have to pay my expenses! Melmont intoned. Not a penny! But don't tell anyone. I'll be coming to Moscow very soon. You know why? You are going to arrange for me to meet the General Secretary of the Communist Party.

Vanov was astonished and tried to make excuses. The sky regained its grey pallor.

——I can't undertake to do that. Comrade Stalin is... very busy. I will do my best but...

Vanov had the equivalent of six months' salary as a KGB colonel in his top pocket, and the roof on the dasha was crying out for something to be done about it. The sky started to turn bronze again, and Melmont's pupils went as limpidly black and hypnotic as when he proposed to the lovely Abigail. Vanov tried to drag his gaze away from the all-powerful Face, but could only get as far as tangling with Melmont's impressive eyebrows, which seemed to be operating a semaphore celebration of their owner's overpowering will.

——I suspect the meeting is… not possible, Vanov gasped.

——The Russian Revolution was for many years 'not possible'. But with faith, anything is possible. Anything, said Melmont, with daunting prescience. It is time for humanity to start taking down these petty barriers of race and country. What we are doing is part of a historic cultural exchange, which always goes on between our nations, whether it is admitted or not. Your Tsiolovsky, as you well know, is recognised as the father of modern Russian rocketry. Almost unknown in the West, would you not say? And yet the ingenious Russian was not closed to the influences of Europe; indeed he obtained his inspiration from the novels of Jules Verne. In Tsiolovsky's autobiography, he claimed, do you not recall, that Tsiolovsky said it was Jules Verne who had set his brain working in a definite direction?

Vanov could only nod dumbly. The ex-tank commander was a stranger to Tsiolovsky's writings, but he was not going to admit it now. Melmont's evenings had not been wasted in the company of the erudite Cole. Cole loved to teach, while Melmont sucked up every word like a sponge.

——Thus the imagination of a Frenchman is the very thing that, in the right hands, could put a Man on the Moon, Melmont concluded, grandly. Vanov frowned at the ridiculous example.

——That certainly won't happen. You tell me men can go to the moon, you're just blowing smoke up my arse, my friend.

Melmont clapped Vanov on the shoulder, stood up and took three steps away from the bench.

——Imagination, my dear Vanov, is the thing that will free Mankind and it alone distinguishes us from Beasts, and it alone is truly International. Help me make this meeting, for the future peaceful development of all nations.

Vanov became aware of the virginal moon sitting palely, three-quarters full, among the leafless branches of a birch grove. The money rustled beguilingly. When Vanov glanced down and up at the moon again, what seemed like a moment later, so much time had passed, he noticed, the moon had moved from the birch branches towards the open sky.

——I cannot take this, Vanov said bravely. Take it back.

He was about to forcibly restore the cash to its owner and add that he, Colonel Vanov, had no way he could arrange a meeting between the supreme head of the Soviet State and a mere wily sub-agent running-dog lackey of a decadent foreign power. But there was no one there. Melmont had somehow withdrawn himself from the scene just as the moon itself now vanished behind a cloud; where Melmont had been till a moment ago was a small flying insect. Vanov, a keen amateur naturalist, watched a lone queen wasp descend and begin probing the roots of the treebase. She would be looking for the fritillary bulbs clustered at such places. Vanov had never seen queen wasps on the hunt for bulbs that early in the year. Perhaps he should not trust the evidence of his eyes. But the money itself seemed real enough, and felt reassuringly ordinary. It was still a bribe, it was just a bribe whose destination had reversed. And what was wrong with that?

In the distance, like fairy bells, there was the sound of the passing trams on a recently repaired stretch of road, as Frederick the Great's dream of a metropolis slowly started to pulse with life again. Vanov also remembered the sound of jays quarrelling behind him in lime trees struck by a sudden shaft of spring sunshine. Then a locomotive started somewhere down by the river, self-importantly, and the queen wasp flew away.

Coming out of a trance-like state, Vanov was told by a little voice that he could accept the money as the reward for ensuring the future of Soviet rocketry. For were not *Vergeltungswaffen-Zwei* treasured so greatly that Werner von Braun and General Dornberger avoided warcrimes tribunals by accepting jobs in the United States? The entire Second White Russian Army, under General Rokossovsky, had been deployed earlier to take the German test station at Peenemunde. Had Stalin then not transplanted all German personnel, thirty-thousand strong, to research stations in the Soviet Union in preparation for building a world-class warhead-carrying intercontinental ballistic missile? So what were a few stray roubles (which Melmont anyhow didn't appear to need) beside that? Besides, Melmont was departing for England with his bride, and Vanov had been forbidden to make contact with Melmont in his adopted country: the island was full of curtain-twitchers so you never knew who might be listening

Melmont watched the puff-puff-puff of Indian-style smoke signals released by a little dockside steam crane as it slowly cranked his car out of the hold of a small tramp steamer in which he had crossed the North Sea from Flushing in the Netherlands to the fishing port of Yarmouth, England, consuming exactly thirteen tons of the best Welsh steam coal. Far more confident of his welcome in England than Dracula, (who arrived at Whitby as a black dog, according to Bram Stoker), Melmont had made the night crossing undiguised.

Next to him Abigail was seated on a pile of their luggage, in a fur hat and a long grey coat, poised for the great adventure of married life. The herring fleet beached in a row behind her was getting ready to sail again. With the U-boats gone away, the fishermen were preparing to wreak renewed depredations on the fishing stocks, which had started to recover during the war. The pinkness of the first dawn of May was being drawn slowly from the sky. Abigail never underestimated the importance of good first impressions. Both passports had been stamped approvingly, she felt, and so the future was full of promise. Furthermore, she was looking forward to wearing her favourite peach silk night dress.

Her pacifist parents had not taken immediately to the fiancé of their beloved daughter, but Melmont had charmed them. Kissing Abigail goodbye, her mother had said to her,

——We think now, after all, you have married well. He'll make you happy if he learns the ways of peace.

If he learns the ways of peace!

Abigail's father wished that his daughter was not being taken from him. He lived only for Goethe, and had advised them to avoid crossing during the storms of *Walpurgisnacht*. But the North Sea was unprovoked over his favourite daughter's departure and they had chugged on arrow-straight and unshaken till the pilot came aboard, a piece of true England with his inimitable Anglian vowels.

Blackheaded gulls screamed in impotent comic outrage overhead as the khaki Dodge with its Berlin numberplates was unshackled from the hauling nets which had cradled it, onto the quay. The car settled crunchingly on its salted leafsprings as if tasting the cobbles mistrustfully beneath its tyres. With its high back quarters, it suddenly looked poised for predation like an exotic animal taken far from its habitat and put down in a strange land where it might wreak ecological havoc.

If he only learns the ways of peace!

The four-berth cabin on the steamer had precluded any nuptial embraces, so the newlyweds spent their first night of true love together in Ware, north of London, famed for its medieval Great Bed. There was however no Great Bed for them. The main street hotel only offered a pair of narrow twin beds, in a tiny half-timbered room where Melmont kept striking his head on the four hundred-year-old oak beams, drawing blood.

He cursed the architects and management in seven languages and mopped his forehead with the chintz bedspread till Abigail gave him a pad of cotton from her bag. A minute later Melmont went to her bag for a replacement pad and discovered that Abigail had packed a contraceptive device. Melmont's brow darkened at the sight of the Dutch Cap. Any barrier between him and his sons was out of the question, and as soon as Abigail left the room he chopped up the offending item to rubberised confetti, with a pair of pinking shears.

Night fell, and an owl hooted eerily outside their window. Melmont was lying down in his Turnbull & Asser silk pyjamas, waiting for Abigail to finish combing her hair. He had not mentioned that he had sliced her family planner in shreds, for *force majeure* does not feel the need to discuss things.

When Abigail got into bed, Melmont instantly raised her nightdress. She watched puzzled as he took a teaspoonful of honey and a teaspoonful of cream, and mixed them together in her bellybutton. This ceremony had not been included in the preliminaries to love, the way her mother had instructed her.

—What are you doing, dearest?

It was something Melmont's grandmother had told him to do as the moon waxed, if he wanted strong sons. He was making his wife's body into a land of milk and honey, where his sons would grow. *Mont du miel, gout doux et léger.* After five minutes, Abigail decided to prepare herself for something more conventional. But when she discovered the crumbs of her Dutch Cap scattered on the floor, she cursed quietly in Flemish, before resorting to French, the language of their courtship, to reason with the monster, who was completely unrepentant. It was their first argument.

—Darling we are going to spend the rest of our lives together and will always be in love. Don't you think that before having children we should at least have a proper roof over our heads?

—Don't worry. We will be rich. Twelve sons.

Abigail laughed, partly because this was ridiculous and partly because Melmont's rough tongue, which had spoken in English, was now tickling her abdomen. He did have seduction skills after all. Abigail, smiling, watched him deliberately licking her, like a vast cat, slowly moving towards that enchanted grotto through which all but Caesar pass at least once.

Her cup of love engorged readily for him that night and thereafter. At the same time, something about the act with him terrified her. Always civil, when he undressed her, a part of her felt stripped naked and pierced by the storm.

—Twelve sons, Melmont would repeat after every love making. *Douze fils. Zwölf sohnen.*

Melmont continued his attentions assiduously whenever business did not keep him from home at night. His preparation was always considerate, though his time of penetration was always short. She did not complain. It was all new, and she was in love with him, though she wanted more physically. Once after he withdrew, she continued on her own, and attained a vaulting orgasm that must have gone on for ten minutes.

—The time is coming. When the stars are right there will be sons, Melmont said. His wife, erotically self-discharged, sighed peacefully.

In Berlin, Eisler was kept busy with a stream of orders from his boss in England. Soon the warehouse was as bare as he had foreseen; all the science magazines had left for redistribution from London. A crucial problem emerged. Melmont it transpired, was failing to mail the science periodicals to the institutions which had paid him in advance, and the institutions were complaining loudly.

Eisler discovered that the only result of repeatedly bringing this to Melmont's attention was to receive a telegram firing him from his job as editor, deducting the last six months' unpaid salary.

Melmont's excursions all over the country delivering *Die Wahrheit* to prisoners of war had become more infrequent as the camps closed down, with one exception. On one of the far-flung farms where German prisoners of war had helped out on the land, Melmont had utterly captivated the farmer's wife who let him have a brace of chickens whenever he visited. Mrs Simpkins, who had lost her husband in the war, even dressed them for the tall, dark stranger who always had a witty remark to put troubles in their place, and went out of his way to charm her.

One of Mrs Simpkins' 'troubles' was the remaining prisoner, a gloomy and taciturn Bavarian, General Trapp, who had now taken up lodgings in the farm. When all the other prisoners had been assigned repatriation dates, somehow Trapp had managed to stay on. He growled, Mrs Simpkins said, whenever Melmont's name was mentioned, or even when his new car could be heard splashing through the puddles of the approach road towards the farm.

——I'd watch out for him. He blames losing the war on you personally I think, said Mrs Simpkins.

Melmont had seen Trapp walk with his hands stiffly behind him on his daily constitutional, grinding unread copies of *Die Warheit* into the farmyard muck with his polished heel. He teased Trapp, in front of Mrs Simpkins, bending down and talking to the chickens, in a falsetto German accent.

——Come away with me, my dears. Don't vaist your lifes laying eggs for Krauts who were so stupid they got caught. Then Melmont straightened and winked, staring at Trapp's melancholy impotent rage from his monocled eye, saying in broad cockney, You don't scare me, chum. I've et peeple bigger 'n' yoo fer brekfus'.

Trapp would shake with impotent rage.

Melmont's funny voices made Mrs Simpkins giggle so much she once wet herself laughing, something she hadn't done since kindergarten. Fortunately she was in the yard at the time, and the lapse passed unnoticed.

——Luther warned us Germans about Jews, announced Trapp to Mrs Simpkins after one visit of Melmont, as the flashy new car drove away.

——Is Captain Melmont Jewish? I didn't know that. He makes me laugh, anyhow.

Mrs Simpkins had little idea of what seeds Luther had sown. To her, the monk was a vague figure in a history lesson long ago who had blown a raspberry at the Pope and told his children that the family lapdogs would go to Heaven.

Trapp and Melmont clashed for the last time over tea. Mrs Simpkins served her delicious homemade currant buns. Trapp, for the first time, refused.

——I'm finished. No more buns. Ever.

Mrs Simpkins raised her eyebrows and made an amazed face at Melmont from behind Trapp's back. Part of the problem of her unwanted guest, in a country still strapped by rationing, was that Trapp had been till now eating so much; almost as much as Melmont, not that she would grudge anything to the handsome captain.

——Are you quite sure, General? coo'ed Mrs Simpkins.

——Yes indeed. I shall show you exactly how, shortly, Trapp barked. He turned to Melmont.

——I have had enough of weasel words in this life. Tell me, Captain, are you a patriot?

——I should say so, yes, said Melmont, smooth as buttermilk.

——A patriot of where? said Trapp, nastily.

——Here. I am English now, just as you are German.

Trapp shook his head.

——My family had lived on the same land for three hundred years. Now Stalin has overrun it and it is the end for us. Ten thousand acres of the best hunting country in Europe. For you to say you are English is rubbish. My family can say it *was* German, certainly, though we are nothing now. But you, can you come to this country and call yourself English after what, ten minutes?

Mrs Simpkins could have sworn she saw a tear of rage glisten in Trapp's eye for a second. There was a long silence, during which Melmont took out and lit one of the last Mont du Miel cigars left in the world.

——If you lose your country, you can always get another one, said Melmont, through clouds of oracular smoke.

Trapp polished the vagrant tear from his monocle, (Mrs Simpkins's suspicions had been correct), and screwed it carefully back into the baby-pink folds around his left eye.

——Will you participate in the governing of this country?

——What does government take? I think I'm brave enough to do it, said Melmont, cheekily.

——Brave? cried Mrs Simpkins, The Captain once wiped out a whole machine gun nest with his bare hands, didn't you, Earnest?

Melmont nodded gravely.

——Not many parliamentarians have done that for England, have they, before they take their seats?

Melmont suddenly had an out-of-body experience of the future and saw himself in a debate in the Houses of Parliament. There seemed to be a lot of people laughing at him, and the ghost of the boy he'd strangled was there too, on the Opposition benches, laughing at his murderer, and saying "For killing me, you never will have sons!" Then the dark vision faded as abruptly as it had come, and he was back sitting in a chintz-covered armchair, facing General Trapp, with everything as it was before.

Mrs Simpkins was undressing the teapot from its cosy to refill it and squeeze the last drop of infusion from some prewar Ceylonese leaf while Trapp's basilisk monocle was fixed on Melmont's face still. He spoke.

——It is no great thing to kill. I have killed.

Melmont shrugged.

——Mrs Simpkins exaggerates. It is also not something I am particularly proud of, either. I only had to deal with one soldier with my hands, and only after my machine gun jammed. Melmont slowly sucked Mrs Simpkins' delicious homemade apricot jam off his puissant, pricklish thumbs, before he added with mock-modesty,

——Our equipment was generally poorer than yours, as you are no doubt aware, so a certain degree of *improvisation* was always necessary.

Trapp knew about improvisation, having commanded a Panzerfaust division on the Eastern front against Russian soldiers. The Russian infantry were not armed, but were sent to the front with instructions only to pick up a gun when the man in front holding it dropped dead. The improvisers of war had won the day there, too.

Trapp rose from the worn settee.

——The future belongs to you, obviously. I hope you can make good use of our legacy.

——Your legacy? What do you mean? Never. I am a democrat, said Melmont.

But Trapp had left the room. Mrs Simpkins smoothed her pinafore and tut-tutted.

——I dunno what's got into him. He won't go home. He should have gone weeks ago but he won't leave, an' till today 'e was livin' scot-free an' eatin' us out of 'ouse-an'-'ome. Mrs Simpkins' vowels always became more countrified when she fell to complaining.

——Maybe I should have a word with him, said Melmont.

——That would be so *kind*. Would you?

——Consider it done, said Melmont.

Mrs Simpkins looked relieved.

——E'll never listen to a woman. And it is time he was movin' on, arter all.

Melmont smiled at Mrs Simpkins. His eyes looked enormous, she thought. Huge, and sensitive.

Outside the door which Trapp had just closed there was the sound of a gunshot, then there was the thud of a falling body. Melmont raised an eyebrow as a small rolling cloud of carpet dust emerged from under the bottom of the door. The labradors outside in the courtyard barked and Mrs Simpkins cried out after them, with the same canine cadence and uplifted face,

——Oh! Oh! Then she added, What's 'e gone and done, now?

Melmont rose from his armchair and crossed the room. When the door was opened, General Trapp could be seen collapsed among the gumboots and galoshes, clutching the barrel of an old-fashioned hammer action shotgun that had been in the Simpkins family since before Mafeking was relieved. General Trapp had shot himself. Incongruously now lying on his side, he looked as if he was practising presenting arms. There was a picture rail above him, high on the dark wall, where the horns of three small red deer hung, killed long ago, now shared the wallspace with Trapp's blood as well as pieces of rear brain. His boots had rucked the dirty carpet in his fall. Mrs Simpkins cried out again, her earlier misgivings fulfilled only too well.

An hour later as it grew dark, Melmont was piloting his brand new Cadillac extravagantly around the twisting country lanes away from the farm. He had been close to death too many times to give Trapp's death much thought. The road straightened and Melmont put his foot down on the accelerator of his pink juggernaut. At the same time, he felt a strange surging restraint, as if something, a giant elastic band perhaps, was slowing the car down. At the same time, the headlights and the dashboard lights dimmed. Melmont cursed and pumped the accelerator, and the car recovered before the cycle began again. At the third fadeout, the power steering stiffened ominously as the engine died. Ahead, in the middle of the road, a flashlight was waving up and down, as if a will-o'-the-wisp was warning the driver to halt.

The car seemed to roll to a stop on its own, its headlights emitting just enough light to show a very tall, gaunt scarecrow-like figure with a pocket torch, standing in the middle of the road, its shins apparently ignoring the threat from the thrusting chrome breasts of the Cadillac's front fenders. As the apparition moved towards the nearside of the car to speak with the driver,

Melmont saw it had a long, pale, melancholy face and recognised Willis Death, the local veterinarian, and friend of Mrs Simpkins.

Death climbed in beside Melmont and sat with dripping raincoat on the handsome beige upholstery of the moveable bench front seat. Melmont, fearless as usual, was the first to speak.

——Know anything about electricals?

——Not these foreign cars, I don't. But even if it was a tractor, I couldn't help you. The Stones are turning you round, see.

Willis Death pointed. Beyond the weak glimmer of the headlights stood the remains of a circle of megaliths which Melmont had ignored and driven through a dozen times on his visits to Mrs Simpkins. Death detested ever having to explain his beliefs intellectually, but continued,

——The road lies straight across the oval, slicing across our ancestor's holistic embrace of the heavens. Every time a car passes, They knows about it. It's loike they made a model o' the universe there, an' everything's connected with it, even today. So it's a place of power, an' these place have personalities, they might loike you or they might not, they might want to hinder you or help you... mainly the force is for good, but not always.

Melmont permitted the rustic lunatic vet to ramble on. There was little else he could do. The rain poured down.

——Many's the time I've taken an animal here and the stones have told me how to cure them. The druids was Pelasgians, I reckon, and they knowed about time through measurin' it. Not unfriendly, like, but they know more 'n' us about before an' after. There's stories 'round these rustic parts, still, that they'd found out the secret of Time itself. Well the secret is bound up with matter, that's a fact because without one there'd not be the other, so maybe they're on to something.

——Whatever it is certainly knows how to stop my car, said Melmont.

——That's because of your Unfinished Business up at the farm. The stones prob'bly know you've got sommat to do there, left something behind, Death added darkly.

——I have a meeting in four hours in London. I don't have time to go back, said Melmont. He was irritated that Death was such a fluent exponent of what was plainly country superstition and rubbish.

——Just try putting the car in reverse, said Death.

Melmont did nothing. He was not about to take orders from Sarsen Blues or any place of dolmen residue. It was not in his nature.

——You can't foight them unless they allows it, they're just too big, Willis added, helpfully.

Melmont finally put the car in reverse and sure enough, a moment later, the starter motor churned, the engine caught and the headlights beamed. Defeated, he went back down the road.

When they arrived at the farmhouse again, Willis Death got out of the car and went inside for a moment, then emerged with a cardboard box full of grey books and motioned to Melmont to open the boot. Melmont pressed the interior electrical release. There was a clunk and a sound of yawning hydraulics and the boot opened as two twin chrome-finish automatic interior lights turned on. Willis Death placed the books carefully in the lighted space.

——That's it, you can go now.

Melmont pressed another button and the boot closed, magically.

Mrs Simpkins appeared in the farm kitchen doorway, with her eyes crinkled against the cold drizzle, holding two fine plucked caponised cockerels, wrapped in greaseproof paper.

——You forgot these. When you left I remembered Willis our vet lives on the Melchbridge road, so I called him on the telephone, to step out in the road, and ask if you wanted 'em.

——I didn't know you had no capons for the captain.

——We was cut off before I'd started explainin' about the fowls, or anythin'.

Mrs Simpkins put the birds next to Melmont.

——What's he put in the boot? asked Melmont.

——It's the books, isn't it? Didn't he tell you? Oh Lordy. It wouldn't have been worth you coming back so soon just for them, but the general has gone and left some books to you. When you left, we had just started cleaning up when I found a note from him saying he wanted you to have them. It must have been what he was talking about earlier, but he wasn't very clear, was he? Poor man!

Melmont drove away. The standing stones gave him no trouble the second time.

॥   *॥*   *॥*

When he finally came to look at Trapp's legacy, Melmont found it consisted of an edition of Hitler's early autobiography, *Mein*

Kampf. Thirtynine copies of that book of racist ranting, in a special printing, unmarked, pristine condition, individually inscribed by the author and bound in human leather, tattoed with numbers. What to do with them? Even Sotheby's, those cynical and glacially incurious auctioneers, would have hesitated before putting them on the market.

Melmont kept the books in the boot of the car, undecided about how to get the best price for them. But he need not have worried: buyers with deep pockets would soon make themselves known to him, dwellers on damnation's threshold. Their diabolic agenda was to use Melmont as leverage, to cast all Existence into Hades. In this, they succeeded beyond their wildest dreams.

For sheer inventiveness in exploiting the equation where Appetite overturns All, I take my hat off to you, hornéd gentlemen.

Melmont the Tycoon

OXBRIDGE IS AN ANCIENT UNIVERSITY TOWN, occasionally confused by the unlearned with Oxford or Cambridge. Oxbridge's intellectual reputation was born sickly, and grew shackled mysteriously, a fact that it seems pleased with now. Smug and provincial, stubbornly outside the limelight, it trails its university sister-cities forever. Its inhabitants claim that it is better than the two ancient centres of learning for it possesses the merits of both without the defects, but they also have a reputation for stretching the truth that reaches into the mists of time.

When the guidebook says the Cotswalls can sometimes be seen on clear day, a blue stripe far away on the horizon, you may choose to believe it, or not. It is certainly true the city is on a plain. They used to make threewheeled motorcars in Oxbridge which worked, they say, until they encountered a slope. Oxbridgers in general are pleased as Punch with their flat surrounds and with themselves, and think anyone who lives anywhere else is mad, bad and dangerous to get in a motor vehicle with. Oxbridgers are suspicious of cars, while the infrequent trains to and from Oxbridge are always crammed, apparently sinking under low bridges far away on the plain towards the coast, or seeming to rise, like distant ships over the ocean, from beneath the feet of the westerly Cotswalls.

Circling both inside and outside the town's new ring road lie the dark earth banks of sluggish canals. The river Oxus runs through the town east to west but appears to lose all sense of direction outside the canalised zone, twirling through the landscape with a complexity that calls on an artist of Escher's disturbing skills to portray accurately. But Oxbridge's greatest claim to mediocrity, which still stands today, is that its dons and fellows and graduates have never produced an outstanding mind or invention. Melmont's decision to move to the area was based exclusively on the town's centrality to middle England.

Ten bowshots west of Oxbridge, he took business premises in what had been once a fancy biscuit factory, Boxly's. Melmont had decided this was the spot from which to reform the way the book trade distribution worked. Not only was it central, the lease cost buttons. Boxly's Biscuits were long gone. The factory had been erected in the days when local sugar beet looked set fair to break the world monopoly of sugar cane, but then came steamships. Its profits declined and the factory gates shut.

Où sont les Boxly Madeleines, d'antan?

Empty throughout the Depression and the war, the ramshackle old biscoterie was now reborn and named Melmont House. Melmont was going to make the country's book distribution 'just like America', centralise it all under one roof, and voilà. That was the plan, anyhow.

Melmont had watched as men on ladders nailed up hard-board signs saying 'Melmont House' over the main entrance, obscuring all but the 'B' of Boxly. Abigail, pregnant, had clung on his arm and kissed him. Then he had left for Johannesburg.

Inside, whether Melmont was present or not, all was bustle, for Melmont's interests were expanding exponentially in all directions from the springboard of science publications. Differently titled enterprises, some nothing to do with books at all, were jammed into cubbyholes and lofts. Melmont Technology Overseas jostled with Melmont Promotions and Melmont Asia Inc. Every landing large enough to handle science magazines had piles of dull and imposing-looking periodicals. Men in suits and secretaries in calf-length skirts and cardigans constantly passed each other, to and fro, up and down stairs, or along the improvised catwalks of scaffolding that had been thrown up to connect Melmont Cape Town with Melmont Reykjavik. All of them marching to a pressing if inaudible tune piped by their tireless boss, the Music of the Future.

One morning, fresh from Copenhagen, the great entrepreneur appeared in the midst of his opera, which was still assembling itself inside the factory. He was observed to open a door behind him, and swinging his arms lightly, go down into the basement canteen where the tea break, a lengthy and enjoyable affair, would be going on, spiced with local gossip and banter.

Melmont marched into the worker's sanctum and banged on a tin mug for silence. Nothing happened. He continued furiously, for thirty seconds, destroying the mug before he got what he wanted. Rows of cheerful working men's faces looked over their cigarettes and cups of tea at the bulky intruder in the suit in their midst, holding a bent spoon in one hand, and a ruined mug in the other.

——Now I have your attention, said Melmont.

Most of them had only the vaguest idea who he was, he had been present so little. But there was a lot of him. Others might complain that the country was still groaning with wartime rationing but Melmont was above such strictures, waxing like a gibbous moon on his mother-in-law's home-cured Brussels ham. He was putting on weight faster than Abigail.

——What's going on here? asked Melmont, as if he did not know he had a canteen.

There was a short silence. Someone disdainfully dropped the remains of an untipped 'Wills' Whiffs' cigarette into their tea with an audible hiss. Melmont repeated the question. Then he repeated it again.

Melmont's English became even more precise and clipped, but it still had traces of Carpathian when he was moved. A ragged and unfriendly silence suddenly hung in the smoke-rich air, by way of a reply.

——Skiffle band auditions! said one wag at length, invisible at the back.

Everyone except Melmont laughed.

——It's a tea break, you not heard of it, mate?

The works foreman, in his donkey jacket office, looked up smiling, wrinkling his forehead, tolerant and amused at the fat foreigner's ways.

——You're doing this on my time, said Melmont, dangerously. I'm not going to be soft-hearted for ever. Get back to work, all of you! Then he turned on his heels, army-style, and left the room.

Behind him, voices exaggerated the local accent to curse him. Most of the men came from Boxly Village and were related, often more closely than bore strict legal scrutiny. It had been ever thus, in rural Oxbridgeshire. But the collective feeling in the room was that Boxly, damned with incest or not, was the heart and soul of England, and we had defeated Hitler, and Boxly feared no homegrown tinpot tyrants. No one moved. There were going to be no dividing walls put up today.

Thirty minutes later, Melmont was sitting in his office having the practices of the British working man explained to him. It was not going well. Mead, the square-faced shop steward with an expression like an intelligent shoebox, should have been afraid of Melmont by Melmont's reckoning, and Mead was not afraid. Melmont, even when he could understand Mead's thick Oxbridge accent, could not find his weak point.

——It's not our job to put shelving up. Never has been. Those lads are chippies. And there's no point in moving the stock now when the shelving's not ready.

——You've got thirty minutes to cure your lot of the British Disease! shouted Melmont.

The British Disease has an ancient international history. The slaves worked to death in Athenian silver mines were prey to it, it is said, even as their enlightened owners talked up the foundations of democracy. Jews recorded in the Bible they were unjustly accused of the local equivalent of the British disease, working under brutal Egyptian pharoahs.

Mead resentfully left to continue to foment unrest among the workers, and Melmont paced the corridor outside his office with furrowed brow. He had not realised a British workforce would be so resistant. On the fiftieth pace, he was buttonholed by a bespectacled young man in a badly fitting black suit, a Hungarian called Stanislav Kirin who had been trying to attract his attention in vain. Finally Kirin reached out and caught Melmont's lapel. Melmont flicked the hand off as if it had been an impertinent bluebottle.

—Can I speak with you please, now, Captain Melmont?

—Who are you, why are you here and why can't you wait?

Melmont gestured to the queue outside his office. A secretary guarded the doorframe, since the door had yet to be hung there. She was speaking on the phone.

—It's Captain Melmont's Chinese visa renewal, yes. He can't come to Petty France because he's in New York.

Professor Kirin tried to jog Melmont's memory.

—You offered me a job when we met in Prague, as translator in your Hungarian department. But there is no Hungarian department here, Kirin added, helpfully.

—There will be, said Melmont, generously. Meanwhile, put these shelves up.

Kirin's academic brow crinkled with misgiving. He had not come fifteen hundred miles to build bookshelves.

—Captain Melmont I would remind you that I am an established professor.

—There are plenty of other Hungarians in this building looking for a job and prepared to do it instead! snarled Melmont, threateningly, and stalked off.

Kirin watched Melmont's back disappear into his office. Then he heard the inventive secretary say,

—Will you ask BOAC to hold the plane at Northolt? His chauffeur is just bringing him.

Inside the office, suddenly tired, Melmont sat down and fell asleep in the chair, cigar in hand. When he woke up an hour later, to his surprise, two plucked fowl were hanging on the back of the door. He had taught Mrs Simpkins to leave the necks on, like his grandmother did, and had forgotten he had them. His spirits recovering at the sight, he plucked them up and opened the door. The queue outside the office had thinned but not dispersed.

Melmont strode past the unlucky few who were going to miss him that day, swinging the chickens by their necks, shouting that his secretary should be fired for not having already sent Mrs Simpkins flowers. Then he halted by a pile of collapsed shelving and heard rather than saw an alarmed Kirin trapped underneath. Melmont leant down and snarled, in Magyar,

——It's just between the two of us, mind, but you're fired.

ffl   *ffl*   *ffl*

The Oxbridge guidebooks never fail to mention Prince's was founded to round off a Jacobean prince's education and to prepare him to wear the hollow crown. Like most plans in Oxbridge it was never to be, for Prince Henry, the eldest and in many ways the most promising son of James I (James VI of Scotland), expired from a surfeit of clysters administered by terrified royal quacks, leaving his brother Charles I to lead the country to hell in a handcart.

Melmont drove his new fat red Rolls-Royce with Mulliner coachwork into Oxbridge, and parked rather closer to Prince's

College than was strictly allowed even in those days. He strode through mock-medieval gothic cloisters built for a regal induction that never was, past the college's Nile Street entrance where one can see Reedy Island bisect the sluggish Oxus, past the Venetian pastiche of Big Bridge till he finally came to a stop in the middle of the lofty seventeenth century quadrangle, beloved of watercolourists and picture postcard sellers alike.

Bach fugues played distantly in the magnificent chapel that made up one side of the quad, while gowned figures locked ancient bicycles to railings in the gloom lest thieves took them while they dined. It all gave a promise of sobriety, learning and continuity to a ravenous sensibility which had come of age wading through blood in the ruins of Berlin.

Holding a plucked chicken by the neck in each hand, Melmont twirled and stared round with benign approval as impacted worms died slowly under his heavy heels. Begun by Inigo Jones and completed by the lesser-known but still respectable Boniface Bacon, Prince's ancient limestone walls oozed serenity and regard for learning.

It was a pleasing prospect, though not everyone in Prince's was prepared to tolerate the admiration of visitors. Melmont had to sedate an irate jobsworth with a ten pound note just to continue to stand on the grass as he stood in rapt contemplation. But the jobsworth had finally retreated to his lodge at the bottom of the stairs, leaving Melmont free to continue his appraisal of the surroundings from the Ground Zero of the grassy quadrangle.

The scent of bruised grass was overtaken by the coarser smell of frying onions from an open window hinting at the jobsworth's own supper, and Melmont woke abruptly from his reverie. Fighting down the temptation to dine alone and at once on raw chicken, Melmont mounted the stone stairway in search of Cole's comfortable rooms at the top. Cole had resisted the family pressure to go into banking after the war, and apparently found his vocation and some happiness as an academic, guiding students along the broad river of European humanist thought.

Melmont entered without knocking. Inside the room Cole, wearing civilian tweeds and a modish bow tie, was listening as a young female undergraduate coolly read out the final page of her essay, without a glance at the intruder.

——"And thus we see in Victor Hugo's championing of Shakespeare, the realisation that the true business of genius is to reconcile Apollo and Dionysus, the grotesque with the sublime, for the combination of the two at once is the only unity that we moderns can comprehend."

Cole nodded encouragingly at Jill's uncertain smile.

——Go on.

——That was the end, said Jill.

——Good! Not just good, but in places, very good, said Cole. He was a born teacher.

——Of course it was the end. I'm here. Now you can start to cook, said Melmont, mischievously. He attempted to pass the two chickens to Jill who, an early feminist, neatly avoided taking them.

——I'm sorry, but cooking is what I came here to avoid doing for the rest of my life.

——What do you like doing? asked Melmont, his eyes burning.

——I like studying, right now.

Melmont nodded as if being handed an amazing truth.

—You'll do, he said.

Cole coughed, embarrassed.

—I should have introduced you. Jill Rysborough, this is Captain Melmont.

—Captain, what do you mean 'I'll do?' Jill asked sharply.

—'Do' for my secretary, of course.

Jill laughed. Melmont sensed resistance. He adored resistance. He only trampled on people if they failed to stand up to him.

—I'm serious. I've only got two secretaries and they both complain they're worked half to death. You want to see the world? One of them has seen the moonlight over the Sumatra Straits twice so far this year.

—Thanks for the offer said Jill, and went out, slamming the door.

Melmont smiled.

—Well, you haven't changed, said Cole.

Melmont dropped the chickens on the table. Their slack necks now stretched down meltingly over the side towards the floor. He picked up the phone.

—Do you have the phone number of some flower shops?

Although the sole Oxbridge florist open at that hour had been closed since noon, since it was early closing in the town, by dint of buying the entire stock Melmont was able to make a gesture of apology, and an invitation to Jill. And lo, she did cook the chickens for dinner and everything else followed. She abandoned her course and worked eighteen-hour days for him, and was even a sometime lover of the great man, and director of his charitable impulses. Prince's had a fine music library but the iron oxide Bach's contemporaries had used for ink was destroying the original sheet music. On hearing this, Melmont promised to provide a grant to stop the rot; which he did. She called him M.

——Never mind your wife, I don't want anyone to know we're doing this, M. Ever.

Melmont loved being called M.

——I promise darling. This is one secret I will take to my grave.

But I am getting too far ahead of my tale. At the time they met, the only thing that Jill had ridden had been a horse.

The auspicious dinner was over, and the table between Melmont and Cole was covered with the debris. Chicken carcases had been ravaged, sundry claret bottles drained. Crumbs of Stilton, like giant's dandruff, lay thickly around Melmont's feet, but though Cole, in a scarlet smoking jacket, could eat no more, the feast was far from finished for his friend.

Melmont performed a rapid solo engorgement of a heart-shaped box of chocolates and dropped the empty chocolate box on the floor. Cole, nodding with amused approbation, leant into the recess of the mullioned window and retrieved a dusty bottle to fill their glasses, with a late-bottled port that Prince's cellar had managed to preserve all through the war.

——Fermented before either of us were born, Earnest.

Melmont grunted noncommittally and spat out a hard centre, missing his coffee cup. Jill having cooked for them was now buttoning up a navy duffel coat with wooden toggles, preparing to depart.

——It's been fascinating meeting you, Captain Melmont, if

only because no one has ever bought me so many flowers. I couldn't get into my room.

Melmont chuckled and relit a Cuban cigar. The days of being forced to smoke his own wares were long gone.

——You're not related to the Gloucestershire Melmonts are you, near Stroud?

Cole laughed and Melmont shook his head.

——Uncle Hymie's probably my only surviving relative. He left for Brooklyn during the Depression.

——I helped Ernest make his name up from a cigar packet, so if he was captured he wouldn't be killed, said Cole.

Melmont's eyes were the colour of night, Jill thought suddenly, and the candlelight made stars in them as he stared at her.

——I meant it, about employment, he said softly. Call me tomorrow.

Jill blushed. She was flattered but did not wish to appear too keen on a career in front of her tutor. She bade them goodnight and went out closing the door.

——Sweet girl. About to get a first-class degree, too, said Cole.

Melmont retrieved a chicken carcase, which had somehow found its way onto the floor and examined it cursorily for flesh, before using it as an ashtray. Cole could tell Jill was no longer on Melmont's incalculable mind.

——So what's new, Earnest?

Melmont looked at his friend and spoke with great emphasis.

——I'm going to revolutionise the book trade by centralising the book repository business. Books are communications. Communications are a field with unlimited growth potential.

The world market, Tristram! I was in China the other day. China! The number of people there is incredible. And did I tell you I was going to be a Member of Parliament very soon?

Cole was amazed. Behind Melmont's increasingly autocratic English he always heard the gutteral roots and had assumed that no one would ever ask him to speak up for them in the Mother of Parliaments. But clearly he was wrong.

——How soon?

——The next election.

——I am sorry to sound tactless, but do you think you will get in? asked Cole. Cole knew Melmont had never voted in his life.

——You don't need that many people to vote for you. Just more than the other fellows.

——How's the book repository coming along?

Melmont did not wish to share his frustrations after such a feast.

——It is the right idea, no doubt about it. There is no doubt in my mind the book trade is ripe for a makeover. It's a full time challenge at the moment.

——Politics might have to come later then, old man, when you jack it in.

——It would have to be a parallel career. I can't live on an MP's salary, said Melmont.

Cole shrugged with the lordliness of one born to the purple of commerce. His family ran a merchant bank.

——You should try living on what an academic earns. It's one of the reasons I'm not going to do it anymore. I'm leaving Prince's, Cole added.

——I say, old man. I thought your heart was in teaching.

—It was.

—Was this a sudden decision?

—Yes, said Cole, telling the truth, though not in its entirety. He had been arrested in a state of undress on Reedy Island, which he had retired to with a waiter. As a murky quid pro quo, Prince's College had accepted his resignation, in return for some high-level intervention which meant the charges of gross indecency were dropped so Cole could reinvent himself, taking up the reins of the family firm without an outward blemish.

—I'll have a merchant banker as a friend. That's good, an honest banker among the crooks, said Melmont.

Cole still had no idea of the identity of the photographer who had come out of the cupboard in Berlin, but assumed that it had been the Russians, and that it had ceased to be important when he was able to rejoin civilian life.

—Did the Russians ever... try anything with you? Cole asked.

—What would the Russians try with me?

—Oh, you know, try to get you to work for them.

The British spies Burgess and MacLean had recently removed themselves to Russia, hours ahead of their arrest. Melmont shook his head.

—In every Iron Curtain country I go, they know where my heart is. I've always loved England. It's time for some shut-eye now. Goodnight, old man.

The two men embraced, then Melmont clumped away down the dark stairs. Cole leaned out from his window as Melmont stood below.

—Bring Abigail down for a day before I leave, and we'll go

out in a punt. You leave that way, he added, pointing past the jobsworth's lodge.

The great swart figure below ignored the direction indicated, swung its arms and stepped out defiantly across the quadrangle towards a twentyfive foot blank wall. And on meeting the wall, according to both Cole, and the jobsworth porter, Melmont disappeared.

We know the night was dark. We can also agree Melmont left the college, somehow, for he was snoring next to Abigail two hours later, for her diary records it. I myself am sceptical that the demons that were about to plague Melmont would have allowed him any latitude with regard to control over matter, at this early stage. It is most likely that Cole, by this stage in the evening was drunk, as was the jobsworth, which is why Melmont was never signed out of Prince's, an anomaly that can still be seen in the visitors' book of fifty years ago on application to the warden today.

&#x0B   &#x0B   &#x0B

Not far outside Boxly there is a small church placed equidistant between the villages of Evengame and Burlingjob. The church is deconsecrated today, but then it was still just possible to glean a congregation from the surrounding country that was greater in numbers than the list of names of the mighty dead on the local war memorials. Melmont, previously immune to the charms of religion, began to patronise the ancient place of worship together with his wife. Afterwards his butler and cook would supervise a post-service picnic hamper from the boot of the Bentley, or Rolls, seasonally adjusted.

During the service, Melmont would sit in the squire's old front pew, magnificent in pinstripes; next to him, those who buttled for him, and behind the servants of the big house, the unmarried mothers and Down's Syndrome youths from Weyhill asylum, adjacent to the church. 'Weoh' is Old English for holy place or temple, so the Norman builders of the church must have been taking over something much older. One Sunday it rained during the service.

At the end of the service the vicar, a lean man with dense grey hair like wirewool, stood at the church door and effusively saluted Melmont as he left the service with Abigail on his arm. The rain was still pelting down outside.

—How nice to see you here. How very very nice. And thank you so much for helping with the roof. Dry as a bone inside, I hope you noticed.

Vandals had earlier scalped the church roof and driven off with the lead rolled up in the back of a van. Melmont had paid for the damage to be repaired. It was very much a crime of its time. Nowadays the bottom's dropped out of the lead market and no self respecting career criminal would consider peeling a lead roof at night.

—Think nothing of it. Can't have the place flooded out before the boy's baptised, said Melmont. Abigail shot him an old-fashioned look.

—Darling, we don't know it's a boy.

The vicar laid a gnarled and experienced hand on Abigail's stomach.

——A boy? Are you sure? Looks like a girl to me.

Melmont started to bristle.

In the rain outside, two Down's Syndrome girls were affectionately sharing a single umbrella as they splashed through the puddles around the scarlet Bentley of the church's benefactor, singing a fragments from a toneless version of *Singing in the Rain*.

——Of course I could be wrong. When is 'he' due then? asked the vicar.

——Soon. And when he comes round to be baptised, I'm telling you, his putz is going to be in one piece.

——Entirely as you wish, the vicar said, it makes no difference in my opinion. The early church thought it profoundly unimportant, compared with the state of your soul. The vicar quoted; half to himself,

"He is not a Jew which is one outwardly, neither is that circumcision which is outward in the flesh, but he is a Jew, which is one inwardly, and circumcision is that of the heart, in the spirit, and not in the letter, whose praise is not of men, but of God."

Melmont's busy eyebrows rose belligerently. The vicar smiled.

——It's just fashion. That's what St Paul is saying. Queen Victoria introduced circumcision in her family because the mad old bat believed that the British were the Lost Tribe of Israel. Then everyone was at it, for a while. But it has no theological meaning anymore—to us. Thank you so much again, Captain.

Melmont nodded and led Abigail to the car by the hand. Above them, the sky cleared miraculously and a little patch of blue appeared which Melmont took as a sign: blue for a boy. Starting the car, in a cloud of blue smoke (another sign),

Melmont announced he would call his son Tamerlane, after Tamerlane the Great, the Tartar conqueror from Samarkand. Cole had told him about Tamerlane. Melmont thought it sounded as if Tamerlane had the right idea.

But when the child was born, it was a girl.

Abigail called the girl Zenocrate, after Tamerlane the Great's beloved, to try to kindle Melmont's affection. Although he later came to love his firstborn above all his children, he dissolved his partnership with The Lord as abruptly as he had cast off Eisler. The birth of Zenocrate was a betrayal and a personal affront, and the flame-coloured Bentley (Connolly hides, but extensive cigar damage on walnut fascia), came no more bearing picnics to Weyhill church's thousand-year-old lychgate, 'twixt the villages of Burlingjob and Evengame, in the ancient and noble county of Oxbridgeshire.

♫   ♫   ♫

Today the same church is the deconsecrated home of an elderly couple who have done the conversion sensitively and respect the church's history. They joke that they are like Philemon and Baucis who looked after Jupiter's temple for him. They farm black English bees on a previously unremarked manmade mound nearby that experts now are convinced was the original 'weoh', a neolithic site of veneration, a mound as old as the legendary ziggurats of Uruk and Babylon.

The black bees of our modern Philemon and Baucis take off

a delicious harvest of different honeys at different times of summer; first yellow, green then August gold will be gathered from hives perched on the weoh. The different honeys made by the bees on the sacred spot are separated by seasonal taste and colour, then distributed to needful friends as unguents for their auras, according to a rather unorthodox interpretation of Goethe's theory of colours: yet it seems to work.

The yellow spring rejuvenating honey goes to haughty retired courtesans, youthful slappers, broke clowns and estuarine conmen.

The dark pine honey goes to depressives, warriors and nurses, the light green to crossdressers, geriatrics, hypnotists and comedians. Former television presenters, disgraced when caught snorting through rolled bank notes, have been willing to go to any lengths to obtain a small pot of Weoh Honey of any colour, hoping it will somehow translate into public forgiveness.

This, to me, proves there is a groundswell of awareness, and an admission that the old gods have well and truly fallen. And the identity of the 'new' gods, or god? It is eminently deducible.

VI

Melmont Unchained

WE JOIN THE FUTURE COSMIC ÜBER-TSAR in his office at Melmont House, where he sits regally, a phone in each hand. The brittle pitch-pine floors resound to the acoustic vibrato of His voice, and the empty factory acts as a vast echo chamber to his commanding Word. In the vibrating air there lingers lovingly faint reminder of vanilla and chocolate, conjuring ghostly hordes of local women dredging sugar dust over long-dead chocolate soldiers.

Behind Melmont's broad shoulder, please note the new secretary, who anyhow will seem familiar. Jill will never graduate from Oxbridge with her First, now. Jill is on the phone as well, adjusting her pearls which lie over a tight blue executive suit, so different to her student wear. She looks ten years older already, though only a few months have passed since Melmont chose her.

——Captain Melmont's about to leave for Los Angeles. I want to check his special dietary requirements in First Class. *Two* lunches is correct.

——I didn't hear that, I'm sorry?

The noise level had risen abruptly as Melmont took a direct

call from Konrad Eisler. Before his former partner could mention the stealing of the stock of science magazines, Melmont started to bellow in an inventive colloquial low German all his own. Excrementally possessed in more than a dozen tongues in ways that Martin Luther at his turdiest could not match, Melmont was the uncrowned Poet Laureate of poop and poo. It loses something in translation.

——What's the matter, uncle Arse-bark? I don't owe you fox-squit! You shitty little Kraut! You couldn't even print bog paper without me! Don't try to tell me my business, blind butthole surfer, when you can't even wipe yourself clean behind!

Picking up the second receiver, Melmont heard the trades union leader Mead identify himself, and immediately growled in Mead's mother tongue,

——I have offered a full set of talks with the union responsible for the stoppage you have engineered in my book repository, which is costing me thousands of pounds every day. If your members wish to become reasonable, then I may re-employ them. If not, then I shall find other workers to do the job for less!

Melmont put both receivers down next to each other. Mead and Eisler's little tinny voices could be heard trying to get past each other. Melmont paused to consider the arrangement but, rapidly tiring of it, tore the phones out of their sockets and hurled them through a nearby wall. This thoroughly frightened Professor Kirin, the Hungarian translator, who was waiting outside the office. Melmont failed to recognise him, and remarked loudly to no one in particular,

——Despicable people! Loathsome! Vile! Unfit to dine upon my excrements! Cunt-*wartzen*!

Kirin nodded agreement and smiled, hoping for reinstatement. The professor had on his one pair of spectacles taped with pink adhesive plaster.

——What are you smiling at? Who are you, sonny? Do you want a job?

Kirin nodded again, wincingly. The accident with the shelves had badly bruised his ribs. The remaining phone in the office rang, and Jill answered it.

——Mrs Simpkins? I'm afraid Captain Melmont is in a staff recruitment interview.

Melmont snatched the phone from her, and the anger instantly vanished as he cooed into the phone.

——Mrs Simpkins, I was going to call you. Your chooka-loos were *delicious*. What do you want to warn me about?

Mrs Simpkins knew her chickens would be delicious, for they were fed on the finest slops that a fowl might enjoy. Only that morning she had been watching her flock clean the melon rinds from the remains of the local Rotary lunch. But she thought the Captain ought to know some strange people were looking for him. As the fowls pecked happily, a grey pre-war Mercedes saloon had driven into the middle of the farmyard and stopped. Suddenly all the chickens had stopped clucking, as if they too knew something was up, Mrs Simpkins added, darkly.

A tall young woman then got out of the front passenger seat. She had dyed blonde hair and a cruel-seeming, twisted face with pale lifeless grey eyes. She and her foreign companions were looking for a "Kept-ien Miel-mont, Em-Cee". Mrs Simpkins had told the girl, in all honesty, that the energetic Captain could be anywhere: Boxly, London or Singapore, as far as she knew, for he seemed to be endlessly travelling for his businesses.

——That's what I said and it's right, isn't it, you do travel a great deal don't you? Mrs Simpkins asked the magnate anxiously.

——Correct, I travel a great deal in business. I have to. A very great deal.

Mrs Simpkins continued with her tale, reassured. The young woman seemed not at all grateful, indeed was greatly irritated, repeating the fact in a whining voice, that Melmont 'ought' to be there. Mrs Simpkins could have sworn that the air temperature went down by a couple of degrees in the farmyard with these peculiar-looking folk, and didn't go up again till they left.

But what she was mainly phoning about were the after-effects. When the chickens that had been standing next to the strange car were slaughtered, their flesh somehow tasted tinny, and the whole batch had to be thrown away. Mrs Simpkins was justifiably proud of her poultry, and nothing like it had happened before.

——I can assure you again, Mrs Simpkins, it was my direct personal experience that both chickens were eminently digestible.

——That's not surprisin' because I gave them to you days before the... the... . I didn't like the look of the visitors at all, Mrs Simpkins reiterated. They say they won't rest till they find you. But they won't say what they want. It's way past my under-standing, that's for certain.

——I truly appreciate your calling and I'll try to be ready for them if they come. God bless you, my dear, and you look after yourself.

Melmont put the phone down, and looked at Kirin.

——An outbreak of fowl pest near the Welsh marches and she thinks it's something to do with me. The English are all barking mad, Professor Kirin, would you not say?

——They are either on strike or insane, the professor duly concurred.

Two weeks after Mrs Simpkins' phone call, the ominous grey Mercedes with its occupants under suspicion of poisoning chickens could be seen halted outside the thinning picket line in front of Melmont House. The strike was down to token numbers over the Easter Bank Holiday. After some discussion with Mead, a person in a long coat was allowed through and shortly Jill found herself facing the young woman Mrs Simpkins had described to Melmont. She had pale eyes, poor complexion and a twisted jaw. She had arrived without an appointment, but still seemed to think it was someone else's fault that Melmont was not there. Jill guessed from her voice she was from Germany.

——I honestly don't know when he will be here, or even free to see you. Yesterday he had appointments in Frankfurt, New York and Peking. Obviously he couldn't be everywhere but... .

——One day on the same day, he will keep them all, the woman said, gnomicly. Jill decided not to try contradicting her, and to get rid of her as soon as possible.

——Today he's actually going to be in Bombay, or Mumbai. But if you leave your name and a contact pho... .

——Where is he this moment, exactly? Is he in Bombay or Mumbai? Why are you being so vague? interrupted the young woman.

——Bombay and Mumbai are the same place as far as I'm aware. He is *exactly* in a city in India, alright? Tomorrow he has a meeting in Moscow, which I know he is anxious to keep, if that's any help. He'll be at the Red Star Hotel.

——Moscow? whined the girl, as if Jill was to blame for the distance it was away from Boxly.

——Yes, Moscow. The number will be available from international directory enquiries. Can I help you with anything else?

The girl looked down at her pale hands with their bitten nails, and said in a low, menacing voice,

——We will find him, don't worry.

——Can I say who called? asked Jill.

——Veronika. It won't mean anything to him, yet.

Veronika's pale goaty eyes looked round the factory past Jill as if she did not exist, then she stood up. The hem of her long leather coat swirled out and fell back as she turned and walked away.

Jill watched the retreating figure with interest. Veronika's walk away on her high-heeled boots was sophisticated, very unlike the angry pale child's face which she had presented. And somehow she seemed to be aware that Jill was watching her walk away. Further away, she appeared to be walking slightly above the uneven knots in the recently varnished floor, as if the industrial floor had never had half an inch of planking scoured off the top over the years.

As the cunning wraith reached the top of the stairs, with the light from the tall windows beyond showing under her heels, she turned and gave a Nazi salute, and her voice suddenly gave a shout which reverberated in the empty factory.

——*Heil Hitler!*

Then the apparition turned, dropped its arm and descended

a spatial approximation of the stairs. Jill felt she should warn Melmont, but he was not to be found on any of the five continents.

Melmont was in fact not in Moscow, nor Bombay nor Mumbai, but close by, with his pregnant wife at his side. He had waited in Moscow till the cherry blossom came out and the Orthodox Easter came and went, but the vital interview he had been promised in the Kremlin had not materialised. He returned to England to find, to his slight surprise, Christ being crucified all over again and a Bank Holiday ensuing. Melmont's second Easter that month was spent fulfilling a long-standing invitation from Cole to drop by Prince's with Abigail. It would be their last chance to take a trip upriver from the college.

Having borrowed the college punt, one of the perks of the Chair he was resigning, Cole embarked with his guests from the Nile Street slipway. Nile Street receded, and fields began to appear on each side. The muddy Oxus, whispering reeds upon each bank, truly dawdles every which way, and Prince's great gold onion-dome of a library roof seemed to loom not much less than when they cast off.

——Are we there yet? said Abigail.

——Almost. We have to pick up my sister and her kids.

Soon a young pale girl and a restless boy in preparatory school uniform were in the punt as well, after complaining they had been waiting on a rotten jetty, breakfastless. Cole did not seem worried about this, or that there still seemed to be no sign of the mother of Dominic and Libby.

——She's like that, he said coolly, nodding to the children. They're terribly neglected.

——Where's their father? asked Abigail.

——No one knows. My sister met him in Cairo. He was a double agent, we think. Or he may just have been a con-man.

——He jumped over a wall at the back of the house when the military police raided, and hasn't been seen since, said Dominic. He squinted up at the figure of Cole above him, smeared to the elbow with green weed. His sister Libby stayed silent, eyes downcast, slim white fingers trailing in the icy water. They were very alike: slight, enchanting, damaged and needy.

——Where are we going, Tristram? asked the boy.

——Well, nowhere in particular, Dominic. I'm hoping to find somewhere where we can have lunch. But the river's course coils worse than the serpents that attacked Laocoön and his sons.

——Who's *Lacoo*?

——Laocoön was a priest of the sun god Apollo. He upset a god, it might have been Poseidon, god of the sea, or it might have been the sun god Apollo, but some god, anyhow decided on punishment and sent giant snakes out of the sea to kill him. His sons tried to rescue him, and they were killed too, Cole added thoughtfully.

——What killed them? Like conger eels?

——Bigger. Gi-normous. Giant snakes which killed a father and his young sons. A conger eel might give you a nasty nip but... .

The mighty apparitions of Poseidon's revenge felt almost palpable to Melmont as he listened, and gave him a sweet tremulous ache in the muscles of his jaw. Cole's nephew and niece then began a piercing enquiry about whether the giant snakes had bitten, swallowed or strangled the men to death.

——The famous statue of the event suggests it was progressive constriction. But that may be just the way the marble was quarried, or what the three sculptors involved could agree on was the most dramatic. You can't have an exhaustive account of a mythical event, you just can't. Specially after two thousand years of bards have had a go at it. The writhing sea-snakes probably derive from stories picked up on Alexander the Great's Indian campaign, about pythons squeezing people to death. Hippolytus was also destroyed by a giant bull which came from the sea, also after a disagreement between two gods.

——So what is your understanding of the real meaning of the story? asked Melmont.

——That men are the playthings of the gods, particularly in a non-Christian era, and men's annihilation is inevitable: the monster we fear most and can do least about.

Melmont loved to hear Cole teach. He looked at the neglected boy, whose attention had strayed to the river bank where a solitary brown-and-white cow stood and watched them reproachfully.

——Listen to your uncle, Dominic. He's a wise man.

——Phooey, said Cole. Though I do feel sometimes I prefer the past.

——This all will be past, in a minute, said Abigail, sleepily.

——What about the baby inside you, does it know that? asked Dominic.

Nobody was prepared to hazard a guess about the unborn child's apprehension of the passage of time.

——Why are you leaving the college, Tristram? Libby asked.

——Money. Professors don't make much and I'm going to

make pots and pots, replied Cole disingenuously.

They slowly went on, grazing the banks, North, South, East and West, till Cole's punting skills improved. It was pleasant in the sunshine. Abigail lay snoozing, in a lacy dress and a straw hat, dreaming of being effortlessly suspended, godlike and beyond time and reproach in the halcyon sky.

The third time the noonday sun swung in front of the bow, it stayed there. Abigail saw that Cole had tethered the punt to a rusty concrete pole under some trees. He was unpacking a picnic on the water meadow. Abigail manoeuvred herself carefully out of the punt, holding her stomach and her back, then immediately fell asleep again on a rug Cole spread for her on the grass.

Dominic shortly proved his uncle's prediction about him needing guidance by pulling the bung out of the bottom of the empty punt. The boy watched the cushions as they started to lift away in the rising water, then turned to find Melmont, who had observed the sabotage with interest, looking at him smiling from under a willow tree.

——How old are you, Dominic?

——Ten, said Dominic.

Melmont winked at him. Dominic realised that here was a possible ally. Melmont might not after all denounce him to the authorities, and smiled shyly. His sister Libby observed a bond forming. Dominic and Libby were twin souls. Melmont did not realise this further subtlety, and only saw himself mirrored in Dominic.

——You're the same age as I was when my father didn't come home one day, said Melmont.

——What happened next? asked Dominic.

——I sat in his place at the top of the table, said Melmont.

——Where did he go? asked Dominic.

Melmont watched Cole rolling his trousers up and wading out to try to save the scuttled punt.

——Where did he go? repeated Dominic.

——To heaven, replied Melmont, then seeing Dominic's suspicious expression, he added, I mean he died.

——What did he die of?

——Heart attack, we think.

The family had gradually pieced together the story. His father, injured in a drunken brawl over a bar bill, had developed acute septicaemia. No one had been found who would treat him. On the third day, friendless, he had been in all likelihood crawling home, but died alone by the roadside. Melmont's voice telling the story became clipped and wooden. But Libby listened with growing horror.

——I'm so sorry. I'm so sorry for you, said Libby.

Melmont nodded in appreciation of her manners.

——My father was cruel but it was how he had been treated. He died like a dog. No one deserves that.

The brown waters beyond the punt suddenly stirred and a woman slowly stood up till she was only knee high in the water. She was clothed only in mud.

——Oh, *there's* their mother! We're just about to have lunch, Priscilla, said Cole with forced enthusiasm.

Cole's sister, her hair full of the river, scrambled up the low bank and stood over Abigail, holding out her filthy hand. Abigail sat up to encounter an ingenuous wide pair of yellowish eyes that seemed to be smiling at a point behind her head from a smeared, elfin face. Priscilla was was not elfin-small, in fact her body was athletic and well-made, but there was also something defiantly fey and unworldly about Cole's sister. Like a water-sprite, she appeared immune to the cold of the water.

——I said we'd meet here, so I swam. It really isn't far and you were going ridiculously slowly. In fact I almost caught you a couple of times. You didn't see me, Priscilla concluded triumphantly, as if the trip had been one long game of Grandmother's Footsteps.

——We weren't looking, said Libby. I wasn't anyway.

——I did see something as a matter of fact, but I thought it was an otter, said Cole.

——That was because I kept *very* low down. Do you have a towel? Doesn't Tristram know he was meant to bring a towel? Why is the boat sunk?

After a towel had been found, Priscilla attacked the subject of the sunken punt, offering to punish Dominic without trial to save time.

——But he hasn't confessed yet, said Melmont, surprising himself with his own mellowness towards the boy.

——But he did it, said his mother.

——I used to be an interrogator, you know. Let me ask him, then. Did you sink the punt, Dominic?

Melmont raised a bushy eyebrow at the boy then winked. Dominic remained silent, and the case was shelved, indefinitely.

Later, after lunch, Melmont performed tricks with half-crown pieces. He made the large, heavy silver coin walk across his knuckles, to Dominic's delight. Then he solemnly pulled the coin out of his right, then his left ear. Dominic was completely entranced.

—Is that magic?

Melmont shrugged.

—Maybe. I taught myself to do it. He passed the coin over to the boy, and another one to Libby.

—Thank you, said Libby, surprised.

As Dominic put the coin in his pocket, his mother suddenly descended on the boy, slapping him furiously. Dominic, clearly used to the attacks, dropped to the ground and adopted a foetal position. Nothing could have offered less aggression. Libby stared at her mother inscrutably.

—Bad, bad, horrid boy. You say 'Thank you', his mother shouted.

—It's alright, it doesn't count, the first time, said Melmont.

Suddenly he stepped forward. Priscilla found that she could not raise her shoulder to get any swing to chastise her son. Melmont had wrapped his arm around her and she could not move. Dominic opened one eye, then slowly rolled away, out of range.

—Say 'thank you' to the nice man! hissed Priscilla.

Melmont slackened his powerful intimacy to allow Priscilla to adjust her towel, then he faced her and said solemnly,

—It would give me the greatest pleasure if I could be this boy's godparent.

Priscilla blinked.

—I should warn you, he's out of control.

Melmont smiled indulgently.

—I'm sure he will grow up.

Dominic sensed an ally in a cold, unfriendly world.

—Say 'Thank you', Dominic.

—Thank you, said a muffled child's voice.

On the lazy river behind them, as if in recognition of an important bond being formed, an upswelling current pulsed once, slowly. It eddied through the smooth surface, spreading out and fading away as it was borne around the bend.

♪   ♪   ♪

In Moscow, one year later, Melmont was waiting to see Stalin at the Kremlin again, but this time it was the real thing. Vanov's superior officers in the KGB had been purged in droves, banished to Siberia and executed in waves of hysteria that included any soldiers who had ever been outside Mother Russia. But Vanov continued to stay alive, partly by playing on the unique importance of his personal contact with Melmont, codename 'Balshoi'. The subtext to all of Vanov's memos and reports was that Balshoi's minder could not be changed because Balshoi was so important. And Vanov made sure no one else came near him. So it came about through attrition, the mills of death ground and ground, and bore Vanov-and-Balshoi higher and higher, till Vanov was close enough to the ear of Stalin to insist rather than merely suggest that it would be in the greatest interests of the Motherland if Balshoi could, after all, finally obtain his longed-for meeting with the little Georgian.

Melmont, in a respectfully dark suit, his wavy hair brilliantined glossily black as his shoes, was now waiting outside a pair of doors for admission to an inner sanctum. Peter the Great had stood on that very spot, during a lull in the beheading of boyars who had omitted to remove their beards.

Melmont touched the decorated, gilded portals of power as if he could not believe he was actually there. And who could blame him for his incredulity? Thirteen years ago he had come to England as a raw recruit, casting his old driver's stick into the North Sea for luck, owning only the clothes he stood up in. And now, at his request, he was meeting with the Czar of the Russias. If the meeting went as he planned, it could turn the former shoeless cowherd into a truly global figure, a mover and shaker of nations.

A suited assistant to the General Secretary called Melmont's name in a nasal Georgian accent, and led Melmont down a long dimly lit corridor with paintings of Lenin and Marx clasping each other in a display of solidarity across the ages. Melmont turned a corner, another decorated door opened and he saw the tyrant.

Stalin was behind a large desk in a small room. The killer of millions was examining a paper, probably a list of names. Stalin notoriously kept the names of those about to be purged on his desk during interviews, and was always amused by people, often relatives or wives, trying to read the names, upside down.

Looking up, he smiled warmly at his visitor who had no relatives living, in any case. Today the dictator was in modest military attire, with trousers tucked into soft leather boots. A vast settee took up much of the floorspace behind him, long enough for the tyrant to sleep on and outfox assassins combing the Kremlin bedrooms. He was said to have twentyseven secret bedrooms scattered around the Kremlin, so that no one would ever know where he slept.

Melmont had prepared himself by pinning his Military Cross on his suit, next to a small tasteful enamel brooch of Lenin above a hammer and sickle. He noticed Stalin's left arm was considerably smaller than the right and his complexion was poxed. This man who killed more people than Hitler was physically unimpressive. Melmont could have easily strangled him. However, he reminded himself, that was not the purpose of the visit. He took the plunge.

——Hitler had a great sense of humour. Know why? said Melmont in Russian, and smiled.

Stalin's eyebrows rose, interrogatively. Melmont delivered his punchline.

——The Volkswagen! He made the first car with a Jewish nose.

The silence that followed the joke was thick as tarred boot felt and twice as dark. Stalin turned enquiringly to his apparatchik at his side, as if to say, and what do you think of that? The apparatchik then repeated the joke, in Georgian. Stalin, the sly Georgian fox, started to smile. And Melmont smiled. The ice was breaking. Stalin laughed. Now Melmont laughed. Stalin's little weak left hand tapped his cavalry trousers in a staccato fashion, suggesting a muscular inhibition, but Melmont read into it an intimation of relaxation and interest.

And he was not wrong. Stalin stood and came round the desk to Melmont, who if he had stood would have towered over him.

——Are you a spy? Stalin said, smiling. He repeated it in English, as if trying out the language without understanding it.

Melmont decided to stick with Russian.

——No. Who would I spy for, anyway?

——Your country, said Stalin. The English spies Burgess and MacLean have recently come to Moscow. Are you here to join them?

——I am a publisher. But I am a Socialist because until I was ten, I had no shoes.

——My father was a cobbler, said Stalin, mildly, as if offering to help, even though it was too late.

——I have a project of biographies which I propose to publish in the West, of the heroes of the Great Patriotic War, including Warsaw Pact leaders, said Melmont.

Stalin walked away two paces, then turned.

——Who had you in mind? he asked, his brown eyes lighting up.

——Yourself, to begin with and then… Marshall Zhukov?

Vanov had served under the great Georgy Zhukov at the battle of Stalingrad, the turning point of the war. Everyone in the army adored him.

——Why Zhukov? said Stalin, beadily. He had jealously banished the popular general to a remote governorship in the Crimea, away from the limelight.

Melmont realised his mistake.

——Perhaps not anyone else but the General Secretary then. It is an important idea. Comrade, your military achievements should be as freely available to libraries the world over in the same way that the advances of Russian science become available worldwide, demonstrating the innate superiority of the Soviet system and its leadership. I also believe that the future of the world will be enormously improved if there is an agreement to share the peaceful developments of nuclear science. I have agreements in principle from the American authorities and I would like to continue to extend exactly the same opportunity to make discoveries public through my network of scientific magazines, Melmont concluded.

Stalin smiled, and then nodded to his apparatchik, and said,

—Very well. Make the necessary arrangements.

Melmont bowed and said humbly,

—This is a great day for Soviet science.

As he was led away out of the presence, he thought he heard Stalin say something to his aide, in Georgian. The apparatchik rapidly caught up with Melmont to give further good news. One million roubles was going to be forwarded by the appropriate department to assist in the biography of the Leader, to cover 'significant costs'. Melmont impulsively kissed the bust of Lenin that sat by the door, before he could be restrained.

—Thank you, Vlad, he whispered.

                    ℳ   ℳ   ℳ

In England, the centralised book depository scheme was going the way of all good ideas ahead of their time. The publishers who had trusted Melmont with their stock lost out, and Melmont's hollowed-out company, which had very little more to it than a short lease on an old biscuit factory, became bankrupt. Creditors would find there was little left to distribute, as

Melmont had parked his financial assets in Liechtenstein.

There was a nasty scene at the final insolvency meeting of the leading creditors, which Melmont attended with Abigail, two weeks overdue. Using Abigail as a shield against reporters, Melmont ostentatiously pushed her towards his waiting car as reporters waved microphones at him in the melée. Cameramen staggered, trying to keep their heavy film cameras pointed at the failing tycoon who was making progress through a crowd composed partly of the vengeful, and partly of the newsmakers themselves. Melmont finally reached the car and was shouting, waving an economics periodical he had recently published,

——If you read my article you will find that overall I have worked night and day to get the trading practices at my firm reformed. But every step of the way the unions have opposed and shackled me!

——How come the firm is bankrupt and you are not?

——That is the meaning of a limited company. The sister company in America is very successful. I never *personally* sold my interest in the firm. The shares were moved to the American branch by a *family trust* over which I have *no control*.

——The bloody crook! Now he's running off to America, look! shouted a voice over the hubbub.

——I would like you to know I am not running away. I will continue to invest in this country, where labour practices permit. In the long run, this country will thank me! I consider myself British to the core!

Abigail was knocked by the jostling crowd and fell to the ground, grazing her leg. Melmont leapt to her side and stood over her, clearing a space for her with his fists, shouting for the crowd to stay away or he'd kill them. There was a sudden hush as he helped his wife to her feet and eased her into the car.

Lying back, shaken, in the rear of the car, Abigail's water's broke. But it was a swift uncomplicated birth, like Abigail's sturdy Flemish forbears. Little Zarustrina, bellowing lustily, arrived as mother and child were being wheeled into the delivery room.

Jill, who had stayed with Abigail, went down to break the news to the father, dreading the reaction that might happen when Melmont learned that he only had a daughter, again. She went to the hospital flower shop and saw Melmont had already bought armfuls of blue flowers, but before she was able to speak to him, the tall and sinister profile of Veronika, the stork-like Hitlerite, cut in, walking fast straight towards Melmont.

Jill could have sworn there was a whiff of sulphur as Veronika passed, or perhaps the hospital just used very powerful disinfectants. With her this time were two companions, a man and a woman, who seemed to share Veronika's liking for shabby leather. Jill wanted to call out a warning, but nothing came from her mouth as the three hellhounds converged in an orchestrated pincer movement on their prey. And now they had him boxed in; there was no escape. But Melmont still seemed oblivious to them, looking upwards wistfully as if he regretted, on reflection, not having bought the whole wall of blue hydrangeas. One of the men tapped him on the back.

—Captain Melmont, my name is Helmut. We have heard you have some financial problem. Well, we will pay two hundred and fifty pounds maximum for the special copies you hold of *Mein Kampf.*

Melmont's financial acumen sprang to his aid. Without pausing for thought he said,

——Five thousand. And you have to buy the lot. You've got two hours. I'm going to Delhi tonight.

Helmut and his female companion exchanged glances.

——What do you say, Hilda? said Veronika.

Hilda had dark hair and was plump, with oily skin and a pair of high-heeled shoes the same colour as Melmont's red Bentley had been. Veronika demi-pirouetted, leather coat flapping like a dead crow's wing on a gate, and whispered in Helmut's ear.

——OK, we will take them all, said Helmut. He was as unpleasant looking as Veronika, with the same skin tone. All three of them looked as though they never saw the sun.

Melmont turned and saw Jill waving to him, uncertain of whether it was her place to interrupt the trafficking.

——It's a girl, Earnest. Seven pounds. A girl, she repeated, expecting an outburst when Melmont grasped the fact. Instead, he calmly pointed to the enormous heap of bouquets which had already been wrapped up.

——Change those for pink ones and take them up to Abigail, will you? Tell her I'll be up in a moment.

Melmont had not thought much of Trapp's strange gift to him since Willis and Mrs Simpkins had loaded the books into his car. Now, at the top of the hospital car park, he opened the boot and examined them again, in the presence of the three peculiar but determined purchasers. The books were all identical, bound in a thin blue-grey, similar to the colour of Veronika's coat. In some places there were numbers inked into the leather. Veronika counted them and announced that there were thirtynine when there should be forty.

Melmont held firm.

——As you can see these are genuine. Not a shadow of doubt they're bound with flayed concentration camp victims.

——Perhaps you have some lampshades from skin also, instead no?

——The *Mein Kampf* price stays the same as for forty, he announced. I am not a furnishings wholesaler madam. If you want lampshades, go to Harrods.

A deal was struck. One of the fiends brought over a Gladstone bag and laid out bundles of notes on the back seat, which was still wet from Abigail's waters breaking.

——Two hundred thousand pounds, Helmut said. Well I suppose it is worth paying that for something which is literally priceless, no, Hilda?

Hilda, suddenly bored and picking her nose, did not reply. Helmut picked out a volume at random, and opened the flyleaf of his acquisition as reverently as any bibliophile allowed to hold a weighty original copy of Shakespeare's First Folio and turn its hallowed pages.

——Look. *"From Wolf"*, that's Hitler's pet name, *"To Von Stauffenberg"*, the very man who would betray him. Tragic, really, no? Veronika sniffed in agreement, and fell to softly humming a tune Melmont recognised as the Horst Wessel song.

It was only when the three had left that it struck Melmont what he had been involved in. Trafficking for profit in human remains. Very possibly his relatives. A spasm of nausea convulsed him and he retched into the gutter at the edge of the car-park roof. Then just as quickly as it arrived, the feeling passed.

A few minutes later Melmont walked to the ward where his wife and newborn baby were on show. Abigail was smiling breathlessly, weakly, feeling absurdly proud and bursting with love for their latest little mite. Melmont methodically started to lay damp twenty-pound notes in a halo around the baby's head. Abigail, relieved Melmont was not angry, spoke to the newborn,

—Look what he's doing! He loves you, little precious girl! You've got the best daddy in the world, did you know that?

VII

Melmont Marxissimus

ONE OF THE UNFAIREST RULES OF THE UNIVERSE IS—
or was—that money begets money; the cash from
the sale of *Mein Kampf* happened to spark a time
of almost miraculous recovery and expansion for Melmont.
The nuclear industry, the monstrous twelve-toed lovechild of
the Cold War, also spawned a printing boom. With monopolies
in nuclear science publications on both sides of the Iron
Curtain, the growing legions of Cold War nuclear research
scientists published in his journals, or they never published
at all. Melmont's publications were essential to both sides,
because they could always be read for covert information on
the progress, or reverses, of Enemies. Terrible mistakes were
made in distant timezones, and narrated later, disguised as
'controlled experiments' in Melmont's science publications; it
was exclusively from Melmont's *International Journal for
Inorganic Chemistry*, volume 13, that the CIA was able to link
the disappearance of fifty villages from maps in the Urals with a
suspected disastrous explosion of sediment tanks in a Russian
nuclear facility.

But even as he waxed fat under the nuclear umbrella, Melmont's old dream of entering politics returned and would not let him rest till like all Melmont's dreams it impelled him to direct action.

Some say Melmont joined the Labour Party a week prior to appearing before the constituency selection board; some say he overlooked that detail entirely. He had no choice of party, for he had alienated the Conservatives earlier. But it was, as it turned out, a good time to be a Labour candidate.

Dressed in a red tie and blue suit so electric that no one could confuse its colour with sympathy for Tory concerns, Melmont faced a host of Labour delegates and named himself as, foremost, the man who would support the then-Labour policy plank, the Campaign for Nuclear Disarmament.

——Choose me and you will be choosing someone who knows this party will win the next General Election. If elected, I pledge to abolish nuclear weapons.

——Order, order!

In the hurly-burly, it had been somehow missed earlier that Melmont had no connections with Barsetshire, the distant rural area that had been recently amalgamated with Oxbridge. But even this handicap was turned to his advantage. Fiddling with his red tie ostentatiously, the great man trotted out his impressive credentials.

——I am originally from farm-labouring stock. And as a businessman who employs over five hundred personnel in this country, I know about all kinds of labour relations, first-hand.

And every word was true, and was believed. Captain Melmont MC was duly selected as Labour candidate for

Oxbridge and Barsetshire. Estate agents in Barsetshire where property prices were half the national average encouraged a rumour he was looking for a house to buy in the area.

Meanwhile Stalin died. As the great political thaw in Russia slowly got underway, Vanov began the process of arranging a prestigious visit for Melmont to the body of the dead tyrant. This would be an enormous accolade, confirming that Melmont was, as far as the new Soviet regime was concerned, One of Them. Vanov's report, which clinched the visit, stated that as soon as Melmont had been elected (which would he predicted happen shortly) to the 'British Houses of Parliament' (both of them, an excusable slip), he was expecting that Melmont's party, in need of a Strong Man in crisis-torn Britain, would invite him to lead the English *duma*. If not, he would at least become a Cabinet minister.

Vanov calculated that the award of the Order of Lenin surely could not be far off for the controller of such a significant source. Such a thing would make him impregnable to enemies inside the department.

After further memos arguing Melmont's worth to Russia as an eye on US developments through magazines devoted to the free exchange of Peaceful Nuclear Information, Vanov finally got clearance for Melmont to view Stalin's corpse, a privilege previously restricted to the Inner Party members. It was to be for a limited time. Ten minutes only or world stability would be threatened. A Chinese delegation, sticklers for protocol and punctuality while being reared from the cradle to be fanatical Stalinists, were due in for worship immediately afterwards.

But then it emerged that Stalin's mortal body was still being treated for its voyage through eternity. However on the day offered, after further frantic string-pulling by Vanov, it was arranged they would still be able to go 'round the back' as it were, and see the work being carried out. Vanov pointed out the honour, though informal, was no less great and possibly even greater.

——Better than kissing the Pope's ring, my friend, said Vanov.

——I am as it so happens in negotiations to write the present Pope's biography, said Melmont. The Vatican is only demanding that we do not cast aspersions on the miracle of the blood of Saint Janarius.

——Who?

Zhukov had allowed his tank captains to pin up ikons of saints inside their tank turrets, and Vanov's crew had had several saints between them, but no Janarius.

——Janarius' dried blood is in a bottle, and becomes miraculously liquid again around the winter solstice. Perhaps they are having the same problem with dear Comrade Stalin going all liquid even after he was hung out to dry. For he was if not saintly, *very* good, wasn't he? added Melmont.

Vanov didn't like it when Melmont made fun of the former great leader.

——You behave right around him. This is important!

Melmont, smirking, agreed to behave.

One bright March morning a procession of four stately Zil limousines swung past Lenin's mausoleum where technicians were experimenting, in order to light Stalin's future bier with a suitably soft and religious glow. Although the museum was closed to the public, outside the squat, polished hematite slab, small gatherings of lumpen, grey-faced people still assembled daily to stare longingly past the goosestepping guards towards the space where Comrade Stalin (to whom everyone owed so much) would shortly, as had been promised, be on show for veneration, education and inspiration.

The limousines turned right into the main gates of the Kremlin. The procession halted and Vanov stepped forward to open the door of the third car. With his large distinguished guest at his side, Vanov stepped in through the sliding doors towards the dedicated Russian medical unit deep within the Kremlin, where Stalin's corpse was being prepared.

The Medical Unit for the Preservation of Soviet Heroes was large, set out like an old-fashioned research laboratory, with dark mahogany benches, test tubes and retorts. The centre had been established after Lenin's death to preserve his outward semblance, though completely against his wishes. Melmont saw x-ray plates of skulls, knees and other, less easily recognisable pieces of human anatomy hung on each wall.

In one room, Vanov whispered, Lenin's brain had been stored in the 1920s, sliced into three thousand sections in order for it to be studied in the hope that one day some doctor would discover, staring into ever-more powerful microscopes, traces of the magical transforming dust of Marx-Leninism that had turned the world upside down.

In the laboratory, white-coated workers, holding files, slides or petri dishes, moved around with grim determination to complete their allotted tasks. Nothing was more important to the Party than the successful prevention of fungal outcrops on the dead leaders, however short of suspending them both in formaldehyde-filled glass sided coffins, there were no easy solutions. Without the stable dry climate that made early Egyptian necrology such a gift to history, the Moscow team faced a continuing challenge. They battled daily waves of microscopic destroyers which arrived on the damp breath and snowy galoshes of every worshipper, but after thirty years of improvisation with wax, Leichner No. 9, injections of dilute Kensington Gore, and the like, change and decay in Comrade Lenin were still the order of the day. Lenin often needed surgery, too, as if, as soon as the last visitor left, the Leader started getting up and moving around, carelessly knocking pieces of his brittle fingers off or losing an eyebrow.

His successor now appeared to have escaped altogether, and no one would admit they knew anything about him. But Vanov persisted, loudly, and finally the chilled and embalmed corpse of Stalin arrived out of cold storage on a stainless steel hospital gurney, trailing clouds of condensation.

It was hardly a sight to cheer the heart. Stalin was not even dressed in a dignified fashion, with an old dressing gown thrown over him. Two assistants lifted the small, unnaturally stiff body onto a bench and started taking swabs around his upper arms.

—There he is, comrade, the greatest man that ever lived, whispered Vanov.

—He stayed true to the principles of Leninism, no doubt about it. Even though he did not have a large *putz*, Melmont added, lighting a large cigar.

Vanov frowned at the irreverence, but no one seemed to object.

The top of Stalin's head had been neatly sawn off, and now

opened with a stout brass hinge at the back. Following the example of the Lamarckian scientists of the 1920s with Lenin's brain, Stalin's brainbox had also been reverently removed. The assistant who had flipped Stalin open was now peering into the cavity with the same kind of torch that doctors use to look in the ears of patients, before removing the specks of verdigris on the hinge with a small toothbrush, which broke in two. Melmont snorted with derision.

The technician went off to find another instrument and Melmont came close and tried to look inside as well, which raised the wrath of one of the scientists, a large woman who shouted at Vanov to take his unhygienic companion and his cigar away. Both of them should be wearing slippers, gowns and masks besides. Vanov replied that the distinguished visitor was at the unit on the highest possible clearance, and it would be unwise for anyone of her rank to be personally responsible for his ejection. However they were well past their allotted time to view, and there was nothing else to see.

As the woman scientist moved to the gurney brake to release it, Melmont tapped the cigar, and a gob of ash dropped into the pan of Stalin's head.

Only Vanov noticed, and while he dared not draw attention to the sacrilege, he was appalled. A moment later Stalin was shut up, and rattled away to the American-made freezer.

As they were standing outside again, waiting for the caval-cade, Vanov asked Melmont if he knew what he had done.

—Of course I *knew*. It was for the people he had killed, the bastard. Half your family went to the Gulags. I was your saviour, and boy did you need me.

——But do you know what a risk you were taking? shouted Vanov, going red in the face.

Melmont shrugged his shoulders.

——I'm not an arselicker when I don't have to be. The stupid bugger's dead and when he was alive I fooled him. Those doctors should be running a waxworks. It doesn't matter how much rouge you put on him, he's always going rot from the inside.

Vanov and Melmont walked across Red Square together in a seething, unsettled silence of co-dependency. Finally Melmont said,

——I'm going public next year.

——Is that good, or bad?

——It is good, of course. Is it good that there are fifty nuclear breeder reactors being built in this country?

——Obviously it is good. Who will want to start a war with an enemy who has ten thousand nuclear warheads? No one!

——No one except the Vietnamese, perhaps.

Vanov said bitterly,

——Brigadier Cole, you say, is a big capitalist nowadays. That photograph you have of him must be proving very useful.

——My dear Ivan Illyich, you don't understand the first thing about me. The liberalising of public attitudes has made the photograph not much more than a curiosity. But if I needed money, I could always ask you, said Melmont, pointedly.

——So is no one blackmailing Cole for being effeminate?

——I would be the first to know. He lives openly with his boyfriend.

Cole had at this time acquired a live-in lover, a camp barrow-boy called Terence. They were an ill-matched couple. Terence perched uneasily in Cole's Thurloe Square house in Chelsea, with its portraits of wigged and ruffed ancestors, country-style hunting prints and satin-covered dining chairs. Everything seemed too large for the rooms and Terence affected to despise Cole's old-fashioned taste, while offering little to replace it. Every two months these differences would come to a head, though Terence was careful never to throw more than the odd cup or saucer, and would return the next day.

——You still don't want to change nuffin? Right, I'm out of here, I can't stand it. Too bleeding poncey for me, and anyhow I got to be at Covent Garden at three sharp or there won't be nothing to put on the barra'.

After one of these breakups, where Terence threatened to accuse Cole of extreme upperclass perversion, through a popular newspaper owned by Midrash The Leveller, Cole was dressing in his pinstripes for the City when a tall lanky boy in school uniform came to the door. Dominic at sixteen was as tall as Cole and had walked from Slough. He ignored the *Daily Telegraph* stuffed halfway through the letterbox, bent down and took the aluminium foil off the pint of milk. He was just drinking off the top two inches of yellow full-cream, when his uncle opened the door.

——I'll get some more milk. I'm sorry, I was thirsty. I've been walking all night. Uncle Tristram, it's me, Dominic.

Cole started as if he had been awoken from a dream.

——Christ! Of course it is. I was wondering who was drinking my milk. Of course, the tomtits have learned to do it the rest of the time. What are you doing here? said Cole.

——I've been expelled, said Dominic.

——What for?

——Wanking another boy, said Dominic, in a throwaway tone, wishing to move into the house. Cole did not move out of the way.

——Oh Christ. Does Earnest know?

Melmont as self-appointed godfather had been paying Dominic's school fees.

——I haven't told him. What does it matter? School's over for me, anyhow now. I phoned little sister to let her know, and she is coming here too. Is that alright? We've got nowhere else to go. Mother's still out of the country, at some loony ashram.

——What about the house she had in St Albans?

——She sold it.

Cole, normally a hospitable soul, started to see ever more inventive headlines leaked to the *News of the People* by Terence implicating Leading Banker with Public School Sex Scandal. He hoped his nephew would go away, but every time the thought rose in his mind, Dominic seemed to drift another step deeper into the house.

Cole was late for a day that started with a meeting with Melmont about the limits to board regulation. Melmont had been trying to bully Cole to bend the rules, for weeks, phoning him at all hours. After that, a complex assessment on a loan for a fabric factory in Turin would be light relief. And perhaps the presence of his nephew and niece would take the edge off the sour hell that domestic life with Terence regularly became.

——You and your sister can stay here for a short while, Dominic, but whatever you do, don't answer the phone.

——Thanks, *mon cher oncle*. You are a brick.

When Cole left, Dominic's eye could have picked up the

breakfast for two, still not cleared away, and upstairs a large bed with sheets tangled. But it wasn't until he found a photograph of his uncle with his arm around a lean young man who had had his nose broken rather often, that Dominic understood that his uncle was half of a couple. Thinking it over, he realised he had actually known for some time. Cole's boyfriend had small wounded eyes under a cowlick fringe. On the back of the photograph was written "Tristram and Trouble, Tangier."

Dominic sat down on the unmade bed and lit up one of Trouble's Guards cigarettes, wondering idly if they were a special homosexual brand. The advertisement went *"They've Got to be Great, to be Guards"* and showed a line of strapping red jacketed fellows in bearskin busbies. Dominic's own experiences with Her Majesty's Guards would be after dark in Hyde Park where sometimes, as he later complained to his sister, there wasn't even time for a proper fag afterwards.

꜒   ꜒   ꜒

Dominic's sister Libby was sixteen as well now; tall, longwaisted with a low voice, lanky and dark haired with a lurcher's suspicious eyes under heavy eyebrows. In eighteen months' time it would all fall into place and she would be model of the year. Till now she had shared a bedroom in her boarding school with an American girl called Amelia Digby. Amelia had been brought up in Maine by her mother and sent away to England to get expensively 'finished'.

Amelia's father was the same wild pistol-toting intelligence officer whom Cole had liaised with in Berlin. Digby was a senior CIA operative, always away in trouble spots. Libby in return boasted about her absentee mother who had spent the last few years in India, ashram-hopping. They both agreed their parents didn't give a shit. The two girls had fantasised a number of ways to escape into the real world, to go to London, and offload virginity as a prelude to true independence.

And now Libby, after the phone call from Dominic, was leaving for real. The liberal regime made escape an unchallenging exercise, but some things are in the blood, and as the daughter of a secret agent Libby was leaving at dawn via the emergency rope ladder from the bedroom. *"For Use in Case of Fire"* it said. Now it was serving the fires of youth.

Amelia watched her friend's preparations. When she spoke it was often in imitation of Libby's eccentrically old-fashioned English accent, one of the few things Libby felt she was happy to copy her mother in.

——Do you think your uncle fancies Dominic, then?

——I don't know. Perhaps he'll tell me if I ask.

——Oh do, but he'll never *tell* you. Fags don't honour women, that's what my dad says. He talks like a hick when he's drunk, she added, imitating her father. 'Fags, Commies an' *wimmin* are the scourge of the world.'

——He sounds quite something, your dad, said Libby. I wonder if he ever met mine.

——The walljumper, you mean. You're better off without him. My father on his rare visits home has given his family every opportunity to hear his Iowa snarl from the bottom of the bottle, and it was why everyone is, like him, most comfortable when they are far away from each other. It's a pattern, we're all fated, I guess, like some Greek fucking tragedy.

Libby pulled on a dark polo-neck sweater and looked out of the window. As they had been talking, the soft dawn light had been starting to pick out the crenellated ridgetiles of the great mock-Tudor roof above the girls' bedroom. It was time to step on stage in her own drama.

——It's funny, I always *knew* I would do this, said Libby.

——Character is meant to be fate, said Amelia. It doesn't give people much room to deviate, does it?

Libby took out a small Campaign for Nuclear Disarmament badge from her chest of drawers and pinned it to Amelia's nightdress.

——Here: CND, said Libby, conspiratorially.

——My father said that all who support the Campaign for Nuclear Disarmament are dangerous lackeys of Communism. Mind you, he's a brain-dead Republican. If your mother calls, shall I tell her where you've gone?

Libby shook her head.

——She won't call, she never does. Wear the badge, now!

Libby embraced her friend, adjusted her rucksack and climbed backwards carefully through the window onto the fire-escape ladder. Amelia leant out of the window and smiled supportively, watching Libby descend. Libby dropped the last few feet into a flowerbed, rolled over like a parachutist, stood up and waved, then trudged off through the dew on the lawn towards freedom. As she reached the far side, she turned one last time. The sun was now suddenly kissing the top of the school's tall asbestos boiler-stack. It looked like a fine day to run away.

Amelia waved again, fondly, and Libby shouted,

——Ban the Bomb!

The shout was unexpectedly loud and the sports hall wall caught the echo and played it back, *boum-boum*, immediately.

——Ban the Bomb!

Fortunately Libby's strict housemistress, Miss Greer, used wax earplugs and continued to slumber through the escape, her papery eyelids closed, dreaming she was young again and in the Artistic Quarter of Paris, called Montparnasse, where she had never dared to venture.

Amelia rolled up the escape ladder to delay detection of escape for as long as possible, then turned on her tape recorder, which she had been listening to earlier. Her father's voice continued,

'*My triple bypass operation went just fine. I hope you are being a good girl where you are, Amelia. I can't tell you where I am for security reasons but it is real warm though they can serve chilled beer. (Distant sharp clacking noise, on the tape.) Welcome to the real world. That there, little girl is the sound of the Commie insurgents' militia downtown, on the other side of the hotel…* '.

Her father was always too busy saving the world from Communism, or too drunk, or just too angry, to write. These tapes at six month intervals were his only form of comunication, and she never replied to them.

VIII
Melmont's Secret Garden

WALKING FROM SOUTH KENSINGTON tube station that same day, London seemed suddenly quieter than Libby remembered it; indeed she could hear the phone ringing from the street long before she got to Cole's house. When Dominic opened the door, she walked in and picked up the receiver, to be subjected to a torrent of abuse.

——Get your arse unplugged and get over here, Colonel Crap-head Cole. I'm making these swap deals with the new shares on my own, you useless little creep.

——You shouldn't have done that, said Dominic to his sister. We're not meant to answer the phone.

——Why?

Dominic shrugged extravagantly.

——It's either Tristram's had a row with his boyfriend or because… , Dominic gestured to the phone's receiver, which was still pouring out coprolaliac abuse.

Suddenly the abuse ceased. Libby said fearlessly,

——Uncle Earnest?

There was a click from the receiver.

——Tristram isn't here, I don't think. This is Libby, said Libby.

——It was him, but he's hung up, hasn't he?

——I suppose so. That is really *weird*, said Libby. What is going on?

A moment earlier, Cole had walked into Melmont's office, and Melmont had put the phone down.

——There you are, he grunted, pushing a wad of papers over the desk towards his visitor.

Cole peered at them.

——As I said, Earnest, I need to take some time to look at these.

——The brakes are coming off in the City now. Are you on the gravy train with me, or with those departing to Night and Fog? said Melmont, aggressively.

——I can't sign these without consultation, Cole said.

——What's the problem, Tristram? I came to this country a penniless outsider. My wealth has been made by hard work and you are not going to ruin it for me. Sign now and save me the trouble of sacking you later.

——Earnest, this is most unusual. Have you approached any other board members with the requirement they file undated resignation letters with you?

——Of course, everyone has already signed.

——If everyone has signed letters of proxy affadavit, it means your board has no power at all. You won't be able to run a public company like this for long, because it's illegal. Someone could shop you, Cole said, drily.

——I'm going to run it any bloody way I like.

——I still need time to study these, said Cole, stubbornly.

——You could have had plenty of time, but you were late!

——I had a family crisis, said Cole.

Melmont grabbed Cole and turned round a silver-framed photograph on his desk. It featured Abigail in a flowered dress and six girls in descending order of height, dressed identically to the mother and smiling palely like her.

——*That* is a family. *You* don't have a family!

——On the contrary, said Cole. I wish I hadn't, but my nephew and niece have just moved in with me. I would ask you not to use such strong language on the phone to Libby.

Cole declined to sign, but in vain. His principles were continuously assaulted and worn down in a campaign over the next few months. He never knew if Melmont would be aggressive or sweetly accommodating, and learnt not to predict. Melmont was a favourite among banking circles because he never quibbled over repayment terms, and Speke & Lazarus would be half the bank it was without his custom. For months, Cole walked a difficult line between resistance and acquiescence.

Summoned to the country by the great man, Cole discovered that Melmont was installing himself in a vast stately home after he had somehow persuaded the Oxbridge council to lease him the huge pile at the outskirts of the town for a peppercorn rent. The enormous site was large enough to develop as the centre of his latest operations, as well as his family home.

——You must come and visit us, soon, old man. The new place is quite something. Fit for a gent.

As soon as Cole relented and obeyed the new country gent's invitation, Melmont took up his insolent tirade. Cole had hardly arrived before Melmont waved papers under Cole's nose.

——Either sign or get out. Who needs fairy bankers, anyway?

Two workmen went by, carefully wheeling a brand-new beechframed oriel stained-glass window depicting Samson demolishing the house of his captors. Waiting for Melmont's fit to pass, Cole looked politely at the coloured glass. Lines of yellow squares, set corner to corner, were the falling pillars of the classical façade which Samson was forever setting a-tumble, bringing the house of the Philistines down on his own head.

——I've often thought that Samson, from the spectacular end he chose, almost could have been a pupil of Gürdjieff, said Cole, pronouncing the name with fastidious correctness.

Melmont's eyes came very close to Cole's face.

——Who is Gürdjieff, my friend?

Cole started to feel slightly weak at the knees, and had to make a conscious effort as if Melmont had acquired Gurdjieff's skills by the act of speaking his name.

——Gurdjieff is, or was, a mesmeric spiritual teacher who instructed his followers to 'always astonish'. His own life was something no one could have possibly invented. He made his first fortune by replacing ribbons on the new typewriters for the Russian army of occupation in his country. He then looked after a large number of people, buying and selling carpets and so on. He said that no one should be a guru who could not support at least thirtyfive people. His writings are opaque to outsiders but he had great presence. The short story writer Katherine Mansfield, in many ways a hard-boiled Antipodean, chose to spend her last days in his Parisian collective where she...

——Only thirtyfive! interrupted Melmont. Then I am a guru *fifty* times over.

Cole noticed that he had surrendered to his teacher. His right hand was in the process of signing the papers held out by Melmont. In exchange for stock options and handsome annual dividends, effective control of Melmont's latest new company now passed entirely to Melmont, who was careful to disparage his legal banditry.

——These letters of resignation, I will never use, I swear. I swear, on my mother's life. Tristram, I cannot do anything irregular, now, look! I am about to become a Member of Parliament! All you need is one of these!

Melmont drew Tristram to a tall gothic window, and pointed proudly to a Land Rover arriving on the broad gravel driveway flanked by lime trees. Cole saw the Land Rover was covered with hydrogen-filled balloons in gay colours with streamers attached. Tall radio antennae attached to the bonnet continued to swing to and fro after the vehicle had halted. On the back of a small round caravan it was towing, a board announced that 'Melmont is here'.

——I didn't know you could be in two places at once, said Cole, weakly sarcastic.

——That caravan contains my Secret Weapon for Election. The Blind, said Melmont.

It was faithful Jill who had found the key to the marginal seat Melmont was fighting: voters in the grim twilight of maculate degeneration. The caravan was filled with big, clumsy manual braille typewriters on small tables exploiting the advantage for all it was worth. Even with the Land Rover in motion, slim fingers still addressed the heavy keys with determination, advising the forgotten and marginalised that their jobs (where employed) or benefits would never go on the scrap heap, should they be guided to the right box to scribble an invisible X or M to send Melmont to Parliament to plead their case.

Cole turned and made his way with Melmont over a vast pale expanse of carpet, in the midst of which a pregnant Abigail was being served tea. As they walked, Melmont gestured across the vast entrance hall, wide as a tithe barn, in welcome to a man in an expensive business suit. It was Gunter Röhl, older of course, and without the hair.

Abigail and Cole exchanged kisses and smiles like the old friends they were.

——I don't understand something Tristram, why is my husband a *Labour* candidate? He has had nothing to do with them till now, and besides, even I know they hate success.

——He's got no choice, said Cole.

Abigail wrinkled her brow, puzzled. Melmont was now bringing Röhl towards them on his arm, as if he had won a doll at a fairground and was going to show it round to less fortunate friends.

——He blotted his copybook with the Tories when his book firm went bust, Cole added.

——When I was pregnant, I remember, said Abigail.

——You're always pregnant, Abigail.

It was so strange that the man who now shook Cole's hand and smiled had once been a prisoner of his. Röhl seemed an old-fashioned gentleman, now; no trace of the military man remained.

——I'm just passing through. I came to see my son, who is on a student exchange here, one of the new Europeans, and I wanted to wish the campaigning Socialist well. What a castle you have here, Captain Melmont, said Röhl, reaching up and clapping Melmont's broad back.

The peppercorn leaseholder beamed, as Emer, the darkly officious Dublin maid, poured dark tea, and added a quantity of full cream milk and several cubes of sugar into a large cup.

—Here's the master's, all brimming now. He likes it Connemara strength, strong enough to trot a mouse across.

Cole noticed that she had poured it into a special cup, the same design as the other teacups, but five times the capacity. The huge saucer held several slices of window cake. Melmont seized the scaled-up container, and stalked off towards the windows of the vast salon, monarch of everything he surveyed.

—The thing about Emer's tea is that it has the beneficial effect during pregnancy of reducing the swelling of my ankles, look.

Abigail's English had become idiomatic, perfect in the way that only some foreigners can speak the language.

—Ach, sure and you're only saying that, Miss Abigail, so's I don't run off and leave you alone with that *divil* of a husband, halfway round the world, as he's sure to be anytoim yer want hem, said Emer, thickening her brogue, in pious emphasis, as Abigail admired her own still-delicate extremities.

—It's true, they are still slim as a girl's, said Röhl.

What Emer had observed was true. Melmont always was away when Abigail's waters broke now, after the disappointment of Zarustrina's sex.

—The astrologers say the seventh will be a boy, said Abigail.

Emer added something darkly to the effect of, given the

fierceness of the master's desires for a boy, mere stars would not affect the issue one way or the other, of course it was going to be a b— .

Melmont, returned, belching a loud interruption which effectively silenced further speculation. Stuffing his mouth full of window cake, he pointed to the carpet. Crumbs of multi-coloured sponge and marzipan rained down and were tamped into the broadloom by Melmont's restless feet.

—You notice it has no seams? This country I love is going to the dogs. Belgium is the only place I can get them to make up carpets of this size.

—What's wrong with seams, Earnest? said Gunter Röhl.

—They're for little people. Now, who wants to see the gardens?

Röhl, pleading hayfever, stayed behind to talk to Abigail, so Melmont and Cole stepped out into thirty acres of construction.

Three hundred men toiled in harmonious labour in all directions around the house. In the middle distance, some were digging foundations with pickaxes; others were pouring concrete and laying paths to rapidly erected wooden huts which were going up over the original vast and famous rose garden.

—I need the buildings there because I'm going to have the editorial staff where I can keep an eye on them.

—How on earth did you get planning permission to do that to a listed garden?

—I offered the council the creation of two hundred jobs, immediately.

—Dominic has left school and needs a job. Is there anything you can do for him? said Cole.

——Tell him to get down here, said Melmont, pleasantly. I need someone to write my biography. He can start any time he likes.

Cole looked at his friend, astonished.

——Are you sure he's up to it? He's only just left school. He's a bit of a dreamer, you know.

——Catch 'em young. I'm going to win this election, you know, said Melmont. There are going to be some changes made to the way this country is governed. We're going to go through interesting times, I'd say. The dreamers are all going to have to wake up.

The peacocks strutted and cried improbably loud in protest at the diminution of their kingdom, standing forlornly at the edge of the building activity in their rain-drenched feathers. Melmont was approached by foremen but refused to hear detail, and waved them away, shouting at the clerks of works that he wanted them to solve the problems, not come to him in tears. Then he discovered that the heating engineers had been told the house was private, and had naturally assumed there would be separate sources for domestic and business. Having told everyone to go away, Melmont now had to perform a personal intervention. He scolded their pedestrian approach and told them to tear up their plans and start again.

——This is the headquarters of a corporation. *One* electricity supply. *One* heating unit! Why should you want to put in more?

Abigail started to approach her husband, helped along past the foundation posts and muddy boardwalks by Röhl. As she reached him, Melmont looked the other way and saw a workman relieving himself some distance away against the wall of a supply shed. Melmont whistled and beckoned to the man, who arrived buttoning his fly.

—You were urinating in front of my wife. You're fired, said Melmont.

—Fired from what, mate?

Melmont gestured menacingly.

—All this.

—I don't work here, I'm delivering a load of sand, mate, said the man.

—Get off my land before I break your neck.

—Earnest, I didn't *see* anything, said Abigail, pleadingly.

The man looked at Melmont's town shoes, then glanced down the muddy ditch still between him and his would-be oppressor. He said, cheekily to Abigail,

—It's not *that* small, darlin'. I could always get it out for you again.

The future MP was, for once, silenced and stalked away, out-vulgarised. A few minutes later, the distant ornamental gates crept open. Cole watched the campaign caravan with its balloons depart behind the Land Rover carrying Melmont. A hooded glass eye also recorded this from under the eaves of the gatehouse, the first of the legions of surveillance cameras Melmont would, in the end, install everywhere.

From the Land Rover, Melmont fought an inspired and inspiring campaign. Having come from apparently nowhere, his energy was intoxicating, his vision persuasive. Which of the hardworking, braille-typing girls and boys working for him did not hope that Melmont might win, and then quickly secure a Cabinet appointment? Minister for Health, perhaps, and then a breath of fresh air, become England's very first immigrant Prime Minister: to drag the class-bound, backward-looking snobbish, inefficient and self-regarding country into the twentieth century?

Melmont the Parliamentarian

THE GREEKS BELIEVED THAT those whom any of the gods wished to destroy, they first drove mad. Happy the Greeks, whose gods noticed them! Our state of mind is of no account to the latest usurping Creator, or He would surely have extinguished any accounts of his serpentine route to Power.

Barsetshire is to the west of Oxbridgeshire, a small sparsely populated triangular county which once contained heavy industry but now only has the scars. Through the market town of Barset flows the once-polluted but now weed-choked tributary, the Rustum, to join the Oxus, a river that itself is often lost in indecision about which is the quickest way to the North Sea. While geographically baffling even to those that live there, the area is rich in late industrial relics, ancient cradles of the industrial revolution which had once sprung up like mush-rooms to supply a world market made suddenly available by steamer and rail.

In the runup to the election, every hamlet of Barsetshire was visited in a campaign of superhuman thoroughness. Melmont and Abigail were now sitting in the front of the campaign Land Rover with Dominic sandwiched between them. For the last fortyeight hours Dominic had listened day and night, it seemed, to an unstoppable Mississippi-like stream of consciousness of the Thoughts of Melmont. The great man, still human, jerked his thumb over his shoulder to get Dominic's flagging attention, as they sped along.

——There are *ordinary* typists in the caravan now, as well. Everyone is able to have a copy of speeches I make even if they were not able to be there. They can have them immediately. I've got the country vote, Dominic. All I need to do is convince the urban Tories round here. Now if they hadn't stopped me buying *The Spyglass...* .

The Spyglass was the daily paper that had once preached Socialism strongly enough to have pushed the old warhorse Winston Churchill out to grass after the war. Melmont and other would-be press barons had recently pursued it, unsuccessfully.

Dominic stifled a yawn.

——It wouldn't make any difference to the campaign now.

——But you know, I'm going to get it too, one day, Dom, said Melmont, presciently.

Melmont leant forward to turn on the TV which had been bolted onto the outside bonnet of the Land Rover. A snowy image appeared on the screen of Ocker Midrash, though the sound was clear enough. Ocker was being interviewed about his latest coup, the purchase of a sleazy British Sunday tabloid, *News of the People,* from its fuddled, alcoholic owner. Melmont swore. He had been after the *News of the People* too, which had been about to fold.

Dominic saw with alarm that his employer was watching the TV screen rather than the road, hunching his shoulders and starting to go purple with jealous rage, all at fiftyfive miles an hour.

The TV screen on the bonnet was showing a cheeky headline which bawled in thirtysix point '*MIDRASH SAVES THE PEOPLE*'. The Land Rover and the caravan were now straying into the ditch unnoticed in Melmont's rage at the TV.

——What's the matter? I put in an equally good bid for that paper. It's a conspiracy, Dominic. One man, three newspapers. Three times I've been pipped. It can't be coincidence!

——We're all going to die if you don't pay attention to your driving, said Abigail quietly.

The Land Rover clipped a beech hedge noisily and Melmont's over-correction caused two volunteers to fall off their seats in the caravan behind.

——There's something you can do that he can never do, which is get elected here, said Abigail, soothingly.

The speedometer, hovering around the sixty-miles-an-hour mark, slowly began to wind down.

——It is true. Midrash can *never* be an MP because he is no true Briton, said Melmont. But he is still bad for this country, even from outside it. He wishes to destroy our institutions and grow rich in the process. But I'm going to break his stranglehold on the media, like *this*.

Melmont took a hand off the vibrating steering wheel, plucked up a bundle of pencils from the open dashboard and smashed their points on the upright windscreen. Pieces of broken HB5s flew everywhere. Abigail began to pull cedarwood splinters from her glossy auburn hair.

——Earnest! I'd only just sharpened all those!

The Land Rover slowed and finally skidded to a stop. A tapestry of slowly moving Friesian cows was filling the road ahead. On a farm lane to the side stood a small knot of farm workers waiting for transport to take them home. Melmont threw open the circular roof opening above the driver's cab and stood head and shoulders out of the vehicle, in a reflex action, to address potential voters.

As he began his oft-repeated spiel from his vantage point, a dry stone wall was visible on which was sprayed an unfriendly message over uneven stones, *'KEEP OXBRIDIGSHIRE BRITISH & THE DIRTY DISARMING FOREIGNER OUT. VOTE TORY.'*

Pointing at the sign, he cried,

——You gentlemen have all read that, I take it? Well so have I. I am standing for election, and I am equally as British as the Duke of Reekie, and the Queen seems to be in a state of contentment about his services as a consort, a husband and a father! No complaints, there!

Beneath them, in the cab, Dominic barely listened as Melmont enlarged on his patriotism in a way they had heard a hundred times before.

——You have to admire his energy, he said to Abigail.

——It's become a lonely life, being married to him. Busy, but lonely. When he's around, of course, it's like the sun coming out.

Above them, the sun started giving its opinion of nuclear power, *fortissimo*, but by now the farm hands were all sitting on a flatbed truck which had arrived for them. The truck was then towed away by a tractor, and only one potential voter was left. Melmont was undeterred.

——We in Britain should be prepared to give up the pretence and expense of a nuclear deterrent that is firstly not independent, and secondly does nothing to deter!

——I am afraid, said Abigail, that if he wins, I will see even less of him.

Above her, Melmont bellowed confirmation of his intentions to his remaining listener.

——So with your passion and indignation, I am going to go to Westminster with the news that nuclear proliferation, which is funded from the Working Man's Pocket, has to cease!

——You know why he likes you, don't you? He wants a son, said his wife softly.

Melmont's remaining audience suddenly removed himself behind the wall and started poking at a bramble bush with a piece of stick. The reason for his interest in the bush became apparent when a cock pheasant exploded vertically upwards with cries of alarm from the brambles and flapped furiously away. The man threw his stick at the pheasant, missed and slouched off.

——What do you think of him, truthfully? asked Abigail.

——I owe your husband a great deal for this opportunity. I see the job as decoding a very complex man, said Dominic.

——Yes, he is complex. One loves him for his complications. He has achieved so much.

——And will more, I am sure.

They sat in companionable silence in the middle of deserted rural Barsetshire. Half a mile away, the pheasant glided to a more secluded field, as above them, Melmont concluded his sermon to the cows.

The next day, the campaign trail led Melmont to a barely functioning railway rolling-stock factory. There was buddleia growing between the rails of the sidings outside the main gates. Beside the rusting tracks, tall weeds and the skeletons of last year's foxgloves waved.

Melmont was standing on the aluminium brightwork of one of the coaches awaiting collection outside. He was waving his arms in front of a hundred workers, watched by his faithful wife and Dominic. The sky was grey. Dominic glanced down at the ragged edges of the tarmac poured onto the earth to make a parking lot, and thought suddenly about the thin cover it made for the round ball spinning once a day in space, and retreated to the car feeling vertiginous.

Melmont was coming to the end of a poorly received speech. His voice was ragged and only the habit of dominance kept him going before the indifferent audience.

——I cannot believe that the British People have become so content with their betting shops and their bingo clubs that they are prepared to watch our once-great nation decline into third-rate obscurity. During the last twenty years Britain has shrunk back in terms of world power to our condition before— Waterloo!

Waterloo was not a subject that came up much in the triangle, even though the foundries had provided the French armies with grey-market bayonet grade steel for both sides in the Napoleonic conflict. Melmont concluded,

——Britain will only survive if we are better than our competitors. Your jobs are not going to go on the scrap heap because when I am elected, this rolling-stock factory is going to stay open! And be the backbone of a properly supervised rail distribution system!

Thin cheers greeted this announcement.

In the Land Rover, Dominic watched the rest of the action through scratched perspex. Melmont emerged from a cursory tour of the acres of machine room to congratulate Jill and others while they were handing out copies of his speech. Dominic noticed anti-Melmont graffiti on the side of the building in the same hand as the first one seen by the side of the road, with some little-Englander and anti-semitic jibes, partly obscured by *'BASH ALL QUEERS'* sprayed over the top. Melmont shook hands with the union officials and climbed back into the cab.

—What happens to those workers if you can't stop British Rail selling the site off?

—The site has immense potential. It has road and rail links and is seriously undervalued. Melmont cocked his head, like a thrush considering a worm.

—Maybe you should buy it, said Dominic mischievously.

Melmont beamed. The thrush had already pounced.

—My dear Dominic, I've put in a bid and have been accepted.

—Did you mention that you were going to redevelop the area in your speech?

Melmont shrugged.

—Once I am elected, everything will be fine here. I shall have the best constituency surgery in the United Kingdom.

It was the last whistle-stop of the day and even Melmont was getting tired. The Land Rover drove straight through the spindly drop barrier of the factory car park and carried it off across the bonnet, as it sped down the road. An electric alarm bleated in the distance as Melmont drove east across the sluggish Oxus, towards home.

Later in the week, the rising moon was almost full. At midnight, Melmont was walking with Dominic in the debris of the underpinnings and temporary and permanent work buildings all around the core structure of the big house, now known officially as Melmont Keep. Melmont was feeling fond of his young biographer, and frequently put a hand across Dominic's shoulders in a friendly and protective fashion. Godson and godfather were, in a straightforward way, fond of each other.

——See all these buildings, Dom?

——I can see their beginnings, said Dominic, truthfully.

In the distance, the peacocks cried. Melmont had bought a joblot of mutant birds which wailed all night.

——I thought peacocks were bad luck.

——On the contrary, Dom; I bought thirtynine. Melmont's voice took on a hushed tone.

——This is going to be a World Communications Centre.

——I thought you were going to be a full-time MP, Dominic said.

——I am going to divide my time between here and the Mother of Parliaments. But this is going to be the hub. In the next decade, publishing and communications are going to become global.

Melmont's arms made a big circle, till they met.

——There are going to be networks of satellites all over the world. That is why you should stay at my side for the coming years. These are going to be truly heroic times.

The sudden and loud beat of a helicopter passing made

Melmont pause. As the noise faded, Melmont pointed in its direction, still using his reverential voice, as if he himself was slightly in awe of what was to come.

——On the day I am elected, I am arranging to have one of those. A chopper. Yes, a chopper will be very nice indeed! And this is where my Lucky Pillar will be, look!

Melmont did a little shuffling Indian war-dance around a hole that a notice announced was reserved for and would shortly hold stanchion 39, as a support of the coming communications empire. Dominic watched as Melmont's lunar wish-shadow danced with its etiolated master, across the duckboards and the unopened bags of building sand around a spot made magical by the private religion of numbers.

——And I will buy *The Moon*, added Melmont.

When Melmont had gone inside again, Dominic wrote in his notebook, by moonlight, in small, precise mirror writing that he used for his most secret thoughts *"Working for madman."*

In London the next evening, Tristram Cole was relaxing, by sitting downstairs quietly in his neat newly painted two-storey Chelsea house, after arranging an expansive loan for Melmont. He had just got back from work, and was still wearing his expensive shiny City lace-up shoes, but had awarded himself a strong whisky and soda, the bubbles of which now swirled in the full tumbler by his side.

Suddenly there was the noise of someone familiar with the front door key opening the door, and his niece Libby appeared with a large number of shopping bags acquired at shops fashionable in the Kings Road and Kensington. Libby had arrived at the house as a schoolgirl, and now was transforming into a mini-skirted siren, borne up through an exponential curve of desirability, a delicious explosion of enviable youth in a haze of slimming pills and booze and glamour, all without paying rent.

Cole took a slug of his whisky. He was fond of his niece, but worried that she would make a nonsense of her life, like her mother. Libby put down her parcels, making her skirt even shorter.

——Christ, Libby, I can practically see what you had for breakfast.

——Don't you like the gear?

——I suppose so.

——What do you really think, though?

Cole followed the progress of Libby's underbuttocks through the front room.

——I'm thinking that Terence is having his rectal warts treated today, so the phone will be free to call your mother and reassure her of your wellbeing. I don't want to talk to her, if possible.

——Why not, out of curiosity?

——She's nuts.

——Dom says that Earnest Melmont is crazy.

——Your brother is just lazy. All empire builders are crazy. They have to be. I'm betting he gets elected.

——How much?

——A grand at eight to one. Ladbrokes aren't going to like me after next week.

——Is it that soon?

——*The trouble with all your generation is you'd rather fuck than vote*, thought Cole.

Libby sat down, fidgetting her divinely shapely thighs and dialled.

—Hello, this is Chelsea 3939. Can you get me overseas, Delhi, India?

Distant exchanges clunked and clicked.

—Mother says her ashram's not ancient at all. It's a concrete one, like a new university.

—I still don't know what the hell she's doing there, and I don't think she does either, muttered Cole into his whisky.

—She said she might be coming back. They sit around crosslegged, drinking their own piss, said Libby.

—To what end?

—I've no idea. Urine is meant to be sterile, isn't it? It may be unpleasant but it is not going to poison you. She doesn't like doing it, anyway.

—She should have gone to university, said Cole, inconsequentially.

—She said someone slipped her guru a triple dose of some drug the CIA developed which makes everything spin like Catherine wheels for everyone else, but the guru never blinked, added Libby.

There was an audible clunk as contact was miraculously made with one of the many ashrams of the Indian subcontinent.

—Could I speak to Priscilla Cole please? I mean Sister Lotus Blossom, I mean Lotus Petal. If she is meditating, would you ask her to call her brother, reversed charges, in London when she comes out of her trance?

Libby went upstairs and found some pills which she thought might be exciting to take, but they were medication: in fact penicillin, she realised, to treat the embarrassing case of clap that Terence had picked up in Paddington along with the warts.

Downstairs, Cole poured himself another whisky. He was certain that his sister would not call back. With luck, too, there would be no phone call from Melmont either, out on the campaign trail. If he won, Ladbrokes would cough up enough to put a swimming pool in his little cottage in the south of France.

Cole watched the summer sun slant yellow over the rooftops, and slowly pass beyond longitudinal ken. The decline towards night aroused inchoate feelings in his bosom; love for his niece, delight in her youth mixed with sadness at the loss of his own, and the ongoing anxiety that Terence, twenty years his junior, would do a runner borrowing his mother's collection of snuff-boxes, in which he had suddenly been expressing an interest.

♫   ♫   ♫

It was polling day and no pundit whose opinion was worth sixpence had expected Melmont to become one of the new MPs. But the tide in the country had turned and the red-rosetted representatives outside the polling booths started to record more and more votes for Labour candidates across the land. This created a collective confidence which people breathed in as they approached the polling stations in steady streams, and many changed their minds at the last moment, not least in Oxbridge and Barsetshire.

Some of Melmont's switch votes were known to him. Willis

Death, the tall pale veterinary surgeon, and Mrs Simpkins, who had grown close of recent years, walked up together arm in arm, still debating on whether personal loyalty overrode a lifetime's allegiance to the Conservatives. Death in his three-quarter length rubberised canvas macintosh was wavering, feeling as he always did when trying to decide whether to put a sick lamb or calf down, when he knew in his heart it would never grow. Mrs Simpkins was insisting he vote for Melmont as she was proposing to do.

——Give him a go. What have you got against him? You're always on about how the laws need changing. Well, how many other *friends* are you ever going to have in Parliament?

That clinched it, and on the way out, when Death saw Melmont standing by the travel-worn Land Rover next to Jill, he gave a thumbs-up, and creased his long face into a smile so extreme the tip of his nose bent down and his small pale eyes almost disappeared into fleshy asterisks.

——Two more in the bag for us, said Jill.

——They're going to get the surprise of their life at their reception.

——They're getting married? How did you know?

Jill looked at Melmont, surprised, since this was a man who never remembered irrelevancies such as birthdays or anniversaries. Then she remembered that the participants in all forthcoming marriages in the local press got a congratulations card from Melmont.

Melmont continued to smile in his secret private joke way when he was unsure of an outcome, half-bowing like a giant automatic marionette to voters who streamed past, whether they saluted him or not. Dominic emerged from the Land

Rover to announce that the blind were still coming in to vote in numbers in spite of the destruction of the support programme late in the campaign. The heavy braille typewriters had all been damaged beyond repair when they fell from a split in the caravan after reckless cornering by Melmont.

—I'm going to win anyhow, said Melmont. Jill, get me the chairman of Icarus Helicopters. He's called Jarvis or Purvis, or something.

Five minutes later, the chairman was being swung into the Melmontian orbit of success as Melmont lectured him.

—My party will carry the country and I'm just winning my seat. If you want your product on the news tonight, carrying the winning team, you will have a unique chance to relocate to a uniquely well-placed site in my constituency. I have a feasibility study here, in my hand, that says you can't expand your capacity where you are sited now. To be ready for the coming boom, all you have to do is move to my constituency; and to move to my constituency, you must have your product ready to go on the news tonight.

Jurvis agreed to look into the availability of a lease on a luxury helicopter from his fleet, but could not promise a pilot at such short notice. Indeed there was still no chopper within ten miles of the packed hall when the returning officer, with wisps of white hair around his dome, stepped up to the dais to announce the results. Even Melmont was nervous about the result, for all his bluster.

—No chopper, Dominic, that's a bad sign. And it's thirteen minutes past the hour.

Melmont was busily altering the time on his wristwatch.

—What should it be?

——Thirteen minutes to. My grandmother said that if you had a watch you can change the time. Mind you she never had a watch.

——Don't worry, darling, you've done your very best, said Abigail.

For Dominic, Jill and Abigail, caught up in the hour, it was impossible for any of them not to want to obtain a win for the capricious vortex of enterprise, from the bottoms of their hearts.

The returning officer's only other time in the limelight was when he dressed as Father Christmas for a local primary school, and he appeared to be in no hurry to shorten his time under public scrutiny and announce the winner.

Finally, the hornrimmed glasses were deemed clear enough to sit on his honest, pink face, and he drew a breath so deep that his badly cut sports jacket started to look out of shape. In a quavering, hoyling voice he began,

——Robert Bathwell Lurk, Druid Party. Fiftyfour votes.

A single ivy-clad supporter of Lurk cheered, briefly. Boudicca lives on in us.

——Nigel Spofforth Borrimer, Communist Party of Great Britain. Four hundred and sixtyfive.

The party of the red flag had never stood a chance in Oxbridgeshire, only one-third of whose population had ever joined a union.

——Oliver Tollemache Venables-Bewley-Hutchinson, Conservative Party. Twenty thousand, five hundred and six.

The returning officer took another deep breath.

——Captain Earnest Melmont, Labour Party. Twentyone thousand... .

——We've done it! hissed Jill.

——Fuck, said Dominic, impressed.

——Five hundred and seven, the returning officer concluded.

The hall erupted in cheers. Through the cheers, Melmont could sense, hyperaudiently, ahead of anyone else the approaching thud of a helicopter.

It was red, Melmont's first helicopter, as befitted a Labour victory, and Jurvis the chairman of Icarus himself was at the controls. Sadly for all of Jurvis' initiative, Melmont's bulk all but obscured the tradename on the side.

——We should have bought a thinner MP, Jurvis later joked to his wife.

Melmont was obviously tired, with bags under his eyes the colour of coal, but he rose to the occasion.

——I feel proud to be called upon to serve this country, and humble, yes humble. And now I hope, after thirteen years in *outer darkness*, the party with which I am happily associated will be able to show its true strengths of leadership.

And Abigail, taken up in the moment, stretched out her hands to the masses and cried,

——He's done it! He's done it for all of you!

The happy couple now stepped into the helicopter and the new Member for Oxbridge and Barsetshire was drawn up into the sky. The downdraft sent tears of happiness zig-zagging down Jill's handsome cheeks.

Dominic's own celebration involved a dark fiesta in Soho, with unprotected sex with multiple partners. He would not know it for some years, but the romp after Melmont's election gave him his fatal infection.

In Delhi, Dominic's mother Priscilla was having ambivalent

feelings about everything, as usual. She was barely aware of the election back in Britain and its landslide for Labour. She had come to India because she did not like anything she saw in the West, and now she was trying to remove herself from Westness, but the ancestral rusty stain ran deep and could not be washed from her soul. She was no happier in her retreat than she had been earlier in her life with the two children who had sprung from her womb with so little gratitude.

And now she was even beginning to resent the tropical dusk, which always rushed the night upon everything without any kind of notice or foreplay. This thought led her to remember the hastily contracted affections of Dominic and Libby's father, and the acute discomfort of sex with him in a sandstorm. His departing words had been, "I'll be back!" Priscilla was bitter. Indeed she was still waiting, should her inseminator prove as good as his word, to give him a piece of her mind. His lack of consideration for her rankled still, even after all these years.

She slouched along an ugly, modern concrete dusk-dimmed corridor towards her little room. Someone was playing a sitar, not very well she thought, in the distance. Her left hand carried a brimming glass filled with her own fresh urine. This was the latest purification ritual they were supposed to do but she had been sidetracked by a phone call from her daughter, who was excited to have landed a modelling job. Ram Baba didn't like them to talk too long on the phone, which suited Priscilla.

——A mannequin, you mean? Take care, darling, I have to go and do something.

She went into her room, and stood without setting the glass down as voices of low-caste cleaners whined distantly in

Gujarati, persistent as mosquitoes. To drown out the sound of India she tuned her Ferguson radio to the BBC World Service with her dry hand, then sat sullenly, still holding the prescribed medicine, wondering if anyone would be able to tell if she simply got rid of it in the street, like the rest of the country.

The radio reminded her of the country she had left, as a band cheerfully struck up *Lullibulero* then as the music faded, a voice said,

——The stockmarket has rallied after Harold Wilson, the incoming Prime Minister, insisted that his party's policy would never be to gut the rich.

How Priscilla hated everything about England, and especially the confident, friendly announcer's voice suggesting social progress. How could there be progress if you believed as her guru did that everything was fixed in advance? Shiva had decreed that an Untouchable was born and died an Untouchable, fit only to empty the latrines of higher castes with a leaking wicker basket. Priscilla's unpatriotic left hand, almost by itself, reached forward and slowly started to pour the contents of the glass onto the top of the radio, which was saying,

——Indeed, he promised immediate action to deregulate many of the City's restrictive practices.

Nothing she had done so far had stopped the nagging voice preaching social progress, so Priscilla poured the rest of the glass over the radio. The voice continued, but increasingly crackly,

——In the House of Commons, praising this, the new Labour MP Captain Earnest Melmont made a maiden speech of record-breaking length which.... .

The radio died with an electric pop, and Priscilla let out a little mew of irritation. Priscilla had a soft spot for Melmont. In a world where so few people knew what they were doing, Earnest Melmont seemed to be the opposite. He was, she felt, all man; a real man. She was glad he was in Parliament. He would shake it up. Priscilla's vestigial mothering instincts were awakened. She swathed the radio in towels, shook it, and begged it to live. But it would not listen to her. It had died.

That night, inside her torn mosquito net, Priscilla fell to her knees and asked God to bless Melmont. In reply, God sent her malaria.

At the same time as Priscilla's prayers from Delhi were being read and weighed by the Supreme Being, whose name was not Melmont—or at any rate, not yet—the Devil, seeing that God was distracted, began tempting Dominic in London, to a breach of trust with his uncle.

Cole was a banker of regular habits but he did not see the need to provide for his nephew or niece at regular times. Dominic, still recovering from accompanying Melmont on the campaign, had come into his uncle's trim kitchen in Chelsea for a late-night snack. After reviewing the contents of the cupboard and rejecting baked beans in favour of waterbiscuits and anchovy paste, he sat down, without troubling himself about a plate.

In front of him was Tristram Cole's carelessly slewed brief-case open on the kitchen table, with a number of papers half out, invitingly on display. From his uncle's phone conversations, Dominic already suspected that something dubious was going on with Melmont's company, which Melmont was planning to sell, Dominic concluded, to impress the Labour government of his commitment to its cause, and thereby obtain his seat in Cabinet. But there was something else going on too.

It sounded from the phone conversations as if his uncle had been trying to dissuade Melmont from some illegal operation to pump up the share price prior to the sale. The papers spilling from the briefcase begged him to read them. Dominic impulsively pulled a selection out and started to scan them.

Inside a minute, Dominic began to see that while the bank's position was peripheral, Melmont was orchestrating a full-blown share support operation which used his parliamentary ambitions as pretext for an overpriced sale.

There is an absolute moralist in all of us when we need one, and Dominic's moral centre awoke at that moment and announced to the impressionable young man that he need not waste his life: he had found his Cause, which was to write the true, as opposed to the approved, biography of Melmont.

At that moment Cole's lover Terence entered the kitchen and saw Dominic going through his uncle's briefcase. Their eyes met. Terence's recent minor surgery had not put him in the mood for love but he still wore a gold-cloth testicular 'posing pouch' bought for seventeen shillings and sixpence in Berwick Street market. He flounced like an amateur Cleopatra to the fridge, opened it and inspected the inside.

—Sweet fuck-all to eat again, I see. D'you think it's a hint to someone to leave, Dominic? You or me—though you're never here, maybe that tart of a sister of yours?

A cat came in and climbed over Terence's bare legs, winding its tail round his thin shins. Terence absent-mindedly took an opened tin of catfood from the lower shelf of the fridge and spooned some into a bowl. The redfaced Dominic was trying all the while to cram the incriminating papers back in the briefcase, but the loose papers were most reluctant to take their place there again.

——I was just… the cat must have knocked the briefcase and I was putting it all back.

Terence licked the spoon deliberately, and started to put the bowl of catfood on the floor. Dominic was lying, he could see that. But what was he lying *about?* Terence wondered.

——I spe-ak no evil, I se-e no evil, I he-ar no evil, Terence droned, using his frontal sinus cavities to the full. He winced slightly, breaking wind on the full extent of his bend.

——Whoops! I should be the one that's blushing now. Sorry. I really should be lying face down, excuse *meeee.*

Terence sashayed from the room, now convinced there was something valuable in the unguarded briefcase which he could use to 'get back' at his snooty older lover. His relations with Tristram Cole were descending to their bi-monthly low point. He would never, he told himself, have gone to Paddington if Cole had been less glacial with him.

A briefcase heist which could be blamed on Dominic, to make even more mischief, would be the ideal opportunity to teach his stuck-up, patronising lover a sharp, much-needed lesson about neglect of loved ones.

Melmont's Miracle of Loaves and Fishes

TERENCE'S PAINFUL POST-OPERATIONAL FART FLEW AWAY, dispersing in the sodium-orange London night towards the River Thames. Its circumference increasing, the fart scented slack water as it wafted gently from Chelsea Creek downriver, driven by an obliging north-westerly zephyr which detoured the freed wind over Pimlico, before allowing it to rejoin the meandering river by Westminster Bridge. Beneath the zephyr now, the tide had started turning in earnest, just as inside the Palace of Westminster, a Labour government was sweeping in and allocating new members for a Cabinet.

As it drifted past the House of Commons, the fart could have written up a trenchant account, as glimpsed in snapshot through the Victorian gothic windows, of Melmont's struggles to have his worth recognised by the party machine. Sadly, farts are blind, and have no interest in politics. Apart from obeying Avogadro's Hypothesis (a law which all gases at room temperature have no choice but to obey), they are Universalists. For each Fart, there is only a brief vocalised discomfort at birth before polite *silenzio* descends for ever, and it mingles with the winds of the world, in a pious ecstasy of loss of Self.

The evening after his maiden speech, Melmont was sitting impatiently at the House of Commons bar waiting for office to be conferred on him by an approaching Labour Party functionary. He fumed inwardly at the delay, even as he half-smiled. The functionary smiled nervously back. Gordon Gordon was a typical Labour MP of the era, which was that of male schoolteachers; the kipper breadth of his red tie spoke of an awareness of fashion even as his gleaming pate and slumped demeanour confessed surrender to youth's own flight.

But to Melmont, the arrival of Gordon, however dowdy, represented a glowing Rung on the Ladder leading to the red dispatch boxes of high Cabinet office. He said brightly,

——So what did the boss think of my performance?

Gordon Gordon looked embarrassed. Melmont turned to the barmaid, who had taken against him already.

——A double pink gin for my friend here.

After an age, the barmaid claimed to be fresh out of Angostura Bitters, an essential ingredient for the hideous tinted cocktail. Melmont's brows beetled, ominously. Gordon Gordon said he actually preferred his gin colourless, and indeed would have drunk the contents of the bar's slop tray to be allowed to deliver his awkward message, and be off to his basement flat in Kennington to practise dark games of brinkmanship of the Self on his own, with plastic bags and satsumas.

As he held his glass of gin, Gordon struggled to find the words to politely express the collective loathing that had arisen in the ranks of Melmont's fellow parliamentarians, who had been obliged to sit through his speech. Having almost no agenda after being elected, Melmont had said nothing in a display of overblown, tendentious horse manure which had lasted over half an hour. Afterwards, there had been no hesitation on the Prime Minister's part in deciding that the pompous windbag should be taught his place by being forced to run the Catering Committee. That would perhaps learn him.

——A great day yesterday, no? said Melmont.

Facing the vast and apparently unrepentant offender, who was able to wiggle his enormous eyebrows without disturbing his expression, like an elephant cooling its ears, Gordon Gordon drew a deep breath and plunged in.

——As a maiden speech, I should say it was… groundbreaking.

Melmont beamed. Gordon Gordon decided to be more frank.

——I don't think Harold was expecting you to speak so soon or so… *long*. I don't think anyone was. You see, you will *learn* when you have been here a while that it is not the place for new MPs… .

Melmont tried to help his visitor out, who was clearly floundering.

——If you have things to say, then you have to get in first, before the other side, no? This country needs a kick up the arse, right up to the top lace, no?

Melmont raised his leg in clumsy demonstration, and rested it on the bar. His foot was clad in a white sock, which a laceless, slip-on leather shoe fatly adorned. Melmont was already getting too stout to tie his own laces comfortably. The barmaid eyed the intruding foot disapprovingly.

——The prospects are not good. Harold admires your sort,

but they frighten him, said Gordon, with a rare candidness.

—So when and where is my appointment, in this glorious new government?

Gordon Gordon looked even more miserable, if that was possible.

—I've been sent to tell you that if you want to make your mark in this government, after yesterday, you are going to have to lie low for at least six months.

—And then?

—Then We Will See, said Gordon, feeling increasingly out of place.

—Six months? Harold Wilson said on the news last night that he was stunned by my victory. Stunned! Melmont's voice rose.

—I'm sure he was speaking the truth when he said that. And I'm sure that in six months… .

—Oh no. I can't wait that long. I want to serve NOW!! Melmont roared. His leg fell to the floor with a crash and the whole bar fell silent, as shocked as if two gunslingers had appeared in their midst with long capes tucked behind their holsters, preparing to draw.

—It's *normal* for first-time members to sit on the back benches, bleated Gordon. There are men who have served the party for over ten years in Opposition, and they are going to be *ahead* of you when Harold puts a Cabinet together. In your case, he realises that you have, er, ambitions so he has invited you to supervise the Catering Committee, Gordon concluded.

It was done. The message was delivered, the picador had lanced the bull and shortly it should fall to its knees.

——The what? Melmont looked blank.

Gordon drained his drink and prepared to leave.

——The House of Commons Catering Committee. It's a very important job, which no one has ever managed to pull off. No one has ever made the books balance. It's always made a huge loss because the greedy sods who sit here are used to getting away with knocking off crates of the booze and when they eat here, never paying for the grub. If you can fix it in under a year it would be a miracle.Well, I'd say Harold could be persuaded to accept your name again for something more prestigious.

Suddenly Melmont grasped what he was being asked to do. And it would not be hard. He understood greed because in some not unholy way he *was* greed.

——Very well, Gordon, he said, calmly. I'll take the job.

Melmont stood up and leant past the startled barmaid. He yanked a bottle of Scotch off the spirit dispenser on the wall of the bar. The bottle still had its optic measure attached. Gordon, thinking that he was perhaps about to be hit over the head, tried to take the bottle from Melmont, who resisted him easily. The barmaid, seeing a fight breaking out over a bottle of stolen Scotch, screamed at the despised Socialist MPs from a safe distance in heavy estuarine.

——'Ere! Whatchoo finkuar? Ge' ar'side if you wanta fi'! Pigs! That's what you are! Pigs!

Coming in closer, she paddled feebly at the two men with a straw broom. Gordon Gordon, thinking he might be crushed at any moment, pleaded with Melmont.

——Earnest, listen to me. If you can turn this place round it will prove that you can do anything.

—That's exactly what I'm doing, said Melmont.

Gordon released his grip and the two men straightened up. Other drinkers watched fascinated as Melmont pulled the optic measure out of the neck of the bottle and started to drink from it. The barmaid's straw broom went up above her head again.

—Put that down seein' as you 'aven't paid, screamed the harridan.

Melmont took no notice.

—'Ere Bev, wass going on? shouted a voice from far away behind the bar.

—Some fat bastard's come in and started nicking spirits!

Melmont put the bottle down again, and pronounced solemnly,

—As I thought, Bev. It's been watered.

—Nuffink of the kind! shouted the barmaid, fiercely.

But it only takes a thief to catch a thief. Bev and her bent workmates had all been on the pull. It was a traditional perk, particularly if you lived south of the river at the edge of the old Battersea marsh, where the inhabitants viewed anything north of the Thames as up for grabs.

—So where's the rest of it gone, then?

Bev lunged forward and snatched for the bottle righteously, but Melmont held her at bay with one hand, like a bear playing with a kitten, till she fell back. He then coolly turned to Gordon.

—The new Catering Committee will make a start now.

Melmont turned to Bev, smiling grimly.

—I'll give fifty pounds to the till for the spirits in all that row of optics. And I want you to pour them away now. I'll watch you.

Bev's mouth opened like a stranded carp, but then she found

herself to her amazement, pouring whisky and gin, and vodka away. There was something about his huge, irresistable gaze. Gordon was impressed in spite of himself.

—This kind of scam is par for the course. Mark my words, Gordon, there'll be some surprises, the deeper we dig, but in the end, it's a relatively simple job because the criminal mind is never that complex.

Bev slipped away to warn Ron the senior wine steward to cover his tracks because a full audit of the cellar would be called for. Ron and the rest of the gang's delaying tactics in the face of Melmont's own probes into corruption were as stubborn and ingenious in their way as the Russian defence of Stalingrad. In the end, Melmont would retire defeated, like the Germans.

Bev whose recorded wages would not have covered the weekly bill for Melmont's cigars, returned, breathing indignantly through her nose. Melmont made sure she heard his next remarks through the noise of crashing empties into the waste bin.

—Yes, it's amazing, the opportunities you have to create financial black holes and cover them up in the catering trade! But if people can't resist dishonesty, it's very simple: they go to jail!

The suggestion that Melmont himself belonged behind bars had been floated in a cheeky biweekly which had received a number of injunctions from the injured party. *The Prefect* was a barbed thorn in the side of the Establishment in the days I worked there. A minor medical condition, which I treated unwisely with gin, was the cause of the outbreak of tearfulness which led to my departure. But there was no ill will on either side and the editor Melquist Shelley has always represented the best of British values: humour, tolerance, decency, love of cricket, warm beer and eccentric dentistry.

Dominic was now facing the editor of the famous satiric magazine across a cluttered desk in the magazine's unruly Soho headquarters. No interview with Shelley was ever complete without his feet in brogues and mismatched socks crossed on the desk in front of him, visible through the ever-open door, and he would assiduously clean his ears through each meeting with a match end, as if worried his hearing was blocked.

—Dominic Cole. Of course I remember you. You interviewed me for the school magazine, said Shelley briskly, and a touch disapprovingly, as ever.

—They cut all the interesting stuff out, said Dominic.

Shelley's expression became pained, and the hand at his ear froze, as if the match had for once reached too far into the interior.

—Was I *at all* interesting?

—The stuff about you despising colonials and 'queers' was interesting, said Dominic, pleasantly enough.

—I just wanted to see if they'd cut it. When I was there, Drabfield was the school of Attila the Hun, politically. Do you remember the school slang for cheating?

Drabfield College, in Pangbourne, Berks, had demanded that the sons of the middle classes who passed through its portals all learnt the school slang on pain of being beaten.

—'Jewing', said Dominic.

—Exactly! said Shelley. But here, I can't say 'jew' or even 'kike' now in my own office any more without being made a laughing stock. They pretend I'm a South African trying to say 'cake'. And there's nothing much worse than being saddled with the persona of a '*Sarth Effrikan*', is there?

Having laid down an impenetrable personal and political smokescreen, Shelley abruptly stood and went to the window. He looked down keenly three floors to the basements of the three-storey Georgian merchants' houses on the other side of the street, then closed his eyes briefly. His breathing became laboured. He is either having a fit, or praying, Dominic thought.

——This used to be a brothel, this house, you know. Mind you, that could be said of most houses round here. And not just in the past tense. Look at the arse on that woman in the black and white minidress. Asking for it! Wouldn't you say?

Silence gives assent, in Roman law. Dominic maintained a politic silence as Shelley went back to his desk.

——What have you brought us then, that *might* be interesting?

Dominic knew he had to get all the information in the headline, or at least the strapline, if he was going to catch Shelley's attention before the next involuntary cataleptic spasm.

——Earnest Melmont, the MP.

——We know him, said Shelley, warily. The mighty porker of Socialism.

——He's involved in a share support operation while he's selling off his company. Except he's not really selling it off. He's faking a selloff, so he can get into the Cabinet, I think.

Shelley's shoulders drooped, and he started to groan. Then one hand went for the patched crotch of his trousers.

——We've been there before. We can't get involved any more. Who's he got lined up to screw this time?

——I don't know if any one individual could do it. There's a group of cash-rich American companies who made a pile when computer leasing came in. But there's only one who owns enough shares to overrule his board.

——Saul Goldfrapp who runs Interlease, said Shelley crisply.

Interlease was one of the names Dominic had seen in his uncle's file.

——Yes, it could be him. Do you want me to check?

——Do by all means but there are so many good stories about Melmont that we can't touch at the moment. For instance, there's a group of ultra-right officers inside MI5 who have proof Melmont is a spy for the Russkies. A specialist in statistical probabilities looked at the number of times Earnest Melmont had encounters with a KGB colonel since 1945, and came up with an impressive 85% probability of Melmont being a stooge in the pay of the KGB.

——Why don't they turn him in?

——They're sitting tight on the statistics till Wilson gives Melmont a Cabinet job, and they sincerely hope the subsequent scandal can destroy the Labour government.

Shelley's eyes twinkled with delight at the mischief in the world and Dominic looked at him with renewed respect.

——Earnest Melmont believes he's got powerful enemies in high places who are stopping his parliamentary career.

——Yes, and twelve of them are in the Cabinet. How did you come across him, anyway?

——I'm writing his biography.

——Commissioned by whom?

——Him.

Shelley's eyebrows arched once more over his twinkling

eyes at mundane mischief and he strode back to the window, scratching at an itch in his groin through his pocket with a deeply thrust hand.

——If you find anything on the Russian side you can prove, do get in touch. It's pointless bankrupting the mag for a stock market swindle, but I would go to bat for the country. Look at that girl on the corner, that's the third punter today, she must have the most *enormous* mortgage. Shelley pointed down at the figure of a heroin-wasted junkie. Dominic thought it was time to take his leave.

He was walking away from *The Prefect*'s offices, down the street through a fashionably dressed crowd. The junkie who had caught Shelley's eye had gone, and there were people who could have all been models or hookers or pop musicians in dark glasses, and they all appeared to be going somewhere in the swinging sixties in Soho, and whoever they were, all seemed to have huge frizzy heads of hair. Dominic was wondering vaguely about having his own lank locks permed when he heard the distant scrape of a sash window pulled open, and a strange, savage cry from behind him. He looked back. High up and far away, Melquist Shelley was leaning out of the windows of his office, waving his hands and bellowing,

——This is the *one* creed through which the English should live. You should *all* learn it. *"Once more unto the breach, dear friends, once more, or close the wall up…"*.

He continued for a while, and then as suddenly as he had begun his oration Shelley stopped broadcasting and disappeared backwards. The window came down with a resounding bang and only then did a few heads turn.

Dominic walked on, wondering if Henry V's battlefield

speech as delivered by Laurence Olivier in the ultra-patriotic wartime film had inspired the young Melmont to storm a machine-gun nest. There had been no doubt that Melmont had been brave; at the same time the rumours that he had made enquiries beforehand about the minimum required to be awarded a Military Cross had never quite gone away.

The handwritten headline for the *Evening News* paperseller on the corner of Goodge Street was 'No TV In Commons: Official'. This meant that while he became increasingly fanatical about videoing everything and everyone, Melmont's own brief performances on the green benches of democracy are lost. The following is a pale reconstruction, from *Hansard*, but think when we talk of heffalumps, that you see them, or at least one, in an electric blue suit, its calves clad in white socks, restlessly grinding its slip-ons on a neighbouring pew, in the Mother of All debating chambers.

Lights, camera, action.

A whiskered Tory rises to speak, having been given leave by the Shadow Minister for Comedy or somesuch, to bait Melmont, who had become rapidly neglected and unsupported by his own side.

——Something puzzles me. We are urged daily by the Honourable Member for Oxbridge, from hoardings and the radio and on television, to 'Think British', 'Buy British' and so on. But a crucial question remains unanswered. My right honourable friend has a large and we must presume successful publishing company. Why then does he continue, in defiance of his public posturing, to have all the publications printed and bound in Czechoslovakia?

Melmont bounds to his slippered feet to hurl a riposte across the floor before the Speaker of the House can interrupt.

——Because it's cheaper there, that's why!

The Tory benches dissolve in mirth at the exposure of the lie at the heart of Socialism. Labour struggles not to follow. Melmont bellows:

——And I'll have you know it's not only cheaper in Czechoslovakia, but also in Bulgaria, East Germany and Romania!

There was something so irresistably comic about Melmont that the laughter spread to the press gallery and soon the Speaker was having to wipe the tears from his eyes. Melmont turned angrily, and started to fold his documents.

——This government does not know how business operates. This government has about as much idea of cost effectiveness as my grandmother's pickled backside!

On another occasion, with no aircraft industry in his constituency, Melmont announced,

——This government is prepared to write off millions of badly judged investments in a supersonic airliner that will never see commercial service. I refer to that Anglo-French *white elephant*, Concorde!

Boos from the Labour benches, excited whistles from the Tories, and cries of 'Order', from the Speaker, as the elephant himself looked around, trumpeting,

——If financing Concorde is Socialism, then I'm a singing mermaid, with big tits!

Naturally, as soon as Concorde entered service between London and New York, the singing mermaid was one of the first to order a ticket. It was in Concorde's claustrophobic cigar-tube of a passenger cabin that Melmont stalked and snared his next Big Thing.

An inexperienced boy, one that had grown rich on the crumbs from IBM's broad table, Saul Goldfrapp was briefly the sixtieth richest man on Earth. His whirlwind romance with the singing mermaid left him disgraced and ruined, with his health and all future sexual relations imploded. As to how Melmont performed the time-honoured trick of parting a fool from his money, but losing much of his own in the process, I beg your leave to tell, O nobly-born; and if you graciously permit, I shall now recount.

XI

Melmont Dances

THE DIGITAL MACHMETER read almost twice the speed of sound, although the plane from New York to London Heathrow appeared empty, as if it were carrying no one at speed to nowhere. Two of the young stewardesses, one blonde and one dark haired, were gossiping in the half dark by the little galley about the disgusting state which the toilet was always left in by one of their most regular customers whether he boarded from New York or London.

——He's here. In fact he's in there now, the dark one whispered, her pony tail bobbing conspiratorially.

——I noticed; hard not to, sniffed the blonde, through her charming surgically enhanced nose.

——The last time there was nasty stuff *on the ceiling*, the dark one said.

——I don't know how he manages it, said the blonde, feeling her shapely leg covertly. With only three passengers on board, she had been planning to use the toilet herself for a shave; with the Mermaid on board, the prospect became less attractive.

——Anyhow, I think your nose looks terrific, said the dark

one, returning to the topic of appearances. She added, I don't see why anyone shouldn't be allowed to alter what they were given if they've got the money. And if you can marry a rich man, it's almost like an investment!

—But do you really think it looks alright? said the blonde, touching her expensive little ski-jump of a nose.

Before her companion could reassure her again, there was a rattling of aluminium panelling, and Melmont burst from the plane's toilet. He too had once been a very different shape, though he more than filled the aisle now, and the inconvenience irked him. He had addressed his ballooning size six months before in a militant fashion, by having his stomach stapled. But the three Evil Ones from the lower depths had no intention of letting him cramp the growth of such a promising organ. After a week of having food by-pass his stomach Melmont could take no more of the smells of vanilla icecream and *boeuf Bourguignon* wafting through his dreams. He phoned the surgeon in the middle of the night, ordering him to take the staples out, and his chef to prepare a post-austerity feast.

The kitchens flew into action with a starter of ten British gallons of Melmont's special Morello Cherry with Turkish Delight, almonds and Raki icecream for the moment his eyes opened after the operation was reversed. The recipe follows a Ruthenian folk-song about the ingredients of a bridal cake, which Melmont's grandmother would sing to him. In the song, the cake turns into a sled which magically bears the bride away from the wicked wizard who used her blood for spells, to her true love, a simple cowherd. Melmont had been a cowherd, once.

Ignoring the pretty, deferential stewardesses, with a tipsy smile to no one which was his one concession to nervousness at new ventures, Melmont made his way down the middle of the plane, his bulk bumping over the tops of the sleek brown leather-tooled seats. Outside the plane, static trailed visibly into the night as the plane's centre of gravity shifted and hydraulic elevons pushed against the rush of supersonic air in compensation, until Melmont reached a spot three quarters of the way down the plane, where a bald and unremarkable-looking American businessman was sitting. Saul Goldfrapp was in the seat next to the window, reading graph sheets as only businessmen can. There was a tasty snack lying untouched beside him.

Melmont toppled into the seat next to Goldfrapp, produced a kilo tin of Beluga caviar from his jacket pocket, and waved it under the nose of his new and startled companion. At the same time, his other hand removed the Concorde snack and dropped it in the aisle with a flourish. Goldfrapp tore his eyes away from the caviar, and stared, amazed at the sacrilege. He had learned not to waste food at his mother's knee.

—You should never touch the stuff they offer you on the flight. Shall I tell you why? The tin has *always* been open too long at altitude, and radiation destroys the bouquet; so I always bring my own. It's Saul, isn't it, said Melmont.

Goldfrapp looked at a man who appeared briefly to have eyes the size of saucers. Melmont's eyes emanated to Goldfrapp not caviar-destroying cosmic radiation but rather the warm promise of the everything that sprang so gloriously from the Nothing that was before. (Acknowledgement of a universal void of time and space prior to creation does not invalidate e<M. The cruel and unnatural location of our present confinement, thanks to

M's uniquely sinister appetites indeed *endorses* its existence. For where am I leading you now with your permission, gentle reader, if not through a Void?)

Goldfrapp held out a manicured hand with flat nails and large cuticles. A computer nerd's hand, artificially tanned.

—Saul Goldfrapp, Interlease: computer leasing. Pleased to meet you, Mister... Midrash?

Melmont's eyes grew huge again, but this time they seemed to be filled with tears. Melmont's voice was halting in an emotion-filled reproof.

—Saul! How could you confuse us? Ocker Midrash is the *other* magnate; the one who deliberately, insultingly snatches the newspaper titles that I bid for from under my nose. It is extremely unfair, and I plan to have my revenge one day when I... My name is ah, Earnest Mmmmm—

Recognition came upon Goldfrapp with the potency of lightning that strikes the tall oak, blighting the living tissue.

—Not... Earnest Melmont? Oh, I have been waiting *such* a long time to meet you, sir!

Goldfrapp offered his computer-friendly hand again to Melmont, in submission. Melmont seized the offered flesh and the alligator (as he would later think of Melmont, for Goldfrapp was born in Florida) beamed its smile of welcome at the coming breakfast. Melmont opened the tin of Beluga, scooped a large spoonful out and thrust it into Goldfrapp's open mouth, saying,

—Shiver me kishkas, Paul, have I got a deal for you!

And as Goldfrapp chewed, before he could even swallow and allow the fish eggs to make contact with his kishkas, Melmont pressed home his advantage with another spoonful, murmuring, "eat, eat". Goldfrapp, surprised, obeyed though he hadn't been forcefed since he was in his high chair. Finally he managed to delay the next mouthful from the heavily laden spoon long enough to say, in a muffled way.

—How opportune, meeting you. We've been shinking of expanding into Eughrrup for sometime.

Far from Goldfrapp expanding into Europe, something nasty from Europe was about to go for his butthole like a pack of starving coyotes, and eat him from the inside out.

—Which particular aspect of collaboration were you thinking about? asked Melmont, with suave politeness.

—Frankly, we've been very impressed by your recent share dividends: fifty percent annually for three years straight. Something's got to be going on, said Goldfrapp, speaking truer than he knew.

—It's a perfectly normal growth rate in my business, said Melmont, averting his gaze modestly. Goldfrapp had gotten rich so quick that he had plumb forgot what normal was. The thought that the dividends might have been tweaked for a dumb cluck like him never crossed his mind.

—Oh, I know it's *normal*. But we've never targeted you for a takeover because your own personal holdings were so high; or, they *seem* to be. Nobody seems to know, said Goldfrapp.

—One way to find out how big my stake is, is to buy it, then you would recover your capital outlay over two years, said Melmont, with breathtaking chutzpah.

—But I thought the share price would take a nosedive without you, said Goldfrapp. He had paid a number of financial seers to analyse and report on Melmont's mysteriously high performance, but none of them had been able to explain exactly why it was doing so well. It must have something to do with the founder.

——I would undertake to remain as director for three years minimum, said Melmont. In three years' time, anyone who is as smart as you would know my business back to front.

——There's nothing particularly smart about knowing more about leaseback than IBM. I just got lucky, said Goldfrapp.

——The luck is still sticking to you, said Melmont, in his serenest and most velvety voice.

Melmont beckoned the blonde stewardess over, who arrived with two glasses and the champagne already opened, but Melmont refused to let her pour.

——I want the bottle opened in front of me.

The stewardess departed crossly, and Goldfrapp was lost in admiration for Melmont's sophistication. He confessed that he couldn't wait to get to London. It was his first trip. He passed a napkin to Melmont, indicating to him a small landslide of caviar that was taking place on the lower slopes of Melmont's shirt. Melmont messily wiped himself, enlarging the soiled area before losing interest in the problem.

Two swift bottles of champagne later Goldfrapp and Melmont had established a drunken camaraderie. (If you mention Krug or Bölinger, they say a case of bubbly may arrive on the lucky scribbler's doorstep. My publishers and I have no arrangement with the firms in question but pigs might fly. One bottle of each brand was consumed.) The young multimillionaire agreed with Melmont that they should go to his office as soon as possible so that Melmont could sell all his shares to Goldfrapp and make him the happiest man in Creation.

The only fly in the ointment was that the plane was going in the wrong direction. Keen to close the deal in a way which would impress his new friend and protector, Goldfrapp beckoned to the blonde button-nosed stewardess to tell her to speak to the cockpit about the revised destination. Soon the co-pilot came and stared down on two drunken businessmen.

——Are you two gentlemen trying to waste my time? We'll be in London in two and a half hours.

——We don't want to go to London. We've changed our minds, said Melmont.

——Yes, sir, that's correct. My name's Saul Goldfrapp and this is Mr Melmont, and we want you to turn the plane around. You're only halfway so there's enough fuel. That's right, go back to New York. We have to do some business there, urgently.

——I'll pay, added Melmont.

——No, no, this is my treat. It shouldn't cost more than a couple of hundred thousand dollars. Hell, my first divorce cost me ten times that.

Goldfrapp already had his chequebook out when the darker stewardess walked away to the other end of the plane, where a forgotten passenger, an old gentleman in an Arab headdress and burnous, was sitting quietly staring at the curve of the ocean. The stewardess exchanged words with the man, and returned with the disappointing news that the third passenger was not agreeable to turning around as he was travelling to England with the express purpose of seeing his horse run at Newmarket tomorrow.

—Lemme talk to him. How much does he want? Every man has his price, said Goldfrapp.

The blonde stewardess was at last able to put the two vulgarians in their place.

—I'm sorry sir, but His Highness the Sultan of 'Qec has asked that he is not disturbed again on this flight.

The Sultan, it was known, had cash reserves so great they exceeded Goldfrapp's and Melmont's pipsqueak billions together by a factor of ten. Melmont, conceding defeat, knew a deep bond could still be formed with shared prejudice.

—Bloody A-rabs, said Melmont, and looked at Goldfrapp conspiratorially.

—Yeah, right, said Goldfrapp, and giggled.

Instead of chortling over whether it was Abraham (or Ibrahim) who spoke with Yarweh (or Allah) two hundred generations earlier, Saul should have looked where we were all headed as the late and lamentable twentieth century sped by, the last one that humanity would ever experience.

Then Saul and Melmont, the sons of Shem both laughed in their sleeves, against the son of Japhet. And lo, Saul knew not his enemy, that Melmont would smite him, hip and thigh, and leave his dwelling desolate. And it came to pass.

If Goldfrapp's well-paid financial analysts had inspected Melmont's style of board meeting, they might have reported differently about the viability of the company. True, these meetings were generally attended by many well-rewarded and sober-suited city gents. But their consciences were paid to sleep soundly through all irregularities, and the coming sale merger which would have called in other circumstances for a degree of scrutiny was treated no different.

Melmont kept postponing the crucial board but was legally obliged to hold a meeting. For some years now Melmont's chief accountant, Gibley, had more or less given up trying to support the ledger figures with reality. Melmont had frothed up his dividend levels from his untraceable offshore funds and kept on the alcoholic Gibley as a pliable creature who wrote what he was told knowing he wouldn't get a job elsewhere. Luckily for Melmont, Interlease was too callow and too greedy to insist on an audit.

When the six board members convened after the ninth cancellation, Gibley was in attendance, swigging openly in his nervousness from a silver flask.

——Who wishes to cancel this meeting and hold it at a later date? asked Cole. Raise your hands please. I see all present vote to postpone. Very well.

Suddenly there was the distant thunder of a descending helicopter, and the raised hands stiffened then fell, knowing that Melmont was about to be in the building. Cole began mentally drafting a memorandum to his bank to play down the bank's exposure. Gibley, in a feeble gesture of concealment, put his flask in his briefcase. The boardroom doors, modelled on Brunelleschi's bronze doors in Florence, swung open, and Melmont marched in as wilfully confident as any Borgia about to assassinate a rival at Mass. Jill was close on his heels.

——This has to be fast. They're holding the plane to Tel Aviv for me. I propose to sell my shareholding in Melmont UK to Interlease USA while remaining chief executive in charge of overseas operations which will be regrouped under Melmont Offshore Communications. Any questions? Meeting ajourned!

Melmont was already turning on his heel when Gibley raised

his hand. His voice was hampered by a nervous stutter.

——J-j-j-j-just a moment. I have detected some problems.

Melmont looked as if he could not believe his ears. He paused, looking over his shoulder. Drawing courage up from God knows where, Gibley continued bravely.

——In the event that Melmont UK is sold as outlined, the share dealings between Melmont UK and the new company, Melmont Offshore, may fall within the terms of an i-i-i-i-illegal share support operation.

Melmont flashed him a look that said 'And what will you do about the fact that the books were cooked by you in the first place, chum?' What he actually said was,

——As this meeting has been ajourned, Mr Gibley, I can tell you informally, that I am selling this company in one month.

Then suddenly, Melmont turned into a redfaced, screaming bully. He stepped up to his errant accountant.

——Do I have to do the accounts for you as well as running round the world, Mr Gibley? I must be mad. My head must be full of chopped worms. Why do I employ a drunken incompetent to handle my m-m-m-*money*?

Gibley thought Melmont was going to hit him. But in fact he was just getting his instructions. Melmont added to the rest of the room,

——I expect a profits forecast of *at least* three million for the final year, or you will all of you depart to outer darkness, leaving only your putzes on the table!! Eunuchs, that's all I have got working for me. Eunuchs!

Icarus Skyways bore the Chairman and Publisher away though Melmont's presence continued to reverberate in the room even after the helicopter turbine faded to the west. Cole alone of all the craven members deplored to himself how the level of collective morality had sunk. He secretly began to despise himself for always being too obliging for his own good, and here he was again, obliging Melmont because he was too weak to do otherwise. He reviewed his past failings with loathing. He had chosen to abandon his thesis on the Versailles Treaty (which his tutor declared would have rivalled Keynes') for a commission because 'his country needed him'. Did it, really? Would it not have been better to have gone into teaching, a protected profession, early and let some other son of the soil risk a bullet?

Propelled by equal quantities of self-disgust and prudence, Cole acted quickly and arranged a spread bet which included speculative short-selling on Melmont shares, held as security in the bank's name. Ten years later he would have been prosecuted for insider trading, but as it was, when the crash came, Cole's quick thinking made the year's balance sheets for Speke and Lazarus, Merchant Bankers, a model for prudent venture capitalism in the City. The bank would be ready to extend the hand of credit again when and if Melmont ever rose from his own ashes.

Meanwhile Melmont, having committed himself to the path of incomplete mergers and plunging share prices, was using the Cold War as an opportunity to grow elsewhere. Being the sole publisher of all government-sponsored nuclear research (there is no other kind) on both sides of the Iron Curtain, Melmont travelled a great deal, sedulously extending his lucrative monopoly in academic nuclear research as the research grants and the university departments enlarged; and now, developing countries withheld bread from the mouths of their poor as they struggled to establish themselves as nuclear players. But it was Melmont's new political position that the KGB now wished to exploit. Melmont the world player was summoned to Moscow, after the Russian leadership's decision to send in the tanks to 'free' Czechoslovakia, but before the tanks themselves rolled.

Vanov's memo to his seniors in the KGB proposed they exploit their British MP as a soothing voice of moderation in the British Parliament. So as the Russian tanks massed at the Czechoslovak border, Melmont was being poured into a limousine from the grotesquely ugly Moscow airport VIP lounge, before finding himself in the Kremlin.

It all looked the same as when General Secretary Stalin received young Captain Melmont MC twenty years before, in the same room. Indeed everything was the same, except for the bust of Lenin Melmont had kissed on the way out. At the start of the swollen and corruption-surfeited Brezhnev decade it had disappeared, 'taken away temporarily for essential repair and cleaning'. It left the country wrapped in a rug and surfaced in 1993 in a flea market in Galveston, Texas, priced hopefully at $15. Things fall apart, the centre cannot hold.

Melmont was introduced by his old contact Vanov to Yuri Vladimirovich Andropov, the ascetic-looking head of the KGB. Andropov had fought against Hitler, then later won his political spurs at the time of the Hungarian uprising. He was, everyone agreed, the future premier of Russia.

Melmont sat facing Andropov, while Vanov sat on a chair six feet back from Melmont. Andropov spoke first. He had a reputation for not beating about the bush.

——How wonderful to meet you Mr Melmont. I have a favour to ask. Some words of restraint from you in the House of Commons will be most helpful shortly in preventing misunderstanding in the Western powers about the so-called 'Prague Spring', an entirely domestic affair as we see it.

Melmont's smile was genuine; a measure of his joy. If his own party despised him, then at least here was someone who knew his value as a democratic Member of Parliament.

——I believe I can help you, comrade. Is there any particular aspect of Russian policy to the Democratic Socialist Republic of Czechoslovakia that you would wish me to emphasise?

——As you know the Czech nation is not foreign to us, we are one large family. We just need, for the sake of international harmony, to be able to settle our disputes in peace.

——You can count on me to put your position as eloquently as you yourself have, comrade. And now, we should be talking about a biography of you.

Andropov looked a trifle surprised. He was aware Melmont made biography offers to all heads of Socialist states, but while Brezhnev was a swollen walking corpse, there was no clear admission of when Andropov would succeed. Had the mysterious Englishman got access to better information than the KGB?

——We need not arouse my vanity. If our dear leader, Comrade Brezhnev is pleased with his book published by you, it would be wise to wait before bringing out one's own story. And now the Praesidium is about to confer, so I must go. I apologise for the brevity of our meeting, said Andropov, standing.

——I wish you luck, comrade, said Melmont.

Andropov scooped up a pile of pinkish-grey folders which contained the detailed running order of the Russian invasion, smiled in a wintry fashion at Vanov's charge, and left.

Later, in a hotel bar, Melmont clinked glasses with Vanov in celebration of the importance of his mission and its role in world peace.

——Long live the democratic union of Socialist republics! Vanov, whose view of Russian military intervention was similar, concurred. But something else was clearly on the rugged former tank-commander's mind. Finally he shared it with Melmont.

——Andropov is going to be leading the country, said Vanov.

——So it was the right thing to offer him a biography, said Melmont. Vanov sighed, exasperated at the shallowness of Melmont's grasp of Russian politics.

——The long-term strategy department of the KGB has analysed the economy and the outlook is not good. Andropov will be one of the last Socialist leaders. The regime is bankrupt. In fifteen years, twenty years, communism will be finished, and then what will happen? Chaos, said Vanov glumly.

Melmont had done so well out of the Soviet Union that he felt ambivalent about its coming collapse, but if news came from such an authoritative source, it must be true. He stuffed a hundred rouble note in the cleavage of a vast waitress who was clearing the next table. The waitress pocketed the money without looking at it, and then banged Melmont over the head with an empty tin tray. Melmont laughed.

——Just get another bottle of pepper vodka and step on it, he said.

——Yankee swine! the woman spat, and flounced away.

Melmont dreamily drew the pattern of a circle in the spilled beer of the uncleared table next to them.

——I sometimes think maybe I should have gone to America, after all.

——Maybe.

——What else has come out of the KGB thinktanks?

——They say you're never going to have power in Parliament.

Melmont nodded.

——I've come to that conclusion too. I won't stand for re-election.

Vanov looked hurt.

——What's the matter, Earnest? We need you there to serve the great cause!

——Parliament's a waste of time. Besides, I am handicapped there. One country is a limited thing. It cannot expand beyond its boundaries.

Vanov looked puzzled. Wasn't Russia expanding into Czechoslovakia, even now? Melmont spread the puddle of beer wider with his finger.

——Country divisions make no sense any more. Media has no boundaries. You start by buying a newspaper. I can do that now. Then it's the next step, logically. Then the sky's the limit, after that.

——I don't understand, said Vanov, firmly.

——There are huge international vistas opening in front of us.

As Melmont was about to share the rest of his vision of the future, a Tom Jones lookalike in a trilby, platform heels and a blue feather boa got up and started singing *Strangers in the Night* with a thick Russian accent, standing aggressively on the podium in the middle of the hotel bar. The singer was backed by a discordant thirtynine-piece orchestra. Melmont turned to Vanov confidentially, and put one great paw around Vanov's hunched shoulders, then bent even closer and cupped his mouth as the massive orchestra wailed. No one could bug the conversation now.

——Vanya, I swear no one but me knows that I don't take the money you are given for me. I don't want it. Take it.

——*What could be the chances?*

——It's yours. But the time and the opportunity has come for you, my friend, to make some *real* money. Listen. I have a buyer who will pay in dollars for weapons-grade plutonium. It's Israel.

Vanov was surprised to hear the buyer named.

——*Exchanging glances, it work out alright*

——I thought they had a viable nuclear programme. They had at least thirty warheads at the time of the Seven-Day War, no?

——That's right. Now they want to mop up any surplus, and so prevent any of the Arab states from getting their hands on a bomb. Here is your window of opportunity, my friend. For every fifty kilos of weapons-grade plutonium you can deliver, I will put a hundred thousand bucks in your dollar account.

——*It work out alright, for strangers in the NI—II—GHT!!!* Vanov laughed, partly to cover his surprise that Melmont knew about his dollar account.

——You can't be serious, Earnest. I'm not going to steal my country's warheads.

——There are ten thousand. How many do you actually need to wipe out the planet? The truth is they're never going to be used, are they?

Vanov shrugged. The cogs of his mind refused to turn and

engage the thrilling logic of the proposal. It was too simple. He said weakly,

——Without any, there is no deterrent.

——Are you seriously going to miss ten? Deterrence will still work without them. Andropov is not the only one looking ahead. In twelve years, believe me, you won't be able to *give* enriched plutonium away. It will become a curse for every country that owns it. For now, you just have to get them to East Berlin. I've got an old Nazi there by the nuts. He'll do anything for me.

Vanov sat silent till the pepper vodka finally arrived. His tempter had gained the ascendancy again. Melmont winked at the fat waitress. This time, when he tucked a further fifty rouble note in her cleavage, there was no complaint.

——You'd corrupt the mother of a saint, Earnest.

Melmont nodded and, reverting to English, suddenly shouted in triumph an old music hall tag a squaddie had taught him when he was first learning English.

——*I should cocoa!*

——Chtoë? —What? said Vanov, politely puzzled, in Russian, trying to draw his friend back into a language they both spoke. It was after all a serious matter they were discussing and misunderstandings could be fatal.

——You are going to do *very* well out of this, old friend!

——OK, we go ahead then.

Tom Jones glanced sharply over his boa at the interruption from the floor. A roistering fat man and his companion were taking turns toasting each other, whooping and drinking out of the bottle.

From fifty feet away, it could pass for a typical Monday night audience with nothing sinister about it at all. The singer shrugged.

The half-cut orchestra crassly took this as the signal to begin the next song, and hastily launched into a brassy version of *So glad we made it*. There was an offkey braying from Siberian trombonists caught offguard and desperately trying to regain pitch control as the world took one more step towards the abyss.

XII

Catastrophe

AS THE SHADOWS LENGTHENED OVER RED SQUARE and the Red Star Hotel (Pis Elegant Rocking Music with Bolshoi Band Tonite!), it was still a warm afternoon outside a crowded marquee in the heart of England. Willis Death and Eileen Simpkins were being waved off by well-wishers at the end of a lavish reception, after having pledged themselves to each other till death did them part, amen. It was Melmont the Magnificent who had sponsored the profligate catering, which had followed on, so unexpectedly, from the exchange of rings in the humble chapel.

The service itself, in the asbestos-sided Boxly Spiritualist Church where Eileen still kept in touch with her first husband after he passed over, had been a touching event. Standing proud and straight at his bride's side, Willis had repeatedly wiped the tears from his deepset eyes, with big meaty hands that had been up more cows' backsides than anyone had had hot dinners, with the possible exception of the reception's sponsor.

The ghost of Eileen's first husband peered down through the mists of the Great Divide, mournfully shaking its head.

The shade must have foreseen how Fate would shortly mock the happy hour, by striking a blow against Melmont's firstborn.

The lethal incident happened close by. After the tiers of wedding cake were sliced and tumbled for the dark bricks of sweetness to be passed out among the sated guests, Willis and Eileen Death (as Mrs Simpkins had now legally become) agreed to leave and mounted into an open landau with a pair of fine greys in harness to draw them away. The rear of the carriage had been lovingly decorated with any number of 'traditional' items, trailing boots and old tin cans, tied to the rear axle with suitably rustic baler twine.

Baler twine! You never see nice square bales of hay in the countryside, tied with two hairy sisal lengths any more, do you? *Où sont les ballots d'antan?* Instead, there are just those obese Melmontian cheeses, cling-wrapped in black plastic, ugly and incongruous cellulose monoliths awaiting the onset of winter, mocking reminders of our jailor.

The newly-weds in the open carriage were unaware of the horror that they were about to come across: they were drunk with happiness, and more than a little wine. Melmont's festive bequest had included uncountable crates of the best vintage champagne, so much so that empty Piper Heidseck bottles would later form an unclimbable mountain completely obscuring the town's little bottle bank, and trumpeting the triumph of excess.

——I dunno about you, but Oi is tight as a tick, said Willis Death reflectively to his new wife. The occasion, crowned by a vintage champagne with an irresistably *more*-ish, chocolatey aftertaste was spreading a delicious balm throughout his senses.

——I don't how many people asked me how I was going to get

used to bein' called Missus Death, said Eileen, not for the first time.

——That was a good do, though. Bloody good, said Willis.

——He shouldn't have done it, he really shouldn't. Musta cost a king's ransom.

——'E loves royalty, so it'd be even more, said Willis, vaguely.

——All those flahrs! said his new wife.

——Even more, if you're seein' double, said Willis, and they both laughed guiltily.

——Do you know that it's not just us. Everyone who gets married gets a card, and births as well, and even if you only get your name in the paper after bein' burgled you get acknowledgement of some kind. I know, it's just one of them Roneo signatures, but still, it's the *fack'* that someone out there's bothered about you, said the new Mrs Death.

——Still the fack, aye. If you're blind and you're sick, when you get the envelope, you open it, supposin' you can, and you just run your hand over the back of the card where it says 'Get Well Soon' and it says it to you in braille, so it's just the same as if you was normal, Willis extrapolated.

——It's them little details that show that he cares, concluded Eileen. She lay back leaning on Willis's strong left shoulder, closed her eyes and sighed. Her hand slid between the groom's thighs, to his pleasant surprise, and he felt a distinct growth in his manhood. All kinds of possibility opened before him. But Death was cautious by nature.

——Don't you think we oughta wait, Eileen?

——Life ain't going to get better than this, Willis, we'd better enjoy it now.

——I'm not saying I don't like it mind.

——I likes your John Thomas better and better, whispered Eileen, and Willis smiled with pride so his eyes almost disappeared and the tip of his nose went down.

As the bride and groom kissed again the Landau's driver turned the corner to find the road was blocked a short distance ahead, and slowed. It had been trailing its tinker's mess reminder of what married life consists of in reality—broken shoes and pots and pans—but the rough symphony of clopping of hooves and the clanking ceased together. Eileen opened her eyes to see what the holdup was.

Beyond the two noble greys of the Landau, a bus and a car were halted. There must have been an accident, but neither seemed damaged. All the same Willis Death got out of the Landau with a terrible sinking feeling where the champagne had been a moment ago. A small crowd was looking at a body on the ground between the two vehicles, and there was a girl's bicycle beyond them, twisted on its side.

When Eileen saw a pink bicycle with cricket pads spilling from the front pannier, she gasped. In a shaking voice she called out,

——Is that Zenocrate's bike, Willis?

Willis made his way around the shocked, silent crowd to find the body of a twelve-year-old girl in cricket whites. Her skull had been cracked open so badly in her fall the brain was visible, between the falling waves of her auburn hair. Her hands seemed to be groping something unknown, out of their gingham sleeves, as she lay on her back facing the sky. Willis now realised who it was and a cry escaped his lips for Melmont's eldest child, the sporting Zenocrate. A white plimsoll lay on the dusty verge of the road. She would never wear it again. The victim was still breathing, but low, and she was a frightful sight.

——Let me through, said Willis. And at the same time, to himself,

——Oh Lord. Why take them so young, with so far to go? Why? *Why?*

Eileen now joined the crowd to see if there was anything she could do. The woman next to her was presumably the driver of one of the vehicles, for she was shaking uncontrollably, saying over and over,

——She just hurtled out in front of me, I never saw her till I hit her, I couldn't stop, I couldn't stop.

Willis knelt, paying attention to the girl's shattered skull. There was a small piece, shaped like a pyramid, incongruously sticking in her hair. If she lived, most likely, she would be a vegetable. Death would be a release.

In the distance there sounded the twin klaxons of the county's emergency services. They had been responding with exemplary speed under their new MP's initiative, but their latest mercy dash would not save little Zenocrate, whose soul was already preparing to depart for angelic realms.

Melmont had been in New York when he was phoned by a distraught Abigail. For a full minute she wailed down the phone, unable to speak. Melmont said nothing, waiting for her to catch her breath. To get him home at once, his assistant Jill had worked miracles. They even held Concorde at Kennedy Airport, its evelons trembling in sympathy as the tragic father-figure was helicoptered in from the World Trade Center.

Six hours later, rumpled and unshaven, Melmont joined

Abigail and the other girls in a vigil beside the bed of their sister. Melmont reached out with his strangler's paws, and took his eldest daughter's sky-clasping hand;

——Speak to us, Zenocrate. Live for me. Speak.

Tears poured down Abigail's face but the girl remained in her coma. After an hour, Melmont rose to go. The poison of disappointment and loss seethed in his veins, but he resolved to be strong and not show it. His life after all had begun in loss. Abigail clutched at him distraught. Melmont pulled away.

——I'm late, I have to go to London, said Melmont.

——Don't go. What for? A terrible thing has happened to us. We need you here. What is more important than that? said Abigail.

——This is terrible, but even more terrible would be World War Three. Russia has gone into Czechoslovakia and I have to urgently address the House. It could make a considerable reduction to our chances of experiencing a nuclear winter.

Abigail watched Melmont's elephantine back as he left the intensive care ward. In her mind she understood he wished for a grand part saving the world—and who does not?—but in her womanly heart he was somehow a traitor, to his offspring, to human feelings, to *everything*.

The motorway towards London was deserted in the cruel dawn light. Melmont had waited till he was alone to weep. Now he wept as he drove, even though Zenocrate's biology had been an enduring insult to his desires for a son. Melmont wept because he was still human, because in spite of her sex he loved Zenocrate, and the love hurt.

It came to him for the first time, that the only way out of the blinding hurt was to *eat the world*.

The thought flashed through his mind and out the other side faster than he could apprehend it; but destiny's bitter fruit had begun its mulct. Like some mighty comet that grazes and blazes past the tranquil earth without touching it, one day the world-eating notion would return, this time with annihilating impact.

Preparing himself for his appearance in Westminster, Melmont located an electric shaver at the bottom of his brief-case, in a mess of broken cigars and foreign currency. He started to shave and immediately felt better. But then, adjusting the rearview mirror to check the left side of his face, to his surprise he saw a motorcycle.

A police motorcyclist appeared to be closely following the bulky car as it careened wildly from side to side up the road, like a schooner abandoned under sail. Melmont, intuiting that the forces of law might wish to slow his progress in some way, stopped shaving and floored the accelerator.

The car straightened out and moved forward like the wind; insofar as a five-litre Rolls can be compared to anything weight-less. Surrounding and protecting their alarmingly massive driver was an aegis of weight; the car's creaking Park-Ward chassis, its vast engine block and syrupy tilting suspension giving heavy orders to chunky radial Dunlop tyres, at a hundred and sixty pounds a set, 'designed and built for customers who consis-tently travel at speeds in excess of sixty miles per hour'. Quite so, your honour.

The police officer turned on his flashing blue lights, but Melmont took no notice. The Triumph 650cc twin (the glamorous bike ridden by Marlon Brando in *The Wild Bunch*) would have had trouble keeping up but the Oxbridgeshire police shaved the cylinder heads to increase compression, added ethanol to the five-star petrol, fitted racing compression rings, ground their exhaust valves regularly and in general treated their bikes like the thoroughbreds that they were, all to trap high-speed traffic violaters and grinning pirates of the road like Melmont.

PC Wootton, (no relation to the Wootton of Blackall Wootton & Sexton, the famous motorbike shop in Theale) knew the outer performance envelope of his bike in the cold, moist dawn air could be a hundred and twenty mph. But he also knew that the police-issue tyres were liable to tear apart at sustained speeds, so he had to act quickly.

He opened the bike's throttle, pulled level with Melmont, and saw the great man shaving again. Wootton, married with two small children, reached out and banged on the glass forcefully with his leather gauntletted hand, praying that Melmont would not start to weave. Luckily the chase was on a recently laid piece of road and the bike was rock-steady beside the big car.

Even Melmont had to concede, with the policeman's fist inches from his ear, that he was going to have to deal with the situation. Wootton pointed to the hard shoulder. Melmont slowed, pulled over and stopped behind the bike. In the sudden silence as Wootton dismounted, the overheated cylinder block started clicking. The exhaust pipes trailed thin whisps of treacly blue upward. Melmont watched the policeman walk towards the Rolls.

Wootton's blood was up at the folly of mankind. Earlier in the day, he had been called to where a busload of pensioners had rammed a bridge support and he was still feeling sick from watching the fire brigade hose down the mess.

——I'm booking you.

——I am a member of Her Majesty's Parliament, officer, and if you wish to hear my extenuating circumstances I have to be in Westminster in half an hour, to make a speech on which world peace depends, Melmont replied.

Wootton noticed all four ashtrays in the car appeared to be overflowingly full.

——Whatcha think you're doing, shaving at that speed?

——There's no time in the schedule set aside for it, officer. And now I must be on my way.

Melmont dipped his hand into his briefcase and came up with a large salad of paper currency. Wootton stared down at the contemptuously proffered fist full of money.

——Are you trying to buy me off with *roubles*?

Melmont realised he had been reaching for the wrong end of the briefcase.

——As your MP, I'd like you to take this as a contribution to the Oxbridge police ball. I can get you a very good rate of exchange on these. Two to one. But there is something you will have to do for me. I shall need an escort to get me to Westminster to speak, and I need to speak before the New York stock exchange opens for trading. You do understand me, don't you?

At Wootton's much-delayed disciplinary hearing, ten years later, after which he took 'early retirement', he swore on oath that he could not remember taking a bribe. Melmont's eyes, Wootton claimed, went as big as saucers, and a sickening green miasma filled the interior of the black and tan Rolls. The policeman, zombielike, then had to obey a sepulchral voice ordering him to do whatever Melmont wanted. The next thing Wootton remembered was forty minutes later, when he found himself on his bike, lights flashing, clearing the way down Whitehall. The intervening sixty odd miles, even under hypnotic regression, were to remain a blank for the rest of Wootton's law-abiding, and not uncomfortable life.

The Carpathian trickster had dazzled and dodged and had now arrived to deliver the speech which was to be the pinnacle of his parliamentary career. Earnest Melmont, shaved, collected and suitably grave, addressed a packed and for once, respect- fully attentive House of Commons, recalled specifically to discuss a very grave world crisis, the recent Russian occupation of Czechoslovakia.

The atmosphere could not be more different to the one at his first parliamentary speech. Melmont felt himself rising to the occasion.

—Honourable Members, I know the country well, very well, having had trading links with Czechoslovakia for twenty years, and indeed having been born near there; not a distinction that many in this house can boast, I fancy. There will be, naturally, feelings of outrage expressed here today; the outrage of democrats who see a small country overrun against its desire, against its will, by a larger and more powerful, more oblivious and predatory neighbour.

Reading the grammatically corrected words now, we can see how Melmont gave the Russians at the time, reading their trans- lated *Hansardskis*, the impression that he was indeed of their party, doing their bidding. Did it help world peace? Who knows?

Outside the House of Commons that night, Melmont was preparing to address a deliciously respectful crowd of journalists and TV cameras. His profile as an MP had never been higher. Even Harold Wilson, seeing Melmont on TV, was won over. Wilson relit his cigar (pipes were strictly for the press opportunities), and watched with admiration. He might even have offered the Catering Commissioner something ministerial, but the government was under constant attack by rightwing lunatic cliques in MI5, for whom Melmont's links with Communist regimes were guarantees of his communist leanings. As ever, the lunatics had it half-right.

With the world listening through the fifty microphones pointed at him the shameless tool of Marxist imperialism spoke. Melmont began gravely; for when, indeed is the fate of the world not a grave issue?

The rich and the poor, tyrants and the oppressed alike harkened. For once, his orotundity was fit for the occasion. It gave hope, like the lodestone that may lead the storm-bound mariner away from shipwreck. It suggested there could be a maturity and dignity in restraining from action.

Woozy Russian premier Brezhnev watched through a fug of disease and vodka, listening to the simultaneous KGB translation, and hardly understood what was going on. But it was obviously jaw-jaw, not war.

KGB chief Yuri Andropov watched stone cold sober, and with relief. The future Kremlin supremo was aware how brittle the 'Evil Empire' was. But as long as the West permitted occasional violent colonialism, internal collapse could be postponed.

Dominic watched Melmont's performance with his uncle, side by side on the sofa in Cole's sitting room in Chelsea. Melmont had been going back over his main points again at some length. Cole, declining to take the moment seriously, was wearing an apron and cleaning his collection of snuff boxes. His disgust with Melmont had deepened since the boardroom incident.

——I advocate to members of *all* parties that it is left to the *individual* consciences of the leaders of the British business community overseas to decide whether or not they will continue their trade with the communist blo... .

Cole switched the sound off.

——Spoken like a man who has just bought two paper mills in Prague, said Dominic.

——Quite so, Dom. He's not improving things between Russia and the West, he's a Cold War budget parasite. He got a science publishing house backlist in Berlin and then developed it as a monopoly on nuclear science publishing. Volumes one to twenty if you want a nuclear programme, and volumes twenty one to a hundred if you've already got one, because you have to know what the other chap is thinking.

The phone rang. The subject of Dominic's biography wanted to clarify his position on the Russian occupation, which he feared might have been misrepresented by the poor editing on the tele-vison news. Dominic should go down immediately to Melmont Keep to collect the great man's thoughts at this turning point in history. But Dominic should also be prepared for the fact that Melmont might be delayed. There was also a rumour, the secretary added, that if the Labour Cabinet lost the confidence of any more of its own backbenches, that Wilson would resign and Melmont would be called upon to lead the country.

——What does he want now? asked Cole, as Dominic put the receiver down.

——He paid for my education and now he thinks he can keep me waiting, said Dominic.

An hour and a half later, having cancelled all social arrangements and postponed two urgent dental appointments and hailed a cab, Dominic was in the vast, seamlessly carpeted drawing room of Melmont Keep, pencil in hand. The prospect of Melmont at Number 10 Downing Street had disappeared back into the rumour mill as quickly as it came. The big house seemed aimless, an exercise in folly without its owner.

Dominic wandered out of the main rooms into an annexe, where there was a study with books covering the walls. There were photographs of Melmont with his family on the desk, but the room seemed little used. Dominic poured himself a glass of water from the carafe on the desk and swallowed twice the permitted maximum of Extra-strength Tylenol. Even through the bitter painkillers and his toothache, the water tasted ancient and musty, as if no one had changed it for years.

Browsing the books, Dominic spotted Samuel Johnson's *A Dictionary of the English Language* high in the bookcase. Dominic had long been fascinated by Melmont's use of words, which was often childishly inventive, at the same time, delivered in the stilted, heightened tones of one who has only learnt to talk 'proper' at stage school. Dominic paused, forgetting his toothache and amused by the idea that his subject might have anglicised himself using the dictionary. Johnson had established the libertarian principle that words were not assigned meaning by pedagogic tyrants, but by democratic usage; Melmont used ten languages, but none of them democratically. Dominic reached up and tried to pull out Volume I, the 1750 first edition, by Longman. It did not budge.

After he tried Volume II, for 'worm' as in 'chopped worms', he discovered the backs were false. But both titles were attached to the back of a small door, the size of a serving hatch. The hatch came away with a small hydraulic sigh, and Dominic saw with great excitement that behind was a brushed-steel handle. He turned it, to discover the whole bookshelf moving. Classical authors from Aristotle to Zeno were real books, shown in a bookcase on a vastly larger door, which now silently swung open onto an inner room. It was a breathtaking moment. Dominic knew down to his tingling kneecap cartilages, that he must be stumbling on one of the secrets of Melmont. But which one?

He cautiously stepped inside. The room, which must have occupied a huge tranche of the ground floor, was window-less and at least seventy foot deep. Rows and rows of grey filing cabinets took up the middle. Dimly lit walls were covered with banks of big Ampex reel-to-reel taperecorders, some of which were slowly turning silently on one-inch wide tape. The tech-nology on view was at least twenty years old, so it must have been going on for most of Dominic's life, he reasoned. Surveillance was not surprising to a man of Melmont's plurality, but the scale was astonishing. Who or what, exactly was Melmont spying *on*? How could one man ever oversee the collection of that much material?

Dominic realised that he should on no account be caught in there, and there would very likely be some kind of recording of who went out and in. In fact, he could have compromised him-self hopelessly already. Stepping quickly out again, he stared round, drymouthed with fear.

He noted a covert video camera behind the desk in the

study, but it pointed out at a passage he had not crossed, away from the false bookcase. He was safe for the moment, unless there were other layers of surveillance: microphones, pressure pads, perhaps? The oak parquet floor had not been interfered with. He carefully shut the main door and wiped his finger-prints off the handle, just before the little dictionary door closed by itself on buffered mini-hydraulics, with another tiny sigh.

Somewhere far away in the house, a dinner gong sounded for supper. Dominic went slowly towards the elusive sound, almost hugging himself with excitement. It somehow fitted. Like Randolph Hearst filling the cellars of his castle in California with treasures he had bought but would never unpack, Melmont had become addicted—to information; more information than he could ever use.

Dominic walked jauntily into the dining room, which had a high Palladian ceiling painted the subtle yellow of a Sicilian sunset. Dominic remembered from previous visits that in addi-tion to the main dish there would always be a lavish selection of grilled wursts and backbacon on the table with chopped green peppers, lamb cutlets basted with a garlic and paprika sauce and other Carpathian delicacies to assuage Melmont's desire for a snack. Ominously, there was no buffet spread ready for the Master. On previous dinners, the eight Melmont girls, identically dressed in gingham and ranged in order of height, had been standing to attention behind their chairs at one side of the long oak table, but tonight, order was breaking down. When Melmont was not at home, nothing seemed to happen on time, or willingly.

Abigail, at the far end of the room, shouted for everyone to sit and begin, but none of her children seemed to take any notice. Some of them even walked away from the table and left the room. Dominic walked up to a pleasantly relaxed-looking grey-haired Jesuit in full priestly garb who was politely examining the wall paintings. Father Cowley was in the process of befriending Abigail. Dominic had gathered that the hollowness of the relationship with Melmont, and his growing harshness to her after Zenocrate's accident had begun to oppress her spirits, and she was seeking divine guidance.

By way of introducing himself to Dominic, the holy Father pointed at the picture he had halted in front of. Commissioned after the accident, it was a full-length oil portrait, much in the manner of Sargent's society 'six-footers', of Zenocrate Melmont aged twelve. A heavenly light seemed to play upon her upturned face and a Union Jack floated in the breeze above her head.

—Would you ever look at what the girl's dressed for, said Father Cowley. She's in white flannels, look, holding a cricket bat and ball. Just think, now, if he'd fetched up and made his pile in Skibbereen, she'd have been dressed for hurling, not cricket.

Cowley was from Cork, so even more than the middling or Northern Irish he felt himself obliged to take a sly dig at his host's pretensions.

—Zenocrate was keen on games, I know she played cricket, said Dominic.

Emer, the Dublin housekeeper, started to have another go at trying to get people to sit down. She walked up to the vast Burmese gong, and beat it again till the girls put their fingers in their ears and surrendered to the order of the table. Dominic sat next to Abigail, at the head of the table. Father Cowley became so confused by the noise that he sat accidentally in Melmont's vast chair, and reached out for the oversized bowl. Emer snatched it from him, and poured in a smidgen of potato soup, and slapped it back in front of him.

——Here, you greedy pig, that's all you're getting, she said.

——I'm sorry it looks like you've had a wasted trip, Abigail said sweetly to Dominic. But he may be down later. He said to tell you.

——It hasn't been entirely wasted, said Dominic truthfully.

Emer banged soup bowls with different amounts of soup in them down in front of the eight girls, according to some secret formula of her own where the smallest got the most.

——Earnest's had to stay in London and do something with… you know he's in charge of the Catering Committee? I don't see why it can't be done over the phone, but anyhow, he left a message. Abigail spoke from an indefinable place far away, a soft infinitely gentle voice.

——We'll make up a bed for you later.

The girls started to spoon up the soup quickly.

——Stop! Have yous got a train to catch? shouted Emer.

——Lord bless this food to our use, and us in its service, Amen, said Father Cowley, and then spoke something quickly in Latin, as if he wished he hadn't upset the natural order of things by accidentally sitting in the big chair and big place setting reserved for Himself, as Emer referred to him.

——Ugh, spud soup. Worse than school! one of the girls said.

——Have some salt. Emer always forgets, whispered Abigail seductively to Dominic. Dominic took the salt, sprinkled some and said,

——Is Earnest a Catholic?

Abigail shook her head.

——No, and neither am I. But Father Cowley's at the seminary down the road, and he turned up in the drive asking for direction, one day.

——I've so little sense of direction I can't find me own earse in the dark, said Father Cowley. But this is how divine guidance works and it's paid off tenfold. Our treasurer was looking for something to mend the roof. Tearing his hair with the estimates skyhigh that arrived. And yer man here. Pointing at the big chair he was sat in,

——Asks me in to supper, and sat where I am now. He told me to tell the seminary to buy shares in his company. That was four years ago. Forty percent dividends for three years in a row. I now come round here to repay the compliment and try to save everyone's mortal soul. Mister Melmont is the first philanthropist I've met, and is in no danger of hellfire, whatever sniping folks say. He's a benefactor of mankind, and under him, the little people rejoice ter fill their porringers, don't they now, georrls?

None of Melmont's brood had any idea what a porringer did, and they seemed to feel no compunction to acknowledge the holy man's questions. Father Cowley continued, undeterred.

——I saw on the news something about a speech Earnest made today. Mark my words, one day someone will make a fillum about your father. He's a great hero, no doubt about it.

The same day he had his hour of glory, the subject for Father Cowley's Hall of Fame had to admit he was losing the guerrilla war with the caterers. Six months after he was meant to have brought order to the place, theft was rife. He may have tweaked

Stalin's nose and got away with it, but Melmont was no match for Bev of Battersea. The cellar continued to be a black hole where drink and money simply disappeared. When foolproof audits were introduced, Bev and her gang simply introduced a new unregistered cash till of their own and emptied it every night, a scam of such barefaced impudence that Melmont might have thought of it himself.

And it was getting worse. The enemies that Melmont had made in his own party were only too happy to buy tobacco, wines and spirits under the counter in a collective effort to force the uppity Member for Oxbridgeshire into failure and disgrace. On the other side of the House, rubicund Tories came to arrangements with venal butlers to fill their car boots for the weekend with whatever was 'available', both sides pretending that the price agreed for the stolen wines and spirits was the result of bulk buying and proof of the success of the free market.

Melmont decided that a money transfusion straight into the veins of the catering department was the only thing that could conceal the situation and buy him time to defeat the thieves. The strategy was nothing if not direct. Having loaded up with money, he waited impatiently for the House of Commons' dining rooms to cash up and close. But he found he had brought the wrong keys and was obliged to jemmy the door open to let himself in, gashing his hand in the process. The damaged door would attract attention sooner or later from Security so to evade awkward questions he dropped to his hands and knees below table level, and began crawling towards a till, which refused to open for him. Forgetting about Security in his keenness to balance the books, Melmont stood up and loudly jemmied all six tills open, forcing them to accept wodges of bloodied fifty pound notes before cramming them shut again and leaving.

He had escaped detection, but the next day the bandage on his gashed hand started to unravel, just as he was called upon for an interim speech to the House on progress in the House of Commons' kitchens.

—My Honourable friend will be glad to hear problems are being identified and addressed in the following fashion. First, so-called crockery breakages.

Melmont's po-faced reports always produced titters on both sides of the House. There was further laughter when Melmont reached up to scratch an itch on his face and it left a smear. The MPs who had had to sit quiet while being told what to think about Russia by this Johnny-come-lately started snorting with mirth as the loser in their midst acquired increasingly bizarre facial markings.

—One area of expenditure which I am confident we can reduce is catering implements. I have discovered on a massive scale, that House of Commons' crockery and cutlery is being registered as broken or missing while actually removed for personal use elsewhere.

Melmont turned to the Labour Party members sitting behind him, who were biting their knuckles to stop joining in the laughter, and barked,

—Some no doubt by the ill-bred gentlemen seated not a million miles from me!

He turned from the thieves behind him to face the Tories again. Picking up a sheaf of papers with his bandaged hand he continued,

——I now turn to to the Honourable Members' questions about special items from the menu. The answer to Question One is: *Oeuf en gelée* is no longer available because there is no demand for it.

There were cries of 'Shame', and guffaws.

——Two. I am still attempting to find a supplier for 'black pudding' or blood sausage, at a price the Honourable Members for Bradford and Derby say they can afford, but there are difficulties in that price bracket of obtaining uninfected supplies of blood.

By this time in the charade, some MPs were rolling on the floor, redfaced. Melmont carried on with his replies to the deliberately trivial queries till he could take no more humiliation. Pretending his duties were at an end, he scrumpled the list up, and retired to a corridor outside the debating chamber, where he slumped and started to weep.

No one came near him to ask him what was the matter. Melmont finally found a Bounty Bar in his pocket, and stopped snuffling. He unwrapped the chocolate-covered coconut confection, and stuffed it into his mouth all at once. He then rose and walked towards his office, where he found Jill employing a rubber stamp with his signature to sign a pile of condolence cards.

Melmont, his jacket over his shoulder, started flicking through them idly. Jill took a tissue, poured eau-de-cologne on it, and started to clean the blood off her boss's face, methodically. Melmont made no protest or acknowledgement.

——The Department of Trade and Industry woman called again over the Interlease share support investigation, Jill said.

The takeover was turning rotten. Melmont's own company shares were plummeting, and at the same time, Saul Goldfrapp's badly mangled bid was failing to complete the takeover.

——Do they think I'm going to waste my time talking to that she-hyena? Melmont wiped his face with his jacket, hung it behind the door and sat down.

——She's actually quite civilised. She was deeply impressed when I told her who would be opening the new hospital wing in Oxbridge tomorrow.

——Has Prince George confirmed he's going to do it, then? It's an insult for those overprivileged colostomy bags to leave an important engagement like my hospital wing to practically the day before. Who do the royals think they are? I'll tell you who they are. This royal family is a bunch of neolithic, craven, uncircumcised, pointy headed, squirming tapeworm-vomiting cross-eyed pygmies!

Suddenly, falling shares were forgotten, and Melmont was his old self again.

——They should have sent THE QUEEN, he roared loudly.

Melmont may have been an ardent royalist once, but he has—albeit in secret—disbarred the whole boiling of royals from any pedestal they might have a claim to in the New Regime. Titles are meaningless now, post e<M. The dimensions have been abolished, and with them the orders of rank. Their so-called 'Highnesses' are no higher up (or down) Melmont's null-dimensional colon of rank than you, gentle reader.

Flicking through the condolences cards in Jill's out tray, Melmont came across a stamped envelope addressed to Zenocrate Melmont at the Children's Wing of the New Oxbridge Hospital. He stared at it.

——Why haven't these cards gone out?

——I'm sorry, I've had my hands full dealing with the robbery last night, said Jill. Apparently the trail of blood led up the stairs to here.

——As Chairman of the Catering Committee, the thief probably thought I would have ready money lying around in my office, said Melmont, plausibly.

——They've established that the intruder broke into the restaurant tills, but cut himself and fled. But they don't know how much he took.

——I can quickly estimate how much he stole. It will be in the thousands, said Melmont.

——The police couldn't believe how much money was left in the tills. They said you should make sure to empty them, last thing.

——I will, next time, said Melmont.

Jill saw Melmont was looking at his daughter's card. His face was dark, full of a sullen sadness.

——Shall I reopen so you can send a personal message?

Melmont shook his great head.

——Send it as it is. She's a sodding vegetable. She'll never know the difference.

Melmont stalked off. Jill noticed he needed a haircut. He had long greasy dark locks trailing behind. Since Zenocrate had been struck down, on a number of occasions she had noticed he was paying less attention to his appearance.

XIII

Melmont the Party Pooper

O N A BRIGHT AND OUTWARDLY AUSPICIOUS SUMMER morning, all was hustle and bustle at Melmont Keep, preparing for the opening celebrations of the new hospital wing. A grand marquee had been erected on the lawn between the workplaces in the garden and the grand old house. The luxurious tent had a pink and white false ceiling, and its walls were being hung with photographs of Melmont meeting important people all over the world. Party designers had hung garlands of dried squash and gilded pinecones on its walls while connecting passages were flanked by corinthian pillars and ornamental balustrades with hanging baskets of real flowers.

The nearby lawns themselves had been judged insufficiently welcoming on their own, so vast oriental carpets were now being rolled out over sedulously watered and trimmed grass, to be edged and pegged before being dotted with recliners, each with its own pistachio-coloured sunshade. Everywhere the eye turned, it seemed no expense had been spared in a dazzling display of considered opulence. Even the most hardened royalists confessed to being impressed by the intensity of preparation for a man who was either twentieth, or sixty-eighth in line to the throne, depending on your view on the outcome in Salic Law of Bend Sinister descent. Nothing else had mattered for weeks, but to turn Melmont Keep and its surrounds into the most luxurious caravanserai, a floating vision of boundless wealth and ease that would fleetingly engage the attention of the 'Ol' Bastard!', as he was known in the gutter press; a spoilt and easily bored prince.

Inside the house, at the top in an old attic bedroom that doubled as a clothes cupboard, Abigail was supervising the fitting of kilts onto her children. The children were all protesting, the smallest louder than the rest. Each of the kilts, from the smallest to the largest, was made from a violently coloured tartan, woven in the same factory, Shagspir & Hoogstraten, as the vast seamless carpets downstairs. Melmont's fear of treading on cracks, lest they opened and swallow him down to Hades' dark kingdom had subsided. Indeed his feet seldom came to his attention nowadays, except in the bath.

Melmont's stomach floated into the little attic room, and he willed the rest to follow, cocking his head to avoid the low ceiling. His children stood barelegged in a half circle, in varying stages of undress. Abigail was crouching by the three smallest, with a mouthful of large safety pins, which were intended to secure the pleated fall of the cloth. The girls kept pulling them out in protest.

—No darling, it's a kilt. It's not broken, it's *meant* to be held like that.

A large box fell off an ironing board, spilling sporrans decorated with fur tassels over the floor. The larger girls immediately began using them as coshes against each other.

——He is coming. Why are the children not ready? bellowed Melmont.

The seamstress had been given the worst migraine of her thirtytwo years from Melmont's shouting earlier, and had had to go and lie down. She now rose from behind the ironing board where she had been lying with her head covered with a wet flannel and looked at her tormentor. A nimbus of light surrounded him, pierced by dark wriggling incunabula, portents of an even worse headache to come. But she could not afford to walk away from this job. The seamstress picked up a three-metre tape measure but rejected it in favour of a five-metre.

——Would you stand still a moment, sir? the seamstress said in a low voice. The time she dreaded, the time for measuring Melmont's waist had come at last.

Downstairs in the main hall, Cole had arrived dressed in a grey silk suit. Libby was beside him in a miniskirt, a delectable young clown, or panda, with a mass of mascara around each eye. Cole was flicking through a programme which described what functions Prince George would perform on that jubilant day of the opening of the hospital wing.

——Who the fuck is Prince George? said the panda. And why should we be worried?

Vague himself on the genealogy of the Fensterkuchen dynasty, Cole tried to refresh his memory by flicking through the lavishly illustrated pages with pictures of the Prince in every conceivable uniform of the country's armed forces.

——Prince George is, I'm not sure. I'll be able to tell you in just a minute… I think he may be *not* the most senior of the queen's nephews, or something, or not the most junior one. There is some dispute about his exact relationship, I know, but I haven't the faintest idea what it is, I'm sorry. If it had been important presumably they would have cleared it up but he's never going to be king unless a charabanc carrying all the rest goes over a cliff. Printed in Czechoslovakia I see, said Cole of the brochure.

——Is he married? Is he the one called 'The Old Bastard'?

——Answer to question one, I don't know. Question two, yes, I believe so.

——Maybe he's the one who's homosexual. Maybe it's your lucky day, said Libby.

——The days of my lucky days are long gone, said Cole.

Libby looked round to see a pale woman with a flannel on her head pursuing Melmont across the great hall and waving a tape measure. The latter, clad only in a shirt, had clearly just walked away from his costume fitting, and was now passing through his guests having lost his trousers but not yet gained a kilt. As he disappeared from view, the still-dapper figure of Gunter Röhl appeared. Now silver-haired, he was sporting a jaunty subaltern's cap cut out of Melmont tartan. A tray of them stood by the door, for guests to pick up as they came in.

Dominic joined his uncle and was introduced to Röhl. When he heard that Röhl had known Melmont in Berlin, Dominic started to stammer with excitement.

——That's very interesting. There were so many aspects of what he was doing even then that Uncle Tristram doesn't know about. How did you meet him? said Dominic.

——It's not a nice story, said Röhl flatly.

——I really would like to talk to a man called Eisler, who owned the science publishing house that Earnest bought at the end of the war.

——The last I heard of Eisler was that he was living over the wall, in East Berlin. He must have family there. If you don't have any ties, they chuck you out at a certain age, so the West can pay your pension. They call them what translates roughly to 'Wall-worthies'.

Röhl chuckled, as though the thought of Checkpoint Charlie filled with bewildered stateless sixty-year olds with cardboard suitcases was a rich joke. It filled Libby with distress.

——It sounds like the plot of a Brecht play, said Dominic.

——Brecht just took the essence of Berlin. He did not invent over-the-top theatre, *pretending* to be real, we were doing un-reality already in life. The Germans are a theatrical people. The SS uniforms were created by a theatre designer, Röhl added, sadly, as if the act had poisoned the mimetic arts for ever.

Abigail came by. Of all the Clan McMelmonts, she alone had made her kilt look as if it belonged.

——You look radiant, my dear. Röhl kissed Abigail's perfumed hand.

——Gunter is the most gallant, as well as the most cultured man in Europe, said Abigail.

Röhl gave Dominic his card.

——Let me know if you need any help finding Eisler, I have numerous contacts in the East, said Röhl.

Meanwhile, Melmont's two-tone Rolls-Royce proceeded grandly down the drive and out through the electric gates as

if collapsing share prices meant nothing, on its way to rendez-
vous with the Important Guest. The gates had scarcely been able
to close for the last hour, so thickly did the vehicles bearing
guests now arrive; the swivelling electronic eye on the eaves of
the single-storey gatehouse would have become dizzy, if it were
human.

Around the same time as Melmont left, the tireless machine
recorded another car, a limousine bearing Saul Goldfrapp
driving up to the house. There's a still from its surveillance tape,
with date and time overlay, in Dominic's book on Melmont.
Goldfrapp is wearing a crumpled white linen suit, and looking
unhappily out of the back window of the car towards the camera,
like a heifer that knows it is going to slaughter.

Accompanying Goldfrapp but unseen by the spy camera was
his accountant, for Goldfrapp could not bear to read the plunging figures himself, and Eva, the diva from Brooklyn, who had
recently displaced Mrs Saul Goldfrapp III in the businessman's
bed. It was Eva's first time in England, and she kept being mis-
taken for Marilyn Monroe, which bizarrely made her feel she
was someone at last. Though she was yet to go to Hollywood,
she *had* fucked one of the Kennedy boys, but she could never
remember which one. Dominic's sober and incriminating tome,
The Book of Melmont (850 pages before you get to the index) is
crammed with all the facts, figures and meetings of Melmont's
double dealings with every dirty little country that wanted a
nuke, but doesn't even mention the delightful and colourful Eva.

Eva would be dead in a year, of a sudden arachnoid sub-
cortical haemorrhage, having been flown out to Hollywood to
be discovered. Taken ill after lunch in the Beverley Wilshire

Hotel, she could not speak to tell them her hotel room number so she was thrown in the LAPD drunk tank where she—mercifully—died quite quickly. One of the morgue attendants who assembled like vultures every day for a month to ravish her unclaimed, astonishing Venusian body was an enterprising fellow. He streamed his fellow-workers' serial necrophilia live onto a pay-per-view website. One smart guy! He must be a millionaire now.

Eva laughed at herself as she got out of the car, adjusting her vast panama hat. As she raised her arms, much of her magnificent chest was on view, for her cleavage and Saul's shares plunged alike. She scrunched across the priceless gravel in expensive fuck-me pumps, to inspect a large and imposing inscription, apparently carved in stone. In a loud fearless voice she read out,

——"This Cranolithic Stone Co-memorates the Earnest Melmont Cryo-genic Wing of St Swithin's Hospital, which was opened", blah, blah, "by His Royal Highness Prince George, Duke of Rockall and Shannon, Who in Accordance wid Royal Custom an' Tradition of Healing Laid His Hands on Zenocrate Melmont with Prayers for Her Benefit, which Took Immediate Effect"… . Hey, Saul, dig this! D'ja think we missed it? Oh wow, the prince can do miracles!

——Maybe he can do one on Melmont's share prices, said Goldfrapp, close behind her, peering over her shapely shoulder. Goldfrapp's late alcoholic father had been a funeral mason, and beater of his wife. As Goldfrapp's mother screamed, his father would ritually recite the names of all thirtynine types of memorial stone commercially available in the US, in a thick

Ukranian accent. The adult Goldfrapp might have swallowed the historic Royal Miracle, carved in stone before him. But his anger, and his father's early lessons in geology now merged to struggle against the Melmontian miasma.

——Wasserfuck's Cranolithic? Some kind of patent granite?

——Honey, you asked the wrong person. I didn't even graduate charm school.

Goldfrapp reached out to touch the inscription and it fell forward, revealing that 'Cranolithic' was in fact a mock-up polystyrene bas-relief panel, painted to look like granite. The large dot of the 'i' on 'Prince' had been drilled through and in the recess behind was a video camera whose basilisk eye was lined up at groin level. Goldfrapp put the inscription carefully back in place so the camera lined up again.

——That's exactly how it was, right? I don't want him charging me for breakages on his spy cameras on top of bankrupting me, said Goldfrapp, sourly.

——You go bankrupt and you've had your last blowjob from *me*! said Eva lightly. And why d'ja call it a spy camera? He prob'ly just wants some footage of people enjoying themselves.

——How the fuck can I enjoy myself when the bastard's killing me? He won't even talk about what's happening either.

——Maybe he knows what he's doing and it will all be better tomorrow.

——Believe me, it won't, said Goldfrapp bitterly.

To cheer Goldfrapp up, Eva mugged at the hidden camera, provocatively smoothing her skirt down, then cast round her with her hands in mock-horror, saying,

——Oh, my, Mr Melmount, if you'd told me you were shooting

from there, I woulda bleached my tush! Shame on you! Bad boy! But look at this mark on the back of my dress! I had to steal a towel from the Ritz Hotel but it weren't enough, I'm getting so wet for you!

——Save it for Fox, snarled Goldfrapp.

Eva immediately pretended to go down on all fours on the expensive gravel, hissing and growling, to Goldfrapp's alarm. By 'Fox', Goldfrapp had meant the film company, Twentieth Century Fox, which had expressed an interest in screentesting Eva. But 'Fox' or 'the fox' was also their pet name for a snappy little bedroom game they used to enjoy together with his-'n'-hers tasselled butt plugs. Not any more! Eva's dead, and Goldfrapp was last heard of living on welfare and under heavy medication in the bluecollar underbelly of the New World, convinced that someone whose name he dare not utter ate his soul.

Guests still continued to arrive at Melmont Keep like a colony of migrant bees to a new hive, approaching from improvised carparks on foot, cramming the air with chatter, the women thrilling the eye with varieties of summer clothes, all asking when the Prince would come. But just as in apiculture, the Monarch is not the first to arrive in the swarm's new home, in human affairs, the Prince's arrival would be later, after he had opened the hospital wing. Melmont was now escorting the tall fair-haired figure, slightly stooped, down the main passage of the new wing of St Swithin's after the main opening ceremony. While his exploits had already been set in polystyrene, His Royal Highness had no inkling about what Melmont intended him to do now.

For Melmont, it was all going to plan, except the Prince was followed by an entourage which included two young detectives, who had already warned the philanthropic tycoon against touching the Royal Person.

——The rule is, sir, he can touch you, but you can't touch him.

Melmont smiled his most sphinx-like smile. He needed only to lose the two unwanted guardians while steering Prince George into the cryogenic ward where the remains of his beloved Zenocrate lay. He would then get the prince to touch his daughter and bring her back to life.

——Gentlemen, this is my hospital. I built it. It is all *safe* because I would not allow it otherwise. My rule to *you* is, I can talk to *you*, but don't *you* try to talk to *me*.

And his arm went up again around the prince, and on they went down the spotless passage. The Prince alone seemed to tolerate Melmont's bearlike embrace of the Blood Royal. Melmont's appearance was even stranger than usual, because he had rejected the kilt as insufficiently becoming and was wearing a pair of vast, hastily sewn Melmont Tartan trews, held up by red braces.

Abigail brought up the back of the little procession, trailing behind the two detectives. The thick-necked creatures growled to each other as they mooched down the corridor, seething with resentment at their charge's connivance and Melmont's very obvious contempt for the rules which the rest of us live by.

——This is *meanterbe* fukken security, innit?

——It's well out of order.

——Wot if 'e 'ad a gun?

——Yeah, right.

—Well out of order.

One of the goons saw Abigail smile to herself as she over-heard the exchange, and said angrily,

—You can laugh. One mistake is all it takes and that's our jobs gone. That's it. Years of starvation wages and then kaboom. You're out on your ear. Screwed by The Firm!

—I am smiling because my husband knows about bravery. He is loyal enough to protect the prince without a need for guns, said Abigail.

The young detectives, oblivious of Melmont's army career, stared contemptuously at his bloated back.

—Your Highness, there is one part of the wing that is not on the Official Schedule, that I would like to show you briefly now before Luncheon, Melmont boomed at his most unstoppable.

Prince George looked up at him, watery eyed and nodded. The brown envelope that had been passed to him earlier made all kinds of informalities possible.

—As long as it doesn't take too long.

—It won't take a moment for you to see what is being done there.

They turned the corner ahead of the escorts. Melmont swiftly pulled the prince in through a side door and shut it before the prince realised what was happening. The grumbling detectives rounded the corner a moment later to find there was no prince. There was only a passage with a sealed blue door without an outside handle. Stencilled on the door was 'CRYOGENIC UNIT NO ADMITTANCE'.

Inside the unit, the lighting was dim and reddish. Melmont led the baffled prince towards what looked like a large zinc bath filled with carbon dioxide smoke. The influence of the royal minders had been gratifyingly reduced to warning, muffled bangs offstage as they beat without avail on the sturdy steel of the door.

——I understand Samuel Johnson was taken to London as a child by his mother, to be cured by a monarch's touch of his scrofula. I would be grateful for a similar favour from the monarchy. Touch my daughter and she will, naturally, recover her faculties, if you are who you say you are.

Melmont gestured to Zenocrate, his eldest child, who lay in suspended animation in the middle of the swirling mist, a spotlight on her angelic face. The best plastic surgeons in the land had repaired her so her skull appeared whole again. There was not a mark on her. A frosty chart gave her name and the date of the accident. The Prince tried to appear interested, but was uneasy at the increasing distraction coming from the other side of the only door.

——Blue Blood Alert! Blue Blood! Open this fukken door! Oorright! Jump to stage four. Get backup!

——I think my people need me to go back, said Prince George weakly.

Melmont thought otherwise. He held the prince tightly as he recited rapidly,

——In the future, Sire, there is hope that Medical Science will be able to revitalise Persons who today are written off as Cabbages. But for now the last resort of hopeless cases is the Seed of those what can perform Miracles. I am a Monarchist. Lay your hands on my daughter and cure her, or else you are a fraud and a chopped worm! Melmont said, his voice suddenly rising.

The very last time anyone had spoken to him like that, Prince George had been eight and his father's tone had set his toilet training back by several years. He hesitated. The banging on the door increased. Melmont's tones became honeyed but urgent.

——You do realise, don't you, that I love the Queen. Our dear dear Queen. It makes me so upset when she is criticised in the newspapers. When I own a paper, I will never.... . Please, if there is a god, you'll do it for me. She's related, I know. At least your aunt, or is it great-aunt, isn't she? Well that should do it, whatever it is. A touch, that's all. Won't cost you a bean. In fact I'll give you another five grand.

The thought of the money was clearly appealing to the prince, but he was also aware that if he failed the offer would be cancelled.

——I don't know what I could do. She doesn't seem to be even breathing, Prince George said.

Melmont put his hand beseechingly on the Prince's sleeve.

——She breathes. In and out. At low temperatures it's just slow.

The prince, in spite of himself, had started to raise his arm in Royal blessing when the lock suddenly broke on the door, and the minders burst in. Their emergency training snapped into place, and they were calm as they surrounded their precious charge.

——This way please, sir.

The Prince gave Melmont a sad look, as he was being led away; as if he had wanted to help but knew it wouldn't have made a blind bit of difference.

Melmont followed him out of the room, and very shortly the

gate camera of Melmont Keep recorded the arrival of the last five cars, one of which, sporting a pennant and with a Bend Sinister coat of arms on the passenger door, was bearing His Royal Highness Prince George towards a lavish celebratory lunch. The Ol' Bastard was welcomed into Melmont Keep, where the memorial to miraculous royal healing powers had already disappeared. In its place was a waist-high amphora filled with lilies, for purity.

XIV

Melmont in Extremes

F OR THE VISITORS WHO STAYED after the meal, the Melmont children had been rehearsed to provide entertainment in the great hall. The white carpet had been removed and they danced a reel to the bagpipes on polished parquet, their numbers making a hypnotic swirl, seen from the top of the great staircase. The dance ended, to applause, then the band in the minstrels' gallery struck up again immediately. The youngest daughter began an animated sword dance over two crossed claymores. Bars of yellow light splashed down across the floor from the great vast window depicting Samson's suicidal moment, mixed with patches of royal purple in the robes of those high-caste philistines who Samson was taking down with him.

But Melmont, heavyhearted at his failure to get his royal visitor to pull his weight and act the part, could not enjoy the spectacle. He floated outside onto the gravel, stopping at the gold-fish pond in the rockery where the drive now divided into two, with the newest route going towards the clutter of one-storey offices that Interlease was now poised to take possession of.

Goldfrapp followed him out and was about to hail Melmont

when he realised that Melmont was relieving himself in the lower basin of the massive ornamental fountain. Above him, the lead statue of a small naked cherub joyfully released a further jet, as if in relief for all the years the cherub had spent drily in architectural salvage. Goldfrapp paused politely till Melmont's tinkling ceased.

——A nice place you have here, said Goldfrapp. If I had a place like this I'd be really happy.

——I'm happy, said Melmont. Pointing down at some agitated goldfish, he added, those fishes know what I think of them.

——Really fancy grounds. We need to talk, sir. Could we take a walk?

——I'd take you round, but looks like rain to me. Those fair-weather cumuli are retreating before a cold front, or I'm a chopped worm, said Melmont, as he groped to zip up his fly.

——Beside the weather turning nasty, the *other* downside is that we still haven't had the final accounts from you to complete the purchase of your company, and all this time, the bottom is falling out of your shares, said Goldfrapp bitterly.

——I don't see why that's a downside for you, said Melmont. You'll just get the shares more cheaply than the ones you bought before you announced the bid.

Goldfrapp had been secretly hoping to offload his illicitly obtained earlier share purchases at a great profit when the takeover was announced. Now the shares were worth a quarter of what he had paid for them, and he couldn't even use them as collateral, because the general perception was that Melmont Inc. was going bust.

——I *can't* complete the purchase if you don't open your

books. Right now I am committing financial suicide. It cost me about ten thousand bucks just now, waiting for you to finish your leak, Goldfrapp whined.

——I suggest you withdraw your bid then, if you are unhappy with the terms, said Melmont. His face wore an innocently inquisitive expression, as he watched the elongation of a dark and ragged cloud which had suddenly materialised from the direction of the Welsh Marches.

——I *can't* withdraw now, without getting my ass kicked in by my board in New York! Wake up, Earnest! That's not coffee you're smelling, it's the fucking building on fire! You're *dying* here, as well! Goldfrapp was red in the face now, and shouting, standing close. I can't believe I've gotten in a deal with someone who is determined to commit hari-kiri!

——Don't you mean, seppuku? That's when I chop your head off first, Melmont said sweetly.

——Whatever, snarled Goldfrapp. You sure got the right stained glass up there! Samson at the gates of Gaza, pulling the whole load down on himself. That's *you*, buster!

——Paul, what did you think of Prince George? Melmont always misremembered Goldfrapp's first name, unless he was exonerating himself with the DTI.

——It's Saul, for the fortieth time. Ah, *fuck!*

In additional mockery, a chill gust of wind now flicked a stream of water aside from the naked cherub above to the side of the fountain, and ornamental piddle rattled down smartly in big droplets onto Goldfrapp's bald pate. He drew out a folded cotton handkerchief and angrily began to dry himself off.

——I don't give a shit about Prince George. I don't give a shit he turned up to open your lousy hospital. I live in the *real* world, where if you don't look out you get sucked down the toilet fast. I warn you, if I'm going, you're coming too, buddy!

Goldfrapp wagged an aggressive finger at Melmont's midriff, then turned to go. Melmont still stared at the sky.

——If he'd just stretched out his hand, he could have saved her, he murmured to himself.

It was said too softly for Goldfrapp marching away across the terrace to hear. The ruined salesman turned scrunchingly one last time on the meticulously graded gravel. *All stones to measure between 12.5 mm and 14.4 mm along their axial length, incorrect stone to be removed at contractor's own cost.* There had been uncountable tons of it and it had ended up costing, weight for weight, more than the best smoked salmon, Melmont's accountant had said. Melmont had just laughed.

——Face it, you deserve to be ruined!! Goldfrapp screamed.

Melmont didn't answer. He appeared to be gently reaching out to something over the goldfish pond. He was off in a world of his own, doing what even God is not supposed to do, to change the past. Zenocrate was going to rise from the dead and stand before him. In his mind, as he moved his hand, Melmont was going to play God, a kinder one than the brute who made this narrow cruel world.

——Rise, Zenocrate. Be well. Embrace your father. But it was not Zenocrate who came to Melmont before the year was out but others, the Evil Ones with roots below and beyond the Veil.

ffl   ffl   ffl

Melmont, returning from America, had not even noticed whether there was anyone else on Concorde, then suddenly, over Greenland just before dawn, there they were, the horrid Hitler-worshipping Harbingers, who all those years ago had purchased General Trapp's volumes of *Mein Kampf* bound in the skins of Germany's victims.

Melmont woke with a start to find their three evil faces staring at him with bright, mocking expectation. It had not been a good six months for him. The senseless feud between him and Goldfrapp had dragged on into the winter and looked to finish them both off.

While he was twice the age and thrice the weight he had been at his last encounter with the Evil Ones, they didn't seem to have changed at all. Their hideous leather clothes were the same too, looking as if they had been lifted none too carefully, from some SS officer's burial ground.

——Surprise! they chorused rustily. Cavernous-cheeked Veronika and her graveyard chums, Hilda and Helmut, all sniggered, as Melmont's bosky eyebrows shot up.

Behind the ghoulish trio, the Machmeter confirmed the spectres had no trouble keeping pace with a plane going faster than a speeding bullet. Melmont concluded he was dreaming; but then Helmut, who had a swastika emblem on a great knuckleduster of a ring on his right hand, reached out and rubbed the ring painfully on Melmont's nose. The touch convinced him that they were real, or real enough to do business with again, though Hilda laid her fingers on her lips, warning him not to speak yet. He intuited her singsong voice,

——*Soft, hear our balm in these, your troubled times!*

—Am I finished? Melmont asked her, with his eyebrows.

Hilda's thin mouth moved to answer, but it was the strange, half-strangulated helium-high voices of the other two together that came out; a voice from eternity, chilling and yet reassuring.

—*My eldritch witching child, be comforted!*

Close that prophetic eye. Bright one, it hasn't happened yet!

Great Melmont's fall is yet to be!

For now, remain our treasured instrument!

Melmont was about to point out that he was nobody's instrument except his own, when Veronika reached out a ghastly hand and stroked Melmont's shoulder. He felt the tension draining away from his body. A feeling of warmth and ease suffused him. It was delicious. He had no worries, suddenly. Veronika pointed out of the window.

—*Stay with us, keep the faith and you will get Everything.*

Everything sounded good, to Melmont.The voices from the eternal shades continued,

—*Behold our solemn covenant,*

Great Melmont rules, in Never-Never Land!

Outside the plane window, the Northern Lights glowed and wove themselves into a mighty 'M' in confirmation of promised power, the same sigil of Mannaz that Eric the Red's chronicler recorded ten centuries before. Then the Mannaz sigil seemed to be floating in the air in the main cabin. Melmont reached out for the enigmatic green rune, now about the size of a man's hand. Though it was more tactile than Macbeth's ethereal dagger, it was slippery and eluded his capture, then vanished.

All this time, the plane's nose had pointed firmly east, towards the pink spot of a rapidly arriving dawn. The horizon was rapidly lightening now as the plane sped away from the night. Melmont suddenly felt tired. He closed his eyes. He knew Veronika and Hilda were still there, because someone was tucking a blanket around him. He was not on his own. Someone cared for him. Veronika's hypnotic, smeary tobacco-deep rasp reassured him,

——*Sleep, master. Your great time is to come!*
The present is a bubble. Let it burst. Let money… disappear!
You will get more.

——But will I ever have *The Moon*? Melmont whispered restlessly. He sensed Veronika had disappeared, and it was Hilda who now bent close to speak to him, for her voice was higher, softer, with almost a religious tone.

——*Warrior Lord of the Forties, the Eighties cower before you, and are abased!*

——But will I ever have *The Moon*? Melmont repeated, and opened his eyes to see that only Helmut was left.

Helmut telegraphed instructions into Melmont's frontal lobes, with masculine abruptness.

——*Be swift. The night recedes. Your question fruitless, ask a better.*

But Melmont had no better question. He began to repeat,
——Will I?

Helmut held up his hand. He was becoming more ethereal by the second as the light became stronger. His lips did not move, but Melmont heard the voice in his head.

——*Since you insist, know you will never have* The Moon.

——Why not? Who's to stop me? said Melmont, suddenly belligerent.

——*The Man in The Moon is your undoing*, intoned Helmut. And then he was gone.

The sun's first horizontal rays flooded into the cabin, then abruptly checked, without a cloud in the sky, as the supersonic plane flew past the penumbra into the ground-zero footprint of a total solar eclipse. Looking out at the phenomenon, at the fleeting moment of complete occlusion, Melmont glimpsed the cheeky features of Bruce 'Ocker' Midrash superimposed on the dark disc of the moon. Ocker was wearing a hat with corks suspended round the brim, and he winked at Melmont and mouthed a 'G'day!' before his apparition faded.

The Evil Ones' reassurances were the only outside support Melmont received, that cold winter. In Melmont Keep (UK), there was a war of occupation going on, with Goldfrapp's Interlease in partial occupation but neither side giving in. Melmont, whose family still occupied the main house, had been forbidden access to all data by Goldfrapp until he declared his accounts. Since, unsurprisingly, nothing was forthcoming, his staff had their instructions to stay put night and day, denying Melmont physical repossession of the unheated temporary buildings which were Goldfrapp's remaining toehold from the disastrous merger. The electric gates had frozen, half-open and the cold weather only appeared to stiffen resolve on both sides. Outside the grounds, the easterly wind off the Urals mocked Oxbridge Council's penny-pinching omission to invest in snow ploughs, while inside on the majestically laid out approach roads, passing cars from both sides of the war skidded into each other helplessly on thick icesheets that had formed over the expensive but poorly drained gravel.

Goldfrapp, fighting his own board battles in New York, issued a fatuous challenge to Melmont to 'get his cowardly fat ass home and face the music'. When Melmont declined to dance to this tune, Goldfrapp appointed whale-watchers to every terminal in the country, as if the 'coward' Melmont might try to gain an advantage by slipping into the country unobserved.

Thus it was that more than one 'spy' witnessed a suspiciously bulky figure heave-ho'ing down the narrow access stairway portside of the slender white supersonic plane just arrived at Heathrow's Terminal 4. After arranging to share the handsome bonus for first sighting, the agents then delegated a spokes-person to segue to the nearest phone, dial in a prearranged number and speak the key words.

—Big Turkey's hit the ground. His limo driver says he's got a meeting in London, but he could be home tonight.

Crackling in the agent's receiver, an artificially bright voice could be heard to reply, from the snowy depths of Oxbridge-shire,

—That's OK, we're ready for him anytime. I thought he might have been here earlier because someone crept in during the night and poured plaster of Paris into the toilet bowls.

The Department of Trade and Industry's investigation panel was waiting as Melmont swept in late, swiftly and grandly, having not paused even to dust the snow from his shoes. It was cold enough for the snow to linger even on the pavements of the South Bank. Melmont did not behave like a suicidally careless business man who was about to have his reputation stripped from him. He was openly amused to see that the leader of the team was a woman. He smiled his most patronising smile at her.

——How can I help you, my dear? Would you like to hear a vindication from a simple business aspect first?

——Mr Melmont, you are here to answer questions from our agenda. We vindicate from over here, said Tessa Prufrock. She had risen from the ranks of the civil service by talent alone, and was well up to punching the full twentyfive rounds with the great bully.

Some hours into the investigation, the attitudes of both sides had not changed. Tessa found they were making as much headway with the former interrogator as an Inuit bone arrowhead would make on the chain mail of an invader. There was always a huge glacier of undisclosed information which somehow Melmont was able to use to distance himself. He always had a right reply, with an infinite resource of mitigating and unforeseen circumstances which, apparently, covered every irregularity that they had been able to cite.

By the third day, even Tessa was starting to despair of getting to the bottom of the matter. The investigation was in danger of chasing its own tail, and time was running out.

——Allow me to explain, said Melmont for the fortieth time. Saul Goldfrapp saw my dividends payout every year and so he invested in my company, like many other fortunate people. Saul authorised Interlease to buy a third of the company's shares, before the sale to Interlease was announced. When the share price became depressed, he did not have the money to complete the deal.

And they were taken off to where it all was supposed to make sense, on the wings of eagles. And it did seem to make sense, until they landed again.

——What about the number of shares sold to Interlease by you in the weeks prior to the collapse, from some of your unlisted companies?

Melmont shrugged.

——Again, it's very simple. I anticipated a decline in share prices once I had left the company.

——Did you ever intend to leave your company?

——I had undertaken a year's stewardship once Interlease was in the saddle. I was going to stick to that, until I found out that they didn't have enough cash to complete the sale. They have to withdraw now. There are American officials illegally occupying my buildings. But I am looking for an amicable solution. I am not seeking their arrest and deportation which I am entirely at liberty to do, calling upon the police to act for me, naturally, Melmont added graciously.

——Mr Melmont, do you consider you acted wisely in all this?

Melmont stood and put his coat on. He felt like banging their stupid heads together. Instead he said, sweetly,

——My reputation is very dear to me. I will remind you that I would contest, with punitive and exemplary damages, any defamatory statements. I am now leaving for my democratic duties. I have to vote now, as this investigation, rightly, was not considered important enough to arrange pairing in the House. Good day, gentlemen, and one cow.

With that, the former cattle drover left ostensibly for Westminster, but without his briefcase. The shocked officials were still talking among themselves as they slowly gathered up their papers, when Melmont swept in again, having 'forgotten' to pick up his case.

None of this was accidental. Inside the briefcase was a voice-activated taperecorder, to pick up unguarded remarks after his departure that might indicate how close his detractors were to the truth.

In the carpark, Melmont handed over the briefcase to a waiting technician. Melmont had generously taken on Frank twenty years ago, although, or perhaps because, the youth had 'form'—breaking into cars with coathanger wires. Frank occupied the position of court jester, able to say the unsayable to Melmont.

—That kid pokin' his nose into corners could be the def of you. Why d'joo want a biography of your life anyhow? If you want it to be like those biographies of tinpot despots you do which get pulped unread you'd better get yourself anuvver Orfer. An' if you're in the market for a warts-an'-all job, a lot of the subject matter is quite tasty, I mean you do sail close ter the wind, Ernie. So that's a high risk. And believe me anything written about you by a queer public schoolboy who's never 'ad a proper job is bound to be knocking copy. Because, what's his experience of life, at his age, apart from taking it up the arse?

—It will make a man of Dominic. I'm giving him a start in life, like I gave you a start, Frank, said Melmont, unanswerably.

♫   ♫   ♫

The S-Bahn overhead light railway carried Dominic twenty feet in the air above the ugly concrete of the Berlin Wall, as it had been doing nervelessly for twenty years. Apart from Checkpoint Charlie, it was the only official route between East and West Berlin. The wall itself which they flew over appeared unimpressive, viewed from the shabby carriages. On alighting in the East, Dominic had his bags searched by a pimply young Ossi in uniform who stamped his daypass without even making eye contact, before being released to the Communist Bloc.

Dominic was young enough to be excited by the idea that Konrad Eisler had been a dissident, though the fussy old man who greeted him in his cheaply furnished apartment didn't seem like an anti-Nazi hero. His wife had died ten years before of lung cancer and Eisler lived alone, inexplicably cheerful. With his beaky face, shrunken frame and yellow cardigan he reminded Dominic of a friendly canary.

——Life could be worse. I'm not dead, yet.

Dominic, as instructed by Röhl, had brought fresh vege-tables, delicacies which only the higher ranks of the Stasi had access to in the East. Eisler hailed each one as Dominic lifted them out of the bag.

——Carrots! Manly carrots! And a lettuce too. And leeks! Gifts from the biographer of Captain Melmont! What indiscretions will I be tempted to? Just *look* at that fine kraut! During the war I lived on a much smaller one than this for a whole month. His old hands tremblingly stroked a hard white cabbage, the size of a skull.

Later, with a glass of schnapps apiece, settled into child-sized uncomfortable armchairs, Eisler started to tell Dominic what he knew of Melmont's early life.

——He had several *noms de guerres* in those days from ciga-rettes like Du Maurier, so if the Germans caught him they would not know. He was Corporal Goldflake for a week, but it was too Jewish. When he became Melmont he also became the British Army censor, and he was very restrictive of many stories, in fact he would black them. The way to get things through was to mention *him*. That characteristic is the one I think that is still strong in him. Of course he betrayed me after rescuing me. Later, he took the stock and carried everything off to England with him in an army truck. War booty. Like the Elgin Marbles! We were to pretend to the Americans, if we were asked, that the Russians had stolen them, but when he reached England it turned out it was Captain Melmont who had exported the whole business and we were left with nothing.

Eisler laughed at the memory.

—How did you meet Gunter Röhl?

—I'm sorry, I've never heard that name.

Eisler cupped his ear and then pointed to the central light fitting and the telephone, to indicate the position of likely microphones, adding,

—But we could still go for a walk if you don't mind the time it takes me getting downstairs.

In the street, Eisler creakingly led Dominic to an open empty space, opposite where a vast ruined facade of a church brooded. Trees were growing through it, out of the brickwork and stucco, silver birch roots digging into the tops of the crumbling walls of the nave. In the East, God was definitely dead.

—I once ran down this street with *forty* Brownshirts after me, said Eisler, as if he wanted Dominic not to forget the exact number of Brownshirts. They slowly walked on. In the distance appeared the Brandenburg Gate, forming part of the Wall, now.

—We can talk here. I have no proof, but I believe Gunter

Röhl made a deal with Melmont to conceal something in his past. It was not uncommon, of course, because those who conducted interrogations had wide discretion and could do what they liked. Melmont told me he had bought back photographs of his commanding officer and a rentboy from the Russians.

Dominic realised with a small tightening of his stomach that the commanding officer the Russians had been seeking to blackmail would have been his uncle. Had Melmont been black-mailing Cole? Dominic could have sworn the relationship was friendlier than that.

—What happened to the photograph?

—I don't know. I doubt if it has very much relevance today. It took place all such a long time ago. Over there, look, is where the Russian section ended. History passes so quickly.

A football stadium nearby began voiding its mass. On the main street the crowds suddenly thickened, with men all walking determinedly in the same direction, oddly quiet and subdued for a football crowd. In the cross-streets, drawn back forty yards from the main road, Dominic saw the turrets of heavy tanks.

Eisler followed his glance.

—*That's* why we don't have your exhibitionistic football hooligans. Oh, and the other depressant is that one in three of these charming people around us will be a Stasi informer. To return to Röhl, he has done very well for himself since, I know. He is probably good at exploiting the conflict to make money, and would not see it as wrong. It's the oldest game in the world, since before prostitutes dressed as Helen of Troy and stood out-side the town walls.

The crowd was getting thicker and Eisler said he was tiring.

Dominic thanked him, shook the hand of the frail old man, and walked towards the S-Bahn. When he looked back, a minute later, Eisler was still there, leaning on his stick and waving to him cheerily. The crowd flowed past the old man, with its composition of thirtythree percent government informers. The distant human mix was duncoloured, and alarmingly robotic, following a route controlled by discreetly parked army tanks. Turning around again, Dominic realised that an older man had stopped and was staring at him from twenty feet away. Dominic stared back. Eye contact, at last. There were six hours to go before his daypass expired and his rudimentary German need not stand in the way of his getting laid by a goodlooking robot.

Something is Uncovered

OUTSIDE MELMONT KEEP, under slate-grey skies, Goldfrapp's executives, dressed in arctic Parkas, were carrying camping equipment and stores of food from a hire van into their offices, preparing for a lengthy siege. They were supervised by Gary, a tall blonde youth with a highly strung nature who had taken the phone call. As the vital stores were accounted for, Gary noticed a large grey Mercedes roll up and park in the distance outside the big house, but did not recognise the distinguished, whitehaired man who got out. The chill red sun had set and Gary had unloaded the final item, a pair of portable toilets, when there was the sound of a second large car approaching less cautiously through the frozen gates. Melmont's black-and-tan Roller made its way over the ice sheets and halted next to the Mercedes.

The visitor in the Mercedes, the courteous Gunter Röhl, had thought he was merely coming to pay his respects to Mrs Melmont, but Melmont who arrived shortly afterwards had another plan. Demanding abruptly that Röhl follow him into the depths of the cold, icy house, he led the way in silence, holding a vast altar candle that had been donated to his wife by Father Cowley. When he was in a spot he judged sufficiently remote, Melmont announced in a stage whisper that he had received news that Vanov had at last arranged for the theft of a nuclear warhead from a laboratory in Murmansk. When it arrived in East Germany he would need Röhl to make sure it got to the West. Röhl felt his stomach tighten a little in nervousness at the boldness and novelty of the enterprise. Not to speak of its dangers if the perpetrators were caught smuggling weapons grade uranium.

——Where is it going after that?

——I won't tell you. If I say Israel, that'll make up for all the poor Jews you worked to death in your factory and why should you have a good conscience about that? said Melmont.

——I don't feel that great about making it available to Pakistanis who are dying to drop it on Indian Hindus either, said Röhl.

——Just do the job. Allow me to worry about the ethics for you. You do the technical stuff, *jawohl*?

Getting a nuclear warhead over a border without detection occupied Röhl's ingenious (if morally quiescent) mind over supper. His solution, which arrived with the port and stilton, was to dissolve the highly enriched uranium in nitric acid and pump it through a stainless steel pipe which predated the wall, from one of his refineries in the Eastern section, close to the border, to a second holding tank in the West. When it reached the West, it could be reconstituted for onward transport, all without arousing the suspicions of border searches and geiger counters.

Melmont was sceptical. Forty years of nuclear research had come up with the broad truth that there was no telling what nuclear substances got up to if they were left to their own devices.

——That is a butthole stupid idea. You are just making a concentrated soup of nuclear particles where the rapid decay particles all settle in the same band of sediment, and before you know where you are, the nitric acid boils and pouf!

——We minimise the sediment with an agitator paddle in both tanks. You immediately take the acid off the other end anyhow, with vacuum boiling.

Melmont slowly came round to the idea of slipping Russian warheads under the Berlin Wall in liquid form.

——Alright, go ahead. But your Nazi putz is on the chopper if it fails, said Melmont, darkly.

——It won't fail, said Röhl, drily. He had got into the habit of ignoring Melmont's preposterous and uncivilised threats.

In Murmansk, the low-security military unit was breached that very night, as the deteriorating weather conditions gave cover. At thirtynine degrees Fahrenheit below freezing, the savage night wind blew horizontally through icicle-strewn perimeter fences, a metre deep in snow. The nearest watchtower had been dimly visible, till the electricity had failed. Now two heavily wrapped figures were clumsily cutting their way in through the fence unnoticed, using bolt croppers. They hissed curses as they slowly chopped through the rolls of razor wire, half buried in snow, in the dark. After twenty minutes they were inside the compound, leading an empty sled towards one of the darkened buildings.

A few minutes later, they came back, dragging the sled with difficulty. On the sled were leaking bags of heavy weapons-grade uranium, wrapped in builder's lead sheeting. This was totally inadequate protection for the two moustachioed thieves, even if the weapons-grade uranium had not been in loose powder form.

The thieves returned to the gap in the wiring still undetected, and departed dragging their nuclear prize into the howling four-month dark. Behind them, a guard lay dying by the smashed laboratory door: his corpse would be frozen solid by morning but retribution would come swiftly. Struggling through the snow towards the getaway Lada flashing its lights through the forest, both men had already inhaled enough radioactive dust to kill a football crowd, and would shortly be dead.

A less-driven, more reflective and altogether gentler kind of snow was falling the next day on middle England, and particularly on the marble angel in the yard of Pargle and Son, Decorative Masonry. The founder, the present owner's great-great-grandfather was descended from masons in nearby Boxly. He had left, expanded to Oxbridge and survived the dip in sales at the end of the Victorian era by diversifying into garden gnomes. The firm still supplied headstone ornaments and other funereal pieces, though much of the work now was for marble kitchens. They had pulled out all the stops for the commission from The Big House, as Melmont Keep was known locally to anyone over seventy.

In the wide and untidy yard in front of Pargle's marble-cutting rooms the snow swirled about a massive special commission from Melmont of a winged angel, a young girl with long hair and drapery sensuously tumbling off her shoulders to reveal swelling breasts. Melmont had finally given in to biology, and allowed the doctors to sign his eldest daughter Zenocrate's death warrant, but he had stipulated to the masons that her memorial must show an angelic archer, a sport which the young girl had excelled in. The assembled piece was ready to go out, but the addition of a bow made it too tall for the workshop.

The Carrera marble was glowing and suggestively translucent, even in the wintry light at three o'clock with the snowflakes whirling around the mason's chisel. A young mason, the eighth generation of Pargle to work in the yard, had started chiselling an inscription into the base, mittened against the cold, just as the two radioactive thieves in Murmansk had started coughing up alarming quantities of arterial blood.

'Zenocrate Melmont, Beloved Daughter'

The stonecutter's father looked on, rolling a cigarette with his right hand, having lost the tops of the fingers of his left in a works accident, which had kept him out of National Service. A pessimist, he saw the end of the yard's life coming soon. He reckoned the eight-and-a-half percent Value Added Tax which had just come in was going to finish off a number of family businesses.

There being no point in risking his son's spelling on a job this size, the father had carefully spaced out the rest of the inscription in pencil for his son's chisel to follow:

'… of Earnest and Abigail.

Blessed are the Pure in Heart, for they shall see God.'

—Oi just hopes we gets paid, said the father, in a deep rural Oxbridgeshire accent.

——Why wouldn't we?

——'Es goin' bankrup'. 'Es still got the Americans occupying 'alf the buildings.

——Cor, bugger. *Still ?* said the son, politely. He was careful not to show a different opinion to his father in most matters even though his heart was secretly lost to motor racing, not marble. He worked carefully down the main stroke of the 'P' in Pure, only stopping as the light failed at quarter to four.

As young Pargle was finishing up, Dominic arrived outside The Big House. The first thing that he noticed was that an eight-foot-wide radio dish was being hoisted onto the roof, next to a neo-Tudor chimney. Dominic was beckoned up to the roof by Frank, in charge of a small team of local fitters who were making heavy weather of securing the unfamiliar installation.

——It's a transceiver, Dom.

——What's it do?

——You can send and receive pictures all over the world. He probably just wants to watch the expulsion of Goldfrapp's boys live from his yacht.

Melmont's surveillance supervisor always seemed to be without any discretion about his employer, which made him a useful friend for Dominic to cultivate.

——Who's winning the war, Frank?

——We are, no question.

——Has it damaged him?

——No question. But when two crooks are both running share support operations there's bound to be tears, isn't there?

Down on the driveway, an executive saloon drew up and a chauffeured woman got out of the rear seat. Frank pointed.

——That's the DTI lady. She's called Tessa something.

——Has the Department of Trade and Industry got anything on him?

Frank shook his head.

——Getting knobbed by some bird at the DTI is no worse than having your arse tickled wiv a fevver. Mind you, if a tenth of the stuff that Earnest did ever got out, it would be the nick for him, if he's lucky.

——So the DTI investigation is nothing compared with what could come out?

——Right. If half of what is on those tapes I edit for him is true I reckon he's into nukes.

Dominic felt the hairs on the back of his head stand up.

——What do you mean?

——I'm not against it mind. In this world it's every man for 'imself. Radioactive material's a commodity like anything else, innit? That's what 'e does. He buys and sells. Everything's the same for him. He's one amoral *cun'*, an good luck to 'im.

On the gravel drive below, a second car drew up behind Tessa's, and Tristram Cole got out and went into the house.

——Would you help me find out more? Dominic asked hesitantly.

——If the price is right. Could be time for you to put your hand in your pocket, said Frank cheekily.

Dominic produced a box of Panzer 'Mignon' cigars that he had purchased at the duty-free in Berlin, and offered it to Frank.

——Come on Frank, I'm fucking broke, said Dominic.

——I'm not being no Deep Froat for no money. I can't afford principles. You musta had a decent advance, said Frank.

——Three years ago. I've spent it. I do nothing else. The trails go everywhere. I just got back from Germany.

——You 'ave to learn, young man, that everything has its price, said Frank. And wot I know is worth more than some crap cigars. If I tell you everything that's my job gone.

——But if he's trading nuclear devices, people have a right to know, surely, said Dominic. After all we may all get deaded, thanks to who he sells them to.

——If I told you what I know, he'd fuckin' terminate me I reckon.

——I won't reveal my sources, Frank. I promise.

Suddenly the straps holding the big bowl of the radio antenna to the chimney parted, and the antenna fell, bouncing once on the parapet before beginning a giddy glide to the driveway below, where it crashed between the two cars. Frank turned to the shamefaced fitters who had been in charge of the dish till a moment ago.

——You stupid yokels. You stupid hayseed cunts.

——Sorry, Frank, one muttered.

Frank peered after the antenna and said sarcastically,

——If you're going to do that, why didn't you go the 'ole 'og and land it on the DTI's fucking motor before the bitch gets out?

Dominic was not sure from the remark whether Frank had been earlier downplaying the threat to Melmont from the Department of Trade and Industry, but on reflection concluded Frank's hatred of Tessa was probably just consistent with the reflex misogony of his class. That was the trouble with sifting information. So little of it was clean.

Downstairs, apart from a falling satellite dish, a visitor from four hundred years ago would have felt at home. It only needed fleas in every bed and mandolins strung with catgut and a madrigal player in the gallery for all of Olde Englande to come back as if it had never been away. Candles threw their little light on to the snow outside as they guttered messily in the mullioned windows. Tessa, unaware of her recent narrow escape, was attempting to warm her hands at the fireplace, a vast draughty erection in marble. In the middle of the fireplace was a log fire, basting a sucking pig that Abigail was turning on a spit. With the heating gone, Abigail now had chilblains on her ears, like her mother had had during the dreadful winters of the war years.

——I'm sorry, Mr Melmont has been delayed. What can I show you?

——You can tell me something. I don't understand the setup here. Is there no power because the bills haven't been paid?

Abigail stopped turning the spit.

——There are two switches. The lighting switch for everything is in the new buildings and the heating switch is here in the house. So when the Americans turned off the heating, we had to do the same with the electricity.

——That means he must have been heating the house with his business account, said Tessa, scandalised.

——Yes, but not any more, as you can see, said Abigail.

Cole walked in and shook hands civilly with Tessa, and enquired what brought her out in such inclement weather.

——I wasn't getting the answers to my questions in London. Mr Cole, does your bank have enough confidence to continue trading with Mr Melmont, should he sort his present problems out?

——I can make my recommendations, but that's a question for the Board, rather than individuals, said Cole diplomatically.

——And what would your recommendations be?

Before Tessa could discover, there was the further scrunching of gravel and a car was heard to halt. A second later, through the still-open door, Melmont's rear view covered by a vast three-quarter length sheepskin coat could be seen departing the terrace where his Roller had parked, towards the temporary offices.

——Do you want to talk to Mr Melmont? Shall I ask him to come here? asked Cole.

——No thank you. I just wanted to see the layout. I've done a lot of talking with him over the last weeks. It does not go anywhere, said Tessa. She started to leave, then turned at the door.

——Enjoy your sucking pig, she said.

As Tessa's car negotiated its way past the hopelessly deformed radio transceiver, Melmont was confronting the frightened and chilly American executives who comprised the remaining rump of the occupation in one of the unheated temporary building's offices. Three of them had their feet in sleeping bags, like derelicts.

Melmont threw away a half-smoked cigar, and ostentatiously lit another one before exuding a gout of smoke towards his cowed opponents worthy of a steam engine that though still stationary, is being fired up to accomplish its task with glorious, still-accumulating Force of Expansion.

——Paul didn't tell you about the English winter, did he? It can be suddenly arctic. And with these short days! I bet you can hardly see to work after lunch in here. Chilly!

Melmont dug in his fleecelined pockets and produced a sheaf of airline tickets.

—I've just been in Florida. I think I can treat you all to the weekend there to think about whether you want to continue this charade.

Gary, the leader, had been warned by Goldfrapp himself that Melmont was full of guile. Gary swallowed.

—You may be using us to try to send a strong message to Mr Goldfrapp about the control of his company, but he asked me to ask you to reflect on what you are doing because very conceivably you could destroy both companies in the process.

It was true. Melmont's tactics were suicidal to any sane person. Melmont smiled like Set the Egyptian crocodile god of death, chaos and adversity.

—If I was self-destructing, Mr Goldfrapp would be the last person to know. He is like a little boy who catches a lizard by the tail, only to find that the lizard is smarter than he is. He is the one who is going to be left with nothing. The lizard you see can shed its tail and grow a new one, but Mr Goldfrapp will never be able to grow a new lizard from the bit he is holding. I suggest you five consider very carefully what I have said, and let me have your answer about this continuing trespass and incursion. But I swear I shall never force you to leave. It has to be entirely voluntary.

The five agreed to consider what Melmont had said, and Melmont prepared to remove himself, dropping the airline tickets on the chair he had vacated with a flourish.

—Your chance for a new life, gentlemen. And a better one, if I may say so.

Later, Gary was trying to type a letter on a manual typewriter. The most junior of the surviving team, a young Presbyterian called Jeff came in and lit a portable gas ring which after a long while might deliver water hot enough to make coffee. He suspected he might have frostbite in one of his toes, but was afraid to look. Presbyterian business school had not prepared him for anything like this.

Jeff watched the bubbles forming at the side of the saucepan as Gary desultorily typed. Spirits were at an all-time low. Melmont seemed to have sucked all hope away. Jeff now terribly regretted not taking the easy option as a store manager in the Encinitas Radio Shack on the new mall, on the balmy shores of the Pacific.

——Is that your resignation letter? Jeff asked in a low voice.

——I only wish it could be. Two weeks ago I was told by New York to trace which of Melmont's offshore companies own what stock. But all the dockets relating to ownership go round in circles. It's driving me insane.

Jeff nodded in sympathy.

——He is one *evil* motherfucker, concluded Gary.

Upstairs under the servants' quarters in Melmont Keep was a suite of rooms where Frank had been expanding his electronic empire as fast as the Evil Motherfucker's desire to record everything grew. Immune to power cuts, with its own generators, the surveillance headquarters could pick up everything said in or around the temporary buildings through a series of planted bugs. A battery of sophisticated rifle microphones now pointed through an open window at the office where Gary was typing. Frank stopped the tape recorder as Melmont walked in.

——Let's hear what the little pissabeds are saying about me, said Melmont.

Frank spun the two reels back like a DJ on a mixing desk, then pressed 'play'. A voice said, very clearly,

——It's driving me insane.

——Ha! They're cracking. I used to be an interrogator, Frank. They won't be here this time tomorrow. I'm off to London, said Melmont.

——OK, boss. Frank handed Melmont a tape.

——Listen to this one. Tessa at the DTI, last week.

——Where's my biographer?

——The boy? He went home, he complained of not enough action here, said Frank, blowing on his fingerless mittens.

——You didn't let him up here, did you?

——Of course not, said Frank. Otherwise he definitely woulda stayed I imagine.

Overhead, the clouds were clearing and the stars were coming out. Abigail watched as the car's double headlights swept through the stalled gates. A part of Abigail wondered what would happen if the electricity never came back, would the human race actually be happier without technology? Certainly humans often used it simply to make each other wretched. But how would you stop, and where? In the eighteenth century like the Amish? Or before the discovery of fire?

Thanks to Frank, there was to be no rest for Gary and his crew. Technology guaranteed that speakers in the grounds delivered long loud speeches to Goldfrapp's trespassers by Melmont, Churchillian monologues that were calculated to demoralise them even further. Jeff and Gary's little crew had learned to dread the nights. First, martial music would sound; something from Shostakovich's *Leningrad Symphony*, and then Melmont's stentorophonic voice would announce,

——Cold! Cold! Cold, as the retreat from Mos-*kow*! Your tinpot Napoleon, Small Paul Shitpants Goldfrapp, is already in retreat, but he has not told you underlings yet. That is the kind of *nebbish* you are working for. Saul has decided he cannot afford to buy my company, but he will sacrifice all of your jobs one by one, rather than bow to common sense, and the inevitable. Melmont Communications is a laterally and vertically aligned company dedicated to remaining united and powerful under its original creator and true owner, a businessman and publisher who understands and nurtures information systems which are the lifeblood of modern wealth. Get out of my life, you miserable chopped worms!

This was repeated hourly at ear-bruising volume, interspersed with lugubrious classical music.

The author of all this torture was several miles away, in his warm motor car, declining to dip his lights for oncoming vehicles. Melmont slipped the DTI tape into the cassette player and turned up the volume. A male voice said,

——I don't think I've ever seen such neat footwork. All without notes.

Tessa's voice could then be heard saying,

——Agreed, but the accounts he gives of the same actions when he's asked to account for them on different days don't ever tally. He's improvising.

——He'd make a brilliant jazz player, though, the male voice said.

——Yes indeed. But I shall write in my report that this is someone who is quite unsuited for the chairmanship of a publicly quoted company.

The Roller swerved dangerously on the crowded road as Melmont swallowed the insult. The driver of an oncoming truck, perilously overloaded with straw bales, was forced to brake and honked his deepening horn furiously as he went past. Melmont snarled,

——Threats of straw, Tessa. From straw people. I'll show you.

Melmont, unknown to Abigail or anyone else, was travelling to London that night specifically for an appointment with a fertility specialist, and the fact that Melmont was four hours late for the appointment, and that the assistant who had been left to lock up could easily have stored the specimens needed went for nothing. Distinguished Harley Street practitioner Doctor Christian Knobb had been looking forward to the second act of *Don Giovanni*, when he was located in Covent Garden's crowded upper bar—they've expanded it since, but it always seems to be full of the most repellant corporate types: who else can afford opera nowadays?—by a minion bearing his name on a placard. The irritated sperm specialist was then whisked off back to his place of work to supposedly supervise Melmont's solo efforts. Since Melmont had already provided one sample for Melanie, Knobb's presence was redundant and his pretty Australian nurse was delegated to tell the patient to come back another time. Meanwhile Knobb slipped away just in time to enjoy hearing how Don Juan putting his jism about led him to a Bad End.

——Mr Melmont, the centrifuge technique has successfully pioneered the separation of male from female sperm, but it needs a considerably greater volume before we can guarantee success. I know you and your wife have successfully had a number of girls, but several visits are needed so we can put it all on ice for you.

——Get me another test tube, Melmont growled.

Later, having stored the results of Melmont's next *petit mort* in liquid nitrogen, with genuine sympathy in her voice, Melanie said,

——You'd have a better chance of helping yourself if you left it alone for a while. The body needs a chance to recover, she added.

Melmont shook his head.

——Not my style. I'm hands-on. Let's wrap this thing up. How many more do you need?

Common sense finally prevailed and a truce was called at midnight. Melmont went to Jill's flat and knocked on the door. She opened it, unsurprised.

——I provided thirteen specimens today. Abigail can only have one more child. So this is the last chance, unless the technology improves. She shouldn't get pregnant till the Americans get kicked out. She might drop it. We're living under siege, he added.

His subsequent copulation with Jill was miraculously functional, but as perfunctory as ever. Afterwards he rolled over and lit a cigar.

——Call whatsisface and tell him I'm coming to get that medal. Now.

Jill stepped out of the shower to discover that Melmont had gone. She picked up the phone and dialled.

——This is Mr Melmont's secretary. He has been invited to your country to receive the order of the Righteous Friends of Israel for his services to the country, by the Prime Minister. He has asked me to tell you that he has concluded his business in London and is now flying to Tel Aviv in a chartered jet, so he should be with you within hours.

A distant Israeli voice welcomed the news and Jill put the phone down, her duty over. They might sound welcoming to her boss and lover in Tel Aviv but Melmont had, once again, overstepped the mark in her small flat and confiscated any spermicides and contraceptive devices he could find. She had warned him that if he did it again, it would be the last time but the business with the fertility clinic had pushed him over the edge. If Melmont now could not stop himself, she would no longer sleep with him, she resolved. Jill worked for him for another year but the affair was dead.

Alone in the dimly lit surveillance room in the upper echelons of Melmont Keep, Frank nursed his ulcer through the night, overseeing the flickering dials of the output levels of the microphones trained on the temporary buildings down below, to catch the slightest indiscretion of Goldfrapp's dispirited troops. Then on the hour, he would trip a speaker switch. Earplugs would be in vain, and all repose in the wooden huts would be shattered by the hundred-decibel 'Thoughts of Chairman Melmont'.

——Pygmies and wageslaves of the puny semite incompetent from overseas, hear this before you plunge, lemming-like to your doom! There is only *one man* who can lead the company away from the abyss. You must throw yourselves on his mercy. There is *one man* who can save your firm from Outer Darkness, Night and Fog... .

The voice blocked out all other consciousness. Lying in his sleeping bag, Gary knew he was being taken over by another's ideology, in the way that Hitler's speeches carried the unwilling along with them. And after midnight, whenever the voice ceased and silence reigned, after a second the peacocks in their cages would all start shrieking, as if a dozen foxes had broken in and were now preparing to rip the show-offs' gizzards out. At three in the morning, Gary, desperate for sleep, ground his teeth together and broke a crown off.

As Gary's tongue explored the vast jagged and unfamiliar biosphere that his tooth had suddenly become, a sun was rising shyly over the Holy City of Jerusalem, wondering which true faith it would shine on most brightly that day. Armoured bulldozers burst into life and went about their democratic holy work demolishing Palestinian houses and olive groves, while the intact heads of vapourised suicide bombers lay where they had fallen undetected on inaccessible flat roofs. Inside the armoured, smoked-glass window of a hotel suite reserved for foreign celebrities, Melmont, who had already packed his bags for departure, was on the phone, excited. The struggle with Goldfrapp was forgotten. A Scottish daily newspaper was suddenly for sale.

Dominic had volunteered to meet Melmont at Heathrow to drive him home, but Melmont, freshly arrived from Israel, waved Dominic out of the driving seat. Dominic noticed they appeared to be travelling towards Scotland, but characteristically decided to say nothing. After two hours, Melmont reached in his bag and produced a flat blue box, which he proudly passed to Dominic. Inside was a medal of a small boy with a slingshot standing on a vast dead adult warrior.

—David and Goliath. Given to me by the Israeli government.

—What for? said Dominic, unable to stop himself.

—For my efforts for the peace process. It's nice, isn't it?

Dominic affected to admire the curious item. It was hard to see how Melmont was contributing to peace by obtaining nuclear warheads for the Holy Land, but Dominic was never sure how much he was supposed to know of Melmont's extra-curricular activities.

——Are you thinking of moving to Israel? Dominic asked.

——Don't worry. I shall never abandon England in her hour of need.

After two more hours driving towards Scotland, Dominic started to doze. Melmont suddenly said,

——I am cursed in my sperm. They don't think I can produce a son.

——I'm sorry for that.

——Do you know why you are here?

Was Melmont proposing to adopt him? Bugger him? Dominic, unable to second-guess his employer, pretended to be asleep. Melmont said,

——I'll tell you why you are here, Dominic. If Socialism is not to die in this country, it needs a Voice. Dirty Digger Midrash decided to put himself behind the Tories. How many leftwing papers are there? You don't need fingers, an amputee could count the number with his arsehole! Nil! Nought! There are *none*!

Melmont's emphatic redundancy reminded Dominic of the Psalms, which he had chanted in the school chapel. '*Lift up your heads, oh ye gates, and be ye lifted up, ye everlasting doors, and the King of glory shall come in.*' Was Socialism, then, Melmont's god? But Melmont didn't have a god, strictly speaking, beyond Opportunity. Dominic let his mind wander. A light drizzle began, and the intermittent windscreen wipers on the car became upside-down swinging golfclubs which failed to knock the falling rain away. It was a pleasant, if pointless, game.

Melmont interrupted Dominic's hypnogogic reverie to explain the puzzle of their journey north.

——Do pay attention. You are here Dominic, to record a Turning Point for Socialism in this country. I have Bought A Newspaper.

Melmont the Newspaper Tycoon

MELMONT HAD BID SUCCESSFULLY for the *North Briton*, a 'troubled' daily newspaper published in Glasgow, and one whose circulation was declining so rapidly that even Ocker had refused to touch it. Before they arrived at the *North Briton*'s offices, Melmont pulled off the motorway for refreshment. In spite of being officially his biographer, Dominic was unable to record exactly how much breakfast Melmont ate. At one stage he thought there must have been a pile of at least twenty fried eggs on the magnate's plate, but they were gone in a twinkling, and double bacon, sausage, extra neaps and fried bread, were called for three times.

Dominic was not the only one to be dazzled: the serving hatches of the all-night motorway caff were filled with the red, beaming faces of cooks who had never seen a single man consume a whole hour's output from six frying pans before. When Melmont finally rose, belching and wiping his lips on his sleeve, the kitchen staff, down to their last pound of lard, could be heard cheering as if Scotland had scored a winning goal against the Sassenach.

In the car, Dominic noticed that Melmont had acquired two haggises, perhaps in grateful recognition of his services to cholesterol. He was consuming them raw, as he drove. Dirty tranches of slush spurted out from under the big car's wheels on each side as Melmont, approximate as ever in his driving, fought the increasingly foul weather.

—Dominic, you are to bear witness to the rebirth of the people's voice, Melmont intoned. We are living in stirring times! Nothing is stronger than an idea whose time for ovulation has arrived! The Labour Party has given its mandate and seal of approval to the workers' cooperative that is now running the *North Briton!*

Melmont's enthusiasm was contagious. Even so, when Dominic heard the words 'workers' cooperative', he wondered if his boss knew what he was taking on.

But the behemoth was so confident of his imminent grasp of a daily newspaper, Dominic discovered, that he had already ordered the celebratory champagne. It was being carried into the building as Melmont arrived appearing as confident before the reception committee as any Roman Emperor taking his seat at the games.

—Mr Melmont, how will you deal with the cooperative that is now effectively running this newspaper?

Melmont positively glowed with imperial assurance at the members of the newspaper's board, who in theory had the power to veto his purchase.

—In their hearts, they know it is in their interests to support me. Particularly when I have the agreement of you gentlemen here.

——We think you are a very suitable owner. But I don't understand these figures you gave. How can the purchase price of the paper's site be reduced further?

Melmont smiled, secretively.

——Because, Mr McGibley,——and I tell the board this in confidence——I am able to reduce the purchase price of the site by obeying the letter of the contract, which does not mention Value Added Tax as exclusive.

McGibley looked as baffled as everyone else. Melmont explained.

——If VAT is not mentioned as *ex*clusive, then I have established that by law it is *in*clusive, so I have already saved the cooperative one hundred and eleven thousand pounds.

Since there were no other bidders, the feeling of the meeting was a profound relief that someone was taking the workers' collective off their hands. To the victor, the spoils. Melmont had his newspaper at last. He rose from the table, shook hands all round, then snapped his fingers theatrically.

——Action! he cried.

Immediately the rear doors of the boardroom opened and waiters with eager demeanour and slicked back hair glided into the room. Some were carrying recently filled champagne glasses, while others bore luscious canapés of artichoke hearts, jellied asparagus heads and paté, or was it *terrine de veau*?

The newspaper's boardmembers were amazed to find themselves in the midst of celebration before an agreement had even been signed. Dominic's reporter's pad came out for a smirking catering traitor who confided that this manna from heaven had actually been assembled so rapidly that some of the appetiser items came from tins of Whiskas.

——But in the hoopla no one's going ter notice, are they? The fat git had most of them. I can show you the tins if you like.

The discovery of the incriminating tins of catfood in a secluded part of the building led to a blowjob behind the wheelie bins, during which the fêted and sated board members departed, deeply relieved that a Socialist millstone was no longer around their necks.

By the time Dominic returned, the fluted champagne glasses had been removed and the boardroom doors closed, leaving the new proprietor in charge, revelling in his role of ring-master.

——Action! cried Melmont, as before.

The doors opened again immediately, this time to admit the workers; a rabble of inky Scots print workers who filed round the walls of the room as if to keep a distance from Kapital, the bulky edifice of Melmont, alone at the conference table. Dominic doubted any amount of champagne would win over the chippy workforce.

——I've ordered us some refreshment, gentlemen.

Melmont snapped his fingers and suddenly the same smart waiters flocked into the room. But this time, they were pushing trolleys, on which were already poured, foam-filled pint mugs. Other trolleys brought up the rear with aluminium kegs of the best local beer, after heavy-laden trays of delicious sandwiches arrived. They were made this time, Dominic noted, with the freshest soft white bread, filled with grated cheese and pickle, rare thinly sliced beef, egg and cress, and ham and lettuce. There were even Coronation chicken sandwiches, which proved popular even among the hardline republicans of the chapel.

——Gentlemen, we should begin as we mean to continue, as friends, so be my guests, Melmont said. We should all dig in. The workforce needed little encouragement.

Melmont seized and devoured a particularly large lobster sandwich, of which there only appeared to be one, and looked round after his snack, smiling.

——Everything alright so far? No complaints? I am the man you should address any complaints to from now on.

——A pleasant surprise, this heavy, Dominic heard one printer say, looking at the descending froth inside his empty mug. Immediately, a waiter was at the man's elbow with a fresh glass which the man accepted silently, and drained as quickly as the first. The mood of the room was definitely mellowing.

When many bevvies had been downed and only the universally loathed mackerel sarnies were left——Was*sat*? Fush?? Tastes like col' *cunt*——Melmont judged the moment was right to establish his monarchy. He stood and tapped on a brass table lamp for silence.

——Gentlemen, as a Labour MP, I am well aware your cooperative is along the Socialist lines laid down by eminent parliamentary colleagues of mine. But that does not mean the path ahead will be easy. I give you my word that I will not rest, night or day, to keep the liquidator at bay, but in order to keep this paper a going concern, the chapels of each separate trade must give me unequivocal control of the following factors of production.

A ripple of suspicion went through the room.

——One, editorial content, and two, advertising. And I have to say, gentlemen, that the days of overstaffing are gone for ever. If you accept my terms and conditions, some of you *may* have jobs tomorrow.

Melmont looked around, a challenging smile on his face, in the shocked silence that followed. Finally, a Glaswegian voice spoke out. With the crippling masculinity of the Gorbals register, a strangulated half-octave below the rest of the male world, it boomed its defiance.

——Stuff yer fukken ultimatum! This is a cooperative, pal!

——Yes, and a cooperative is where you cooperate with me. Action! Melmont cried, and snapped his fingers a third time. His eyes were coldly glinting.

There was the gutteral clack and clatter of what sounded like truculent two-stroke motors being yanked into life nearby, to the printers' surprise. Then the motors were eased up from idling speed to the maximum revs in a second.

Then with a howl and deafening yatter, the far wall of the boardroom was pierced by the keen blades of three eighteen-inch chainsaws. The printers sprang away from the walls, and watched amazed as chainsaws sliced through an otherwise unremarkable picture of some stags at bay, and rapidly hacked out a wide entrance through the uprights and plasterboard. The midsection of the wall fell down in a cloud of plaster dust.

The chainsaw gang behind the new opening stood away to allow six burly men dressed in boilersuits to bring in a huge carved sleigh bed, already made up with a Melmont Tartan quilt cover, which they put down in the middle of the room before departing, marching two by two at the double. On the backs of the boilersuits was printed 'Melmont Solutions'.

The building dust was still drifting around the shocked and

amazed faces of the printers. Melmont spoke into the silence.

——I hope you don't mind my bed being delivered. As you can see, I do not intend to leave the building until I have the *North Briton* in profit.

When Dominic wrote, describing the bizarre scenes at the *North Briton* to Eisler, the old man cautioned him to keep copies of his mansuscript. Dominic wrote back in acknowledgement,

...I don't think that the North Briton *is going to be the big break that he wants. The paper is dying under him, though it's not entirely his fault. The Department of Trade and Industry is meant to be supporting cooperatives, but in fact the civil service has seen to it that the red tape strangles them at birth. Since Melmont is one of the damned even if the DTI can't put him away, they are unlikely to make his life owning a newspaper any easier. If you come across any more information about his early exploits, please let me know by whatever routes. I will always be grateful for your help and encouragement. I have tested HIV positive so I have something of a race against time to finish the biography of Melmont.*
Yours very sincerely,
Dominic Cole

The letter was returned after six months, overstamped 'Addressee Deceased', with Teutonic triumphalism. The realisation that Eisler's time had been called before Dominic's focussed his mind. He now found himself inspired to rise ever earlier to finish the work, imagining Eisler beside him in his canary yellow jumper urging him on to track down leads with a lop-sided smile that Melmont, forty brownshirts and the rest of life's vicissitudes had not managed to erase.

In Melmont Keep, the electricity and heating stayed off, while the peacocks continued to yowl their vanity through the dark hours. Willis Death had been called in but had not been able to find out why the peacocks cried all night. As a country vet, ruminants warmed Death's heart but peacocks, he confessed to Abigail, left him cold.

——They are birds Oi could have allowed God to remove from creation without any protest on my part. All outward show, and nothing inside.

Abigail thought it might be trapped wind.

——Oi changed their diet but it don't make a difference.

Emer slept through all disturbances.

In London, Libby was amusing herself as only those with youth and beauty to burn may do: having made enough in three months of modelling to live for a year, she partied. She had moved out of her uncle's flat, but sometimes came round to see 'the old bugger' as she called Cole cheekily to his face. The previous night, Libby had run into her old school friend Amelia at a 'truly groovy' party. Libby realised as they talked, that Amelia's father, the delinquent CIA operative who had known Cole in Berlin, was exactly the kind of spook that Dominic should be talking to about Melmont's early life. Accordingly, Libby called round to her uncle's, hoping to find Dominic and give him the lead.

She arrived to find both Cole and Terence extremely drunk. Terence had a towel wrapped around him and was weeping.

Cole was fully dressed, and icily judgemental. Dominic had, earlier in the day, taken a decision to move into an office basement with all his files and without a forwarding address. A large white van had already come and gone. Something clearly serious had happened. Cole was saying,

——If you're going to be taking papers out of my briefcase, Terence, and trying to sell them down the public house, it's very simple. House rules. You can't stay here, Terry.

And Terence, whose face was red and ugly with gin and emotion and selfpity, selfloathing and underdoggery, blubbed,

——You didn't mind when your snotty little nephew shoved his nose in your case though, did you?

——Did you see him do that? said Cole.

——Of course I did. Where d'you think I got the fucking idea?

Cole exchanged shocked glances with Libby. Cole shook his head.

——But Terry, why is it that the only time there is anything *missing* from my case, it's being punted for sale by you in a pub a hundred yards away?

——Gimme a last chance, said Terence.

——But you're a thief, Terence, said Cole, priggishly.

——Your fault. I don't have a job any more, because you *tol'* me to give it up.

——You know that's not true.

——You don't take any notice of me if I don't have any money, said Terence.

——Terry I don't give a shit how much money or not you have. I just don't want you stealing my documents and selling them down the road.

——It was Dominic's idea.

——Did he tell you to do it?

——Of course.

——These lies get you nowhere, Terry. I'm afraid I can't have you in the house anymore.

Terence ran upstairs and slammed the door. Cole sighed.

——I don't know what's got into him. I got them back but it could have been very embarrassing. The bank has to be so careful about what it knows publicly.

——Careful about what it knows?

——Earnest is being investigated.

——Good heavens, what for? said Libby.

——I rather think that's his attitude too, as you can't jail MPs, or at least, not easily, said Cole. It's what was happening exactly when he was meant to sell out to Goldfrapp. It would have been embarrassing if, say, *The Prefect* had got hold of what Terry was flogging.

As Terence sobbed angrily in Cole's bathroom, Melmont, unaware of his latest narrow escape, was lying on the vast sleigh bed in the boardroom of the *North Briton* watching black and white video footage of a workers' meeting of the staff of the *North Briton*. The bed was covered with the remains of pizzas, and in one corner, a complete salmon skin minus the head. With him was Frank, a skinny minnow to Melmont's mighty turbot. Melmont's 'bugger-in-chief', as Melmont teasingly called him, had taken a break from subjecting Goldfrapp's junior executives to sleep deprivation, and was trying to improve the sound quality of the bugged meeting tape. A Welsh voice seemed to be able to rise above the audio difficulties on its own.

'What the government's recognition of the collectives means is power now truly resides in the people. This is an extraordinary concession, to admit that we *are* the process of work itself. There is no other way of defining it and for anyone to set themselves up in authority above us, is to take a step backwards to the bad old days.'

The Bad Old Days turned the monitor off, dismissively.

——How's the retreat from Moscow, going, Frank? Are they dead of cold yet?

Frank sniggered.

——The snow's still thick down south, which helps. On the lawn, I counted four abandoned sleeping bags, before I came up today. There's only one voice being recorded left. A bloke called Gary. He spends time talking to his wife in Portland, Oregon.

——Cut the phone.

——You're better off with the information he gives. I don't think Gary's going to make it through the weekend.

Melmont started to prowl about the damaged boardroom.

——I want a mike in the editorial offices here.

——Easy to do you a video job too. There's this new little fibre optic lens which you can push through polystyrene tile ceilings: It's a bit more expensive, mind.

——Just do it, said Melmont.

——You know what? I think you should try to make the paper more consistent. With all the different ideas and prices and editors flipping around, people don't know what to expect.

Melmont raised an incredulous eyebrow.

——Frank, what do you know about *anything*, apart from poking wires around?

Frank smiled, ferretlike.

—Well, f'ra start, I know all about *you*, said Frank.

And Melmont and Frank both laughed, two villains together, both knowing there is no honour among thieves.

Down south, the cold continued and the sluggish Oxus froze so hard that the old custom of whippet sleigh racing revived, to the great entertainment of hundreds of locals lining the curving banks each Saturday afternoon. Father Cowley had taken to visiting Abigail more frequently since the heating failed at the big house. They would go for walks before dusk to visit the plot of land where Zenocrate's angel on its plinth now stood in the middle of a large clearing. Melmont's original plan had been to have a family vault in the church, but when he turned against the Church of England and commissioned Zenocrate's towering monument, there was no thought of where it was going to end up. For the moment, it had its own place, charming in its own way, in the midst of a beech wood, awaiting the legal clearing for burials in unconsecrated ground. The plinth had been dropped down on poorly levelled ground where the stumps had only just been grubbed out, and was already starting to lean.

—Zarustrina loves it here. She can't wait for her sister to be buried here. She already brings flowers.

Cowley sighed, sympathetically. He had great difficulty in telling the girls apart. On the way home, after Abigail stopped at the local shop to buy candles, Cowley said,

—Have you given any more thought to the matter of your faith?

—I can't decide, Father.

——It's just that if you're planning to have any more children, now, it would be a fine thing to *start* them off the right way, said Father Cowley, gently.

A distant cheer could be heard in the frozen air. Young Pargle, the inscription's sculptor and would-be racing driver, had been the first with his panting dogs to cross the finishing line drawn in Oxus' ice by Reedy island, in a home-built sled. To the victor, the spoils. To the baptised through our Lord Jesus, an eternity of bliss.

——I can put my hand on my heart and say, there won't be any more, now, said Abigail firmly. Her days of fertility would indeed have been over; however, she had not reckoned on her husband's determination, hand in hand with the march of science.

That night, the peacocks were particularly intrusive. Their cries cut into dreams for miles around like blazing fractal scimitars. At three in the morning, Gary, trapped closer to the cages than other mortals, decided he had to act to get some sleep, or he would go mad. Perhaps he was a little mad already, who knows?

He slowly got out of his sleeping bag. The cold did nothing to still his desperate resolve. First, there was a Swiss Army knife in his rucksack, which would serve for the deed. Gary found the fat red penknife and peering down through bloodshot eyes, broke two nails opening its longest blade. When the blade finally and grudgingly obeyed him, he let go a little whinny of acknowledgement. The deed could now be done. Gary crept out into the freezing night.

A bare twenty minutes later he was back in the room, carrying an extinct candle. His eyes now were strangely unfocussed while his hands, forearms and T-shirt were smeared with blood. He dropped the still-open knife point down onto a beech- wood chair, where it stuck, perpendicular, the coagulated blood in its many crevices declining to run down the blade. The phone rang. Gary picked it up delicately, to avoid dirtying the receiver. It would be his wife calling. She was the only one who called at this time.

—Gary?

—Yeah, it's me. Hi, hon.

His voice sounded strained, his wife thought. Maybe they had all left and the calls were being transferred.

—Where are you now? I called you fifteen minutes ago.

—I went out. I'm still here. I'm the last one here, hon. The very last one.

—You went out? I thought you were locked in.

—Naa, I went out.

—Why?

—The peacocks were driving me crazy.

—So what did you do?

—I brought them back here so they'd be quiet.

—So you're keeping them quiet?

—That's it.

—Well I can't hear them, certainly.

—Yeah I know. I got plans for them though.

Gary's wife's voice now took on an edge.

—I have to go see my analyst, now. But you're not going to do anything to them, are you? Gary? I know it's late there. Have you had something to drink? Are you on drugs?

——I can't talk over the phone, hon. It's company policy not to discuss policy. I'll tell you about it… someday. Soon.

Gary put down the phone, and went back into the nether room where forty decapitated peacocks were neatly piled up on an office table. Ignoring the blood that had seeped onto the floor, Gary started to load the peacocks into one of his fellow-worker's abandoned sleeping bags, humming *Moon River*.

Gary slowly dragged the heavy, bloody load out of the temporary buildings. Melmont's two-tone Rolls-Royce was parked outside the house on the gravelled driveway with the rear doors unlocked. Gary pulled out two dead birds and threw them in the back, then with grim determination, tugged the rest of the silent dead birds, towards the dark house.

The following morning, Emer awoke from her sound and un-disturbed sleep with an uncharacteristic feeling of foreboding. Having a drop the previous night had never been a bother for her but this morning something was not right about her sleeping arrangements. There was so little room in her narrow bed she was reminded of how in her childhood, a ceilidh ended in Tipperary with her mother, all the McPherson boys and her together in one bed. Emer pulled back the covers to discover a large amount of blood on her night dress. Her first guilty thought was that it was her own — her mother had most memorably beaten her at her first menstruation, and the shame had stayed with her. Then she saw the bright tail of a peacock.

If there was one thing she hated it was peacocks. She couldn't stand to see the animals let alone touch them. Emer screamed, sounding rather like a peacock herself, and thrust at the bird, but could not dislodge it from the bedclothes. She swung her feet out of the bed to get away from it, and realised as her feet touched the floor, that she was standing on another bird. She saw the walls of the room were flecked with blood. But if the animals had been alive and pecking at her she could not have been more frightened. She screamed again, hysterically. The touch of the long eye-like feathers was the most repulsive thing she could think of, after the McPherson boys.

Emer knocked into the wardrobe, and the doors juddered open to allow several more dead birds to fall on top of her. She fell to the ground sobbing, only to see a headless peacock that had been balanced on top of the half-open bedroom door dislodge itself in wingless slow motion, to land triumphantly on her face, its cold claws probing her lidless eyes.

The shock expelled her sanity in its entirety.

Inside a minute, Emer was transformed from a slightly old-fashioned housekeeper, though overfond of Passport Whisky, to a gibbering idiot who had so little control over her central nervous system that she was only able to leave her bedroom on her back, pushing her body along with her feet, uttering hoarse cries.

This was the sight that greeted the Melmont daughters, who slept next door in one dormitory and had ventured out in their white night gowns, curious at the bumps and frantic screams.

The eldest girl went to wake her mother. A doctor was then called, who sedated Emer with an injection. Then the girls watched as gentle hands put their former housekeeper onto a stretcher which was wheeled to a waiting ambulance. She would never come back to work for Melmont.

Till the day he died, Gary believed that he'd put the birds in

Melmont's bedroom, but he was killed after his return to the US by armed intruders high on crack cocaine, who were disappointed at only netting the $169 in his wallet. Coincidentally, the departing psychopaths used the same triumphant phrase as Gary had used about Melmont, after leaving off the dead peacocks;

—That showed da fat *fuck.*

While not as fat as Melmont, Gary's experiences in Melmont Keep had led him to divorce and depression, and he had become severely overweight, dying with his arms locked protectively around his post-lunch snack, a family pack of Bobs' Big Boy cheesy chicken nuggets and fries.

Meanwhile, as his derided and bloated enemies were exiting in hails of bullets, the Fat Fuck Himself was inexorably approaching his own unique apotheosis, that would destroy the context for life, leaving only false consciousness intact.

XVII

Melmont the Priest

ABLY ASSISTED BY MELMONT'S ENEMY, the Department of Trade and Industry, the *North Briton* was being destroyed from within, by the workers' collective who were more interested in exercising their principles than turning out a readable product. Their fat proprietor found himself unable to stop the paper's readership shrinking week by week. The definitive revolt happened while Melmont was down south. He was able to watch through surveillance cameras as the workers took over the boardroom, and his huge bed was toppled from the top of the building, to crash into a skip six floors down. For Dominic, who was present in the flesh to witness the revolution, it seemed to take for ever to fall, as the Melmont Tartan coverlet blew away in the direction of Oban.

The dream died, but Melmont was unrepentant about any part he might have played in the fiasco, striding about the empty printing shop with Dominic his sole audience, cursing the excremental government for turdist conspiracy in the suicide of the cowpat-collective.

——I'm not prepared to have my nice clean plans for a newspaper empire smashed by a bunch of alcoholic shit-eating Trotskyists. Stalin had an icepick driven into Trotsky's brain. Now we know Stalin was not all that bright, but I now see it was one of his smarter moves, said Melmont, grimly.

——How smart do you think Stalin was? asked Dominic.

——Not as smart as me.

Behind the brave rant, the former cattle drover was exhausted. Fearing Melmont would fall asleep at the wheel, Dominic refused the offer of a lift, so Melmont drove south without his biographer.

As his Roller left the motorway and reached the fringes of Barsetshire that midnight, Melmont became aware of an overwhelming need to relieve himself. He stopped the car with the headlights illuminating some large grey standing stones. When he got out he became aware he was not alone: there was a crowd of chanting, white-robed people in the middle of the ring, but they took no notice of their visitor.

Melmont leant against one of the outer circle of the Reelwrong stones, making water as the Druids distantly chanted. He watched indifferently as their High Priestess, personating the Great Goddess, took her clothes off and invoked the moon, praying to the celestial body from the centre of the egg-shaped circle. She was improvising a tender ecstasy of love and devotion for the world and its wellbeing, and all the creatures it carried as it whirled through the mightiness of Space. Melmont, badly bruised by his brush with the collective, was sulking and unmoved by the realisation he was in the same place as he had been all those years before, when his car had stopped of its own accord and Willis Death had come forward to tell him to go back to the farm to collect his poisoned chalice; Von Trapp's human skin-bound volumes of *Mein Kampf.*

The Evil Ones were watching him, as they often were, given permission by the angels that guard the Earth and now the trio visited Melmont via telluric current, entering the stairway to his consciousness through Melmont's channel of micturation, easy-peasy, up from the sacred stones. Then they walked into his cerebral cortex, their mission as always to lead the tycoon towards the pure equation of Greed that would then enslave all Creation. But they needed his help to do it; their evil alone was a weak spiritual thing, not of the coarse plane of matter.

The moon itself now came out from behind a cloud, as if summoned. Thanks to Helmut, Hilda and Veronika's machinations with Melmont's nervous system, the silver disc's vivid appearance prompted an immediate reaction from their host body.

Melmont started to moan and dribble at the mouth, looking at the moon's brilliance. He felt faint. His car headlights appeared to fail. He clasped at the stone now with both hands to stop himself falling to the ground, and as a result experienced a most unexpected and painful orgasm. He groaned. Young probationary Dark Lords of Hades, who were watching the possession as part of their apprentice studies, snickered knowingly at Melmont's bewilderment, shame and discomforture in the loss of seed.

The three expert Evil Ones now put it in Melmont's mind that the apparition of the moon was a promise from them that he would soon own the newspaper *The Moon.* A suspicion arose in Melmont's mind that promises made by Evil Ones are not kept, but was ruthlessly suppressed. An inner voice whispered seductively that *The Moon* would soon be his for the taking, from Midrash.

——When will that be? asked Melmont giddily.

——As soon as you show your bottom to Saint Peter, the nasty trio chorused. Then the loathsome *prana* parasites swung lightly down the ropes of Melmont's drooling snot, back into the earth and down to hell again.

＊＊＊＊   ＊＊＊＊   ＊＊＊＊

Melmont did not have long to worry about how to carry out the base and sacrilegious rite specified by the Norn, for his work had been cut out for him, as tailors say. En route for Israel, his 747 was in a holding pattern, waiting to land at Rome Airport. On the ground, there had been a serious incident involving a plane which had failed to take off on the main runway, though no further details were given to passengers for the moment. Suspended in the aircraft in its thirteenth pass above the Vatican, Melmont, bound for Tel Aviv, was on the deserted first-class upper deck when he felt a strong stirring in his bowels.

As soon as he had moved to address this call of nature, he realised he had fulfilled the letter of the Norn's stipulations, for St Peter surely would be able to see through an aluminium bulkhead. Where then, was the newspaper? The tycoon crossly resumed his seat and demanded brandy and a cigar in compensation. But no sooner had he lit the cigar, than it tasted suspiciously like a Mont du Miel. Melmont made a face, and plunged the offending tobacco into the brandy. The Italian stewardess was shocked.

——Is sum-sing wrong, sir?

——Take 'em away. They deserve each other, but I don't deserve to be kept waiting for what is mine.

The stewardess picked up the glass and explained in a hushed whisper that the reason for the plane being kept in a holding pattern was that an aircraft had exploded on takeoff from *Roma*, *morte cinquecento, forse molti cento,* 'ow you say, *sfera di fuoco*, fireball, and it was still ver' ver' dangerous to land. Though no man is an island, Melmont did not look remotely sympathetic or grateful for the sad information on the deaths of his fellow men.

——I suppose the bloody fire brigade's all off at Mass. Typical. Bring champagne, *apra la bottiglia in cui posso vederlo*.

The stewardess brought the champagne and as instructed opened the bottle in front of Melmont. She carefully filled an extra-large glass right to the brim, and left with tears in her eyes for the many unknown victims of the disaster that had just occurred.

Melmont became aware that there was a bubble in the champagne which was not ascending. He was about to call the stewardess back and give her a lecture about foreign matter in his drink, when the bubble started to grow.

And grow, and grow. It was clearly a hole in Reality, and very shortly he could see through into another world, as if through a fish-eye lens.

In the other world, Helmut, Veronika and Hilda appeared

naked. Corpses hung behind them on meat hooks in rows, but they appeared unconcerned, playing cards on a butcher's slab. Helmut casually took up a packet of cigars and lit one. Melmont saw they were Mont du Miel brand, something that had not existed in the real world for a third of a century. Nostalgia momentarily plucked at his heart.

Acknowledging the importance of the cigars, Helmut winked at Melmont, and lit a match by friction on Veronika's pubic hair. She protested sluttishly, but then smirked and seemed to accept the insult. Hilda, sat between them, held out her hand of cards to Melmont. It was a royal flush in hearts. Helmut and Hilda gave the thumbs-up sign. Melmont intuited that he was going to be lucky in cards soon.

——Be prepared to win *The Moon!* a throaty voice said, as the vision faded.

As it did so, the bubbles resumed their upward march.

And now Melmont noticed that sitting on the tray next to the champagne glass was a brand new and unopened pack of cards. He touched the cellophane wrapper with trembling hands. They were exactly the same as the cards the Norns had been playing with! His throat dry with excitement, ignoring the Norns' earlier prophecy in his greed, Melmont shoved the magic cards into his pocket.

The five hundred victims of the plane crash, all new arrivals to Hell wept when they learned on arrival in Hell that they had been holocausted for the fine-tuning of Melmont's Appetite. But the Norns, (who have full discretionary powers in the upper districts of Hell, though answerable to Hecate) were so pleased with the way the sting was working, they delayed general torment for the five hundred, setting up a huge plasma screen in the central square, so the new arrivals could all relax watching the re-runs of their spectacular plane fireball before they started their eternity of torment.

Like a masterly move in chess that frees up the deep structure of the winner's game, the plane crash had also stranded Midrash, with time to kill at Rome airport. Almost as soon as Melmont stepped off the plane he spotted his rival, the rubberfaced, wiry Australian, in a phone booth. Midrash had discovered a newsworthy incident and was dictating it to his headquarters ten thousand miles away, and pretended to be unaware that Melmont had seen him.

The polished marble floors went every which way, and a tiny fear still tickled Melmont saucily whenever he came to the edge and had to cross over a paper-thin crack. But he kept going and crept up, silent as an elephant in the night, till finally he was almost within touching distance of his rival. Turning his back deliberately on Melmont, Midrash was saying,

—Headline, "Jumbo Jet Horror". Strap, "Hundreds feared dead". A hands-on newsman to his fingertips, Midrash was proud that he could still dictate copy fluently without notes better than most of his subs,— Text. "At least five hundred people are believed to have been killed when a fully loaded Kinky Nippon Airways jumbo en route to London exploded after takeoff from Rome Airport, a hundred feet in the air, in a fireball that ignited the tarmac. The airport's firefighting team was joined by five units of the Roman fire brigade but it is feared there are no survivors. Foul play is suspec…".

Suddenly something foul slammed into Melmont's knees. He

could see the legs of a lean, dirty bronzed woman in a cheap Indian cotton dress who must have had her arms around his legs, because he couldn't move them. Then the woman released her hands, shuffled backwards and put them together prayerfully, kneeling in a position of oriental submission. It was Priscilla. She had no shoes on and the soles of her feet were black.

——Earnest Melmont, it's Priscilla Cole. Remember me? I've been in India, but it didn't work out. The guru turned out to be a sham. I don't know why I didn't see through him straightaway, but they really want us for sex or money, don't they? I've just had the narrowest escape. I should have been on that plane which crashed, but I was spared. My boarding card was number thirteen. Look.

Priscilla rooted in her Indian tooled-leather drawstring bag and fished out a crumpled boarding card.

——It's number thirteen! So I didn't go. It sometimes helps being superstitious. Not all the time. But what do I do now about going home?

Melmont smiled his sphinx-like smile and took the boarding card.

——It's *my* lucky number. I tell you what, I'll buy it off you. Call the local Hilton, tell them to send the bill to me. I'll have my secretary in London arrange a first-class ticket to London.

——They say people entertain angels unawares, and you must be an angel. I'm going back to England. Do you know why? We need to get rid of Americans using us as a nuclear base. You were a nuclear disarmer as an MP weren't you? You did your bit, didn't you?

Melmont's voters had heard his opinions on nuclear disarmament before the election, but they had been the last to do so.

——I am no longer an MP, said Melmont, though I think I may have helped a little averting a nuclear crisis when Czechoslovakia was invaded. You should do one thing very quickly now if you haven't done it already, which is to claim for your luggage. The tag is on this card. Take it back, for now.

Priscilla's mouth dropped open.

——My luggage!

Melmont handed her boarding card back, and she scurried off just as Bruce Midrash hung up the phone and sauntered out of the booth. His eyes met Melmont's.

——Business must be thin, Ocker, if you're having to do all the reporting yourself, said Melmont.

Whatever you do, don't call him Ocker, new employees of Bruce Midrash were warned.

——Are you here because they're going to roll you out to clear the runway, Trannie? responded Midrash. Midrash's paper had never come up with a really good nickname for Melmont. They called him 'Trannie', for his Transylvanian origins, but it had no real bite.

——Guess not. Means we'll be here a while.

Melmont pulled the pack of cards out of his pocket.

——Poker. No-limit game, Ocker, said Melmont.

——Hey, I wasn't born yesterday, I'm not playing anything with marked cards, said Midrash.

——These are new, see?

Melmont's thumb scratched at the clear plastic wrapping. Ocker's eyes a pair of canny beige adding machines narrowed slightly.

——You're on, Trannie. Suits me. It makes the time pass if

you're having fun, said Midrash. No cheating, mind. A big bastard like you could keep any number of marked decks between the cheeks of his arse.

——I expect you could do with some easy money for alimony, that's all you lazy Ozzies do, play around, joked Melmont. When they carry you out feet first, there's going to be the mother of all legal fights over who's going to inherit.

Ocker's weakness was for setting up successive families on every landmass where his beady eye had spotted circulation potential.

——Frankly Trannie, if it's after I'm dead, I don't give a toss. If they want to screw the whole thing up, let them. But at least it'll be a fight between *men.*

They settled down to play, Melmont squatting, Midrash cross-legged, on the marble floor. Inside fifteen minutes, Midrash had forgotten all about the air disaster and even his latest Pacific-Rim sheila. He had a fullscale disaster of his own. The Trannie had bluffed him holding a rubbish hand to his two aces, and he was more than a million dollars down.

𝄞   𝄞   𝄞

Amelia and Libby were slowly lifting Amelia's tetchy and incurably ill father in his wheelchair up the staircase in Prince's College, after supper, helped by Dominic. Amelia, Libby's American close chum from boarding school, had been appointed a Reader in modern history at Cole's old Oxbridge college, in the same rooms at the top of the stairs as Libby's uncle. Digby was not making his ascent any easier, thrashing uselessly with his arms against the Grim Reaper.

—Stop trying to fly. Calm down, dad.

—I'm as calm as it gets. This dying is a fucking drag.

Hearing Amelia and Dominic talking about the room's earlier occupant, the old soldier barked,

—I knew the bastard. British army, right? Another faggot.

—But not a Commie, said Dominic, loyally.

—I think Dominic might be sensitive about the f-word, father.

—Plenty of Commies work in banks, said Digby, snarlingly. Commie faggots.

Amelia rolled her eyes upwards for Dominic's benefit. As the wheelchair took the turn in the stairs, Digby's frail hands beat on the undemocratic ancient walls in rage like an angel with broken wings.

—Stop, father!

—I'm *helping*. You're doing nothing, and it's not going to happen on its own.

They finally got to the top landing, and wheeled Digby into Amelia's rooms. The quadrangle below them was floodlit, and Dominic noticed that undergraduates of both sexes were being laid out in rows.

—Most peculiar. Looks like they've been gassed. Should we be worried?

—No. They have to get legless before the party ends at eleven o'clock. College rules, Amelia said lightly.

—Screw the view. I don't have much time left. Let's get this over with, said Digby.

—Colonel Digby, I'm so sorry. I'd like to thank you for

agreeing to meet with me, said Dominic, at his most appealing.

——I can see you look a bit like your uncle, kid. What do you want to know about Melmont?

——Anything you care to tell me. I've been commissioned to write his official biography.

——I'm not going to help whitewash this guy.

——I understand. But you met him in Berlin. What was your impression?

——Oh, what is it that Thomas Carlisle the historian says? "Coming events cast their shadows long before." He struck me as a crook then, in other words. People don't change.

——They grow old and die, that's change, said Libby.

——Horse's ass, replied her father.

——Did you know Konrad Eisler? said Dominic.

——Never heard of him.

——Melmont's science journals editor.

——Oh him, yeah. Prewar Commie. Showed his colours when he stayed over the wall. Dead now.

——He thought Melmont had some kind of hold on Gunter Röhl.

——What for?

——To get Röhl to do stuff for him.

——What kind of stuff?

Dominic took a deep breath.

——He's trading highly enriched uranium.

Digby nodded, satisfied for a moment.

——It's actually WGU, weapons-grade uranium. I've been telling that to people for thirty years.

——The way to make a case against him is to bring out a completely accurate book where he will sue. But the facts have to stand up in court, so I need anything you have.

——I've been keeping files for years, young man. But he covers his tracks pretty good. It's like you crawl and you crawl, but where's the wall that proves you're in this dark cave? I don't know how much more I care. The fact is, Dominic, I'm dying.

——You're not the only one, said Dominic.

——You too? I'd forgotten. Sorry, said Digby. He paused for a moment, then held out his hand. Amelia had never seen her father apologise before. Dominic took Digby's lean pink leathery paw and held it. It was warm, as if the skin was almost too thin to hold in the hot rage of its owner's blood. Digby said,

——I'll let you have what I know as soon as I know it. Let's see if we can take this mur'fucker down before we go!

Outside Prince's College by Big Bridge, the sharp-eared vegetation of Reedy Island heard Digby's battle cry. It was the same malicious plants whose rustling had once betrayed Cole to the local constabulary, forcing him to leave Oxbridge for ever.

These treacherous reeds all now conferred, and were about to elect a body of reeds to warn Melmont he had sworn enemies in hope of some future reward. But Winter, overhearing them, resolved to punish the upstart reeds by depriving them of speech during his time of office.

Accordingly, each year as plovers give place to greylag geese and Autumn begins her retreat from the flood plain of the Oxus, Winter blows in but the dry leaves of the sedges can only clash together uselessly—*Shhhhhhhhh.*

The warning is ignored, in any case, by our absentee Governor, *Rex-Imperator Omniphagus.* Melmont On High needs no craven informers, nor seeks vegetable alliances, for He is immovably enthroned now.

The day after Dominic and Digby formed their alliance, Digby flew home and Dominic drove to interview Willis Death and his wife. The road to their farm rose gradually till it passed through the uplands and the big stone circles. Dominic had borrowed an E-type 2+2 Jag convertible from a gallery owner friend of his who had gone to Paris for the weekend. The powerful sports car was now doing one mile an hour, behind a herd of bleating sheep. Amelia was sitting in the apology for a back seat; Libby was in the passenger seat looking at her brother's transparent complexion in the sunlight. The cold wind was ruffling his thinning hair.

—Was our father bald, Dom?

—Fuck knows, said Dominic.

—Is this woman we are researching really called Mrs Death? said Amelia.

—Now she is. She's a war widow who married the local vet. She used to be the cook at the prisoner of war camp which was on the farm.

—It's funny, I look at my father and I think, your whole personality, your whole life, everything is shaped by the last war, said Amelia.

—It's why you became a historian isn't it? said Libby. The past making sense of the present, or something.

—It's a hard job making sense of life when the only difference between us and the fucking sheep seems to be that we know we're for it, and they don't, said Dominic.

The silly sheep suddenly acquired knowledge of life and death, parting like the Red Sea as Dominic accelerated purposefully through the gap. Shortly the car carrying the young searchers reached the farmhouse and they were given a warm welcome by Mrs Death (née Simpkins), who led them into the homely front parlour of the sixteenth century cottage.

In the corner of the room, Willis Death was on the phone. He was looking suddenly older than Dominic remembered seeing him when he had come to examine the peacocks six months before. His hair was completely white now, and his hands shook even as he held the phone. With Parkinson's disease, it had become more and more difficult with livestock, but he was still able to give younger vets advice and the benefit of a lifetime's experience, which he did freely and with pleasure, gripping the receiver in both hands to replace it.

——Sorry to keep you folks, but I've become a world expert suddenly in birth complications in Friesians.

He gave his visitors a warm smile as he rose with difficulty from his chair. He shook their hands one by one, saying he was pleased to meet them, his deepset eyes twinkling humorously.

——They ring you up from all over the world, dear, don't they now?

——Yes, it's a strange feeling, seeing as how before we was married I had hardly bin to Lunnon. A good feeling though. Boggered if I'm taking all this hard-earned knowledge with me, and the kind thing about Doctor Parkinson is that if you can cope with the shakes, he leaves you with your brain. So which one of you is the writer?

——I am, said Dominic.

——I wouldn't know how to do that. I can talk, mind, but

putting one word after another and just having it lay there on the page, staring at me fills me with holy terror, said Death. I can tell people how to do operations, down to the larst details, but... .

——They ring you up from all over the world, repeated his wife, lovingly.

——You wouldn't believe the places they got Friesians, nowadays. Tibet. China.

——It's not like I'm making anything up, said Dominic.

——So it's all going to be true about him?

——As close as I can get.

Willis Death appraised Libby's slender sprawl terminating in pink suede Biba boots.

——You're very beautiful, my dear, he said, sweetly.

——She's a model, said Amelia.

——But so are you. You could be a model, too, said Willis Death, gallantly.

——I don't think she'd like the waiting around, said Libby.

Mrs Death fetched in tea and homemade Eccles cakes, and told of Melmont's generosity to them.

——He surprised us completely with a wedding reception, in a tent it was. It had a marching band, and everything. Lovely it was. But then we left and saw that poor girl in the road.

——Zenocrate, said Death.

——It was a strange thing to happen, that reception, because it was like getting everything you wanted, but then you had it, and your happiness, and it was all taken away.

——It's right, no sooner than we got married, I started to get this, the friggin' shakes. Never had a day's illness in me life before. Couldn't get a mortgage on this farm, then.

——We got into debt, said Mrs Death, showing the whites of her eyes, round and protruberant as table tennis balls.

——But the Captain couldn't have been better to us, he stuck by us thick and thin. He guaranteed our mortgage for us. Talk about a friend, Willis shook his head.

——Have you ever done anything for him that he might consider useful?

——I wouldn't say so. I'm only a country vet. I've not qualified to treat the likes of *him*.

——I'm going to ask you about the German army officer who killed himself.

——That was a long time ago!

——Would you tell us about it?

——I don't think we got nothing to hide, said Mrs Death.

——You had to call the police, even so, in those days, said Willis.

——Well it's no different now.

——It is for Germans though. You said the police came by and because he was a German, it was like, "good riddance!"

Willis and Mrs Death then took the three young people through the dramatic tale of long ago, the death of Von Trapp outside that very sitting room, whose violent dislike of Melmont was expressed by spitting and stamping on copies of his newspapers. He had not only left no ghost in the hall, there was the continuing enigma of why the disappointed Prussian war hero should have left Captain Melmont any books. It was all strange, almost inexplicable. And yet life went on.

——Can you remember anything about the books? Dominic asked.

——It's gone clean out of me head. Sorry.

——There was a box, wasn't there? You told me you'd put the box in the boot of the car, said Mrs Death.

——When did I say that? What car?

——I don't know, the car he drove away in.

Willis and his wife exchanged frowning looks. Then suddenly Willis stood up.

——Got it! I think I know what you come for!

The old vet walked out of the room, and returned in a moment with a greyish leather-bound volume, dusty and slightly battered.

——I never seed that before. What's that? said Mrs Death.

Willis peered at the spine, then opened the book. Whether his hands were trembling with disease or excitement it would be impossible to say, Dominic thought. Both, perhaps.

——I found it the other day in the hall. It's definitely one of them. It's in German. It's old Hitler's *Mein Kampf,* look, he said excitedly. His shaking hands tore the rice-paper cover protecting the photograph of the author. Willis snorted with irritation, then closed the book and passed it to Dominic.

——The set had dedications, I understand, said Dominic. But the flyleaf on the remaining copy had been torn out.

——So whose book is it, then? said Mrs Death.

——It should go to Earnest, it was left to him. But I dunno if he wants it any more, said Willis, it may not be worth anything on its own. Funnily enough, I found it that day when the boy slaughtered all the peacocks. It was at the bottom of an old game bag on the hatrack I was throwing out.

——I'll take it to Earnest, if you like, said Dominic.

——That's a good idea, said Willis. I remember now, there

were thirtynine others. I must ha' thought I'd packed them all up when Earnest counted them.

——You remember he counted thirtynine? How come? You couldn't remember a thing a moment ago, said Mrs Death, a little sharply.

——It's the medication, dear. One door opens, another closes. Earnest said thirteen was his lucky number, and thirtynine is let's see, three times thirteen. He was more'n happy to take them just as they was.

——I hope this last book getting found don't mean his luck's running out, then, said Mrs Death, darkly.

What Willis Death did not tell his visitors, from not wishing to appear a superstitious hayseed, particularly in front of the two pretty ones, was that when he had first found the book, there had been a triangular dried bone fragment of skull adhering to the book cover, from the general's suicide all those years ago. Far thicker than the piece he remembered from Zenocrate's accident, the relic had given him a strange, uneasy and atavistic feeling. He had carefully prised the bone off the book, and then buried the fragment of self-slaughter within the perimeter of the Reelwrong Stones. Death was a cryptic animist beneath the nod to Christianity, and if anyone had asked him what he was doing he would have explained that the Pelasgian Druid sentinels who guarded the stones would take away any curse, and make sure Trapp's soul after his terrible self-immolation was reborn in a better form at some stage. Not in his lifetime, probably. Maybe not in your children's. Didn't matter. Does not the Lord's Prayer end, *"world without end, Amen?"*

XVIII

Stomach Speaks!

ROME AIRPORT HAD COME TO A STANDSTILL after the crash, as Melmont continued to take Midrash to the cleaners. Midrash was ten million dollars down when the departures board reconfigured itself at six in the morning, to announce flights might begin again sometime that afternoon. At midday they had been playing continuously for eighteen hours. Melmont counted his chips, pleased.

——That's thirteen million you owe me. I think I'll stop there, said Melmont.

——Chicken, Trannie. Play on, said Midrash.

The game continued. Even Midrash's hardboiled assistant, Joe Mellors, started whispering in his boss's ear about the advisability of packing it in to limit the damage, but Midrash waved him away. Almost immediately he lost another million.

——That must have been the most expensive minute of your life, Ocker, said Melmont.

Midrash grinned grimly and said to his assistant,

——Alright, it's a wrap. If you see me at another card game ever I'd like you to give me a good hard slap.

Then to Melmont, he said,

—At the price they're at this minute, you could use your winnings to buy back all the rest of your shares. Will a cheque do?

—A cheque would be acceptable, if you have some form of identity, said Melmont.

Instead of writing a cheque out, Midrash tore open an empty cigarette packet, wrote on it, and put it down between them. Melmont could not believe his eyes. Midrash had written 'The Moon'.

—Want me to slap you now or later, boss? said Mellors.

—Calm down, Joe, I'm just seeing if I can get Wide Load here to miss his plane.

Mellors now saw what Midrash had written on the paper, and gasped.

—That's my job on the line there, boss, suppose he wins? He won't want to show mercy.

—You're spoiling my concentration, Joe. If you don't pipe down you'll find yourself back on the *Woomera Advertiser*.

—Your job will be safe with me, Joe, depend on it, said Melmont, magnanimous in what he thought was victory. To the victor, the spoils. He could always fire him later.

—I'm certainly not staying to work for that lard-arsed pinko swine, said Joe, pointing at Melmont.

He just wouldn't respond to their insults, Melmont thought, and in a minute he'd have a newspaper all of his own again.

—When you closed the *North Briton*, Trannie, tell me, was it because it was too rightwing? said Midrash.

Melmont said nothing, following his new plan.

——Na, reckon it was his body odour, said Mellors. After a day
and a night of cigars and poker, Melmont was certainly riper
than when he first squatted down to play.

——Oh, was that why the *News of the Screws* owner wouldn't
go near him? Midrash said, facetiously. Midrash had, earlier in
the year, scooped a Sunday tabloid from under Melmont's nose.
Melmont thought there was a conspiracy against him. Indeed
there was. The Norn had seen to it that the owner of the paper
had been so drunk by breakfast each morning that he had not
realised that Melmont was offering even more money for the
paper than the Australian.

——Shall we stop these childish games and play? I'll see you,
said Melmont. He poured all his chips into the middle of the
table, so they covered the cigarette packet.

——Hey, *The Moon*'s worth more'n a piddling twenty million,
shouted Mellors. If you want to gamble with the paper I love,
boss, it might as well be for its market value! Get him to put
more in the pot!

Midrash gave a weary smile and cocked his head.

——Leave it out, Joe. Trannie doesn't have access to *that* kind
of finance, and never had, said Midrash, patronisingly. By this
time they had got Melmont thoroughly riled.

Melmont tried to bluff again holding a weak hand, lost, then
watched in disbelief as Midrash scooped back all the millions he
had lost. Next, Midrash recovered the piece of cigarette paper
with his paper's name written on it. He ceremonially burnt it in
an ashtray, saying coolly,

——That's the last time I'm doing that, Joe, I promise. But I
wasn't being entirely foolish. I had a plan all along.

—You had a plan to whip Trannie? You coulda fooled me.

—My father taught me the trick in poker is only to think about winning, and never what's in the pot.

—Thank Christ for your dad!

—Life's a risky business, Joe, too much so to take seriously, said Midrash.

The Australians prepared to leave. Melmont flushed hotly and stood up.

—Play again! he said, commandingly.

Midrash was walking away now, laughing. Melmont took a step towards the tycoon. Suddenly he remembered what it had felt like to collapse the throat of the wounded German boy, and his thumbs itched to do the same for the mocking Bruce Midrash, if he could get him within arm's length. Melmont started to move towards the slight Australian with his hands extended. Midrash laughed and danced away.

—Joe, you're going to have to stop Trannie from following me.

—No way, I could get run over. If he's bothering you, just lead him through the revolving doors over there; he's bound to get stuck.

—Sorry Trannie, that's the Sydney flight being called. Thanks for the game, it passed the time pleasantly.

The two men walked rapidly away. Melmont stayed rooted to the spot, ignoring all boarding calls in whatever languages. Waves of disappointment, anger and humiliation broke over his head. Elegant young Italian security guards, heavily armed, with sallow complexions and expensive haircuts, wandered over from time to time, but in the main, the airport left him alone, a ballooning blackness on a Carrera marble grid. He would have stayed there for ever, if a voice had not spoken from within him. It was the voice of his stomach.

—Feed me, the voice growled, miraculously, though the subtext was ominous. There had been a power shift. While other people had stomachs, Melmont's stomach now it seems, had him. Increasingly, it had gained power over the years. And now its Trades Unions were making their presence felt with unprecedented vocal demands.

The day after coming so close to owning *The Moon*, the talking belly's proprietor was sitting with and behind his stomach outside a café in Jerusalem. Melmont was wearing a yachting cap at a jaunty angle, and apparently not a care in the world, to judge from his expression. His companion was a more serious-looking greyhaired, bulletheaded man in a silver suit. Zak was Melmont's contact in Mossad, and had been a frogman: his service to Israel had included personally sinking several British ships as they rode at anchor. The café, with its noisy traffic close by had been chosen specially by Mossad, who had been approached with a discreet offer by Melmont of weapons-grade uranium, the substance without which no small, beleaguered democracy can ever feel itself complete.

The sun was shining. Thirteen expresso coffees had been ordered and drunk, and now it was time for business.

—My friend, it is no secret; my researches tell me the reactor in your country will not be producing sufficient weapons-grade plutonium for a warhead for some time. I'm here to tell you, you don't have to wait. I know there are meant to be restrictions on obtaining nuclear materials but in practice they can always be got around. I have been offered several Russian warheads, said Melmont, exaggerating only a little.

—What kiloton yield? asked Zak, softly.

—Between twenty and forty kilotons.

—And how many warheads do you have?

—Thirteen, said Melmont. Melmont figured some could always be lost in transit, emphasising how lucky Israel would be to get any at all.

Zak said nothing, so Melmont said,

—I'm buying a newspaper.

—But Earnest, every time I see you, you *always* say that. You're always pregnant, but you never have the baby, Zak said with cruel sarcasm.

—This time it's different, I'm buying *The Spyglass*, the only remaining daily to support Labour in Britain.

—How are you going to pay for it?

—Money, money, money. And now for the last time, do you want these warheads? They could be gone by tomorrow.

—I'd have to get back to you, I don't have authority to recommend that kind of purchase, said Zak. He felt there was something untrustworthy about Melmont's approach. The offer could be a blind to discover the real state of Israel's nuclear potential.

—Just remember, my friend, how the chain of this offer works. The condition of sale to me is that I find a buyer on this trip. Otherwise, they will go elsewhere for their broker. And if they use another broker, these things could end up anywhere, even in the hands of the Palestine Liberation Organisation, said Melmont.

The PLO was recently in the habit of drawing attention to the Palestinians' injustices at the hands of Jewish butchers by allowing suicide bombers, in the Islamic *hashashin* tradition, to board buses full of Israelis. Though Zak and Melmont both knew the PLO was unlikely to strap on a nuclear warhead in the same way undetected it was always a possibility. Most things are possible in Jerusalem, including miracles; indeed the Holy City was about to play host to yet another miracle in the café.

A mere twentyfour hours after it had first found its voice, Melmont's stomach could be heard again and this time it was singing. Melmont recognised a snatch of *Ave Maria*, before it seemed to realise this was a provocative choice, in the circumstances. The stomach then came up with *Food, Glorious Food*, which it sang with feeling in a pronounced yiddisher accent, as if to convince Zak of its owner's pledges to Zionism.

——*Foo', glorious foo'! 'Ot sossidge an' mus-turd!*
Woil we're in ver mewed, cowelled jilly an' cus-turd!

Fortunately the traffic noise made the stomach's travesty inaudible. As soon as Zak left, the singing abruptly stopped and a woman's voice said, piteously,

——Feed me. Feed me.

Melmont realised it would have been unseemly to search himself in public for lips, to find and silence them. Seated in the little café, Melmont replied disengenuously to his stomach from the corner of his mouth.

——In due course, my friend. In time. Be patient. All in God's good time. Shut up for now, will you?

Zak was not the only one to feel that Melmont's conversion to the cause of Zion was opportunistic. In London, Dominic had received a home movie-quality tape from Digby's archives entitled 'SLEEPING WITH THE ENEMY'. It began, not unstylishly, with a handheld shot showing a helicopter descending among date palms, creating a dust storm out of which Melmont stepped to embrace a trio of Arab sheiks.

Dominic immediately stopped the tape and phoned Amelia.

—This is too good to watch alone. Your father's put together the smoking gun.

Then he rewound the tape while he phoned his sister. When she arrived Libby noticed the remains of many takeaway Chinese meals lay crowded on top of the television. At least he's eating, Libby thought.

Digby had appended his own crude subtitles to the scenes. The first one read 'MELMONT KISSING THE ASSES OF TOWELHEADS'. The narrative then moved jumpily on, with covert surveillance shots intercut with more conventional footage of Melmont, obviously the guest of honour of the sheiks, ingesting hospitality in his unique fashion, at a succession of profligate and gargantuan feasts.

Feast followed feast in the Saudi Arabian desert, datable by the technology to Early Video but with stars so bright they were registering even on smudgy footage, each gesture leaving its ghost, like the record of the first men on the moon. Then, better-quality recorded feasts in gilded hotel rooms showed Melmont in a turban, beaming, surrounded by the houris and belly dancers of the occasion. There were also feasts among marble colonnades of princes' palaces, where fountains played.

Clearly Melmont was a man whom Saudi princes believed in. There was also covert footage, painful and unpleasant to watch, of Melmont's insulting usage of prostitutes in imperial suites, the women being used momentarily and then immediately thrown out. Sometimes the women were forced to depart often before they could rearrange their hair or even fully dress. Sometimes the old boar didn't even touch them before he snarlingly ordered them into banishment.

——He's not impotent, look, but he seems to think in his head he's fucked them already, said Dominic.

However ungallant Melmont was, the strange leitmotif of these brief liaisons was that wherever he was in the world at the time, Melmont seemed always to have been supplied with a version of a Third Empire sleigh bed, the very same kind that had been ignominiously pitched from the *North Briton*'s roof.

The soundtrack of the compilation was patchy. At one banquet, Melmont was lying on his side in the Roman style. Digby had subtitled the sections with an English translation. Melmont's knowledge of Arabic appeared to be good, delivered through mouthfuls of lamb and accompanied by graphic if not elegant gestures, throwing bones, half-chewed over his shoulder at the same time, and reaching for another delicacy;

——Captain Melmont, is it true what we read, that you have just sold a hundred thousand sets of encyclopedias in one week, in India?

——Every word is the truth, my prince. It may be even more.

——These sales figures strike us Arabs as almost miraculous, because you appear to have included an out-of-date map of the subcontinent, without a division for Pakistan.

——My prince, the figures are true. We prefer on occasion to be old-fashioned, as you call it, rather than insult Islam, and so we do not recognise the secular partition of Pakistan, for is she not truly better known as 'The Land of the Pure'?

A smooth answer turneth away wrath, the proverbs say. A smooth answer leads Sunnis and Sh'ites alike by the nose to Melmondia. The prince appeared to be satisfied with Melmont's excuse, and Melmont continued,

——It is this kind of statistics from a publishing company that makes the company attractive to investors, who are no fools!

——Agreed, my friend. Whatever our reservations about credible stock movement, sometimes we should accept the verdict of the market.

——If investors are fools, my prince, there's an awful lot of them out there. When I went public, shares were oversubscribed twenty times.

——That's a lot of smart investors! Now I understand you, sir!

——And I have consistently rewarded these sage investors with forty percent dividends for the last three years, and will do the same this year. You may rely on it.

——Ah yes, the future. *Insh'Allah*. If Allah wills.

——If Allah was on my Board, Prince, I would have him sign the same agreements with me as everyone else.

The scene abruptly ended there.

——Must be all pre-Interlease, said Dominic.

——Machiavelli would have loved this guy, said Amelia. But he hasn't said anything yet that would get him taken out by Mossad. Pre-1948 maps of Israel might have posed problems but selling out-of-date maps to the Arab world is the sort of thing that gets you Israeli medals.

——Let it roll. According to your father, he incriminates himself plenty.

The tape continued to play. Another desert, another feast, in a tent. This time Melmont was sitting next to a decorated, clearly high-ranking military Arab, who was in personal charge of feeding Melmont with a succession of sheep's eyes. Melmont was clearly enjoying himself, and the number of sheep's eyes remaining on the plate continued to dwindle throughout the short scene. The subtitled conversation with the general was highly disturbing.

——Mister Melmont, do you have links with Israel?

An eyeball went in. Melmont chewed and swallowed.

——My children have been brought up in the Church of England.

——So they're now supposed to think he's not even Jewish, goddamit, said Amelia. Sometimes she sounded very like her father.

——He wasn't, for a while, said Dominic.

Onscreen Melmont paused, as if waiting for the interruption to finish, then said,

——As far as I am concerned with respect to Israel, I have never visited that artificial country.

The general was clearly relieved.

——It is getting very hard for us dealing with the Israeli war machine. They are quite prepared to wage nuclear war, we know. We know the reactor is much larger than was agreed.

——Which one? said Melmont.

Fortunately for him, the general did not notice the slip.

——They only have one, in the Negev Desert. But it will be able to produce warheads very soon, if it has not done so already.

One of the sheep's eyes in Melmont's mouth split as he bit down, and a jet of hot jelly vaunted into the air and passed onto the robes of the general, who mopped himself without comment and continued.

——The Americans are simply the tools of the Jewish lobbying machine and will do what they are told. President Johnson will not let us have what we need to protect ourselves against this new nuclear state. We are naked and unprotected, crying out for help.

Melmont looked suitably grave and responsible for a moment, then spoke.

——There is another route apart from the White House to achieve a nuclear shield. As you know I have extensive contacts with the inorganic chemistry fraternity.

——Irrespective of their country's allegiances, I understand. It is a unique achievement to have built a global network in a divided world.

——I have always operated on the premise that science should be above politics.

——We have no facilities for enriching uranium, which I understand is a very lengthy process.

Melmont nodded.

——I would agree.

——We are in haste.

——My fortunate state does mean that I have access to a number of sources of enriched uranium.

——In which case we would be very interested in negotiating a possible purchase price.

——It would make me more than happy to help your country counter the Jewish threat.

Melmont suddenly turned to the camera and said sharply in English,

——Here, is that thing on?

The screen went to black. Blocky handwritten captions followed, in Digby's angry scrawl:

THIS DEAL ABORTED BY CIA.

THE GENERAL WAS KILLED. BUT

IN THE LAST THIRTY YEARS THERE HAVE

BEEN TEN THOUSAND NUCLEAR WARHEADS

MANUFACTURED IN THE FORMER SOVIET

BLOC. THIS MAN HAS TO BE STOPPED.

The videotape clunked to a stop then started to rewind noisily in the stunned silence.

——So he's just sorta offering them round like toffee apples, said Amelia.

——I don't understand. When he ran for election, he was *against* the nuclear bomb, said Libby.

Suddenly Dominic uttered a deep groan. Then he clutched his stomach hard, as if he had been punched there and fell to the floor, white as a sheet. Libby was at his side, almost before he settled on the ground.

——What's going on? cried Amelia.

——It's these cocktails of stuff he has to take to control his symptoms and he crashes out sometimes.

Dominic opened his eyes. Five minutes later, he was making himself a coffee, apparently recovered. Amelia was still looking shocked.

——This happens, he said. Libby knows it's not serious.

——But Dominic, if that's so, should you have been driving like you were, never mind passengers, last week?

Dominic looked sheepish.

——It's not happened when I'm driving. Only when I get very tired or emotional.

——Oh, so it's a reaction to the video.

——I suppose so. Blame Melmont, said Dominic. I do, for everything.

Searching for something to eat, Libby found a giant catering pack of baked beans, but nothing else in the kitchen.

——Is this supper? I thought you didn't like beans, she said.

——Right, I can't stand them, said Dominic. But eighteen months ago I had a brief relationship with a boy who stacked the pallets at a cash-and-carry. He came round and thought he was going to win me back with the beans and the offer of unprotected sex.

——And did you? said Amelia, unable to stop herself. Dominic shook his head.

——I've probably killed enough people, as it is.

Amelia took them all out to supper at the local Indian. Libby held Dominic's hand, and then fanned her finger over the purple flock wallpaper, without which no standard Indian eating house dared throw its doors open in those days. Dominic drank red wine, and felt better. They toasted life and Dominic's quest, and their friendship, and honour, and freedom. When Libby went home she cried into her pillow for her brother till she fell into a dreamless state beyond sorrow from the coming separation of the twin to one's soul.

In her rooms in Oxbridge, Amelia's dreamlife drew her into

another world where Prince's College hung fantastically in the air, a giant Indian Rope Trick, only reachable by thin, tiny ladders woven from hemp. Then later she dreamt that Oxbridge had drifted back to Earth again, and she was about to conduct the rehearsals for an operatic ballet about Stalin, staged in Princes' own vast gilded oriental dome.

The opera set in Amelia's second dream consisted of twenty-seven settees, with a bedside light in each one. When the dictator lay down and closed his eyes, in his imagination he became a popular Tsar who was never assassinated but threw grand balls in the Kremlin with countless Archduchesses begging for a moment of intimacy with the great man. That was the first act.

How the work ended was still being decided. The music for the performance had been chosen from the scores Melmont's bequest had rescued from oxidised oblivion in Prince's music library. Amanda reflected that the composers would have known nothing of Stalin, though they would have known of Ivan the Terrible and Peter the Great. Perhaps that was enough.

In Amelia's dream, she stepped onto the conductor's podium and glanced down at the score. In reality, she could not even read music, but now the orchestra was looking up at her expectantly, and the only thing to do was play her part so the bearded boyars on stage could perform a Mazurka.

Amelia boldly pointed her baton at the strings section. Magically, on command, the acoustically perfect dream-dome above resounded with the rich opening downstrokes of twenty erotically charged dream violins, as History began its great dance for her.

XIX
The Hissing of Serpents

THE WEATHER HAD TURNED FOR THE BETTER at Melmont Keep after the last of the American invaders finally fled, but though the heating came back on, the social atmosphere inside the house remained chilly in the extreme. Emer's twin sister Biddy had been sent as a replacement for Emer after she went insane. While her sister knew her way around the pantry and had only drunk herself senseless at night, Biddy drank all the day as well, while calling out to herself the words of sentimental ballads. Something in her found the yoke of domestic service unbearable, for vacuum cleaners and polishing machines seemed to perish as soon as she touched them.

Melmont, making the wind his posthorse, blew in briefly to find his wife sitting alone at the long baronial table in front of an untouched plate of corned beef and diced beetroot, Biddy's idea of a 'spread'. The huge table stretched out into the gloom. Somewhere in the distance Biddy's voice rose and fell, sending its message through the empty corridors, a particularly plangent song from the third Irish potato famine, *The Tatties Are So Small, Over Here*. Hidden away, the banks of voice-activated tape recorders with their giant spools stopped and started and stopped again, undecided on whether Biddy's toneless keening constituted a conspiracy about to be hatched in any of the seventyeight rooms.

Melmont did not notice his wife was weeping. Abigail rose, and to cover her tears turned on a small electric kettle on the sideboard, next to a jar of instant coffee.

——How was your trip, dear?

——Which one?

——Weren't you in Israel?

——Among other places.

——Well how did it go?

——It was good. You have to bang heads together though and stamp your feet to get things done. Not unlike Russia, though of course the country is smaller.

The kettle sighed, increasingly loudly. Melmont, distracted, stared at it for a moment.

——Where are the children?

——It's termtime, said Abigail bitterly. You said they all had to go to boarding school, even though I wanted them with me and you're never here.

——You sound upset, said Melmont.

——You should know why I am upset.

——I don't. But perhaps I have a right to know. Can I do anything about it? Why won't you tell me?

There was a long pause before Abigail felt she had enough strength to continue.

——I heard it on the news. Gunter Röhl is dead. He was murdered outside a supermarket this afternoon.

Abigail noticed that when she announced Röhl's execution, Melmont's thumbs never ceased to pry a bread roll apart.

—Really?

—You don't sound very upset. Or surprised. He was your friend too, wasn't he?

—These things happen over there like that. Bloody German anarchist gangs are always taking out heads of corporations. It's their version of football. There's someone I found in Israel though, who will interest you.

—Who's that? said Abigail in a weak little voice.

—A doctor who can guarantee boys, said Melmont. He'll put a spring in your step.

Abigail felt faint. With the certainty of the abandoned wife, she knew her husband had had a hand in Röhl's death. And now the monster wanted her, in her sixth decade, pregnant again.

—Earnest, haven't you forgotten something? Biology. I'm too old; Abigail almost added 'thank God', out loud.

—You'll do it if you love me, said Melmont.

The rest of the spartan meal passed in silence. At the end Melmont rose, lit a cigar, and set off towards his study. As he passed Biddy, who was mopping, and moping and mithering disconsolately to herself, Melmont said,

—And tell her she's fired.

—Who? said Abigail nervously, thinking Melmont might be referring in a roundabout way, to a divorce. That would be a blessed relief, never mind if Father Cowley said it was a mortal sin.

—The housekeeper.

—You want me to fire Emer, or fire Biddy?

——I can't remember her name, That one. The one who drinks and makes terrible soup.

——They both do.

——She's standing in front of you, THAT ONE, snarled Melmont, pointing at Biddy.

——That's Biddy, who has kindly come to help out. Emer's in hospital.

——In a pig's arse, snarled Melmont.

Biddy stopped singing and stared at the big man. The electric kettle on the sideboard clearly knew something was up, for it started to hiss loudly in an agitated way. Melmont, deprived of a telephone to throw, unplugged the kettle and hurled it at the wall past Biddy's frightened head. Hot water splashed down the wall and lay smoking in puddles on the floor as Melmont stamped off, shouting something about snakes.

Biddy took umbrage, and the ferry back to Cork from Cardiff the next night. When her sister made her welcome but expressed surprise at seeing her so soon, Biddy replied,

——It's no time of my life to be having a violent master, insane, who says that a little kettle, no harm to a soul, is talking back to him.

The next morning, Abigail woke to see her husband at work at the side of the ornamental lake in front of the house. Having cut open a pair of chest-deep waders to get himself into them, and fallen down facefirst in the black mud, Melmont was a frightful sight, wielding a hedge trimmer.

——What does he think he's doing? said Abigail, to herself.

Melmont, whose interest in gardening had always been slight, was trying to cut all the dead sedge down because all through the sleepless night he had put up with its insistent clashing. It is those who have guilty secrets who most fear the hissing of serpents. Like the little kettle, the sedge had been offering sibillant warnings; whispers of further enemies in the ear of the murderer of Gunter Röhl.

ᛗ   ᛗ   ᛗ

Usually there was a sort of gentle joy for Dominic in walking home along the Notting Hill pavements carrying a Chinese meal, the day's work done, often another piece of the Melmontian puzzle fitted, feeling tired and contented, vindicated, in fact. But Röhl's death puzzled him as it had puzzled the choleric Redland Digby earlier in the day. He stepped down into his basement flat carrying a pack of three-minute egg noodles (37 New Pence from the shortlived "VG" grocery chain) in one hand, rolling a joint in the other. He really needed to get stoned to eat, and so it was a few minutes before he picked up his messages.

—Dominic, it's Redland Digby. It's midnight your time, I know. You saw the news about Röhl, I guess. Mossad was blamed but they shouldn't be getting the heat. In fact, the Iranians took him out. They'd been promised a delivery of you-now-what. They'd handed over money to Melmont who then... had him terminated. It's weird, I don't understand why he would do that, because Röhl was such a keystone of the whole business. Unless he's found another way of doing it.

After Dominic had another joint, he put on Vivaldi's *The*

Four Seasons, took a medium-soft lead pencil and started systematically to make ten thousand marks on a piece of paper, one for each warhead owned by the bankrupt Union of Soviet Socialist Republics. When Vivaldi had told the story of a year, Dominic was up to five thousand, and tiring. He marked out the last of the missiles, long after midnight, to Jim Morrison singing *Strange Days,* and sat back to look at the hoard. From the size of the missile cache and the resultant poverty of the country's subjects there were probably as many ways of getting missile heads out of Russia as there were missiles.

♩   ♩   ♩

Meanwhile the subject of Dominic's investigation was once again close to his dream of owning a national newspaper. *The Spyglass* was a superior Socialist tabloid that had brought the troops home and Labour into power in 1945, then abandoned its role as educator and slid downmarket, and now it was about to fall even further, into Melmont's lap. With a smaller circulation it was still the chief tabloid rival of *The Moon,* though it would never rival Ocker Midrash's vulgar pastiche of a tits 'n' arse anti-monarchist bluecollar, voice-of-the-proles redtop. Melmont was able to buy *The Spyglass* because the Board didn't want to sell the paper to Midrash, who was perceived as loutishly Thatcherite, as well as owning far too many papers already.

Just as in the days before his election to Parliament,

Melmont's character seemed to have the effect of creating a desired outcome by an exercise of will that steamrollered all obstacles. Like a shark scenting blood, Melmont moved into a hotel suite opposite *The Spyglass* building in Fleet Street, and a swarm of apparachniks followed, wheeling in fridges, telephone exchanges and every item that a successful tycoon could need to complete his purchase of a further major communications asset.

Tristram Cole was in the meantime providing Melmont's lesser bankers with the kind of thrilling inside information bankers like to hear.

——I suggest that we can confidently offer Melmont Communications another ten to fifteen million, not least because our audit appears to have seriously underestimated the assets of the real estate and the pension fund. I know Mr Melmont has a very stringent agenda as regards cost control, which he was almost successful in implementing in the case of his previous acquisition, the *North Briton.*

This time, because of the equity, the purchaser would be acquiring in effect for any purchase under a hundred million, there would not be a problem even if the editorial as well as the printing staff left.

The City fell into line, its short memory obliterating the Department of Trade and Industry's dour assessment of Melmont's probity, thirteen years old now. Lucky thirteen! After Cole's warm words, the available war-chest for acquisition of *The Spyglass* was considerably increased. As was Melmont's girth, by a constant diet of chicken tikka and icecream and doughnuts and trays of deepfried samosas, waiting impatiently for *The*

Spyglass board of directors to bow to the inevitable. Melmont sat occupying most of a black leather sofa as he munched, but still stared hungrily at the building opposite, which he had even checked was structurally able to have a helipad on the roof. The paper was already, in his imagination, his. Why, oh why were the chopped worms delaying?

Night fell on the scene and the neon lights of *The Spyglass* came on and spelt out its name across the street at his eyelevel, but not brightly enough for him. Melmont tore down the net curtains that hung grubbily in front of the plate-glass windows, and bundled them up in a ball before opening a window and pushing the lot out into the street. Jill came to his side. The only news was that there was no news of capitulation, yet.

——Telex *The Spyglass* Board with a final offer of ninety million, deadline midnight, growled Melmont. His saliva glands ejaculated audibly as he bit into another overstuffed doughnut. A sous-chef had been seconded from the Savoy, a few hundred yards away, and had been given a cook's syringe and instructed to saturate the insides of a hundred doughnuts with a special confection.

——But they've already got jam in them.

——Never mind; he wants *more* jam, and not just any jam, it has to be Morello cherry jam. There was a Morello cherry tree in his grandmother's garden and he used to mitch the fruit before the birds got it, before it was ever ripe, and *now* and forever is the time for that elusive ripeness, that succulence. Melmont took another doughnut, and the red dart of jam squirted out horizontally to leave an ambiguous sigil on the plate-glass, the only thing which stood between Melmont and the other object of his affection.

——Mr Melmont, the Board hasn't acknowledged the previous eighty million pound bid yet, Jill said. She was one of the few people round Melmont to stay calm.

——In that case, send the higher bid individually to their homes, at eleven thirty, exactly, said Melmont.

As Melmont's increasing blandishments went out to Mayfair or the far 'burbs, across the way in *The Spyglass* boardroom was a scene of conflict between two warring interests within the newspaper. The editor, Hector 'Spittle' Stilgoe was a man of small competence and less charisma, who had been appointed by a board that needed someone to 'deal with' the print unions. And now, facing him, Stilgoe had four printers in a state of calculated umbrage, deliberately making a mess of the nice white sofa, having carefully inked themselves before ascending to confront and go into battle with the management. Stilgoe was trying in vain to rise above the provocation of the class warpaint.

The four printers sat with their lower lips thrust forward and their blackened arms crossed. They possessed the swaggering pride and confidence of a hereditary working-class elite: men of note; sons of the men who had printed extra editions when Germany invaded Poland, and grandsons of the same printers whose fathers had typeset Jack the Ripper's murders on the very day they happened. Socialists were routinely astounded when they discovered how much the printers took home each week.

Though no one was listening to him, Stilgoe was saying, in a characteristically defensive monotone,

——If it don't get printed, nevermind how good the stories are, how can the bloody paper make enough money to survive? The people owning this place, will just close us down. The share price will go up in that case too because the building won't be losing money.

When Stilgoe's selfserving staccato had ended, Eric Boniface stood up to deliver a response. A short, aggressive redhaired Cockney, his wide mouth was set upon a small body with a tense but turret-like belly. As he spoke Eric waved his forefinger, sometimes ahead for emphasis, sometimes behind the *tempo* of his argument.

——*Hiff* we're talking share prices 'ere, then wotabaht what you lot 'ave been getting on with up here? Five-hour lunches you have to be carried back from. Champagne an' tarts coming in the back door by reg'lar delivery. I'm not standing here gettin' a lecture on how to run a farkin noospaper, with people what should know better behavin' like that; stands to reason.

Eric sat down. Stilgoe said, greyly and wearily,

——There is a foregone conclusion to this discussion, which is that the Board is going to unload this paper if it can. It will only consider not letting all of us go hang if your three unions together provide a no-strike agreement.

——Three unions? Have you counted the union representatives here? There are four! shouted Eric.

——The number doesn't matter. However many there are.

——You're against the unions! shouted Eric. Class-fucking traitor!

——My father was a trades union official, Eric, said Stilgoe, wearily, wishing that he had stayed at *Woman's Realm.*

——You're still against the unions. The unions that you ignore is the one Fing that stops the working classes bein' thrust into the Abyss! shouted Eric.

Stilgoe put his grey hands, holding a ballpoint pen, through his greasy hair for the hundredth time that evening and spoke with all the sarcasm he was capable of.

——*Abyss*? Your holidays in Spain and the new cars you get every year in this job is the *abyss*?

The gap between Eric the Red's wages and the national average was ten to one. The paper had exposed the cancer in its midst when it printed them in self justification, on the last week of production. This had not endeared the printers to their employers.

——I'm not having anyone puttin' our wages in the paper again, either. It's well out of order, said Eric. On top of the printers' wages, the paper had revealed that the worksheets for each shift included generous cash paypackets made out to phantoms cheekily entitled Snow White, Bambi and Mickey Mouse.

Stilgoe and the printers were unaware that Melmont was watching and thanks to Frank could hear every word. As he stared hungrily across the street, Melmont heard Stilgoe say,

——The Board knows that as things stand it can't control you without an agreement, and it is going to get rid of the paper if it can, so you're someone else's problem.

——Someone else? What, you mean that fat git, cried Eric the Red. Leave it aht! You must be jokin'! It's on the statutes. They 'ave to protect the labour movement from mad bastards with no conscience an' sell to a Conglomerate!

Having accomplished nothing, the militants all left the editorial suite, Eric last. Melmont watched through binoculars as Stilgoe lit a cigarette. The smoke hung tangled in slowly moving loops round his head, like his own wretched fix.

—You, stupid bastard, will be the first to go, said Melmont, softly. Then turned to Jill.

—Telex the Board again. Move the deadline to six am and make the bid a hundred and five.

There was the sound of a drawer being opened then a glugging noise as Stilgoe poured himself a stiff editorial. Then the phone rang in the boardroom. Melmont leant forward to listen.

—Hector Stilgoe? Bruce Midrash here.

Melmont gasped at the Australian's amoral opportunism and listened horrified as an admittedly unremarkable editor was poached from under his nose.

—I hear you're in a spot of bother. Why not step this way? How would you like to edit *The Moon*?

Having decided that firing Stilgoe would be the first thing he did he was now being thwarted by his rival from indulging in one of life's pleasures. Melmont went red, and Jill for a moment thought he was going to rashly try to hurl himself across the gap between the two buildings, as the conversation between Midrash and Stilgoe grew chummier.

—And of course, you'd have a free hand with the editorial policy. I don't like to interfere, said Midrash, a trifle inaccurately. Midrash liked his editors to guess his preferred approach and only made trouble if they got it wrong.

—That's an extremely kind offer, Mr Midrash. To tell you the truth, I was kind of dreading working under The Fat Controller.

—Who? Oh, Trannie.

Midrash was just too old to have read the Reverend Awdrey's delightful *Thomas the Tank Engine* books.

——Leave him alone! I'll break your legs if you take my editor! shouted Melmont. Fortunately the speaker Frank had rigged was a one-way device.

Ten minutes later, still fretting over having lost his insignificant editor, Melmont was called by Cole with smooth and welcome news. As he listened, Melmont felt honey was being poured into his wounds.

——You're not just getting what you want, Earnest. It's turned into Christmas. Calm down. You're *there*. Just keep quiet about the fact that you've bought it for a song. Everest has been scaled. Now, don't fall off.

——This takeover is going to go down in the annals of history, said Melmont. Socialism and journalism at last together. Where is my biographer? He should be here!

If Melmont had still been sleeping with Jill he would have hugged her. Instead, he hugged himself, and realised that in the excitement, he had neglected his bodily functions. One of them was extremely pressing.

——Order twenty linen napkins, would you?

The napkins arrived on a silver salver, brought in by a smiling but baffled room service.

——Is this what you ordered, sir?

——Yes. I'm going to do a big poopoo now, he announced to the maid.

Afterwards, Melmont left the building to take possession of his new toy from the air, arriving in style on top of *The Spyglass* building in his helicopter.

Thrilling, specially composed music played and teams of fluorescently dressed abseilers danced down the sheer sides of the newspaper building as searchlights blinded those who looked up. The searchlight's position meant that few saw that Melmont's idea of conquest was to make water from atop his latest domain onto the obediently cheering crowds. Like Melmont's lovemaking it was over in a few minutes. The super-fit abseilers rewound and stowed their Mylar compound ropes and collected their specialist clamps, the lamps went off and the speakers fell silent.

Almost before he had rebuttoned his flies, Melmont had gone within, knowing his great challenge lay before him, to impose a working relationship on an ancient technocratic elite, the print unions. He faced the same four printers across Stilgoe's desk as the ones who had been there the day before with Stilgoe. Stilgoe's desk was cleared already, with the exception of an empty gin bottle in the lefthand drawer.

—Where's Stilgoe? asked Eric, uncertainly. His old enemy had gone and been replaced by something dangerous resembling a Kodiak bear in a suit.

—Your editor will not be returning. I have paid a hundred million pounds for this paper. But if the notion took me to close it, I could do so tonight and still not lose a penny. What do you say to that?

Eric remained silent. The helicopter was thudding on the roof, as if suggesting that the great man had given orders for an imminent takeoff, if offended.

—However, closure is not my intention. I am going to make *The Spyglass* into a leading paper once again. I remember it was, when I was in Berlin during the war. You printers have a unique chance to become the most highly qualified volume printer workforce in the world. With wages to match. We will look forward, rather than back. For instance, gentlemen, we are going to be the first daily newspaper to use colour!

The idea of new printing skills were the last things on the printers' minds.

——That's well and good, always provided, Mr Melmont, that you accept that our present wage levels are the basis for future negotiations, said Eric the Red.

——I can assure you that the new technology will bring greater rewards than you can dream of. But I do want you all to observe some self-restraint.

Eric blinked behind his big glasses trying to work out what was being said. Melmont had shifted and become an unfamiliar bear, uttering weasel words. The dancing bear then became a polar bear. Melmont reached into his pocket and brought out a stuffed Mickey Mouse.

——The first rule is no more Mickey Mouse, said the bear, smiling dangerously at Eric. Then waggling its murderer's thumbs, the bear effortlessly tore little Mickey to shreds, till there was nothing left of him.

XX

Ocker Throws a Snit

MELMONT WOULD NEVER DEFEAT THE PRINT UNIONS, and the lesson was not lost on his deadly rival, Ocker Midrash of the calculating beige eyes, who saw the fight against the unions was unwinnable by conventional thinking. So Ocker, in great secrecy, began to plan the news empire Melmont was only dreaming of; and Ocker's empire, when it came, had smooth outward walls offering no niche or toehold for inky Eric and his kind. The 'electricians' who ran Ocker's new machine all had to get on their knees and swear they would not make trouble. To the victor, the spoils.

As he strolled by the editor's slab of *The Moon* that night, Midrash saw a news story about Melmont. Above the jocular goofy caption was a photograph of Melmont's helicopter making its appearance on *The Spyglass* building's roof.

——The Trannie Has Landed!

The clowning and punning of his cheeky little newspaper suddenly grated as inappropriate. Midrash felt suddenly miffed that Melmont was on the front page of Midrash's own publication. He decided he was not going to give his rival free publicity in future.

—Inside page, straight text, no bold, fifty words max, early editions only, he barked.

Two editors sprang towards him and hovered nervously one at each side, as Ocker's bony reptilian finger identified the offending mock-up.

—Right you are, boss!

—And dump the picture, Ocker added, cruelly. Then he was gone.

Weeks later, when Melmont's habit of using the rooftop of *The Spyglass* as a pissoir became the gossip of Fleet Street, *The Moon* received pictures from their highest-paid battle-hardened celebrity photographer of Melmont's huge bottom sticking out of the side of his helicopter. But the very same day, the scoop of Melmont crapping on Fleet Street was trumped. The picture desk was offered a sweetly charming colour picture of a *very* young Fensterkuchen prince with flaxen blond hair (colour printing had just come in, as Melmont had predicted). The little prince had his trews down and was fulsomely urinating to camera, in a pretty arc that caught the sun.

If both pictures appeared in the same edition, they might have led to questions being raised about the paper's true pre-occupations. Faced with a choice between a sweet royal with both hands on his piddler to steer the flow, and of even more publicity for his morbidly obese rival defecating, Ocker chose once again to pretend his rival did not exist.

Melmont's publications meanwhile printed pictures of the Publisher, fully clothed, at every opportunity. At any time, there were up to fifty court cases on Melmont's behalf proceeding through the courts and pictures of Melmont victorious in injunction were given particular prominence.

I was in a room recently with roughly two hundred of Great Britain's lawyers in it, celebrating an old friend's elevation to becoming a Queen's Counsel. The guests, in conversation, to a man, would deplore Melmont's exploitation of the legal system to gag criticism. Looking around I realised there was probably not a lawyer in the room who had declined to have his palm greased by the Melmont Shilling.

Supported by *The Spyglass'* able photographers, Melmont's profile increased, and endless injunctions ensured that his habit of keeping his accounts in Liechtenstein was no more eccentric or criminal than Ocker's penchant for keeping his accounts off-whatever-shore he was trading on. Abigail suspected that Melmont was implicated in the death of Röhl, but still had no proof. She submitted grimly to a sequence of post-menopausal pregnancies, but even the New Biology still was able only to conjure up girls from Melmont's loins.

Melmont's sixtieth birthday loomed. He was determined to outdo the celebrations which Prince George had graciously attended for the hospital opening. A disaster loomed over public relations supremo Ira Bleaver's failure to obtain the heavy hitters of the Fensterkuchen clan for the party. Melmont fretted.

——Shiver me kishkas! Tell that useless little runt to get on the phone now, Jill, and put a rocket up their fat Kraut bottoms!

That runt, the famous Ira Bleaver, resigned saying there was nothing more he could do.

——I'm off. No point in continuing, really. I've *told* him there isn't a brown envelope in the world big enough to have whoever it is that he wants, but he won't listen, so that's it.

The Spyglass ran a story the next day saying Melmont had re-hired Bleaver for 'an undisclosed sum but bound to be in excess of £250,000' with a picture of the Publisher shaking hands with the famous stoat-faced PR, taken before the rift. While it was completely untrue, there were no hard feelings on either side. Porkie or no porkie, it was a valuable piece of advertising for them both.

Meanwhile, the party preparations were gathering momentum in Melmont Keep. In keeping with the threatened no-show of royal cover, Melmont assumed a new title for himself for the great day, issuing instructions he was no longer a newspaper owner he was a Publisher, and should be addressed and always identified accordingly from henceforth.

The temporary buildings had gone that had briefly housed the doomed Melmontian appendix, Interlease (septic, critical, burst, excised, now obliterated from memory). The shallow foundations had been grubbed out and fresh rosebeds planted to make ready for The Day.

Fresh peacocks, bred to be fully tailed the year round and guaranteed not to succumb to night-shrieks, were being delivered on a lorry loaded with their ornamental cages, one to each bird. But the new birds were the most quarrelsome creatures imaginable and promptly tore each other's tails out. The devil is always in the details.

——There's a problem delivering one invitation to your birthday party, Publisher. Priscilla Cole is camped outside Greenham Common and the Post Office won't deliver there.

——Don't come to me with some chopped wormage about

postcodes. That's not a problem. You solve it!

Jill drove down to Greenham with the invitation.

Greenham Common was one of the many places which had been commandeered for airstrips by the American forces when they came over in strength to prepare for the invasion of Europe. Then the runway was extended so that mighty B52s could use it for pilot training. The thrill of seeing one of these huge noisy eight-engined dragons on training flights, with their undercarriages down and brake parachutes open, straining slowly across the sky was religious, a pagan epiphany for small boys living nearby. But the B52 warrior-gods went away to bomb Laos and Vietnam and Cambodia, and the station was mothballed until it became a centre for Cruise Missile carriers.

Cruise was the successor to the earlier V1 or 'doodlebug', a pilotless plane that self-steered to its target, which Hitler had hoped would teach London a lesson. The Greenham missiles had large mobile launchers which would drive out of their reinforced silos through Berkshire, Barsetshire or Oxbridgeshire's leafy byways, and release their lowflying missiles to wing under the radar of the enemy and strike at the heart of his Evil Empire. In peacetime, the missile launchers still had to cross the station perimeter in rehearsal of their war-dance, and this is where the Greenham Women camps sited their protests.

The camps were peopled by women, who tended to simplify armed conflict as male, with Woman a non-belligerent, redemptive force. They claimed that even the occupation of the land by the Americans was illegal (which it was), and they harassed the personnel going in and out of the camps, and hung coded folk-offerings on the perimeter wire: little dolls (to remind the soldiers that they were human); mirrors (to do the same); and wild woolly webs like something made by drugged spiders, which were perhaps potent Earth magic spells; certainly they testified to a self-consciously low level of spinstering skills among the politicised single-sex community. Some of them were anti-men, as if women somehow had had nothing to do with bringing men into being beyond submitting to rape. Some of them had been raped and had forgiven their oppressors. Some were actually mentally damaged, but probably not as badly as the staff whose job it was to maintain the instruments of mega-death on the other side of the perimeter fence. Frankly I remain in awe of their courage, and suspect that the madness they practised is perhaps the only kind of sanity left.

Jill changed from her court shoes to a pair of sensible green wellington boots for the trudge around the main camp, which had blossomed, untouchable in law, on the aforesaid common ground in the churned mud alongside one of the missile access roads. Around her, women were tending to their low tents made from polythene and sticks. Some were rudimentary. Some were well kept inside and clean, with separate cooking areas and neatly piled plates with portable gas stoves, as if going camping and saving the world were one and the same thing.

Jill had been given a photograph of Priscilla taken in Cairo thirty years before by a studio photographer, with a curling painted backdrop of the pyramids. In the photo, Priscilla sat looking like the Sphinx itself, pictured behind her, with a wry enigmatic expression on her face.

Twenty feet away there was a wild, coldlooking grey-headed woman in a sleeveless quilted jacket, tending a fire. Jill looked down to check the photo, wondering whether the young

Priscilla was the earlier self of the crone who poked the fire, 'othered by time', as Coleridge describes the difference. Before Jill could approach, a rough gonging noise started and the woman Jill was looking at stood up and rushed away.

Someone was beating an oil drum. Summoned by the noise, women now started pouring out of the benders towards the road. At the same time, the wide metal gates of the base opened, two hundred yards away, and a huge multi-wheeled missile carrier rolled out. As the gates closed it accelerated towards them, changing its many gears. The women moved away from the road and waited. Jill noticed that their arms were filled with jam jars and balloons filled with paint, which they now prepared to throw. Jill started to feel afraid: the approaching carrier looked as though it had been designed for a war-crazed boys' shoot-em-up game. It was the size of four large removal vans stuck together, with high massive sides. No one dared jump in its path, but a fierce keening arose from the women.

——Killer! Killer! Killer! Killer!

The killer roared by loudly, still gaining speed and the women pitched their paintbombs. For a regularly practised ritual, which it was, the Greenham Women's aim was wretched, and there were few hits on the immense, almost unmissable khaki sides. The memory of Zenocrate throwing a cricket ball time after time to hit a single stump twenty yards away, flashed through Jill's mind. It was after his firstborn had hit the stump thirteen times in succession that Melmont, laughing and applauding seated on his shooting stick, had commissioned the full-length portrait in virginal cricket whites that still hung in the great hall.

As the mobile nuclear weapons launcher lumbered away,

the women joined hands across the road again, in a magical affirmation against the horror that had just passed; of their lives, and of their wombs which they affirmed should bring forth a sensible race of women-children only from henceforth.

The Cruise carrier returned ten minutes later, when the whole dangerous game was repeated, but in reverse. Finally Jill found Priscilla where she had first seen her poking a fire.

——They don't seem to go far, if they are meant to be escaping a nuclear strike, said Jill.

——They are just trying to frighten us, but they don't succeed, said Priscilla, who had scored a hit on the returning carrier's windscreen with something bloody.

Jill had seen the strike and complimented her on her aim.

——Only ox liver, sadly. Last week we had a human placenta, but I don't imagine the drivers can tell the difference.

She wiped her hands. Jill handed her a large white envelope and she drew out the stiff gilt embossed invitation card wonderingly.

——Of course I will come. He has been so good to me. But what is this? Has he been made a knight, or something?

The Publisher of Melmont Keep had awarded himself the titular freehold of a Manor, which came with a coat of arms. A quartered shield with a book, a sword, a tusking boar sangliant, and beside the boar, a shining city on a brown hill, which had prompted Frank to gently rib his enormous employer.

——Is this a broad hint to the world about the dangers of radioactive excrement, my Lord?

——That is the shining city of Jerusalem, Frank, which certain crusaders put on their escutcheons. They also had to personally defeat three Saracens.

——How many Saracens didja take out yourself?

——I have been to the modern Jerusalem many times in the course of business, the difference between me and a crusader being I am not obliged by charter to liberate the indigenous populations, and I go there bearing gifts, in peace.

Frank pointed to the motto floating below it on a swirling banner:

——Look, fuckin' Latin! Aren't people going to think you're a stuck-up cunt wiv one of these?

——I think not, Frank.

Melmont's new motto, '*Scienta Melliflorissimus Est*' translates as 'Knowledge is the sweetest thing of all' not a bad motto for a science publisher. Really, it's easy to be snide about purchased titles and other gong-chasings, but didn't Will Shakespeare, The Master, who has no need for accolades, decorations or titles, fix himself up with a crest? Melmont's little snobbery makes him *plus anglais que les anglais,* walking in the footsteps of the Bard of Avon.

And the Bard himself would have been delighted, I have no doubt, to see the road past Ann Hathaway's cottage featuring as an emergency access item in the Greenham Common Ground Zero nuclear dispersal plans.

♫   ♫   ♫

The rotund nuclear salesman's sixtieth birthday dawned bright and clear, a perfect English summer's day. The lovely violet-blue around the Morning Star slowly faded as the sky lightened, and King Sol not only announced his intention to rise majestically unclouded by Neptune's fogs from the sea, but for once kept his word, another sign it was going to be a scorcher.

The Sun, also known as Apollo, or Phoebus, the Shining One (My Lord Melmont of Boxly Manor, Evengame and Burlingjob is not the only Urge to help himself to more than one name) soon broke the horizon's circle to light the eastern flatlands of great Boudicca's territories. Then, great Phoebus-Apollo's car revealed itself in all its profligate glory, soaring west-wards with the hoofbeats of its blazing steeds spreading plasma and countless neutrinos through the firmament as well as the blessings of visible diffused light from a gloriously blue sky.

In the middle of Oxbridge, the goldleaf-clad copper panels of Prince's great onion dome creaked as they warmed, and the carp and mullet in the Oxus moved from their night-grazing upon surface-hopping insects, to root themselves ruminatively in the abundant deep soft mud of the river away from the pitiless noon rays.

Long before noon, Nile Street's crooked mile was choked with airconditioned coaches blowing diesel fumes into the sullen crowds on the pavement. Cleopatra's mannequins followed the queen on her round track out through the doors and in again beneath the face of the famous Waterclock in Nile Square as it struck twelve. Cole took one look at the heaving thorough-fares in each direction, and decided against trying to purchase Melmont a last-minute birthday gift. He walked down back streets till he found an entrance to the towpath along the Oxus to the pub opposite Reedy Island, which was mysteriously deserted, with the surrounding fields and river as quiet in the afternoon heat as they would have been towards the end of God's week of Creation, before talking animals appeared.

As Phoebus-Apollo relented and the shadows lengthened again, the talking animals were unquestionably in the ascendant in a spot outside Oxbridge, on a south-eastern swell in the river plain, now Melmont's Seat. Fitters, riggers, liggers, whiggers, butlers and civilian sutlers, caterers, their kith and kin all bustled around the great house, preparing for the celebrations. Half a ton of fireworks had been lashed to an enormous trellis at the end of the gardens, and when the signal to light was given an hour after sunset, they would spell out in a blaze of catherine wheels and multicoloured flames, 'HAPPY BIRTH-DAY EARNEST MELMONT MC 60 HAPPY YEARS'.

The impressive guest list contained both Great Ones as well as Melmont's old friends whom he had not forgotten. Several Sheiks would be present, and even a Sultan. There was, true, a sad lack of major native royalty to ratify Melmont's citizenship of John Bull Island. Ira Bleaver had hit the nail on the head when he said that there wasn't a brown bag large enough. Ira often used the truth, when it suited him.

Dressed in a dinner jacket, Willis Death was being helped from his car nearby by the juddering light of the fireworks as they ignited. His Parkinson's disease was even more pronounced, but he was happy and proud to be there. His wife took his arm to help him cross the immaculately graded gravel path, and they both looked with pleasure at the brave display in letters ten foot high, in a font derived from *The Spyglass* front page headlines. For a minute or so, it lit up the house in a way Phoebus himself would have approved.

——Aow, Gawd bless 'im!

All in all, everyone agreed it was a fitting tribute, though afterwards the smell of burnt feathers filled the air. The new peacocks had earlier made nests in the walkway above the rear of the fireworks. The sudden holocaust caught the foolish birds unawares. This accident was the source of the story that several peacocks were roasted on the spot for Melmont's own consumption. However Ira Bleaver suppressed such gossip about his porcine client by offering redtop editors other choice cuts from his well-stocked larder of scandal.

Inside the house, Melmont was resplendent in a wing collar and tails. No peacock gizzards or specks of gravy stained his shirt. The invitation had indicated that medals should be worn. His own decoration for bravery was pinned over his heart. He greeted his distinguished guests as each one was announced with a smile, a wave, a handshake or a humble inclination of the head.

Priscilla arrived on the arm of her brother in a tattered evening gown of no particular colour. Cole was wearing a dinner jacket but was without decoration; his own Military Cross had been stolen by one of the young panther-boys he had feasted with, and he had not replaced it, feeling that the medal aged him, and tied him to a long-gone conflict.

Melmont beamed at Priscilla widely; she felt bathed in his warmth and affection and almost girlishly weak at the knees.

——Priscilla, I am *deeply* honoured. How are you and what have you been doing?

——I am watching the world gear up for Armageddon. The British soldiers who are brought in to protect the airbase from us because they say we are dangerous, they drive slowly in their buses past our camp and have all got their trousers pulled down with their anuses flat against the glass.

Melmont tut-tutted.

——We are the conscience of the nation and we are edited off the news. You should send a photographer down to cover it, said Priscilla.

——I will, said Melmont.

The crowd moved on, and Cole and Priscilla were borne away towards the glittering chandeliers of the first refreshment tent, where Libby stood, looking glamorous enough to be a prince's consort. She was indeed on Prince George's wish list. His wavering loyalty to the party was secured on the further promise that Libby, one of the year's top models, was going to be there.

Prince George's detectives were standing at the sides of the tent with what passes for discretion among minders, as dishes with venison and wild boar's head were borne past. Oblivious to the display, they were looking forward to the time later on in the evening when they could slip away and snort some coke, but now their master was in conversation with a goodlooking commoner and the agenda could change in a twinkling. The prince had a particular weakness for assignations in carparks, which required all the minders' training to conceal from public scrutiny. They were, in their way, experts in human frailty.

——She's on the troll. I'd say he was in with a chance.

——*Well* in.

Libby passed up on the carpark offer and waited a week before sliding between the sheets with Prince George. She was disappointed that royalty snored, she told Dominic.

——Of course they snore. What I want to know is whether his *cum* tasted any different to the *hoi polloi*.

——Not really, said Libby.

Prince George was complaining gently to Libby about how his duties were really quite a slog and how nothing exciting ever happened to him. The rumours of how he had been separated from his minders and trapped in the cryogenic unit by the megalomaniac who threatened to strangle him unless he brought a dead child back to life had been greatly exaggerated.

——I wouldn't be here if he'd tried to hoodwink me. I think your godfather's a very lively man. There was an unplanned deviation for the inspection of a cryogenic unit and they hadn't yet fitted a door handle, that's all.

As if in punishment for his failure to raise the dead through a royal miracle, he would be recalled in Emperor's New Clothes by the artful Midrash tabloids, five years after it all happened. 'TOP MODEL GOBBLES OL' BASTARD', the headlines would announce. 'Royal Cum "similar to rest"'. Well, Libby would say that, wouldn't she?

Behind Libby's yet-to-be-tried pouting mouth stood Melmont's would-be Russian 'controller', Sergei Vanov, increasingly portly, waiting to hail Melmont. Vanov was in a dinner-jacket with enough medals on it to suggest he might have won the war on his own. But put on the scales, even with his wives and children thrown in, Vanov would never come close to matching the weight of his host and secret benefactor. Vanov approached and embraced as much of Melmont as he could get his arms around.

——Old friend! My wife almost killed herself for disappointment that she could not come, said Vanov. She has heard so much about you.

——You'd better make it up to her, or she'll turn you in, you two-faced old capitalist, said Melmont to Vanov, and laughed, though Vanov only smiled politely.

Everybody who was anybody was there. Ira Bleaver was there, naturally. He and Melmont had now made it up for real. In a profile piece, a not infrequent event for 'Hire A Believer' as the self-propelled little so-and-so was known in the columns of *The Prefect*, Ira announced his reconversion to Melmontism.

——I was wrong about Earnest. Someone told me something bad about him and I believed it. Well, that's easy to do, isn't it? Given the aggravation he's had, and the unjust accusations, it's no wonder that he resorts to law so quickly to defend his name. But he was publicly vindicated recently after a vile personal attack, and now I'm glad to say I'm going to be working for him again, with special emphasis on expanding the profile of his global communications, not forgetting his work for charity.

Quite so, Ira. Quite so.

When Melmont's assembled guests sat down to feast at the long tables, they found on every place setting a lavishly bound, gilt-inlaid copy of a book. Under the book on the plate was a bag containing a toilet kit, with a teeny pair of nail scissors which unfolded then refolded into themselves till they practically disappeared, accompanied by masses of foil-sealed scented disposable wipes.

——He obviously is worried that some of his guests won't be clean or have long dirty fingernails, said Prince George, and his minders both politely laughed. The joke was later included in *The Wit and Wisdom of Prince George*, published as damage limitation when it became clear that the palace had nothing substantial to offer Ira Bleaver in return for keeping Royal cum off the front page. The book sank without trace, as sometimes happens, even with Royal books. The cum, on the other hand, is now part of our rich folk heritage.

Libby, to her alarm, found herself sitting opposite her weatherbeaten mother.

——*Christ, am I going to look like that one day?*

Priscilla's head was bent, her long, wild greying hair wrapped carelessly around it as she studied the outside of her copy of the handsomely tooled menu, with its heraldic shield showing the Holy City.

When are you going to see Dom, mother? He's in hospital again, you know.

Priscilla ignored the question.

——I say! What can *this* be?

——It's the menu. Mother, what did we do to deserve you?

——Oh, you mean Dominic's health. He'll be out in no time, I expect, said Priscilla, turning to the book that had been under the menu. When it was opened, it revealed itself to be *Earnest Melmont, the Little-known Facts* by one Andreas Rommos.

——Darling, if someone has written a biography already, isn't Dominic wasting his time?

——No mother, he is not wasting his time. Also I don't think when Dominic's version comes out Earnest will be giving copies of it away at his birthday party.

——Then what is this?

——It's a cuttings job. Some hack has been hired to cut and

paste every time Melmont's name gets in the papers. Unlikely to be critical, or read.

——You don't think Earnest will like what Dom will write? Whyever not?

——Because he's found some quite bad things that Earnest, that Melmont, has done.

——All gossip. And I don't believe your brother has AIDS. Earnest wouldn't employ him if he had. He has morals, you know.

Libby's jaw dropped deliberately but her mother was turned away from her, peering shortsightedly at the entertainment. One of the little Melmont girls, surely the youngest of all, had clambered up on a central table and a hush slowly fell on the room as a pink spotlight picked her out.

——My name is Thophie Melmont, with a Thed, the little girl began, lispingly. I am theven years old. I have three thithters, all born on the same day. Daddy *THTILL* forgetth our birthdayth. (Laughter from Daddy, and from guests). He ith a Thtrict Daddy but thometimes he can pretend to be Nithe. I wote thith thpeech mythelf, Zophia concluded.

The miraculously *in vitro* fertilised tot knelt without further ado and got off the table, backwards, showing her white knickers and chubby legs to an applauding crowd. As Zophia descended, another little triumph of biology was being coaxed onto the table by Abigail.

——My name is Zebediah Melmont. I am the same age as my three sisters. Our mummy had us all at once when she was over fifty, quite old. This is a brave thing to do because you might die. Mummy was sent to Italy by Daddy and had some special injections from a nice doctor.

Try as they might, with the fastest centrifuges in the world, the doctors had not been able to create what Melmont required, a boy.

The boy in the hospital bed next to Dominic's had just died unexpectedly, too soon to put him in the bed next to the doors. The nurses swung into action, donning rubber gloves in the middle of the room. To distract attention from the mucky business of Death, they put screens around the bed in a matter-of-fact way, and turned the television on loud to cover the doctor's swift and matter-of-fact autopsy.

There was Melmont on the box, as large as life, with Abigail on his right hand in the midst of his birthday party Dominic gasped. Ira Bleaver, publicist and puppetmaster, was seated prominently nearby, as a sign of his renewed favour.

—My dear friends and family.

—*Cardiac arrest.* The autopsy came through underneath, from the bed to Dominic's left, as an uneven counterpoint to Melmont's measured tones.

—Yes, family! There are some values we cannot lose in this sceptred isle.

—*Extended fungal growth.*

—Fair play is one. Decency is another. The family is a third, not forgetting that great family at our head, the Royal Family.

—*Ocular lesions.*

—Apart from my family here tonight, I can see captains of industry and commerce…

—*Karposi's sarcoma.*

—And trades unions leaders, able politicians, popular music stars, not forgetting the cream of British football and the renowned publicist.

The corpse next to Dominic was finally wheeled away, as the spotlight played briefly on Bleaver, who looked up, suitably modest.

——Ira Bleaver, champion of the downtrodden, knight in white armour to those who have not the money to fight for their rights in court, unlike myself, Melmont added, to a ripple of laughter.

A friend of mine was called in to write a movie script for and about Bleaver, which exposed his borderline legality, but the rampant little sod wanted to be portrayed as a stud as well as a knight in shining armour. Ira binned the project.

——Not enough sex!

Well, he would say that, wouldn't he?

Melmont continued, jestingly,

——There are people here who have at one time or another tried to put me in jail. Suddenly the spotlight was swung away from Bleaver and picked out the DTI inspector, steely redoubtable Tessa Prufrock, who realised at that moment she had been compromised by accepting the invitation. She blushed scarlet.

——Welcome here tonight, Tessa, boomed Melmont. Your allegations have long been refuted and are now laid to rest. Under your plate I think you will find, if you look, invitations to join no less than three of my offshore corporate boards, with guaranteed first-year bonuses!

In the applause, Tessa could be seen looking under her plate, but then she decided to resist the money-mujik's charms. She laid the plate down and beckoned for a microphone to be brought to her, and then spoke bravely into it.

——I should like to thank Mr Melmont for his offer. I should

make it clear that as a former DTI board member, I won't be able to accept his offer to sit on any of the boards.

——You will, Tessa, you will! said Melmont, to general laughter, as Tessa sat down again. Melmont adjusted his spectacles.

——I want to share with all of you, important tidings. A revolution as potent as Gutenberg's print revolution is taking place as I speak, and a new world is opening before all of us. The opportunities this new world offers are literally boundless. But if these new communications systems continue to fall into the wrong hands, I need mention no names, we may wake to find Great Britain is Great Britain no more.

——The cultural intruders in our midst can and must be vanquished! That is why I am taking up my trusty sword now, like Saint George, on your behalf, the behalf of everyone here tonight, to do battle for everything we hold dear.

The curtains behind Melmont were drawn up smartly to reveal a large revolving globe of the world, with the countries in bas-relief, surrounded by numerous satellites which blinked rapid pulses of light to indicate radio communication. Then the globe stopped rotating and opened. An enormously tall Brazilian transsexual in a leotard and six-inch red heels rose up to sing. The orchestra struck up *Happy Birthday to You*, and Abigail and the girls led the applause. Dominic watched the credits roll as the cameras cut back repeatedly to Melmont's beaming face with a fat cigar tucked in at the corner of his smile. He clearly was having a wonderful birthday.

So much to do, muttered Dominic, so little time.

XXI

Faithful Jill

MELMONT'S SECRETARY JILL and Tristram Cole were having lunch together at her request in Cole's club, where the shepherd's pie, following an old wartime tradition, was middling to poor. Jill was leaving hers, and Cole was preparing to be indignant on her behalf.

——I should have warned you.

——It doesn't matter, Tristram, I'm really too upset to eat. My world fell apart yesterday. I left to go shopping early morning, which is when I like to get it done, and I forgot something I was going to take back. When I went back into the house, there was this ratty little man.

——A burglar?

——Much worse, said Jill, a *bugger*. Earnest's bugger. I haven't slept with Earnest for four years now; I haven't worked for him for two.

——I thought you set his party up for him?

——Alright, but I went back as a *favour*… The point is, Earnest is *still* bugging my house.

——Earnest is bugging your house? said Cole, a sinking feeling in his stomach.

——This chap, Frank, says he's been working for Earnest for yonks.

——What does he know about Earnest?

——Everything, as far as I could tell. Do you know of him? He's quite small, and has crossed front teeth.

——Haven't met him, I don't think.

——He was there because he thought I was out for the day, which I normally am.

——So he knows your movements, said Cole, thoughtfully. What was he doing?

——Changing the cassette in the spy camera in the light fitting above the bed. It's activated by body heat apparently.

——That's the most terrible invasion of privacy, Cole said.

——I feel like telling the newspapers, said Jill. I have nothing to lose.

——Which ones?

——I don't know. *The Prefect*?

——They may be injuncted from mentioning him.

Melmont was already suing *The Prefect*, which claimed that the great man was rigging the Spot-the-Ball competition in his newspaper. When the timing of the announcement of the 'winner' was delayed yet again, Melquist Shelley, the editor of *The Prefect*, took legal advice and pointed out truthfully that the only clear winner, yet again, would be the litigious E. Melmont, Publisher.

'Spot the Ball' was a game where you had to guess where the ball was when the photograph of a game of football was taken. Nowadays with data search and real-time computer reconstructions offered from the Internet, any booby with a modem and enough gigabytes on their hard drive can find the ball in any photo, from every angle of every goal ever scored, so it's history, like nine men's morris, flock wallpaper in standard Indian restaurants and Cruise missile protests. Melmont sued, but it looked like this time he was going to lose. If he lost, his legal stranglehold would start to loosen.

——Has he spied on anyone else, do you know? Cole asked Jill.

——*Everyone*, said Jill. According to my bugger, it's an epidemic. Not just his wife and the accountants and the journalists but the milkman, the petrol pump attendant. More tapes than he can see in a lifetime, Frank says. It's crazy.

——He's certainly borrowing an awful lot of money, Cole said, thinking, He's expanding way too fast, and not looking where he's going.

——He's going insane, Jill said simply. In fact he went insane a while ago. It was just that no one noticed.

Dominic discharged himself from hospital when it looked like Melmont was going to lose, and walked straight to court. Looking haggard and blotchy, he slipped into the visitors' gallery of Number Thirteen, where Melmont was more than filling the witness box. Crucial evidence had just been presented to the jury. In a period of hushed indeterminancy, inseparable from any real legal process, the twelve just men and women were examining a Spot-the-Ball photograph from *The Spyglass* pasted on a board.

The judge smiled benignly on the mainly elderly jury, as they exchanged long- for short-range spectacles to peer at the blotchy black-and-white photographs of the ball-less struggles of two unidentifiable teams.

——Take your time, ladies and gentlemen.

Melquist Shelley, sitting below the visitors' gallery, was biting his nails to the quick, desperate to have and hold the victory for free speech that so many times had been denied by the obese bully in the witness box. It was not terribly English to care about principles, but like many staunch defenders of the English way of life, Shelley's family came from elsewhere, Sicily in his case; perhaps this was why he enjoyed a feud. Morrish, the lawyer retained by the magazine for the defence, had assured him that the trickery was blatant and *The Prefect* would be vindicated. Their costs would be awarded.

——The fat crook has done this heist in broad daylight, no question. There is no way, under English law, he can get away with it.

Until he had become ill, Dominic had had little time for human frailty, but now, looking down on the back of Shelley's neck as he chewed his nails, Dominic noticed that the skin was pitted and deeply scarred, and he felt a stab of sympathy for the eccentric editor.

The jury had finished examining the photographs and Morrish was invited by the judge to launch his legal broad-sides upon Melmont's daylight robberies. He began smoothly.

——It would be helpful to the jury if I clarified the sequence of your actions, Mr Melmont, leading up to this present court action against the satirical paper, *The Prefect*, for libel. Mr Melmont, was it not *after* your rival paper, *The Moon*, began a bingo competition with a large cash prize, that you instituted a Spot-the-Ball competition for your newspaper, with the written promise of a prize of one million pounds?

There was a pause as photocopies of the front page of *The Moon*'s bingo offer, with the date ringed in felt pen made their way round the jury.

——I'd had the idea *first*. I had the idea before *The Moon*, to run a competition, said Melmont, belligerently.

——The jury have seen for themselves the result of the competition in your newspaper, on the thirteenth of June this year. Now, exactly one week later, on the twentieth of June, after the competition had closed, your newspaper *The Spyglass* could announce blithely that the ball had in fact been in a square *no one* had chosen. Is it not the case that by delaying the announcement of the prize as you did, you were able to artificially place the ball so no one could win, *after* the entries arrived?

——I would never do that.

Melmont's lower lip started to jut out but he pulled it back in. He continued.

——I do not think the public are gullible. I love the public. And if it was done in the way you are deliberately suggesting, I would not know anything about it, in any case.

Morrish, a former Winchester College scholar, smiled a polished, wintry Wykhamist's smile.

——Come come, Mr Melmont, I put it to you that you are the very much hands-on proprietor of this newspaper, and no stranger to its workings as you seem to be suggesting. You are trying to jump up the circulation by advertising large cash prizes which you will make sure are never awarded. Perhaps because you cannot *afford* to pay them, the Wykhamist concluded, tartly.

Even the judge looked secretly pleased that Melmont looked rattled.

——I am the Publisher of the newspaper. I do not editorialise. I do not seek to editorialise.

After the lunch break, Dominic was joined in the public

gallery by a clearly disturbed man with a heavily bandaged head wearing a thick pair of spectacles. All Dominic could see of his face were his bad teeth, which were familiar, but Dominic could not remember which mouth he had seen them in. The mummy-like figure shook and twisted as Melquist Shelley took the stand to be assaulted by Melmont's suave and expensive legal retinue.

——It is my client's submission that there has been a campaign of consistent and scurrilous vilification of him by you, under the assumption that he is a rich and powerful member of the Establishment. How would you characterise him?

Shelley took a deep breath. *For Christ's sake don't say he's a kike,* thought Dominic. The whiff of knee-jerk public-school antisemitism always hung around Shelley's newspaper, like stale deodorant.

——We seek to expose wrongdoing wherever it happens. It's not confined to the wealthy, or the Establishment. Plenty of crooks come here from abroad.

Melmont's counsel turned suavely to the jury.

——Rich my client may be, powerful he may be, but I would draw the jury's attention to the letter in the magazine which you have all been given copies of. The letter purports to come from Mrs Abigail Melmont, my client's wife. The supposed letter asks, as you will have all seen by now, whether there is a similarity between the plaintiff and Adolf Eichmann, who personally supervised the extermination of European Jews in their millions. Now it is well known that my client is Jewish.

——It is also true, that in the time he stood as an MP he very regularly was photographed with his family coming out of

Christian services, said Shelley, looking on the godless Melmont with withering scorn. The judge was delicately enquiring whether the learned counsel was saying his client was of the Jewish *race* or simply the Jewish *faith*, when the twitching man wrapped like a mummy suddenly stood up in the gallery and cried in a coarse London accent,

——Pity Eichmann didn't finish the job he started at Buchenwald!

The voice was unmistakable. Under the bandages was very obviously Melmont's bugger, Frank. Dominic stared at him, horrified. Frank put his fingers to his lips, and allowed two court ushers to bustle him from the gallery.

Dominic was appalled at the cynical manipulation to obtain sympathy for Melmont. His stomach started to hurt, and he almost fainted again. When he looked up again, Melmont was meant to be holding forth. But he was in tears, sobbing. It was perhaps the only time he ever wept over what had happened to his family. Rivers of water seemed to pour down his face, reuniting him with his humanity.

——Take all the time you wish to compose yourself, the judge was saying.

Melmont sniffed once, and launched into the prepared counter-attack.

——I have been yoked by innuendo with a *monster*. My family was *destroyed* by Eichmann. Mother, father, brother, cousins. All of them. Blotted from the book of life. If this is a just and fair treatment, to dismiss my action against this malicious fort-nightly, then I'm a chopped worm!

Shelley caught Dominic's eye and shook his head. Frank's

planned intervention had worked and the decent, fair-minded jury now had to weigh *The Prefect's* right to tasteless schoolboy irresponsibility against the monstrosities of Auschwitz. Naturally *The Prefect* lost and was heavily fined.

The failure to pay out prize money had been passed over in court, but it had been a warning to the bank. Cole's memo to his fellow directors did not dwell on the possibility that Melmont might end behind bars, but he was instructed to keep his client, who had borrowed massive sums for his newspaper purchase, on a short leash in future. When it looked as if Melmont might lose the case, he agreed to abide by the new guidelines the bank had laid down, in return for extending his loans. Relieved, Cole reported to his fellow-directors that the client was cooperating. Then Melmont announced on the day after the trial victory, that he could not keep a meeting with Cole to reschedule debts.

——I am scheduled to visit my old friends, the Deaths. I swore I would do it as soon as this case was over. Willis is not well, not well at all. It is a matter of the heart, and of family.

Cole pointed out that the Deaths did not have a packed schedule and could be visited at any time, and were not in fact related to him, but Melmont was not to be swayed.

——My dear Tristram, they are related in a sense, for a man needs grandparents. If they have been ruthlessly exterminated, then one must simply start again.

Cole said, sarcastically,

——Then you might as well drop in on my sister in Greenham. But remember to take your own tea, they were out of PG Tips when I went.

——Consider it done, Tristram! Melmont bellowed.

Cole looked suspicious. Melmont laughed, and slapped his incredulous old friend on the shoulder.

——You think I would mislead you? Never. Your sister is a genuine heroine. One of the regrets I have about my time as an MP is that I did not ensure the government's undertaking to abolish nuclear weapons was carried through, once we were in office.

——You would have met your match there, it would have been impossible, said Cole. Melmont, future achiever of the impossible, nodded sagely.

The sky was dropping small, chill translucent missiles in infinite numbers when Melmont stopped by Greenham Common. It was Nature's way, from clouds black and heavy with rain. Water sluiced into any bender whose builder had been unwise enough not to clad the roof with generous plastic overlaps or elevate the floor.

At the same time as the windows of heaven were opened, the perimeter of the camp was being broached by bulldozers whose pretext for the demolition of temporary dwellings was that they had to clear the verges of all vegetation, reducing the 'fire risk' to any passing missile convoys. Even the prophet Elijah, who insisted on everything being soaked before he called down fire from Heaven, would have thought twice before asking God to set light to a passing missile carrier from a roadside camping stove in the middle of a Berkshire deluge.

The Greenham downpour came in waves, as if the modern weather-god, keen to establish a new record for the amount of rain that could fall, was filling a giant celestial waterbucket and emptying it overhead, to help the downpour along.

In the midst of this invasion from the sky, Priscilla Cole was being chased, though she had broken no law, with several other defiant muddy figures, all of whom had had their primitive shelters demolished. They had been trying to sit in the road to protest against the demolition of their dwellings, and when ordered off, they fell back on another section of road, and regrouped. Lightly clad and slippery with mud, Priscilla was in her element and on high moral ground. Shouting threats and imprecations against her pursuers who were handicapped by beer bellies and heavy macintoshes, not to mention prejudice and ignorance of common law, she managed to avoid being detained for longer than the others, though she was finally brought down by a brutal rugby tackle. The weather-god chose this minute to relent the rain's intensity.

Priscilla screamed with pain and anger, and bit her attacker through his thick jacket, on his arm. His response was to club her savagely about the head, to make her let go. The tall gates to the missile base opened and the big rocket carrier rolled in and back to its warm cosy pen. Even so, Priscilla's attacker held her down, telling her that if she tried to get up she would get arrested.

Face down in the mud, Priscilla did not see the vast figure emerge from the car. Melmont was suddenly standing by her.

She screamed, again.

—Oh God! Is there no justice?

And suddenly there was. Her oppressor took one look at Melmont's brow, coiled in biblical wrath at the blood pouring from Priscilla's head.

——*Who hath dared to wound thee?* The guilty malefactor scrambled away from the judgement to come as fast as the greasy conditions allowed.

The rain halted. Melmont let his umbrella fall. He knelt in the mud, and took Priscilla's bloody head between his hands, and pressed it to his chest, stroking her filthy, matted hair. He felt again what he had felt when Priscilla encountered him at Rome Airport, a rich, intoxication of Self. Once again, he had saved her. His heart was filled with love and emotion. If it felt that good to save one person, how must it feel, dying to live again, to save *the whole world?* After a taste of godhead, Melmont would take his chances.

——Weep no more. You are safe with me, Priscilla. Weep no more.

Back in London, a little corner was being lifted on Melmont's god-like aspirations to observe all of creation.

Cole had made discreet enquiries in the *Yellow Pages*, and immediately afterwards, for some hours after dark, plain vans with special parking clearance were parked outside the elegant Speke and Lazarus buildings in Threadneedle Street in the City of London. When they had wrapped their cables up from the faux-classical atrium, the drivers drove the vans directly to Chelsea where Cole had his house debugged. The microphones they discovered there were older, and some had become inactive through being painted over, twenty years before.

——It's the same system as you've got at Speke's, the chief engineer assured Cole.

Cole called up Jill and when she came over, showed her a

bulging shopping bag which trailed wire.

——Here are the excised cancers of his perception. Stay for supper, he said.

Actually what Cole wanted to do most was show off and introduce his new, petite, and pretty Filippino wife, Jade, who served them. She must have been forty years Cole's junior. She spoke little, and smiled a lot. It was, surprisingly, a love match and her family were wealthy too.

——I went to the Philippines to look at some shrimp farms we were investing in and met Jade. It's funny, I'm only beginning to realise now how lonely I must have been.

——What did Earnest say when he heard?

——He made a three-hour phonecall to me. Nobody knew in England, but still, it was as if he knew I was somehow getting away from him.

——My family went crazy, said Jade, they thought all this phoning was from his boyfriend and Tristram was getting wet feet about marriage.

——Cold feet, darling. But I wasn't. Cole smiled tightly at Jill.

——All the same we almost missed the altar, said Jade, and laughed as if it was the best joke in the world to nearly miss your own wedding.

Jill decided she rather liked Jade. Then the talk turned back to Melmont again, as if it couldn't get away.

——I think he is incredibly dangerous, said Jill. My bugger says that Melmont has got a contact in the KGB and he gets this man to organise, inside Russia, stealing warheads. He's not only trading plutonium, he doesn't give a shit who he sells it to. He's been at it for the last decade.

Cole was reluctant to be convinced of Melmont's threat to world peace.

—He's probably no worse than the lunatic fringe of the CIA who sold Semtex to Gadaffi.

—If you match the explosive power of one to the other, he's worse by a factor of several thousand. Someone has to show him up, sooner or later, said Jill. What about this book your nephew's meant to be writing?

Cole shook his head sadly.

—Dominic will not finish a thing in this life.

—So what will you do?

—I don't know, said Cole.

Cole and Jill both fell silent, pondering the fires that Melmont was conjuring.

—I just wish it weren't true, said Jill. I wish I could wake up out of this. I wish it were all a bad dream.

—Power without responsibility is a terrible thing.

—It gives me the heeby-jeebies just sitting here thinking about it.

—You would have thought that someone would have caught onto what he was doing, said Cole.

—The most important thing you ought to do is make sure the bank is covered, said his wife.

—You can't insure against nuclear war. But I've always arranged insurance against him going down, and none of this criminality is proven, yet. We'd just say if asked, we knew nothing about it. And officially, that would not be a lie. As bankers, you don't need to know the full facts. It's sometimes better if you remain in ignorance, actually.

♫\   ♫\   ♫\

Later that night, Prince George escorted Libby upstairs. A formerly loyal palace servant snapped the gobble, whose publication later shook the Windowcake dynasty to its furthest-flung duchies. The fact is, The Butler Did It. As to reasons, some say he was touched in the head, jealous and possessive of the prince's affections. Some say the butler himself needed something to bargain with to avoid dismissal as rumours abounded of his merciless predation on below-stairs buttocks. Perhaps he thought the act of love made a nice picture. Perhaps the event in question did not take place and the butler just had a friend who was good at photomontage. Cameras are so clever nowadays they are able to prove that the truth is a lie, with its trousers on.

In complete contradiction of his uncle's casual dismissal of his abilities, Dominic had assembled all his research and finished his damning and damaging book. He became possessed of the wish for Melmont to see it before he died. His sister was appalled by the idea.

——That's *madness*, Dom. He'll bury it. You told me yourself how the legal system of this country has been paralysed by Melmont's writs.

——Suppose I die tonight?

Tears came to Libby's eyes.

——Wait till he's in jail, at least be like the Mounties. You'll get your man. And you could live for years! They're always finding new drugs!

——Libby, believe me there's nothing in there he doesn't know or I can't prove. I want to see and hear him squirm. I could do with some fun.

In the end, the dying man's wishes prevailed, and his sister reluctantly agreed to get a manuscript copy to Melmont, personally.

Melmont the Royalist

FOLLOWING HER BROTHER'S INSTRUCTION with an increasingly heavy heart, Libby arrived at the Concorde desk at Heathrow. She was about to turn round and go home, when five minutes before the last New York flight of the day, as Dominic had predicted, Melmont hove into view. He was wafting importantly along while talking into a phone. Around him, a gaggle of his personal assistants were struggling to define his progress, like the ground crew of a partly inflated barrage balloon trying to restrain it as it rolls across the ground. In Melmont's case he was partly secured by a long lead to a bulky mobile radio-phone which an assistant at his side was carrying in a huge briefcase. Another assistant on the other side of him was piloting a huge fax machine, on castors. A third assistant was carrying the massive heavy batteries for the fax machine.

Nowadays, of course, any dull dog can do all of that and more on the move with something the size of a pecan, without the need for a supporting flotilla, but where's the drama in that?

As he talked and walked, Melmont, Man of the Future, was perusing the end of the long scroll of paper which was spilling out of the fax machine. Libby stepped back wincing at the sud-

den loud screaming of the dot-matrix printer on the vast fax
machine as it drove past. She set off in the baggage train of the
magnificent bustle. One bag porter was carrying, inexplicably,
three bright red golfing bags. As they swept on, a large piece of
fax paper got torn off, and falling to the floor, was trampled.
Libby picked it up to see that the lead story of Melmont's rival
paper, *The Moon*, had broken.

'Keeper of the Queen's Pictures Exposed as 5th Man', *The
Moon* trumpeted. The 'fifth man' was the Communist spy
long believed to have haunted the Establishment. But it hardly
mattered. The broken old aesthete, long past passing secrets on
unless they related to Poussin or Velasquez, would merely hand
back his knighthood, and retire from the public eye. Libby felt
rather sorry for him.

Looking up, Libby realised that she had stopped to read the
piece. The gaggle of suits around the big man was fifty yards
away, on a moving pavement. Libby swore, and set off in
pursuit. The faster she walked, the faster Melmont seemed to go.
It was impossible to run in her tight skirt and pumps, it was
unthinkable to remove either to solve the problem, particularly
in a public place where there could be photographers. Libby
teetered on at the back as the procession swept forward at an
unsteady six and a half miles an hour, just close enough to hear
Melmont bellowing instructions to his editor for a counter-
thrust to Ocker's republican jibes.

——I don't care what the facts are. Tell the toothless little
schmegegge to write a proper feature, *now*. No, I want it *yesterday!* We are a Newspaper that Supports the Royal Family! I have
provided a Pledge. When the Duke of Arschborung-schiesse

burns up Windowcake Castle lighting some naked footman's farts, I want 'Homeless Corgis Fear' as the headline on the front page. Not interviews with muckraking specialists in sexual perversion in the Fensterkuchen dynasty. Do I make myself clear?

Suddenly, the group was going through passport control. Libby had no passport to offer. She tapped on the shoulder of a forty year-old man, the last in the retinue.

——You have to be Frank.

Frank smiled seductively, as he imagined. Libby could hardly tell him she recognised him from her brother's detailed description of his nicotine-stained crooked teeth.

——Hello, darlin'? Are you comin' on the plane wiv us?

——No. But Dominic wants Earnest to have this.

Libby held out the fat manuscript. Frank stared, horrified at four hundred pages of indictment, single spaced and held together by a fat rubber band.

——He's mad. He's fucking mad. He can't show it now. He'll get us all fucking killed. D'you know what happened to Gunter Röhl?

——Personally I agree with you, but Dominic wants to see the effect, said Libby.

——It's alright for him to be fucking brave. But *I'm* not dying. Tell him not to be such a selfish bastard. I'd be a dead man. Tell him I got to have time to prepare a fallback position. You can't just... .

Frank drew a line across his throat, took his passport and ran crouchingly after the fat man in the big black suit who walked with such determination towards the tilted nose of the parked supersonic plane.

Libby arrived back at Dominic's basement flat to find a whirlwind visitation on Dominic by her mother was taking place. She had, somehow, got wind of the fact that Dominic was proposing to blacken her hero's character. Dominic was reclining, in a relaxed pose. As Libby came in, Priscilla was standing over him wagging her finger.

——You can't just lie there and tell me the book is finished when there are so many charitable causes that he supports. I bet you haven't mentioned *one*.

——Of course he supports Third World literacy, mother, he sells books, doesn't he?

——I mean fighting the good fight at home. I bet you haven't written about that. The Ministry of Defence was prosecuting us, and then, in the middle of the case, when everything seemed completely lost for the Peace Camps, we heard that one of the country's foremost Queen's Counsels had been assigned to the defence and this man was being entirely paid for by Earnest Melmont. A *very* clever man. A Wykhamist, called… Porridge.

——Morrish, corrected Dominic. And not *that* clever. Melmont wiped his arse with him when Morrish defended *The Prefect*.

An old feud was about to re-erupt over Dominic's deliberate failure of an exam, aged thirteen, which had caused him to detour to the relatively undistinguished Drabfield College, with its pungent traces of institutionalised anti-semitism.

——It was such a pity you weren't clever enough to go to Winchester, Earnest would have paid the extra, said Priscilla.

——Fuck off, mother! shouted Dominic. He was trying to lever himself off the bed with energy he did not have.

Libby swiftly intervened to help him to the lavatory, and

when he was seated on it, she returned to the room, saying brightly,

——You were saying you had this marvellous QC, mother. I didn't know you'd been in trouble. What happened?

——There were thirteen of us, and we were all going to prison. But this man, Morrish, *completely* destroyed the prosecution's case.

——It can't have been any case at all, then, said Dominic, through the lavatory's open door. Approaching death was not mellowing him towards his mother.

——Morrish went to the Land Registry and discovered the original enclosure was illegal, so Greenham was *still* common ground in law. We had as much right to be there as anyone.

——Any of those pariahs in horsehair wigs could have done the same for you, said Dominic.

Priscilla angrily shut the lavatory door, but Dominic pushed it open again immediately.

——We were saved. This is the *third time* that dear Earnest, who you are apparently trying to destroy, has descended from the clouds to rescue me. Now you put that in your book, if you dare!

Priscilla swept out, in the highest dudgeon possible. Dominic went and lay back on the bed.

——Frank refused to take the book, said Libby.

——I didn't say give it to Frank, said Dominic, angry.

——He said wait six months.

——Alright if you've got six months. Look at me!

——He said it was more than his life was worth, said Libby.

——I don't think Frank's life *is* worth that much, actually. And he's a fool as well. He'd be safer if Melmont knows that it's all in the fucking book, and he can't keep the lid on it by putting Frank in a concrete overcoat.

—But you're not trying to save Frank's skin, are you?

—No, dear sis. We're getting close to the blue tunnel time. I am not interested in some wrong that's righted after I cease to exist.

Libby sat on the bed and held Dominic's hand.

—You want to see his face when he reads it, don't you?

—I do want him to know that someone else knows.

—Knows what?

—Everything he's done. Dominic closed his eyes. The struggle with his mother had worn him out. Libby looked at her brother's lean profile as he settled on his back, with his jutting adam's apple and his big prow of a nose, which was getting sharper by the day.

The opportunities for catching Melmont in the country were few, for the next few weeks. He had not been home for two months. Abigail, alone in the vast house without even Emer for company, went and sat at Melmont's big desk in his study. In one of the drawers was a dusty tape recording, which she took through to Frank's secret ground-floor recording domain. She had earlier discovered the small Johnsonian door to the inner room, but had never wanted to cross the threshold. Now she had a reason, to find a reel-to-reel tape recorder. They were stacked, floor to ceiling inside, but none of them was plugged in. The technology had moved on and now the room was being used mainly for tape storage.

After some fiddling, Abigail revived an ancient Grundig,

threaded the lead tape around the heads, secured it to the spool, and pressed the 'play' button. Two voices came out, cracklingly, a man and a woman's. The man's accent was slightly foreign. He said, commandingly,

——Twelve sons. *Zwölf Sohnen.*

And the woman said,

——Oh my darling. Oh oh oh. Don't stop.

Abigail listened to herself having an orgasm, more than thirty years ago. She stopped the tape. There were some things best not to be reminded of, and joy with the monster was one of them. As she took the spool off the machine and put it back in Melmont's desk drawer, the phone rang. Once, Father Cowley had been a frequent calming visitor and spiritual guide during Melmont's absences but now he sounded flustered, without being willing to say why, over the phone.

Abigail entered the rather nasty modern church that passes for Catholic on the main Oxbridge road, just as Cowley, behind the confession screen, was replacing the nicotine patch under his cassock. He recognised Abigail from her scent before he saw her. He had been eaten up with anxiety since making a discovery the previous week, so much so that he had almost broken his undertaking not to smoke three times.

——Bless me Father, for I have sinned, said Abigail.

Father Cowley raised his hand and tapped on the screen.

——I'm going to stop you right there, and I'm afraid you're not going to like what's coming, he whispered, removing a small dark object from his battered old Sweet Virginia tobacco tin. Cowley fed the incriminating item through the ornamental grating between them.

——Can you tell me what that is, Abigail?

It was small and black and it hung from one of the two wires that sprouted from it. It was very obviously a microphone. Abigail sobbed, involuntarily. She had been coming to Father Cowley for spiritual assistance, abandoning the sparer faith of her fathers with reluctance, only to discover that Melmont had been sifting the succour on offer, for treachery. Where would it end?

——Where was it found?

——Here, right here in the confessional.

——I'm sorry, said Abigail, as if she was responsible for her husband.

——It's not your fault in the slightest, said Cowley.

Earlier, Abigail had told Cowley of the vast recording chambers she had come across inside the house. Was it right to pry into her husband's affairs, she now asked him. If she suspected he might be endangering other people, Cowley suggested, it was her Christian duty not to look the other way. But only if.

Back in Melmont Keep, Abigail thought of Röhl with his kind greyhound eyes, and took her courage in both hands. She went to the Johnson Dictionary door, and turned the handle. She sensed a resistance this time in the big tape vault door, but she had simply forgotten to move a table which had been placed against it. She went in, turned on the lights and started to sort through the tapes piled high in the drawers of the cabinets around her.

The amount of material was dauntingly large but she rapidly broke the simple code of the dating system by remembering when things changed, or when cars and people looked different. The first two one-inch tapes were simple surveillance tapes from the gatehouse. Later, the number and kinds of recording equipment used multiplied. But there was nothing of much interest. She began to suspect that any sensitive material would have been in the big walk-in safe in the room upstairs that Frank used. She had never been interested in breaking into anything before, but she had been using some of her empty hours to teach prisoners at Oxbridge Jail to read, and she encouraged them on their discharge to keep in touch by letter.

Abigail had drawn the line till now at asking the criminal classes up to the house. But now her husband was a criminal, she would set a thief to catch one.

Two days later, Tosh, an amiable former burglar from Barking, came up the drive with his friend who apparently had always fancied a crack at a safe. Abigail swore them to silence inside the house, and fed them a light supper of smoked salmon with cream cheese and some strong Trappist beer that her father had been fond of, before they set to work. Later, when Tosh's friend set off a controlled explosion to take out the deadlocks, Abigail shot at rabbits in the vegetable garden, to confuse any recording instruments. Afterwards she gave them both five hundred pounds in cash, and offered to drive them to the railway station. Tosh thanked her for the offer, but said shyly they were planning to knock off a motor and take it to London.

——Oh Tosh, Abigail said, *must* you?

——I promise if you drop us in the centre of town, this is going to be the very last time, Mrs Melmont.

——It's a victimless crime, y'know, his friend added. The people who can afford the sort of motors we can shift are generally well insured.

Leaving Tosh and his friend to be chased by PC Wootton on

his Triumph 650, Abigail returned home and looked through the tapes in the big safe until she came across one marked 'Compilation, Lhör.' Again, the code was so childish: Gunter Röhl's name simply spelt backwards! It was as if Melmont wanted her to find it. What she saw when she played the cassette confirmed her worst fears. She was married to a murderer.

The picture quality of the black-and-white tape was good, except for a slight fisheye effect in the corners. Offcamera, there was the sound of a closing door. Shot from the ceiling, Melmont's Mossad contact, who Abigail remembered dimly from a party, came in to greet Melmont seated in an anonymous office suite. Melmont rose from the desk to greet him warmly.

—Zak, my old friend. How was your flight?

—It was good. Is this room clean?

Zak was looking under the surfaces of tables, presumably for bugs and secret cameras like the one filming the scene.

—I have it swept every week. So what's this important problem that can't wait?

—There's a man called Röhl involved in a uranium shipment to Iran. We've found out he's told the German police you're connected with the deal.

—I didn't do a deal with the Iranians, Zak. What kind of friend of your country do you think I am?

—Did you take money from the Iranians for this shipment?

—I swear on my mother's grave, no. Röhl must have set it up for himself behind my back to compromise my dealings with you.

—He says they've paid you half already.

Melmont shook his head.

—I've only had dealings with your side my friend. I'm sorry.

I didn't realise that Röhl was going to be the weak link.

——So what is going to happen next?

——I'm going to pick up this phone and tell the Iranians where Röhl lives.

——You might find that we get there first.

——I don't care. I really don't mind who takes him out. I'm through with him. There are twenty routes out of Russia that don't use his stupid pissing little pipe that's always silting up.

——So are you agreeing he should be killed?

——If he's giving out my name to German security saying I'm dealing with Iran, I don't care what you do with the punk.

Zak stood up.

——It'll happen soon.

——My friend if you want to do it this afternoon, that's no problem. Röhl, after this, well, he's like something you have to wipe off your shoe as fast as possible, something unpleasant. In fact his death would please me. It would mean that he's screwed my wife for the last time.

Abigail watched as Melmont picked up a phone and dialled. From the conversation, it seemed to show that Melmont was still rather more involved in trade with Iran than he wanted his Israeli contacts to find out.

——Doctor Muhammad Bar'Iq please. Gunter Röhl is no longer handling your shipment of H.E.U. That is what you ordered my friend. Highly Enriched Uranium. It is easily upgradable to weapons-grade. There's going to be a delay while the routing is rearranged but I'll have them with you next week, guaranteed.

The tape changed to one of a supermarket carpark shot from

low down. Abigail noticed the cars had German numberplates and the time and date were three days after the first time-coded scene.

Before it happened Abigail knew what the end was going to be. Gunter Röhl came into sight carrying bags of groceries, his arms full, with a white macintosh draped over his shoulders. He opened the boot of his car with his remote key, but his macintosh which he had put on against the rain was hampering him loading the bags and he seemed undecided.

Then things happened quickly. A man in a balaclava arose from behind a nearby car and started shooting at Röhl with a submachine gun. There was no soundtrack, just the quick flicker of bullet openings in the cloth of Röhl's jacket. The momentum spun him round clockwise, and he turned and fell. The bullets kept flicking into him, scattering and bursting his groceries. It looked as if he died in a dark pool of blood, but it was raining heavily, and it might equally have been a puddle.

Abigail called Cowley to arrange a meeting early the next day, and came quickly to the point.

——What would you advise if I came across evidence that my husband had committed a murder?

——Did he do it himself?

——Not directly, but as good as.

Worse than directly, Abigail wanted to say.

Cowley groaned. He had joined the church to avoid the hard choices of real life, and here they were coming after him again.

——I don't know. We're neither of us detectives. It's a considerable allegation. I wouldn't do anything, yet.

Abigail went back to the big house and sat while suicidally

bold rabbits assaulted the rows of lettuces outside the kitchen door. She had not got the strength of mind to load the gun and kill a harmless creature. Melmont had said he would be back that evening. She sat till it was too dark to see, wondering what she would do if Melmont himself now walked through the door.

Melmont's delay in arriving home that night was caused by the impulse purchase of a football club. It proved an unwise purchase, like most of his later ones, since it was not a good football team, indeed, at the bottom end of the league table. But the exercise provided him with a whole night's amusement, in a life which innocence had largely forsaken. It happened in the following way.

He had been visiting the country's largest nuclear reprocessing facility, prior to a bid to run it. Seascale is on the coast of Northumberland. The plant employs several thousand locals and apart from farming, the plant, notable as a local health hazard and terrorist magnet, provides almost the only employment. The afternoon meeting had gone well, and the plant's directors had intimated that the government was keen to privatise reprocessing. The sleek car left the heavily guarded facility, and was following signs for a heliport through the dingy back streets of Seascale, when it passed under the shadow of a stadium. Melmont order his chauffeur to stop at once. He had taken to being chauffeured lately because the steering wheel no longer agreed with his stomach. He was getting too fat to drive.

He hoisted his enormous bulk out of the vehicle, which groaned with relief, and made water in public, leaning on the stanchion supporting the grandstand of a poorly maintained ferro-concrete football stadium. Unaware there was a game in progress, he gazed up at the stadium above him, wondering idly how much it would cost to do up and sell on. Suddenly he heard a deepthroated roar from within the stadium itself. It thrilled him to the marrow, instantly.

Hearing the noise, he briefly became the crowd in the Coliseum baying for more blood. He was *there*, instantly, wherever 'there' was, beyond Rome: it was here, and everywhere, in all times there were and ever would be. Suddenly energised, he prowled his way in the shadows underneath the primitive stands, looking for a way in to where the glorious Noise lived so he too might revel where he belonged in the warm radiation of the masses.

Inside the stand, in the manager's sparsely decorated box, Lobos de Rio, the balding moustachio'd manager for the Seascale Athletic football team was dejectedly staring out as Millwall hammered his team flat, pumping another Estuarine goal into the net. His slightly built assistant beside him with his head in his hands looked like a man who had lost his antidepressants some time ago. But their fortunes were going to be shortly altered from a direction they never expected.

The Seascale supporters were there in strength, for the game was on home territory. Melmont wandered among them, apparently aimless. Here he would help himself absentmindedly to the popcorn from a depressed Seascaler's giant cardboard container, there he would take a bite from the vagrant end of a two-foot hot dog that the owner carelessly let drift towards The Aperture, but in fact he was gaining ground and advancing by magnetism towards the manager's lit box, where Lobos and his suicidal sidekick were jointly confronting a bleak future. Melmont himself was smiling slightly as he did when he was nervous. But he was not nervous now. He was certain.

He paused to draw breath in his ascent by a young female Seascale fan. She was wearing a denim jacket, cut away to show her waist under a Seascale football scarf, which had a smeary Paisley pattern in the middle of it. Melmont reached out and fingered the rayon item, with something akin to reverence. The girl turned, ready to slap him.

——My favourite team, he said to the girl. What is their name?

——Seascale. You can keep 'em. The cunts are two down already, the girl said savagely.

Two female companions of the girl, bulkier and with shaven heads, moved to their mate in protection to match the giant threat of the Incomer. Melmont still held on to the scarf.

——How much do you want for this? he asked.

The girl spun round in the midst of her friends, once, twice. The scarf fell from her.

——You can have it, gran'pa, she said.

Melmont's brow creased. Sudden lack of loyalty always troubled him.

——What's the matter, darling? Don't you love your team?, Melmont said.

Then his eyes went as big as saucers.

——This could be a dream come true for you. I happen to be buying Seascale Athletic, this very evening.

The idea had just occurred to him. Those were always the best ones. He continued,

——If you give me your name and address, I will make sure you are secretary of the new supporters' club. You can help to make Seascale a household word, just let me have the T-shirt too and we can have copies made.

The fan scribbled her name and address down, and then abruptly took off her Seascale Supporters' T-shirt and handed it to Melmont. She was bra-less. Around each breast was a tattoo which read 'SEASCALE'.

——These cost thirty quid each to have done, she said.

——We shall be able to get the cost down if we have a full-time tattooist working for the club. I won't forget you.

Melmont looked at her roundels, and then at the paper with her name on it, then up to her, again.

——Grace.

Melmont finally stepped into the manager's box, having purchased an inordinate number of supporter's items of clothing on the climb. Seascale knickers unwashed since the team last won were pinned in rows like medals on his chest. But Lobos de Rio and his assistant, sunk in melancholy, could not even bring themselves to turn around. Melmont coughed, then twirled a football rattle he had been given. Finally Lobos glanced over his shoulder, and said contemptuously,

——Oo are you, then, the Michelin Man?

——I am Seascale's Salvation, Melmont replied. But for the rescue operation to be successful, the Fat will have to be Carved Away, he added darkly.

——Speak for yourself. Get out of here.

——No no, believe me, it is *you* who are out from now on, what's-yer-name.

——I am Lobos de Rio, the team manager. This is my box. Get out.

——You're fired, Lobos. One month's salary is all you're getting. I'm the new manager.

Suddenly, against all probability, Seascale's goalie punted a desperate high ball which bounced wildly once, then dropping into the corner of the opponent's net, scored without any defender touching it. It was discovered afterwards to be against the rules, but by that time, no one cared. The Seascale fans went wild. Some mutilated themselves.

——See? The effects of better management are always felt *immediately*, said Melmont.

Lobos turned and stared at the intruder opened mouthed. He had been outclassed by the Melmont metaphysic. The score was one all.

——My side will win decisively in the second half, announced the publisher and football team owner.

At halftime Melmont made himself known to the rest of the Seascale supporters, and the fans sang the Seascale anthem. It uses their own ironic words, to the delightful tune of a ballad made famous by Rod Stewart. *Sailing* was a hit around the second time the Norn appeared to Melmont; that means nothing though, beyond the fact that time flies, while songs stand still. Do you remember *Sailing*? Don't mind the other people in the carriage, sing it, please, to these words:

> *We're disgustin'*
> *Seascale mutants*
> *Radioactive*
> *We don't care...*

In the second half, Seascale scored again, a six-fingered 'hand of Seascale' cheekily helping the ball into the net, making them a goal ahead, as Melmont had predicted.

—First goal under Seascale's new colours! Melmont cried. He was wearing a Melmont scarf around his head, as if it were a Kamikaze headscarf emblazoned with the divine deathwish.

The unexpected victory made Melmont the Lord of Misrule in Seascale for the evening, which was just as well, since he could not have left quickly. The chauffeur had returned from tracking down fish and chips to find the car with all its wheels missing, resting on plastic milk crates. Melmont was borne in triumph out of the stadium past the astonished wheelless chauffeur, on the shoulders of twenty panting Seascale fans who had stripped to the waist and were wearing torn shreds of the new tartan as favour round their white bare arms.

Photographers who had been at the match heard that Seascale had a new owner who had worked the miracle, and the prodigy is on film, carried along chuckling on his back; one clip even suggests he was tossed as if in a blanket. How could they even have carried him, let alone thrown him in the air? But there it is on video so we have to believe it. It is a puzzle, certainly, this strength found in joy.

Their mascot finally proved too heavy for even the victorious Sons of Seascale, and they unceremoniously tipped Melmont into the front flowerbed of an obscenely tidy-looking bungalow owned by one of the semi-retired technicians who used to show the public round the nuclear power plant, and preach the miracle of nuclear engineering.

As the singing fans went away up the road, lights started coming on in the front room of the bungalow, with angry threats to the great gurning lump in the front garden, that it should stop damaging the statuary and impacting the topsoil, and the po-lice had been called, hopefully for a swift arrest.

The Lord of Misrule, having fallen off his horse, ignored all reproof, snoring among the garden gnomes. He had been transported briefly to Oblivion. The stars winked down on all this; knowingly, according to Tetrode. I leave the future Abysmal Ruler to his stellar-observed Seascale slumber, and turn to the death of his biographer, Dominic, in the next chapter.

XXIII

The Death of Dominic

D OMINIC WAS DYING, but like any assiduous journalist
was still making the best use of his sources, with
pencil and paper poised ready to take notes off a
radio broadcast. He was in a hospital bed, in a pleasant single
ward. Its window looked out onto a tree, planted expressly by
the National Health, which had discovered that patients who
looked out on such things found more reason to live, though the
noble provision also gives a comfort to the irreversibly stricken.
Dominic had asked for the window to be opened and although
it was cold, the dying man's wishes were complied with by the
cheerful nurse.

The radio was on by the bedside, and Dominic was listening
to Melmont's appearance on *Desert Island Discs*, a long-running
BBC programme where the honoured guest, wherever his nativity
occurred, is received into the nation's mythic Heartland, with
his story interspersed with a number of his favourite records.

From the radio, Dominic heard Melmont say in a persuasive,
rich warm voice,

—In answer to your question, I was awarded my Military

Cross some time before my family were, as you say, 'put into cattle trucks' for the concentration camps. In fact, I knew nothing of their fate till after the war.

—Next song?

—My next song will be *Land of Hope and Glory*.

Dominic, dreamy, felt rather than heard birdsong flood in from the sunny square of cold air. It mixed in a strange colloidal symphony with the regular muffled pomp of the marching music. It felt strange, but not unfamiliar.

Then suddenly things became unpleasantly familiar. The ward door opened and Melmont was in the entrance with a bunch of asphodels. He looked like a mad bison. He wanted something. Dominic's remaining braincells were astonished.

—My God, I've started hallucinating early.

—Don't worry about a thing, Dom. We'll have you up and running about in no time, said the mad bison, and turned off the radio where his doppelgänger apparently lived.

—As a matter of fact there is a pharmaceutical company I own in Israel which has made some really startling advances in combating your virus. I'm proposing to put a lot of money into searching for a cure.

The enormous bison sat on the bed. Christ, he was huge.

—When you've made as much money as I have, the bison continued, you want to leave the world a Better Place. What have you been writing about me, then?

Dominic turned his face to the wall in reply.

—I'll give a quarter of a million pounds to AIDS research if you let me publish your book. I'll edit it personally with you. Consider the cheque to be in the post.

Dominic gritted his teeth. Through his fever, he knew he

must never let Melmont suppress the truth about himself.

——This could be the most expensive hospital visit anyone ever made! Half a million, then, to AIDS if I can be your publisher. And that's a floor, not a ceiling. Any higher bids, anywhere in the world, I'll match them. Don't give the rights to anyone else. Promise.

The bison surveyed his fallen adversary, and concluded he had won.

——So it's a deal. You get well soon, you hear?

When Melmont left, Dominic opened his eyes and checked under his pillow. The fat manuscript was still there. He drifted off to sleep.

He woke an hour later to find Cole in the room, an unobtrusive presence.

——We've been trying to get your mother to come, she got the message but she's in Tibet, Cole said.

——With a bit of luck, the Chinese will have closed the borders, said Dominic, drily. He pushed the manuscript at Cole with an effort. Cole picked it up wonderingly.

——Christ, is that it? You did it Dom, you did it.

——Gurdjieff says "always astonish". One of your sayings. When we were little.

——I'm sorry, I don't remember.

——When you were at Prince's. Every summer, you took us boating. And you taught us.

——What did I teach you?

——I can't remember.

Slowly Dominic slid down the bed and put the pillow over his ear.

——Can I get you anything, Dommo?

Dominic shook his head. After a minute he groaned loudly, and said,

—It's too much, Tristram, the birds sound like Charlie Parker on speed. Shut the window, would you?

But when his uncle left, Dominic didn't like the silence much, which was too full of potentising possibilities, so his last act was to turn the radio on again. A warm, bisonous voice said,

—My last piece of music is the *Enigma Variations*, because I believe that they in some way plumb the mysterious soul of this my adoptive land.

Dominic's soul began to fold its tent, and he departed this life peacefully to the music.

He had asked to be cremated. Two weeks later, with the aid of an unhelpful heritage tourist map, Amelia and Libby were standing in a deserted muddy field in Wiltshire with not a half-timbered cottage in sight. Libby was holding the urn containing surprisingly heavy ashes. Cole was to have been present, but the inevitable phone call from Melmont kept him away. In the middle of the field rose a small stream which might arguably be the headwaters of the Thames, which was where Dominic had asked for his ashes to be scattered.

—So this is Middle England, said Amelia. It sure feels in the middle of something. But what?

Eventually they plumped for the little stream at their feet as the probable source.

—Really it is an impossible task your brother set you. White Nile or Blue Nile?

Libby upended the urn and the ash fell in lumps which sank and bobbed up again, releasing curious patterns on the surface. The two girls walked away together over the cold boggy field.

——Goodbye Dominic, I love you now and forever, and to-morrow I swear I will make twenty copies of your manuscript, called Libby to the swirls of grey dust being carried down by the stream.

Amelia was shocked.

——You mean you've still only got the one he left you? That's terrible!

——No no. Tristram has one, and there's also another in Dominic's old flat.

——Libby, this guy can do *anything*, I thought. Is three enough?

——No probably not, but I've been grieving, Amelia, I'm not a machine! barked Libby.

♫   ♫   ♫

In Berlin, it was snowing. Colonel Vanov, dressed in a fur coat, was striding down the pavement, which was lined with recently cleared snow in neat piles; so Teutonic. Beside every third pile, it seemed, there was a prostitute, hopping from one foot to the other. The working girls were dressed in moonboots against the cold, and garish nylon ski-suits.

——You got some time, mister? One hundred marks.

What a job, in cold weather too!

Ignoring blandishments, Vanov pressed on to his destination, a plush and expensively dark restaurant. Once inside, he gave his coat to a waiter and looked around. The surroundings were discreetly opulent, with wide spaces between the tables, perfect for diners who did not wish to be overheard. Vanov approached a central dining table where, alone, there was a large figure seated with a huge napkin over its head. The cloth was a special dense-weave Egyptian cotton provided by the management to capture the essence of the scent of the rare and expensive delicacies it served on vast white chinaware plates. Vanov sat down opposite Melmont, amused.

—Started without me, have you? I wasn't that late, buddy.

Melmont, communing with his precious truffles, did not come out from under the napkin. Vanov went on,

—I can tell this is a really *old* spy. You remember how it used to be done? In the old days, in Russia and in Poland, we took lipreaders from the deafmute orphanages, remember, to tell us what was said in public places? C'mon, lighten up! The Wall's come down!

The waiter brought a plate of truffles and laid it in front of Vanov, who put his napkin on as well and inhaled the delicious aroma and looked down. Vanov knew Melmont had finished his truffles when he saw hands with thumbs fat as doorknobs appearing from Melmont's side of the table. One of the thumbs was clearly considering a border raid on Vanov's plate.

—Hey, keep your mitts to yourself unless you want a fork through one!

There was a pause while the thumbs withdrew, then Vanov said,

—Did you know I'm a professor, now? Strategic Studies Unit, in Princetown.

With the collapse of the empire, the Russian diaspora had erupted again. Melmont was suspicious.

—How the hell did you manage that?

——The predictions my department made for the Russian economy were closer than the CIA's. I've handed in my notice.

Melmont lifted Vanov's napkin and stared him in the face.

——I'll put twice your Harvard salary in your dollar account if you stay in the KGB and help me.

Vanov shook his head and dropped his napkin, shutting out the eyes big as saucers, and picked up a fork again.

——So how many more warheads have you got for me?

——Ten. What am I offered?

——In the present world market I can only offer a hundred and fifty thousand, said Melmont.

——That's ridiculous. No way.

Vanov's character was changing. He even sounded more American by the minute.

——My friend, plutonium is not a rarity any more. I'm buying the British Government's nuclear fuel processing plant at Seascale for less than one percent of what it cost to build it, said Melmont.

——It has to be more than that for ten. My wife has a heart condition. It's going to cost us two hundred thousand dollars to fix in America.

——No it won't. The President of Blue Cross is a very good friend of mine, said Melmont. But the boast sounded a little hollow, even to him.

After lunch, the two men went to Check-point Charlie to try to bargain again. They stood on a surviving piece of the Wall, that had in the past been so good to them.

——Just think, all this used to be ours, said Melmont. It was all so much simpler when the Wall was up. And now who is running the show either side? Rabble, my friend.

——I agree. I feel like a dog in the wrong skin, said Vanov.

Melmont was still feeling out the warhead bid, though his heart wasn't in it. They both knew without admitting it to each other, the bull market in uranium was collapsing.

——In one week we can talk again, when you and your wife come to my birthday party.

——It can't be in a week, said Vanov. The boat is already at sea.

——Then let them come and we'll settle a price later, said Melmont, expansively.

Vanov was getting irritated with Melmont's vagueness.

——Listen, the warheads are in their casings, as arranged. The fissile weight is certified. Why do you tell me to wait? My boat is outside Archangelsk, it is not large, a trawler, and the weather will get bad if it stays there, which is dangerous. Today I had a call saying they were having trouble and needed to make port quickly. Either they meet up with your container ship now, or they return. If I don't have a proper payment from you, I will have to tell them to return to port.

——No no, tell them to wait, my ship will come to them very shortly, said Melmont, dreamily.

——What money will you pay?

——Two hundred, and you'll get it when you come to the yacht next week. I swear. On my mother's grave, I swear.

The weather worsened in the White Sea. The warheads in question were lashed in cases marked 'Salt Cod' in a row on the deck of a trawler with a damaged propeller, which was having difficulty facing into the rising waves fifty miles outside Archangel.

Over the next few hours, the battering the crates received weakened their sisal restraining ropes till one by one they snapped and the crates crashed loosely around the deck. As the burly captain struggled in the wheelhouse to keep the boat's bows to the wind, the sea reclaimed the crates one by one, in spite of rescue operations bravely launched by young deckhands, who attempted a makeshift harness. But their efforts went for nothing, and the horrified captain could do nothing to avert the shock of a particularly large wave which slammed into the port side of the trawler, reared over the side and onto the deck.

The wave seemed to have a particularly malefic agenda. It picked up the last crate almost intentionally, and floated it overboard with one oilskin-clad youth still hanging onto it. The high seas made the damaged boat impossible to manoeuvre for a rescue, so death would come within minutes in the chill water.

A rope was thrown towards the young sailor clinging to the crate, but it fell short. The captain cursed. The sailor, a non-swimmer, saw with terror his last hope disappear as the air bubbled out of the sinking crate beneath him. His panic allowed his drowning to be mercifully brief.

Soon the crate and the blonde corpse together were drifting down in the dark beneath the waves to join the rest of the warheads scattered on the seabed in the mud. They came to rest around a sunken British merchantman from a North Atlantic convoy, torpedoed in *that* war; so irrelevant to modern times, so very long ago.

Apart from an occasional dreaminess, which he claimed chicken soup always cured, Melmont showed no sign that he

realised that the bubble was about to burst. At his opulent pent-
house suite below the heliport atop *The Spyglass*, he continued
on a rampage of twentyfour-hour acquisition. There was no
field in which Melmont was not extending tentacles in the effort
to outgrow Midrash's evil empire.

It was midnight, and below in *The Spyglass*'s boardroom,
Frank was changing over the building's surveillance cameras to
colour at last. His unshaved and unlovely assistant with freckles
and flattened hair the colour of putty, sat sequentially in the
different chairs in the boardroom, giving grumpy sound-checks
for each.

——The Pope 'as red socks. The Pope 'as red socks. The Pope
'as red socks. The Pope 'as red socks. The Pope… .

Melmont arrived like a whirlwind, bellowing into a mobile
phone and drowning the assistant's mantra out.

——IT HAS BEEN CLEARLY ESTABLISHED THAT PENSION
FUNDS ARE PART OF A COMPANY'S ASSETS AND IF THE
NEW OWNER OF THE COMPANY WISHES TO DISPOSE OF
THE ASSETS WHICH HE HAS LEGALLY PURCHASED THEN
THE NEW OWNER HAS EVERY RIGHT TO. I AM THE NEW
OWNER AND THERE IS NOTHING MORE YOU NEED TO
KNOW.

Melmont hurled the phone at the wall, where it smashed
dramatically.

Frank tutted.

——Those cost two hundred a pop, said Frank the cynic,
mock-accusingly.

——He got the message.

——Ernie, tell me something. I was followin' your newspaper's
campaign against that Israeli technician who blew the whistle

on their nuclear programme. What have *you* got against Mordecai Vananu?

—Me? Nothing. Never met him. What are you talking about, Frank? He's just a liar, that's all. The Israelis don't have the bomb.

—Except they *do*. It's *strange* that someone with your access to information would be wrong on such a simple issue. Is this something they've asked you to do for them?

—I wouldn't dream of allowing the Israelis to dictate editorial content, said Melmont. As soon as he had spoken he had the same feeling he'd experienced when talking to Vanov, a misgiving that the undertakings that came out of his mouth sounded insincere and hollow. He slapped Frank on the shoulder.

—What's the problem, anyhow, with them having nuclear weapons? They're not going to be targeted on Essex, are they?

—Fuck Essex. I could be in the real firing line. A very good job I got offered is Iraq. Saddam Hussein wants his torture chambers rewired.

Melmont laughed at the terrible enormity of Frank's amorality. It really was too extraordinarily humorous. Frank said,

—It's not funny. I gotta pay off the Spanish timeshare bandits I got involved with.

—Listen to you, said Melmont. The working classes! Houses in Spain and you're all still complaining. You are worse than the print unions.

—Remind me, when am I getting paid by you for this change to colour? asked Frank, pointing at the invisible microcamera installations.

Melmont shook his head.

——Frank, you are greedy and immoral. You are exactly what is wrong with the working classes in this country. Your only redeeming feature is you have no guile.

——You said I was the only man you met who said exactly what he thought. Well, I think the writing was on the wall for the likes of you on Black Monday.

Melmont shook his head, dismissing the effect of the recent stock market crash, the worst for sixty years.

——The writing was on the wall now for the *little* people, he said.

——Alright, then what *is* your equity to debt rating? asked Frank, casually.

Melmont laughed, a deep, booming, laugh.

——Frank, you are *incorrigible*. However, we must continue to love the sinner, even as we hate the sin. Accordingly, I invite you to my birthday party.

——You had one of those, recently.

——This next one is on my yacht. You will be able to mingle with Elizabeth Taylor, and the Aga Khan.

——No, really? Get away!

Frank's extinct roll-yer-own trembled and almost fell from his lower lip.

——They are mere celebrities. You, however, Frank are Frank, my frank friend, and you can fly out tomorrow, first class so you have some holiday.

——I can't go tomorrow. I'm having a barium meal.

——My friend, isn't caviar preferable?

——It'd have to be Chernobyl caviar or it wouldn't show up in the x-ray. You got any?

In fact, Frank, for all his levity was getting an ulcer from worry. He hadn't been paid by Melmont for six months, and he didn't need Dominic's book to tell him the roof was about to fall in. Having fallen out with Dominic over remuneration for the book material, Frank now needed to rebuild his alliance there.

He made his way towards West London from *The Spyglass* on the ever-erratic Circle Line, and got off at Notting Hill Gate intending to surprise his author.

Libby had been working all morning on a small desktop photocopier in Dominic's basement, from which a strong, over-heated, acrid smell now came. Frank was slightly surprised to hear of Dominic's recent death, but not unduly sentimental.

—Face it, we all gotta go at some time. Is that it, then? Frank pointed.

Amelia was addressing envelopes to likely publishers.

—That's it.

—To tell the troof, him and me didn't exactly see eye to eye. And I never thought a book would do anything. A movie, or a mini-series, even a moosical. Nuffin serious. Put Jeffrey Archer in an inflatable costume and tell 'im ter sing.

—Are you a… producer, then?

—Dom used to call me Deep Throat, I gave him dirt. I got some redhot new stuff. I did this tape for Abigail his wife, who came to me and said she wanted proof of everything he's ever had, for the divorce. I thought it could go with the book by some kind of arrangement, so if you're in the early stages of book production, it's just a suggestion mind.

Frank pulled a small high-resolution video camera out of his pocket and plugged it into the television. The screen immediately showed Melmont in a compilation of characteristically brief sexual encounters.

——I don't see how this is going to help sell a *book*, said Amelia.

——Sex sells anything, easy. Put it on a CD and stick it inside the cover. I got five hours of him bonking. It's true you're not going to sell it to cable TV for more 'n buttons, you got to think package, cos actually it's quite borin', it's like watchin' cheap westerns wiv the same Indian fallin' off the same rock over again.

——This is early days. We don't even know if we can find a publisher to risk it. Let alone one who is going to sell it with a porno package.

——Bollocks, this aint porn. It's nuffin. Not even top shelf. The true value is 'oo it is, rather than wot, said Frank presciently.

——How much do you want? said Amelia.

——I was finking a hundred grand, said Frank.

——It's something you'll have to talk to the publishers about, if we can find any who aren't just too scared of him.

——Oh yeah, I forgot, he fuckin' sues everyone to deff, doesn't he? Could be a problem then.

——Yes, it could be, said Amelia.

♫   ♫   ♫

The final straw for Cole in his relationship with Melmont came when he had been waiting outside Melmont's office with a crucial letter from Speke and Lazarus for four hours. All

Melmont had to do was spend ten seconds signing a renego-
tiated debt agreement, and all might have been well. Cole had
reached the head of the queue and had been about to be led in
to The Presence, when a brash young man appeared and was
called in before him, carrying a package. Cole protested, but the
preferred youth was Melmont's supplier for bulk caviar, which
could still be bought off Iranian cabin staff. Shortly a secretary
brought up a set of large silver spoons and some sliced lemons.

Pipped to the post by fish eggs, and uninvited to take part in
their consumption, Cole stood up and strode out. He was so
angry he drove the wrong way out of a multi-storey car park.
When he found the right exit and paid, he saw with a sinking
heart that Melmont had come out after him and was waiting for
him, saucer-eyed, blocking the exit. Determined to have nothing
more to do with the monster, Cole simply tooted his horn.

Melmont held up a suitcase, beaming, and Cole was obliged
to open his window at last, only to discover that the suitcase
was a trojan horse in disguise. Melmont tripped the catch and
suddenly baby clothes from the suitcase were filling the inside
of Cole's car. Then, equally suddenly, Melmont was in the car
beside Cole.

——I heard the happy news! Zophia, who I swear is still a
virgin, knitted this specially.

Melmont held up a knitted woollen pixie hat.

——I'm going home now, Earnest, said Cole.

——I know. You will take me with you. I must hold this golden
child.

Cole drove to his house, grudgingly. Melmont's loud,
voracious greeting of the baby alarmed them all at first, but the

little morsel, initially fearful of Melmont, suddenly started to laugh. Melmont got down on the floor with the infant, tickled its tummy, and put its feet in his mouth and then started to babble baby talk. Within a minute the baby was laughing endlessly, charmed by the enormous clown who had blown in. Melmont peered down the front of the nappy and sighed with envy.

——Of course it's a boy first time! No squirting your schlong into a blender and have them whizz it around, for you! Cole, you are a mensch!

——We have to go, he is being baptised at six.

Melmont stood up and nodded as if he understood the seriousness of the undertaking.

——Have you put his name down for Eton yet? said Melmont.

——No, we are not calling him Eton, he will be called after Dominic, said Jade, firmly, adding, I believe you knowed him.

——Yes, I knew the dear foolish boy, said Melmont. If only he had been more careful. But death does not separate us from those we truly love.

Having uttered this profundity, Melmont gasped and abruptly clutched at his heart. Jade snatched her precious baby back as Melmont slid down and began to spread over the floor. Cole went grimly to phone an ambulance, secretly hoping that its engine would fail or some other act of God would remove the great buffoon from his life. Melmont recumbent showed an unfamiliar aspect, like a mighty elephant tranquilised against its will by bush rangers, which now lies upon its side, its eyelids closing, though still vital and dangerous to approach. But he was also lying on their luckiest wedding present which had been blessed by Buddhist priests, so he was unlikely to die there. Jade squatted down, and patted the heaving lump who covered the woven silk rug in the middle of the room.

——Mistah Mermont, is something Wong?

——Water, gasped Melmont weakly.

Jade filled a tumbler quickly and brought it to the articulated mound.

——Don' worry, you'll be alright.

But as she bowed down with the glass to Melmont's hand, he waved it aside, and said urgently,

——Listen darling. It's not water I'm after. I need half an hour alone with Tristram or I'm finished. Have your boy baptised another day. I'll make it up to you, I swear.

Jade shrugged in surrender. And then suddenly Melmont was on his feet as if pulled up by strings, saying,

——It's alright, Tristram, cancel the ambulance.

XXIV

He Had Always Hated Baked Beans

L ITTLE DOMINIC WOULD NOT BE BAPTISED THAT DAY. Cole went with Melmont to the bank's offices, and sat with two of the bank's assistants to sift and thumb sceptically through a huge, complex proposal that was the last *jeté* of the doomed empire.

——Earnest, I don't understand this. It says, 'The company of Melmont Thermo Nuclear will place a confidential bid of two point two billion pounds for British Nuclear Fuels contingent on receiving government aid in the stipulated areas.'

——I'm going to be the only bidder so the whole industry will go cheap. I'm qualified. They know I'm doing them a favour, taking nuclear reprocessing off their hands.

Melmont pushed the papers over to Cole.

——Now if you look, you will see there will be an immediate repayment to your bank on completion, of thirty percent of the outstanding loan.

Cole got the same feeling that he got in Egyptian markets where the transfer between buyer and seller always had a fifth-dimension Melmontian loopiness. You went into the market looking for a mirror, and came out having paid far too much for a goat you didn't want, and there was no explanation. This time, Cole was determined to resist the proffered goat. It stank.

——Earnest, do you have any indication from the present government about the level of subsidy you can expect to receive?

——You know how it works. Members of the select parliamentary committee for nuclear safety will be on the boat. We'll get it sorted out as we go. You are coming to my birthday party, aren't you?

——I need to ask some more questions, Cole said.

Melmont suddenly announced he wanted the room cleared. Cole raised his eyebrows and looked at his watch meaningfully.

——I am answering every question as fully as I can, so you are in charge of how long this takes, Tristram.

When they were alone, Melmont took a deep breath. His eyes remained cool and calculating, but the rest of him seemed to expand to compensate before he spoke.

——This is in strictest confidence. This country is in crisis, but I have assurances the government will support me. It is recognised by the present Cabinet that *IF* they are *EVER* going to get out of their deeprooted difficulties, responsible people outside the official Cabinet are going to have to take a role.

Cole realised that he was being asked to believe he was sitting alone in a room with a Responsible Person, and one who though he had long left Parliament, still had designs on a Cabinet post.

——You may think this sounds far-fetched, but it makes excellent sense for someone who understands the nuclear industry to be Minister for Power.

——But, Earnest, this could mean the country's nuclear policy would be run from Liechtenstein, Cole said.

Melmont hardly blinked.

——*Firstly*, it's high time we all went into Europe. *Secondly*, I understand white elephants and I can change them into black ones. That's *very* attractive to this government, Tristram. Thirdly, I'm thinking of *your* percentage. I'll make a further share option available to you, personally, for one hundred million shares in Melmont Nuclear. I will also guarantee a dividend of at least eighteen percent in the first year.

——Suppose you get a meltdown?

Melmont shrugged, like Atlas occasionally does.

——It's covered by insurance. I *own* enough insurance companies. Everything's covered.

Cole looked at his polished leather brogues, experiencing a reprise of what he called in later years his 'caviar' moment, when he realised that he had had enough. Then he spoke confidently. For when Melmont went down, Speke and Lazarus, with its firewall in place now, would escape without any investigation or public rebuke for 'irresponsibility', indeed, only the most nominal losses.

——Earnest, the political angle you are pitching is not researched, so we'd have to come back to you on that. And there is the element of the sheer size of what you are attempting. We have been told this year we can't put our eggs in one basket. Not after the recent stock market performance. Why don't you approach one of the really big boys? Credit Suisse, say, or Lehmans, and tell them exactly what you've told me? It might be just the thing they were looking for, said Cole, deadpan.

——Good idea. But Tristram, can we say your bank guarantees

an intergroup loan of two hundred and fifty million pounds for three months, until I've set something up with Credit Suisse?

——It's still too little information. We really do need to see the Government is interested, not just have you tell us.

Melmont produced his wild card. Scrabbling in his briefcase he pulled out an ancient black-and-white eight by ten inch photograph from an equally ancient brown envelope, as used by intelligence officers in the British army, *circa* 1945.

The photo showed the young Brigadier Cole in the buff, in bed with a blonde youth, a German, Cole remembered. Frozen in time, across the bridges of the years, the German was masturbating Young Cole. The lighting was rather effective, school of Cartier-Bresson, Cole thought. A buckled thirtyfive millimetre negative was held to the top of the photo with a rusting paperclip.

——This abomination. We can pretend it never happened. You get the negative as well, added Melmont.

——Earnest, why are you showing me this now?

Melmont took a deep breath, expelling the air with all the sincerity and compassion he was capable of.

——I bought it from the KGB to protect you and so that you would be able to come to your senses and abhor disgustingness, and one day marry and have a family and live without shame. Not like one of those sordid queers the Commies turned, like Burgess, like the Keeper of the Queen's Pictures, whose whole life was a lie. So I am proud of you, but I feel you owe me something. Besides, what if Jade saw this now? Pouf! added Melmont, gravely, flicking his fingers up to suggest an abruptly terminated relationship.

The choice of expletive in the circumstances was unfortunate, and riled Cole.

——They don't give a toss, excuse me, about that kind of thing in the Philippines. And the bank is only interested in balance sheets. I can't see the synergy in the companies you've bought since you sold your publishing company. You routinely pay too much for them, you are overextended and your chosen biographer has some very serious allegations about nuclear weapons trading with non-democratic regimes, said Cole, cunningly removing any Buchenwald factor from the accusation.

——My dear fellow, the Russian Federation has had nuclear weapons for fifty years, the Chinese for thirty, and these non-democratic nations have not started a world war, have they? What has democracy to do with security?

It was as close as anyone would ever get to an admission from Melmont of promiscuously trading in the most powerful weapons of mass destruction known to man on the world market. It might be Israel or Islam, it made no difference to the great salesman of Einstein's patent medicine. Cole said quietly,

——Democracy is *everything* to do with what we are talking about. You are asking for a mortgage for a house built on sand. You want Speke and Lazarus to underwrite you while you're waiting for a government nuclear subsidy to clean up their mess, but what happens in a surprise general election? All the promises the previous government makes can go for nothing. So I would very much like to hear your comments on Dominic's thesis.

Cole reached into his briefcase and dropped Dominic's manuscript on top of the photograph.

——Have you read this? Pouf! said Cole, unable to stop himself.

——I don't have to. The accusations are so many regurgitated rabbit pellets. I'm not surprised the little queer who wrote it is related to you. But one thing is certain from our meeting. I'm going to see that this viperous crap, this tissue of falsehoods and lies never sees the light of day!

Melmont snatched the manuscript up and waved it angrily, as if to throw it out of the window, though for security reasons, none of the Speke and Lazarus boardroom windows opened. For the first time, Cole saw a flicker of desperation, he thought.

——Tristram, I need this to work for me, because my next move is Even Bigger. I'm going to buy out the world debt. It sounds barmy but there's a reason. Very soon all the countries like the US will cancel their debts to Third World countries and I'll be quids in. I'm going to the conference to announce it, now. In Canada.

The man who was proposing to escape his pressing liquidity problems using the mighty lever of World Debt buffed his black loafer experimentally, once, with the palm of his big hand.

——Dominic said you'd end up going crazy. Please Earnest. Prove him wrong.

——You forget, Tristram, that things have gone down around me before and people think I've gone away for good but I always surprise them.

——You are overextended, Earnest. If you have a plan for retrenchment, the bank could support it. But this endless expansion... .

And Cole waved his hands, hopelessly. He looked at his old

friend, and Melmont's face was without any indication of what was going on within him. His expression was as blank as when young Melmont had found his grandmother's house lifeless; blank as the Rune of Destiny.

In Dominic's old flat in Notting Hill, the manuscripts were packed and ready to go out to publishers' readers, but the IRA's fondness for mailing parcel bombs in order to reclaim the Holy City of Belfast meant that for two weeks, all postboxes stood on the London street corners with their lips forbiddingly sealed. Libby and Amelia agreed to return the following day, leaving the precious manuscripts together in the flat overnight.

When Amelia and Libby tripped down the basement steps to Dominic's flat bright and early the next day, the key turned uselessly in the lock. The door was already open, the lock smashed. Inside the flat all the manuscript parcels waiting to go out were missing, as well as the notebooks and every scrap of paper in the place. Nothing else had been touched.

—We're still just alright, I gave my uncle a copy, Libby said bravely. When she found out that Cole had given his copy to Melmont, she sat and cried, inconsolably. She had let Dominic down.

—It's his life's work and it has gone for nothing because of my stupid carelessness.

—Mine too, said Amelia. We wanted to do good, and we ended up doing bad. Kinda depressing. My therapist's a Reichian and he says that shit like this happens when you don't have the right kind of sex. If you don't come it all gets bottled up.

—You means, the book is missing because I gave someone a

blowjob? cried Libby. That is ridiculous.

—Blowjobs are ok. Just another facet of the genital embrace. Just make sure you come.

A learned discussion on clitoral *versus* vaginal orgasm was interrupted by the arrival of a parcel. Amelia picked it up and recognised the aggressive penmanship of the address as her father's.

—This is for Dominic from my dad! It just plopped through the door, she cried.

—It's not going to be the manuscript is it?

—I guess that depends on where your fingers have been in the last ten minutes. No, it's too light.

—Go ahead and open it. He could have sent it on airmail paper, said Libby.

—Why would he do that? Your brother never struck me as an 'airmail paper' kind of guy.

—You're right.

Libby remembered the rare letters from her mother on a single feathery blue sheet which she always managed to tear when opening. They had arrived from around the world, full of incomprehensible injunctions, twice yearly, for twelve years of incomprehensible boarding school.

Inside the package sent to Dominic was a video cassette entitled 'Redland Digby's Last Will and Testament'. Amelia loaded it into the video player. Raddled head to camera, her father spoke.

—*Hi Dom. By the time you get this I'll be dead. Now the hidden subsidy from the evil empire is down the tubes for Fat Freddie, look at the other soft targets he's likely to go for.*

Banking swindles. Bankers are such cocksucking idiots and greedy with it. Shortsighted too. Amelia will help you noose the bastard. With the world filling up with pansies like you, I guess my girl's never gonna get married. Well I'm about to go off to take the long view.

Amelia started to cry.

—I miss you Daddy. I'm going to miss you so much.

Amelia and Libby sat and wept together. Finally,

—This is ridiculous, said Amelia, always the practical one. We still have no book.

On a further search, they found the copy of *Mein Kampf* with the flyleaf missing, that Willis death had uncovered.

—That's a fat lot of use, said Libby.

—Yeah, even if it belonged to Magda Fucking Goebbels. But of all people, Dominic will have known the kinda guy he was up against. He must have had a second line of defence.

—He was depending on me. He died too soon to do anything about it.

—Hot damn! What was your fucking uncle doing giving the manuscript to the one guy in the world who shouldn't have it?

—Dom tried to get me to give it to him, as well, remember. Amelia rolled her eyes.

—Dad's right, we have to noose the bastard.

—If we can't, it's our own fault. If this wasn't a basement I think I would have thrown myself out of the window in despair by now. How stupid can you get?

Libby opened the fridge. The interior was still full of small pieces of rotting food, and at the back, a catering size tin of Heinz baked beans, with a jaggedly open top. Amelia watched in horror as Libby prized the lid up further. There was thick green mould growing on the top.

——Urgh, said Amelia.

In the corner, the Redland's tape finished and the television switched back on, revealing the villain himself in full flow before a rapt audience. Melmont the saviour of the poor had flown to Canada for the World Debt Meeting and was addressing a packed conference hall. Melmont was saying,

——So, in six months' time, maximum, it should be possible given our collective resources, to create a financial platform large enough to take on the world debt, and stabilise it by internal arbitrage as summarised by the plans in the folder you will have found on your seats. This means that multinational companies such as my own, in alliance with the First World banks, can collaborate to create a genuine world credit net that does not penalise those who are already poor.

There was applause. And indeed it was a brilliant notion, the only problem being that it was Melmont who was behind it. Amelia and Libby watched Melmont stilling the applause with his bearlike hand.

——My, my, doesn't Fat Freddie look like he's got all the cream; suppose he'll fool them now, she remarked bitterly.

Melmont continued,

——Debtor nations have been unanimous in their enthusiasm for the scheme which in a time of recession restructures their economies responsibly, in a united global monetary market. I solemnly promise you... .

Here Melmont paused, to let the solemness sink in, so that you could surely have heard a pin drop in the huge hall.

——I solemnly promise you that the human race need never see the end of this wealth which we will have created in this fashion!

The speech ended. Melmont strode down the broad aisle of the hall away from the podium, smilingly acknowledging the applause, which was as wild as if he had won an Olympic gold medal.

——Omygod, he's getting a *standing ovation*, look, said Amelia.

Libby was not watching the TV. She seized her friend's wrist.

——Just a minute, Amelia. I've been thinking. Dominic hated beans, so why did he keep an open tin for so long? Why did he even open it, come to that?

——I dunno. Your brother was not exactly houseproud, was he? Rewind. He was a *slut*. You tell me what he was doing with the beans. You're always going on about how you and your brother think exactly alike.

Libby donned a pair of yellow rubber gloves, took a deep breath of determination, opened the fridge again, and laid hold of the catering pack of beans. She took it out, turned it upside down on the draining board, opened the bottom with a tin opener, then righted it again and pulled the tin away.

A sluglike mass of beans started to move inexorably towards the plughole, but quickly lost their will to power and started to spread out. As they did so, a see-through plastic wallet was revealed which when rinsed clearly had a copy of the manuscript inside.

Flushed with success, the girls embraced.

——It's not just his diet, I should have thought of it earlier. He was a natural conspiracy theorist, said Libby.

—Thank you, beans, for overlooking the feeble nature of our masturbations, said Amelia.

On the news that evening, Melmont's radical plan for reducing world debt had been received with polite incredulity by the UN, hailed by the president of The Gambia, and denounced by three obscenely poor countries whose names no one could remember, though their thieving presidents all had fat offshore bank accounts and villas in Geneva. It takes one to know one.

♫   ♫   ♫

Melmont stood at the stern of a huge fibreglass palace of a seagoing yacht. The sea was a gorgeous blue, the sun shone and the boat still rode at anchor in a rich man's marina of one of the more attractive Balearic islands. Honoured guests had been ferried to the harbour all day, by the ultra-modern yellow beetle-like taxis that plied between the dusty landing strip and the picturesque port; for once the taxi-men's meters were shuttered, no pesetas, *plees*, thank you, all gratis, from the great man's largesse.

Melmont smilingly acknowledged the attention of the prom-enaders performing their late afternoon *volta* while taking bets on his *avoirdupois*. The big man paced about his boat, its clean lines contrasting strongly with the froth of polystyrene and old planks that milled messily in the water, jostling the cast-resin hull. Frank was high above the jetty, putting the final touches to the satellite communications links that would allow a World Debt Arbitrager to command his future empire from the waves. Below the furls of fibreglass over the futuristic bows, a man in a bos'n's chair was hung out over the twinkling harbour waters, carefully painting the brand-new boat's name in gold on the bows: 'Angelic Zenocrate', after Melmont's firstborn.

As in most fateful, fatal voyages, there were signs a-plenty. As soon as her name was completed on the glossy side and the boat cast off, Zenocrate appeared, depending on who you talked to about it. Sceptics deride the rumours, saying she was hallucinated by her father, convinced his cricket-playing daughter could be glimpsed somewhere among the jovial throng. Total disbelievers should note that Vanov's wife, who had never met Zenocrate, and was quite unfamiliar with the rules of cricket, later talked of a dream she had that night, of a lithe young girl dressed in white who was laughing, gracefully striking away apple-red balls with a flat-sided stick, as fast as they were thrown to her.

Personally I believe we are beggars, ignorant of the Universe's infinite dimensions and our actual interconnectedness. Or something. O nobly-born and revered Reader, bear with me, we are close to the end of a rippin' good yarn.

The first guests to arrive in the saffron-yellow taxi shuttle were Vanov and his wife. The taxi wheeled away smartly back towards the airport, and the stout Russian couple were led towards their cabins by a richly dressed Indian Sikh dwarf. Vanov's wife, Dalia, was overcome by the spectacle she had stepped into. She spoke in hushed tones to her husband, as if they were in a cathedral.

—Look at the size of this yacht. It is like the Czar has come back. How can one man make enough in his lifetime to own so much? It's a miracle! God must love him.

Dalia tugged at her husband's sleeve a moment later, and they both paused to look in on a generously proportioned indoor swimming pool in the middle of the boat, where Melmont's brood of girls were preparing an entertainment. All the offspring were wearing one-piece swimsuits of the Melmont Tartan. There were seven elder daughters. Together with the indistinguishable quadruplets, they were being coached in synchronised swimming, while singing a song specially composed in praise of their father.

At the side of the pool, a rehearsal pianist was playing on a huge Bösendorfer Imperial grand piano. This is the plangent, rather catchy song that they sang all together, in their high girlish voices, which echoed through the pool area:

> *If you catch a millionaire*
> *Better hurry, they're quite rare,*
> *Though their names can become household words.*
> *Aristotle F Onassis*
> *Had an eye for the lasses,*
> *But Ari has gone to his eternal reward.*
>
> *Aristotle, tell us what'll*
> *Make you love us, Aristotle!*
> *You're so rich, you're so Greek*

[Solo, hopeful, from Zarustrina]
> *You'd oil me sixty times a week!*

[Main chorus, all, *largo*]
> *But farewell to Aristotle's fame!*
> *Now completely eclipsed by The Name*
> *On a hundred Melmont Communications*

[*Con Vivace*, all, increasing tempo]
> *Network TV, FM stations*
> *Melmont football recreation*
> *Off myriad Melmont satellites*
> *It's a Melmont Global vision*
> *All round the whirling Melmont world tonight!!!*

The song-and-dance ended with a 'wet pom-pom' version of a joyous water-ballet. The girls were upbraided after the climax of the song for slack overall elocution (a growing problem among the young, the pianist asked them not to take it personally) and told to do it again. It sounded even lovelier the second time around. Mrs Vanov spoke only Russian (readers may have noticed her earlier remarks were translated, for convenience) but the close harmonies heard in their fibreglass cathedral of opulence seduced her senses and touched her heart, never mind the words.

    —So sweet, she sighed. So tasteful. All his lovely children.

    —Mind you, he really wanted boys, said her husband darkly.

    Other guests were already boarding from the dockside, so their small guide began now angrily beckoning. The Vanovs humbly resumed their walk through the opulent ship to their luxuriously appointed cabins.

On a lower deck, Zak was settling down to watch the same rehearsals through a huge plateglass window which gave on to the swimming pool. Insufficiently distinguishable the girls might be, but they were attractively feminine, Zak thought, particularly the older and more *zaftig*, as they practised their underwater synchronised swimming manoeuvres, bursting in and out of the water like undines or water sprites:

> *Aristotle, tell us what'll*
> *Fire your dreamboat up, full throttle*

There was a dish of caviar on the table beside him, which Zak tasted appreciatively, before carefully pouring himself a small glass of chilled vodka from the container in the middle. Discretion was called for. Although the immediate surroundings were luxurious and easeful, a cloud was gathering over Mossad's dealings with Melmont, who was demanding larger and larger financial concessions for his companies in Israel. At the same time there were unsettling reports that other less democratic countries in the region had been approached offering easy terms for weapons-grade uranium. If rumours turned out to be true, Melmont at least knew what to expect after the death of Röhl. Zak was unafraid of that conclusion to events. Like the biblical King David, Zak had executed any number of men in the line of duty defending Israel, in his time.

When Zak looked up from measuring his careful pour, his host was also standing in front of the plate glass, looking at the spectacle of his children praising him in song.

——Great caviar, Earnest. *L'Chaim!*

The big man appeared to be transfixed by something in the water-ballet.

——There!

Zak had no idea who he was talking about. Melmont seemed to be pointing to a completely empty area of the pool.

——Your daughters are all very pleasant, and what again are their names?

——I saw Zenocrate! exclaimed Melmont.

——Who? Point her out to me. Which is Zenocrate? said Zak.

Melmont didn't answer. He turned and went upstairs into the pool area, to look for confirmation or contradiction of his hallucination. He was sure he had seen her, lithe and solid, in the joyful flesh of her adolescence. When he walked in by the pool, the alarmed rehearsal pianist redoubled his efforts, and the daughters, waisthigh in the water, leapt around like spawning salmon, but after Melmont had counted them, he ignored their efforts, preoccupied. A thought struck him. If she had appeared, she surely would have been caught by the surveillance suite cameras on the pool.

When the boat was being fitted out, Melmont had decreed a multi-vision room which was a sphere entirely constructed out of inward facing TV monitors. Sitting in the control suite of his empire, he would choose and amplify images from anywhere he chose. But when he passed through the door to check the pool tapes of the last half hour, sitting in the vast tilting chair in the middle, surrounded by monitors, was Abigail.

——What are you doing here? he asked, coldly.

——Frank left the door open. But I can ask you the same question, said Abigail.

——I need to check something, said Melmont.

Abigail stood up.

——I was looking at this cockpit you've created for yourself. Your little world, with you in the middle, with you on your throne. You must think you control it all, when you see it all. What do you think you are doing, really?

Melmont ignored his wife's questions, and sat down and fiddled with the controls till he accessed the pool. He replayed the recent rehearsal he had been watching over a large number of screens, but he could not see Zenocrate. He continued, running and re-running the tapes, backwards and forwards, convinced that there would be a sighting. Behind him, Abigail weighed in, heatedly.

——I don't think I like what you've made, here. It's not nice. In fact it's a throwback. The only other animals that have this multiple outlook you've created are vile insects. All this money and power, and you've used it to evolve into a common blue-bottle, Earnest, a creature of decay and carrion. Bluebottles are small but they always lay their eggs in larger things, spoiling them. It worries me where you are planning to lay your eggs.

——What worries you? Melmont had noticed that there was a small area where the diving board could have obscured one camera's view of an apparition of his eldest, and was seeking another camera's corroboration of the area's emptiness.

——Plenty of things. One of the things is how you can rewrite the past. Calling your boat Zenocrate, for instance. She was nothing to you when she was alive.

——You're so wrong, Abigail.

——You never even remembered her birthday, shouted her mother shrilly.

——You're wrong. I do care about her. I've seen her here, this afternoon, as real as you or me.

——I put flowers on her grave last week. You weren't there, but that's how it is nowadays.

——She must have been diving in the pool or something, said Melmont, feebly. His argument tailed away into the uncomfortable feeling of hollowness. Melmont was unaccustomed to self-doubt.

——Have you thought of seeing a doctor? said Abigail.

——I don't have delusions. She'll be on this tape, somewhere and you'll see. The camera does not lie.

Melmont zoomed in on the pictures on the monitors, more and more. All around them, enormous arms and legs of children thrashed silently as he searched vainly through the exaggerated pixels.

——The trouble is with these images, they're not an exact record, or complete. Maybe she could be behind that pillar, he said, hopefully.

——Have you been faithful to me, Earnest? said Abigail.

The question was so unexpected that Melmont paused before replying.

——On my word of honour.

——On your honour, I see. Abigail produced a silver CD disc from her hand and slipped it in the console.

There was a whirr from the computer, and all the screens suddenly started playing Melmont making love to various

women. Since most of the occasions were of very short dura-
tion, Frank had looped them, making him appear more priapic
with each individual than was so in real life. Seen all together,
they soon became ridiculous, cartoon-like strivings. Melmont
closed his eyes, to shut out the tiresome images, and said
patiently,

——None of this ever happened. It's an invention. I can tell
you, they're all computer-generated montages. You forget I used
to be in intelligence, Melmont added.

Abigail turned the CD player off. The images went back to
showing the daughters in the pool. But still no Zenocrate.

——And to think you had Röhl killed from jealousy, she said.

——No I didn't, said Melmont. I had him killed because he
was expendable. I needed that money for expansion. With Röhl
out of the way, the Iranians wouldn't come asking for their
money back!

——You said to that man that Röhl was making love with me.
First, it's not true. Second, I don't understand how you can be
jealous about someone you clearly don't love.

——Zak is that kind of crude Jew who needed to think that
I had a grudge against Röhl so I would do nothing to stop him
being killed. Röhl's life was mine to take, or not from the beginning.

——You had no right.

——I have every right.

——His blood is on your conscience.

——Come come, Abigail. He was a Nazi. Slaves of the Reich,
all my family died in caves making his rocket fuel.

Abigail shook her head.

——These hands have cooked Gunter dinner, and turned down his sheets for him. His son even played tennis with Zenocrate.

Now both Abigail and Melmont were crying. But she bravely continued,

——The faith you were born into holds hospitality sacred. But look at you! What have you done? I would rather leave and bring the children up on charity, than live with a murderer! Earnest, I cannot see into your heart any more. I am afraid of you. Afraid.

Melmont the murderous war hero twiddled some knobs on the monitor. His daughter's voices came out echoing, mocking and ghostly.

> *If you catch a millionaire*
> *Better hurry, they're quite rare*

——So, what do you want with me? said Melmont.

——I want a divorce. I shall do my best to make the little ones forget who their father is, said Abigail.

——Wherever you go you cannot cut yourself off from me, Abigail. This is what the whole *thing* I am going for is about. One world. Everything linked up. Now is not the time to doubt me. The truth is, I'm going to be arbitrager of the world's debt. Possibly the most important position ever created on the planet. I'll be able to eliminate tropical diseases, stop global warming.... .

——Stop! screamed Abigail. I am not going to go along with it any more. Someone has to say, enough! I am taking the children, as soon as they have sung that stupid song for you, tomorrow.

——I think my children will thank their lucky stars they had me for a father, said Melmont.

Abigail dug in her handbag a second time.

——Here is the document of separation. Don't make it more difficult than it is already. You will sign this, or Interpol will know who killed Röhl!

——They already know it was Mossad. I told them, said Melmont, smiling; impregnable to self-doubt.

——You disgust me. Your are shameful.

Abigail was walking away now. Melmont shouted after her,

——If you divorce me the world will see you for what you are, a hardhearted merciless gold-digging bitch! And tell Frank he's going to have to explain to me what he meant by letting you in here! Tell him to come and see me! He's fired!

Alone in the communications suite after Abigail left, Melmont watched the big fax machine excreting the front page of *The Moon*, with a picture of someone in an unusual position at the windows of one of the royal palaces above a chippy headline 'CRAPPY OLE BAS-TURD!' Later editions admitted coyly, and in small print, the royal defecation caught on camera, far from being a blue-blooded jobbie, was actually the love-child of computer graphics. Melmont read with interest that a lifestyle guru had advised Prince George 'to conquer your fear of failure and death, deposit your morning stools out of the window'. The guru was so confident this would work that the timing of the exercise came to the attention of the paparazzi. So the bum on view was indeed royal, though sadly the prince was costive on the morning in question, hence the need for extra pixels.

Bleaver still managed to skim a cool six figures for arranging it and once again, the imminent downfall of the Fensterkuchen dynasty was predicted by all parties. And still the sky did not fall.

Below the fake turd story was a far more ominous headline 'THORP TO CLOSE: OFFICIAL'. The doomed Thorp reprocessing plant at Seascale had been one of the rungs in Melmont's fantasy ladder of refinancing, which would now be shown for the smoke-and-mirrors job it was. If that was not enough, the page two lead story was 'WORLD DEBT A MYTH'.

Melmont saw he was finished. The house of cards he had built was blowing away before his eyes. He felt his knees buckling.

—Don't do this to me Ocker, please, he whispered, as if his wily rival would, if asked nicely, call back and pulp the edition which announced damnation. In fact, Midrash was still oblivious to the fact that there was enough misfortune posted in his cheeky little redtop to knock his rival out of the ring, twice.

And now the third blow fell. The smaller A4 fax in the corner used for correspondence suddenly sprang into life as if it had just read *The Moon*'s pages too and realised the jeopardy Melmont was in. To the Devil, a deficit. To Earnest Melmont, one page.

Be advised The Bank of Speke and Lazarus has rescinded ALL credit to Melmont Communications Group unless immediate security of £60 million or $100 million is provided in the next thirty repeat thirty minutes. No further warnings will be issued.

Cole had acted with brutal swiftness. Melmont felt himself consumed in a rage against the worldwide conspiracy. He took the emergency fireman's axe from its brand new sling, and destroyed the offending fax machines in a blizzard of blows. Then he still found a great emptiness in him, which was unbearable. He left the suite and walked into the swimming pool, interrupting the rehearsal, rudely pushing the pianist off his stool, and addressing his children severely.

——What you are doing is Spiritless and Weak, Melmont began. Your Enthusiasm is non-Existent. When my Guests watch this Performance, you must make them Understand that I Am Entirely Admirable! Sing after Me!

The pianist watched incredulously as Melmont then attempted to play a piano accompaniment, *without any musical training whatsoever*. His paws crashed stupidly and discordantly on the keys as he roared,

——*If you catch a millionaire.*

Then suddenly, as if not wishing to admit he didn't know more words than the opening line of his own song, he abandoned the big glossy piano and padded away from the pool area.

A door to the upper deck crashed shut, and the children made faces at each other. Melmont was a remote, but not particularly fearsome figure to the lissome pack. The music teacher, on the other hand, found his hands shaking as he lowered the long black wooden lid over the extended keyboard. Indeed, his hands would shake for three days after that encounter.

——I think we need a break, see you tomorrow bright and early at ten, everyone, the pianist said, carefully.

XXV

Valete

THE BOAT HAD LEFT PORT in the late afternoon and was now making its way through a calm, flat sea in the direction of Africa. The sun was setting astern, behind the little island they had left. As the sun died it splashed glorious streaks of orange among the white clouds, a glowing palette reminiscent of a sky painted with fluorescent soft-boiled eggs from giant bantams; godlike freerange hens who had been allowed to roam freely through eternity.

Melmont stood on deck while the boat's powerful engines murmured distantly. He turned from the bows and stared at the bravura sunset, then at the back of his left hand, then at the regular wavelets of the wake. Everything bored him, but he waited in vain for some entertainment from the leaden path he had entered into. Ever and anon, he raised a bottle clenched in his right hand to drink from it. It was a Melmontian bottle, a Jereboam of Lafite. And why not? Life is too short to drink bad wine. To the south, as if mocking the eviscerated magnate, hung a large and impressive three-quarter moon. From somewhere, a recording of the girls could be heard singing,

If you catch a millionaire
Better hurry, they're quite rare

Frank came and stood beside the ruined millionaire on the rear deck of his impressive boat. As soon as he had heard the separation Abigail had been planning was on, Frank had gone straight up to the crow's nest and bolted on a further couple of antennae.

Standing beside Melmont, Frank straightened his tie, pink with pistachio stripes and free with the suit.

——You wanted to see me, Publisher? Beautiful moon tonight. Whoops! Have I said something wrong?

——You've been very foolish, Frank. You will have to write a letter to my wife, explaining how you forged those images.

——In a pig's arse! said Frank, contemptuously. That's you bonkin', and you know it.

Melmont put the wine down and took Frank by the jacket lapels and lifted him up in the air. Frank's Take Six leisure suit had not been designed as a people-carrier. It made a rude tearing noise, and Frank slipped down a few inches, but Melmont still held his face close to Frank's.

——You will do what I say, said Melmont crushingly.

Frank remained unhypnotised.

——I'm sorry Mr Melmont, I'm going to tell it straight. You might be able to get away with faking stiffs, like in the case of amazing dead aliens, but everyone knows how live rumpy-pumpy looks.

Melmont was about to hold Frank over the side, to get him to come to his senses, when the fearless and wily bugger spoke again.

——In case I should lose my footing, Mr Melmont, I should warn you that at least two cameras are recording this encounter, so should you wish to re-engineer the onboard images later, the other side's version is being streamed in real-time to your wife's lawyers in Switzerland.

Melmont dropped Frank to the oiled teak decking with a grunt and turned away. Frank picked himself up, straightened his tie again, and walked off smirking, to report the encounter to Abigail.

Much later, the moon was the brightest thing in the sky, and while he was no longer bored, Melmont's soul was still besieged by melancholy which wine did little to assuage. The ship kept the same heading east towards a sunrise which would also bring slander, calumny and, quite possibly, imprisonment for fraud. Big tears rolled down Melmont's cheeks in pity for himself.

——I know how you feel, my friend, it's beautiful, is it not? said a familiar voice at his elbow. Vanov had joined him.

Melmont passed him the Jereboam, and Vanov drank. After a long silence, Melmont said, hesitantly,

——Look up. Over there. Do you ever see a face, when you look at the moon? I do. I always do.

Vanov peered up at the moon, briefly.

——Foolishness invents these things. Before telescopes, they said there were oceans up there; cities!

Vanov, the post-Marxist realist who had seen Melmont arrogantly drop cigar ash in great Stalin's skull, chuckled at his old friend's sudden superstitiousness and, misreading his mood, continued,

——Earnest, your greatness is founded on the new technology, not peasant superstition. The fibre-optic link all over the world with its giga-giga-gigabites, and you taking a percentage of every one! Soon, you will be a twenty-first century pioneer, leading us to global awareness and away from the base conflicts that have poisoned this century! Or that's what it says in the birthday brochure in the cabin, at any rate, Vanov added, his tone becoming less certain.

Melmont chuckled. But it was a wheezing chuckle, as if his lungs were bored with their struggle to inflate inside that great body.

—Old friend, there is something I want to give you.

Vanov passed Melmont a giftwrapped small box. Melmont pulled the wrapping off and a smile of delight and recognition lit up his face. It was a Mont du Miel cigar packet, held in a frame with handpainted roses all around it. Melmont lightly kissed Vanov on both cheeks. Then he took the little cigar-picture item and hung it on the bulkhead behind them, by a convenient downlighter which illuminated it well. They both admired it in silence for a few moments, then Vanov said,

—My wife said, "Is that all you are giving him, a cigar packet? A man who is taking over the world debt?" So in Geneva she went to a craftsman and he added the frame, for which the bandit charged me four hundred Swiss Francs!

Both men laughed together. Then Vanov said,

—I have to go and make sure my wife is not afraid.

—Afraid of what?

Vanov shrugged.

—Her parents were arrested but nobody told her, when she was little. She waited on her own for many days. Ever after, she doesn't like to be alone.

——Tell her she just needs to press the bell to get what she wants, any time of the day or night.

——She wants to feel safe, my friend.

——I will do my best. I'm sure on this boat she will feel safe.

——My words to her exactly. Goodnight old friend!

Vanov left, pleased that his gift had worked even better than he thought it would. Tomorrow he could take up with Melmont the money Melmont owed him.

When Melmont looked away from the cigar picture to the moon, it appeared to have got even bigger and he could not see Midrash's mocking face in it any more. As he squinted at the huge orb, there was the sound of flapping wings and something passed in front of it. There must be a vast bird following the boat, an albatross, perhaps. Melmont peered out but could see nothing.

But next, there was the sound of wings beating directly overhead, and Melmont was astonished to see an angel descend slowly and almost nonchalantly onto the deck, with no more fanfare than if it had been an ornamental bird alighting on the trim lawns of Melmont Keep. He looked on the angel as it folded its tall wings. He knew that face. It was Zenocrate. She was older now than when she had died and was an angelic young woman, beautiful and tranquil-looking.

A cry escaped his lips, but then his voice seemed to lose control of its register. What came out next sounded almost like his grandmother's voice he had last heard sixty years ago, and in her native language. The voice was creaky with age. But the tone was full of wisdom. It spoke of beauty, and of the burdens of life, and the wisdom of resignation when the time comes for laying down those burdens, to step into we know not what.

Melmont spoke a welcome to his dead daughter without knowing exactly what he said, using another's voice, in a lovely rare, strange, Slovenian dialect. Now extinct, alas, even though it had had its poets. In the vanished tongue, he said,

—Oh, my ineffable perfection. Oh, my soul.

And Zenocrate replied, in the same lost language,

—I am here, I am here to greet you, oh Beloved.

Heaven had been good to Zenocrate for she was clearly possessing a radiant perfection, as well as a loving mind. Melmont pinched himself to make sure he was not dreaming. His gaze appraised her body. Her sportive feet with slightly prehensile toes rested easily on the deck, as if she could flap her wings and cast off at any time. Her robes were long and loose. While a scarf modestly covered her hair, her strong arms were bare.

Zenocrate looked away from her father and started to string a short composite tartar bow, its ribs curling forwards from the handle before turning back, then pointing forwards again. It was thicker and heavier than the token bronze bow that streaked her memorial with verdigris, but the lovely creature from the supernatural realms seemed to have no trouble in stringing it.

Melmont saw her beautifully proportioned shoulders flex as she fitted a golden arrow to the string and straightened up to face him. As she did so, she seemed to wink at him. Melmont remembered she had always been able to keep her left eye open while closing the other; it was her party trick. But now, Angelic Zenocrate's slate-grey right eye was looking over the arrow straight at him, and the wink had turned into her aim. Melmont reverted to English.

——Careful now, dear, where you point that thing.

Zenocrate did not reply in words. She let fly with the thick gold arrow, and it sizzled through the air between them like a fast gunpowder fuse, until it reached her father and Melmont felt it pierce his heart. He started to reel on his feet.

——*What's happening, Zenocrate?*

——Heart attack, father, his daughter sadly pronounced, in her beautiful, clearly modulated Oxbridge High School voice.

Angelic Zenocrate watched sadly as the big man staggered, clutching at his chest. Finally, losing his balance, he slowly pitched over the railings, and slowly slid down the sloping hull into the silver sea.

The splash on entry was hardly audible above the engine noise and the distant rehearsal. The moon started to pass behind a cloud and the boat motored quietly on into the night. Melmont's cameras which should have recorded his last moments were found to have been mis-installed, and Frank's surveillance tapes proved to have been wiped, after being stored by the police enquiry next to a locker of stolen uranium. Thus Zenocrate faded from the scene, leaving no trace behind, apart from this account.

Long before the Spanish police declared the equivalent of an open verdict, Dominic Cole's detailed exposé went on sale in bookbins in every major bookstore in England. Shrinkwrapped inside the hardback, priced at twenty five pounds before discount, was a 'free' crossreferencing CD with video clips, which included Melmont's own assembly of the death of Gunter Röhl.

The looped bonking scenes are, of course, also available on the Net and have no real net value; though they have been used as background material by the publicity-hungry self-mutilating popgroup FatManDies(on-the-job)™, as well as dim-witted 'installation artists' from Santiago to Vermont; to my mind the sex scenes combine the repulsive with passé, but the penny has yet to drop with the art headbangers. The rest is silence, and e<M.

𝕸   𝕸   𝕸

I conclude with Libby's dream. Libby, dressed in a long cotton nightdress, was waiting to get into a covered tent where an Important Entertainment was advertised to be taking place. Over the entrance to an old circus tent was the proof, a garish fairground advertisement in firework colours that never seemed to fade or die. The marquee over the canvas entrance flaps said,

> **See Melmont Burning in Hell.**
> **Show Him What You Think of Him.**
> **3 Throws for a Tenner.**

Everyone that Libby had ever known was there, standing in line so they could hand over their hard-earned francs or pound or whatever, it didn't seem to matter, and get the chance to chuck away and get rid of their anger at Melmont.

Bruce 'Ocker' Midrash was there, in his oiliest incarnation of a fairground barker who had seen worse and better days but not many hot baths. Brucie was taking the money. In exchange a sullen-looking Senegalese in a biker jacket, who Dominic later told his sister was Ocker's latest bride, was handing out hard wooden fairground balls.

Midrash was brassily intoning a spiel to get even more punters to roll up.

——*Ten gets you three to teach him a lesson.*
If your aim is true, you might get a confession.
He's jumping, he's jiving, he's jerking, he's dodging!
Try and hit the dodgy geezer,
Once he was a big crowd pleaser!
Now, as you will plainly see, he's in the red-hot dunney!
The place for rotters who abscond
With other people's money!

Libby stepped up to the grimy magnate to ask his real thoughts on Melmont. Magically, Ocker seemed to be able to read her mind and answered before she could speak. There was no judgement of his defeated rival when he spoke.

——Sometimes it all comes unstuck. It's all just business, Ocker explained, flatly. Now, where's your money?

Libby discovered she had no money, or indeed a place to put it as she patted her thighs through the thin cotton nightdress. She realised to her surprise she was holding a book in one hand. Ocker's latest bride held out three balls as a possible exchange for the book, but Libby refused to part with it. Instead, she said to Midrash, tremblingly,

——I don't know how I know this but I need to return the Magda Goebbels copy of *Mein Kampf* to someone who is going to meet me inside. Can you help? Please?

—No worries, mate!

Midrash waved her through to the tent, turning to the next customer as if Libby's bizarre statement was the most normal thing in the world. He began his spiel again;

—*Ten gets you three, to teach him a lesson...*

Libby found herself on a chalked line on the grass, next to the ruined pensioner Willis Death and his wife. Willis was in a wheelchair, and his Parkinson's was going to severely hamper any accuracy. But he was going to have a go, anyhow, still incandescent with fury about what Melmont had done.

—I'm going to show 'im when I see 'im! 'E went down, and 'e 'ad our pensions in his pockets, Willis cried, inarguably. Mrs Death joined in the bitter condemnation.

—And the mortgage, too! We bin repossessed!

Libby felt enormous sympathy for the thousands of old people who had invested so much in Melmont, and found their financial saviour had now turned out to be a thief. Suddenly the lights went up as the target was illuminated.

It was cleverly contrived. The stained glass oriole window in Melmont Keep showing Samson breaking apart the house of the Philistines had been reproduced as a backdrop. Standing in front of the collapsing pillars, Samson was represented by a cut-out puppet figure animated by wires, but it was Melmont wearing a loincloth. There was a drumroll from somewhere. Fake flames licked the figure from underneath, and it started to jiggle.

People began to throw their wooden balls at the wicked image. Libby saw Willis Death getting excited at the scene before him, and he struggled to rise from his wheelchair. As imitation

hellfire tickled the puppet's feet, Midrash could be seen back-
stage, winding and pressing a clockwork thing that made a
yowling noise, close enough, in the general excitement to pass
for a cry of pain from a tortured sentient being.

——Burn, yew bastard, burn! Willis Death yelled, his soft rural
accent deepening in his wrath.

Everyone now started hurling their balls at the puppet in a
hail of hate. Libby found the manufactory of self-righteous rage
distasteful, but still had her mission. She pushed her way
through the crowd to where she knew she would find Dominic.

There her beloved brother was, not throwing either, but
watching amused, as he watched in life, his hands thrust deep in
his pockets. The noise and shouting was overpowering but she
was happy just to see him. She hugged him. Everything would
be alright now they were together. She shouted above the noise,

——Do you know anyone here who wants a spare copy of
Mein Kampf?

Dominic smiled at her, shook his head patronisingly but
held her by the hand as the puppet of Melmont was stoned
by the crowd. Then a man who was the spitting image of Stalin,
stood up on a rickety chair, pointed at Melmont and cried in
heavily Russian-accented English,

——Comrades! Come, let us exterminate this rootless international filth, and rid our society of it for ever!

But then just as he threw the first ball at Melmont's puppet,
the back of Stalin's head fell open on a hinge, and a cascade of
cigarette butts poured out down his back, far more than his
empty head could contain. It was, Libby thought, enough to fill
a couple of dustbins at least. But Stalin seemed unaffected by

the loss. When he stepped off his chair he was immediately ankle deep in cigarette butts, but he did not lose his footing and his aim was true. The puppet shook violently as successive wooden balls found their target.

Stalin's announcement and assault caught the mood of the crowd, which now redoubled its efforts, pelting the cutout furiously. Libby noticed that Midrash, who had been crawling around on hands and knees collecting his wares to resell, was now setting up a projector pointing vertically upwards. Suddenly it came on, brightening the roof of the tent. Stronger than sunlight, it was actually projecting a picture of the moon with Midrash's face on it. It dazzled Libby, and the crowd fell silent. Then the light went off, abruptly.

As the light died, the crowds all magically disappeared as well, as did their suffering target. And now only the Norn were in front of her and all was silence. She recognised Helmut, Hilda and Veronika from the description that Mrs Death had given of their visit to her farm.

Dominic had also vanished with the crowd but she did not feel afraid, even though as if to prove Mrs Death's worst fears about the chicken-poisoners, as they stood in front of Libby they all slowly sprouted horns. Then grey feral tails whisked into view. Throughout their transformation, their strange eyes, with squarish, goaty pupils, were dilated with eager devoted expressions towards what she was holding: the cursed volume, bound with human skin, probably sawn off a still-living sentient creature. Without a word being said, she knew these shapeshifters were here to collect the book she had brought.

Helmut finally stopped morphing and stepped forward with

his hand out, and she gave the book to him. She felt a strong sensation of relief as the three of them turned away to examine it. Addressing the trio's bent backs, the lovely dreamer said,

——I'd like to know one thing. Where is it going?

Helmut half turned back to her, and smiled a bucktoothed crooked smile.

——Why, to the library of a Certain Gentleman.

Then the damned trio quickly trotted away from Libby on their newly minted hooves, with their acquisition, and climbed onto an ancient, muddy BMW with a sidecar. Helmut started the bike with a kick from his cloven hoof, and skewed the front wheel as far to the left as it would go. He let in the clutch, and with a jerk, the trio went whooping round and round the grass enclosure of the inside of the tent three times, in an ever-quickening circle. Libby started to feel giddy but kept looking keenly. They did not change shape again, but the wingless bike lifted off the ground, and they were most definitely flying as they passed at thunderous speed out of the tent through the flapping canvas door.

Libby ran to the entrance, intrigued. She watched the trio on the motorbike intently, but they quickly vanished up into the sky, leaving only an oily smell on the wind. The dwindling putt-putt of the bike engine was finally drowned out by the noise of a cash register ringing behind her.

Ocker was tallying up the night's takings as his wife stacked the plastic chairs and swept the arena. Libby, emboldened by her successful question to Helmut, wanted to ask what part Ocker had played in the book's return. She took a step towards him but then halted. Some invisible force was stopping her.

Ocker looked up at Libby, not unfriendly. As before, he seemed to know what her questions would be. But this time, he was not disposed to answer. He winked at her deliberately, then turned his attention to deep uneven stacks of notes of dollars, yen, euros, rupees, rands, English pounds and Kenyan shillings, on the table before him. To the victor, the spoils. As the dream faded, Midrash was patiently sorting the paper money he had been paid for his mixed-media entertainment, with a practised, inky thumb.